Pathos of Murder

A Bekbourg County Novel

by Sherrie Rutherford

VENCIN Publishing

Venice, Florida

Bekbourg County Novels

Pathos of Murder

Bookends of Murder

This book is a work of fiction. Names, characters, places, events, incidents, business entities, and organizations are the product of the author's imagination or are used fictitiously. Any resemblance to actual places, organizations, business entities, events, incidents, or persons, living or dead, is entirely coincidental.

ISBN: 978-1-7345992-1-3

Library of Congress Control Number: 2020909027

VenCin Publishing

Venice, Florida

This book is dedicated to my parents,
Wanda and Dwight, for their love and support.

Acknowledgments

In this book, I would like to extend special thanks to:

Larry Goetz, my love, whose imagination runs through these novels as the pages are turned. Larry's inspiration and devotion made the Bekbourg mystery stories possible.

Gary Steinhilber and Pat Goetz for being readers and for their encouragement as I was writing the Bekbourg County novels.

Family and friends for the outpouring of support for BOOKENDS OF MURDER and their enthusiasm for the publication of PATHOS OF MURDER.

Clarissa Thomasson, my editor, for her guidance.

Cross Ink, Corp., for cover design.

To all the people who read my novels.

Pathos of Murder

A Bekbourg County Novel

By Sherrie Rutherford

Chapter 1

July 4, 1980

Byron Thornton whistled, “Man! Where’d you get *those* fancy duds?”

Leo Davis laughed, “Didn’t know I had it in me, huh?” Leo was carrying a duffle into the living room and dropped it on the floor.

“You’re really leavin’?”

“Yep, sure am. Just finished packing. There’s a few things in the closet you can have if you want ’em.”

“Does Roger know you’re leavin’?”

“No way I’d tell Roger. Didn’t want it to get out. You never know what Roger might do. If he’d spilled the beans, I might already be on my way to the big house.”

“Huh? What’d you mean?”

“Just got back from being summoned by the judge.”

“What? You mean Sophia’s dad?”

"The one and only."

"He doesn't know, does he?"

"No way, man. But he knows that Sophia and I have been seeing each other, and that's plenty for him. Doesn't want his precious daughter being seen with a 'lowlife' like me. He had one of his minion deputies track me down. Pulled me over after leaving my uncle's house this evening. Told me to be at the judge's office at eight o'clock sharp. You'd think he'd have better things to do on July Fourth. Shows how much he wants me gone."

"What happened?"

Leo puffed up his chest in mockery of the judge and lowered his voice, "'Sit down, Davis.' 'What? No warm greeting, Judge?'" Leo was getting into the theatrics, "'Listen punk. I know all about you, how you operate. Think you're a ladies' man with that silver tongue, but there is no way that you're going to take advantage of my daughter. She is too young to know about con men. I'm not going to let her fall victim to scum like you.' I said, 'Judge, don't you think Sophia should make up her own mind?' That sure got a rise," Leo was grinning.

Lighting up a Camel while enjoying Leo's theatrics, Byron laughed, "I bet. What'd the old man do then?"

Leo was on a roll. "'Davis, I have in this file here a list of all your run-ins with the law. Some can easily be re-opened. I'm sure you can be tied to some other cases, too. Life behind bars for a pretty boy like you won't be fun, but I'm willing to make this easy on you. I've got $10,000 in this envelope. You leave town tonight and never show your face around here again. No contact with my daughter ever. What's it going to be, Davis?'"

"You're kiddin'? $10,000? You lucky SOB." Leo was grinning. Byron stopped short, "Wait. You took the money, didn't ya?" Leo's grin grew larger. "Don't tell me you didn't take the money?" Byron blew a smoke ring.

Leo laughed, breaking the suspense. "Byron, you don't actually think I'd turn down $10,000?" he asked—pointing to an envelope lying on a sports jacket draped on a chair back. "You bet I took it. I made it look like it was a hard decision, that I didn't like him threatening me, but yeah, I took it and told him I was leaving tonight."

"So, that's it? You're leaving Sophia?"

"Come on, man. You know me better than that. Yep, I'm leaving, but I'm not letting that pompous jerk threaten me. My future father-in-law just gave us a nice nest egg to start our new life. Joke's on him." Leo was in good-humor. "Say, I got you something." He walked into the kitchen off the small living room and brought back a bottle of Jack Daniels. "Don't drink all this at once." He handed it to Byron. "Now, I've got to finish clearing some things out of the bedroom. Then Sophia and I are off to a new life."

Leo shook Byron's hand, "Take care of yourself, Byron."

"You too, Leo. We've had some good times." Ready to go tie one on, Byron nodded to the bottle, "I'm going to get a good start on this Jack and head to Knucklepin's. See what's happenin'."

After hearing Byron's old jalopy pull away, Leo slipped the money the judge had given him in the sports coat pocket and slung it over his arm and picked up his duffle to put it in his truck. After he loaded those things, there were a couple of final things he needed get out of the bedroom, and then he would take one last look around the house.

As he walked to his truck, his thoughts were on Sophia and their future. He didn't notice the hot, humid night or the fireworks smoke that had drifted and hung heavy in the air. So focused were his thoughts that he wasn't even tuned in to the occasional fireworks sounding off in the distance. He opened the door of his pick-up and started to put his duffle in the cab. Something, some sound, yanked him from his reverie—a footstep on the gravel.

Chapter 2

May, 2004

Like many small towns in the Midwest, Bekbourg, Ohio had experienced an economic roller-coaster ride. Farming had been the predominant way of life during its early history. Over time, other industries emerged in the region, such as lumber, paper mills, coal and iron-ore mining, and brick-making. The 1840's brought a major boost to Bekbourg's economy. In order to stay competitive with other cities in the region, the City of Bekbourg decided to construct a railroad, the WVB&C, from Cincinnati, Ohio to Wheeling, West Virginia. After building the railroad through the center of town, they also built a switching yard, a freight house and a passenger depot. With Cincinnati one-hundred-twenty miles to the west and fast access to the east coast markets, Bekbourg was positioned for major market expansions. Around the turn of the century, two large factories, the Bekbourg Springs Milk Company and G. E. Geisen Paper Products, were built—ensuring steady economic growth.

Bekbourg prospered through the early twentieth century and even held its own during the Great Depression. However, like much of its surroundings, Bekbourg was not prepared for the economic forces of the second half of the century.

By the 1970's, it was in a steady decline and needed to do something to avoid the fate of numerous rust belt towns.

Its economic turn-around started with the nearby construction of two major highways. The paper plant was purchased in the early 90's by a group of investors who retooled the plant to produce polystyrene products—which proved profitable as demand for those products grew in fast-food restaurants and other food-related services. During the same time period, Bekbourg began to promote tourism because of its proximity to Hocking Hills, Wayne National Forest, Peatmont State Park, and the Scioto River. Businesses opened in Bekbourg in response to its tourism outreach, which resulted in a rebirth of the old downtown. Early development included a stunning restoration of the old boarding house into a B&B and a popular coffee bistro next door.

Gentrification of the residences near the downtown gradually began in the early 1990's. Kye Davis and her husband early on recognized the benefits of relocating downtown. They sold their house in an outlying area and bought and remodeled a duplex to rent one side to supplement their retirement income. Cheryl Seton and her fiancé, Sean Neumann, rented the other side of a duplex from Kye.

Cheryl Seton was returning from a long walk with Buddy, a Chocolate Lab, who felt proud, having chased a fair number of squirrels up trees. His tongue was hanging out the side of his mouth, and the look of success and happiness showed in his face and prance. Cheryl was nearly at a jog trying to maintain Buddy's pace. When Buddy saw Kye sitting on the front porch, his excited lurch caused Cheryl to drop the leash as he bounded ahead to greet Kye. Cheryl got there just in time to see Kye give Buddy a treat that she kept at the ready for just these occasions.

Cheryl had her dark hair pulled back in a pony-tail. She looked like a model, tall and athletic, in a tank top and running shorts. She had spent the first fourteen years of her life in Bekbourg until she and her mother moved to Cleveland to escape the notoriety of her grandfather's guilty plea to murder. Her career as a newspaper reporter for the acclaimed Cleveland newspaper, *The Presenter*, had brought her back to Bekbourg a year earlier to cover the killing of five members of a family with drug connections. Although she still worked for *The Presenter*, Bekbourg was now her home, and she commuted between Bekbourg and Cleveland.

"Good morning, Kye. Isn't it a glorious morning?"

"Yes, it surely is. May is one of my favorite months. I was expecting you and Buddy. Coffee's made. Get you a cup and let's sit and catch up."

Kye, a retired high school English teacher, had taught Sean during his junior year. Sean had been a star quarterback for the local high school and was set with a scholarship to play college football when he suffered a devastating shoulder injury that ended his football career after high school. He had worked for the railroad a couple of years and then enlisted in the Marines. After Basic Training, he decided to specialize in law enforcement and signed up for special training in the military police. During his career, he was sent all over the world and worked his way into the elite military investigative unit. After losing his partner and nearly dying himself in a deadly trap in Kuwait, he retired from the Marines and returned home to Bekbourg. His best friend from high school, who was the local sheriff, Mike Adams, persuaded him to join the Sheriff's department. He rented the duplex, and when he and Cheryl became engaged, she moved in with Sean and Buddy. Sean was now interim sheriff for Bekbourg County.

Buddy was lying on the porch chewing on his raw hide, listening to Cheryl and Kye and watching for passers-by. "Mmm, this coffee hits the spot. Thank you. Sean had to leave early this morning to go to Columbus for a meeting, so he missed our morning walk."

"You both are so busy, Dear, so I'm glad that I get to watch Buddy when you're both gone."

At hearing his name, Buddy perked his ears and looked up at Kye. Cheryl and Kye laughed, and Buddy looked at both and then returned his attention to the raw hide.

As they talked, Cheryl noticed that Kye seemed preoccupied. After a while, she asked her if something was on her mind.

Kye sighed. "I'm sorry. I don't mean to let my mood spoil your day."

"Of course you're not spoiling my day. Please tell me what's wrong."

"To be honest, I'm worried about something. I don't know if you saw Saturday's *Bekbourg Tribune*, but there was an article about a development that is planned up near where the golf community was built several years ago."

"Yes, I read that story and saw the news clip on TV. It was the groundbreaking for the second phase by Bekbourg Enterprises to build weekend homes and cabins and recreational amenities. Harvey Bennett, the President, really talked up this new development. There was a lot of fanfare. All the County Commissioners were there—along with some other big wigs from the county. It's near their first development that included the golf course and a gated community of luxury homes."

"Yes, that's it. It's going to be called 'Lake Meadows.' I own about thirty acres that belonged to Cecil's family. Cecil and his brother Lester grew up there. When their dad passed away, Cecil and Lester inherited the place. Cecil was working on the railroad, and I was teaching, and we already had our own home. Lester's wife had died, and he was raising his son Leo, so they moved to the old home place. A few years later when Lester needed money, Cecil bought his interest, but Lester and Leo continued to live there. When Lester died, Leo stayed there until he moved to Texas in 1980. The property had the old house and a barn that sat a good distance behind the house. Cecil said that his dad used to put up tobacco in the barn. He even used it to store an old car. I think Cecil thought if Leo returned one day, he might fix up the old house. Anyway, when I read that article, I wondered how close the development was to our property. I haven't been to see the property in years. After church on Sunday, my friend Milly and I drove up to see it. I couldn't believe what I saw. The house and barn are gone. There were stakes in the ground, and someone has even graded a road."

"Oh my, Kye, how is that possible?"

"I don't know, Cheryl, but I'm upset. I went down to the courthouse yesterday to see what I could find out. They weren't helpful at all, but they told me that it sold at a tax sale. I don't know how that could have happened. I may be old, but I stay up on things. I paid taxes on this place. I would have paid them on that property. Last night, I went through our files. Cecil always handled all our financial matters, but when he got sick, I started handling things. I wasn't as much as a stickler as Cecil was, but I know that I would never have failed to pay taxes on that property.

"I found some old tax invoices. I guess because Bekbourg is such a small county, they always put the invoices for both this place and our acreage in the same mailing. Our canceled checks show that Cecil wrote one check for the taxes on both properties. I did the same. What's confusing is that when I went back through the files last night, I noticed the invoice for the acreage taxes had not been included for the last three years. I have tax invoices for this place but not for the acreage."

"Surely, they can fix this. Can I do something?"

"Well, Dear, I appreciate that, but I've already put a call into Owen Donaldson. I'm meeting with him this afternoon."

Cheryl laughed. "I hear that he is a textbook definition of curmudgeon."

Kye laughed, "He is a sour puss."

They both laughed.

Cheryl was perplexed by how this could have happened to Kye. "Well, if you need my help, just let me know."

Owen Donaldson was both an attorney and CPA and had practiced in Bekbourg for about forty years. Those who knew him were accustomed to seeing him in frayed pants and wrinkled shirts that bunched like elastic beneath his suspenders. Very little tread remained on the bottom of his worn tennis shoes. He self-styled his hair by whacking his bangs high on his forehead and chopping it the same length, more or less, below his ears. His portly face had red splotches made more pronounced by his frequently-unshaven white whiskers. Judge Bergmann's required courtroom decorum was the only reason Owen owned a suit, which he had repeatedly donned over the past two decades. Owen's tall frame supported a hefty pear-shaped physique.

Because Owen was a fierce advocate, clients tolerated his crustiness and abruptness. In fact, some clients retained him with the idea that their opposition would rather cave than fight with Owen. Although he handled general civil and criminal cases and fought to protect his clients against the county and state in tax and zoning issues, he was considered the local legal expert on fighting for environmental causes.

Leaning back in his chair, tapping his pencil on the desk, Owen listened as Kye described the situation. “When I received the tax invoice, I just assumed that it covered both properties, that they had consolidated the amounts.”

“What about the assessments? Do you have copies of those?”

“I looked through all my records. The yearly assessments also stopped coming for the property the same year. But I have them for the years before the county stopped sending them. The year before the assessments and invoices stopped, I paid taxes on both properties.”

“Was there anything different? Had you changed the property from Cecil’s name to yours or something like that?”

“No, it was nothing like that. When Cecil bought Lester’s interest, he went ahead and had both of our names put on the property, and it was like that the last times I paid taxes on the property. It is Cecil’s family’s home place. I can’t think that I let this happen. Will I be able to get the property back? I have money to pay any back taxes.”

“Those people in that tax department don’t know what the hell they’re doing. Some of the most incompetent people I know. So, it’s hard to tell what they have done. I’m not going to sugar coat the situation, Kye. That Bekbourg Enterprises group that is developing your property is planning to make money off of it. They have deep pockets. It could be expensive to fight them. I'll look into this for you and see what I can find out, and then we'll decide what to do."

The Bekbourg County courthouse was located off of Main Street in the old downtown. In addition to housing the county courts and judges, it also was home to the county commission with its meeting chambers and offices. It was one of the largest buildings on the street, just across from the grand old hotel where the only operational part was the GilHaus restaurant, Bekbourg's most upscale eatery, which provided the grandeur of the early 1900's with opulent crystal chandeliers sparkling across white tablecloths, crystal goblets and china. Behind the courthouse on Court Street was the county services building, which contained the tax office, treasurer, county engineer, auditor, recorder and all other county offices. The police station and jail were next to the county building.

When Owen entered the Treasurer's office area, Charlotte Mooney knew that her day was going to take a turn for the worse. She glanced to see if she could make a dash exit, but there was no one else manning the counter.

As he reached the counter, Owen demanded, "On what basis did you take Kye Davis' property in a tax sale?"

Charlotte meekly asked, "Whose property?"

"Kye Davis. She and her deceased husband own thirty acres, and when she drove out to look at it on Sunday, she saw that robber baron outfit has staked it out and plans to build vacation homes there."

"It's part of that new Lake Meadows development?" Charlotte asked.

About that time, Pauline Kaufmann walked up, having heard Owen's booming voice. "Owen, what is this about?"

"You heard me. Kye Davis drove out to her property on Sunday and saw that it has been staked out for development. When she came in here on Monday, she was told that her property was sold at a tax sale and is now part of that Bekbourg Enterprises development. Kye is an upstanding citizen and pays her bills. There is something fishy going on here. She is willing to pay any back taxes, but she wants her property. It belonged to her late husband and was in his family. Now, how do we get this straightened out so she can have her property back?"

Pauline was the County Treasurer. "Well, I am not familiar with the facts here, Owen. I'll look into it, but if she didn't pay her taxes and it sold at a tax sale, there isn't anything that can be done. The purchaser owns it."

"Don't play me for a fool, Pauline. I know you know darn well what the facts are. I will be back tomorrow, and I want an answer, and the right answer is that there has been a mistake, and the property belongs to Kye. Just to make sure the ball is rolling, I need to see the tax invoices, paperwork and notices and all the tax deed auction documents connected to this property. And before you say it," he thumped down a handwritten sheet of notebook paper on the counter, “I have a written request right here. That’s a bullshit requirement to have to put it is writing, but I don’t have time to argue.”

Charlotte and Pauline both looked at the paper—Charlotte as if it might somehow materialize into a biting reptile. Pauline replied, “This could take some time, Owen. We’re reorganizing the county’s files, and most things are in a warehouse.”

“This better be ready tomorrow.” Owen’s voice always projected, but his volume ticked up a couple of notches, “You all are trying to steal property from an old lady. Let me tell you right now, I’m not going to let that happen.”

After Owen ambled out, Charlotte picked up the list, but Pauline took it from her, “Don’t worry about that crackpot, Charlotte. If he raises it again, let me know, and I’ll handle it.”

After Owen returned to his office, he poured himself a whiskey. He called Kye, “Look, Kye. I’ve read everything you gave me. I need to file for a temporary restraining order to stop them from moving forward with that development until your property rights can be sorted out. I just got back from the county offices. Even though I gave them a list of documents I need, they’re not going to provide a blasted thing. That’s the way they are. I’ll keep working to get those documents, but I had two aces up my sleeve to get at least some information. Two other county departments keep copies of court filings. The sheriff’s office keeps copies of the Sheriff’s Sales, where property tax foreclosures are sold, and the Clerk of Court keeps formal court files. I went to the Clerk's office and found the court documents that pertained to your case. Those files had copies of the assessments, the tax invoices and the notices of delinquent taxes for the time period covered by the foreclosure and all the court foreclosure documents. Now, these are not all of the older documents that I want to see, but at least I could see the ones they used to support the tax foreclosure. This part is a darn mystery. For some reason, all of those documents were mailed to the old house address. Did you change the address with the county?"

"No, of course not. How can this be? They always mailed things to us at our home. I still get the duplex tax documents there. I don't see how that could have happened. They used to put invoices for both properties in the same envelope, and those were mailed to our home. I don't know why there was a change. If they mailed it to the old address, I guess it must have been returned to the county. I wonder why they didn't look into that when it was returned to them."

Owen thought to himself, *They probably didn't want Kye to get the information, so they intentionally mailed the invoices and assessments to the wrong address*.

"I don't know, Kye, but I'm going to keep digging. I told the Treasurer and the County Auditor that something wasn't right. Another thing I did was to check the legal notices the county published in the *Bekbourg Tribune* for the tax foreclosure sale. Those were plain shit as far as describing the property. No one would know whose property it was."

"I feel so bad about this, Owen. What do we do?"

"A couple of things: first, I'm going to quickly file for a temporary restraining order to try and stop them from doing anything else to your property for now. When I file for the TRO, I'm also going to file to force the county to give me the additional documents I need to see what went on. There is something else that I think we should do quickly—even before I file for the restraining order. We need to get some public opinion going on your side. If you want to move forward, I'll call my good friend, Saul Timmers, at our TV station here and set up a news interview with you for tomorrow. Those are my immediate plans. After I get some more information and facts, I'm going to file a lawsuit that claims the county wrongfully took your property. The first priority though is the request for the restraining order."

Kye felt she couldn't let the matter drop. She couldn't live with herself if she let Cecil's property get away from her. Cecil had thought that his nephew, Leo, might someday return to Bekbourg and need the place to live. Well, the house was now gone, but Leo could always pull a mobile home on the property if he ever came back. She told Owen to work on the TRO and set up the TV interview.

Kye's TV interview aired that evening on the local news. With Owen by her side, she told about how Cecil had grown up on the property with his brother, Lester, and how Cecil's father left the property to them when he died. She explained her sentimental feelings for the property and the shock of seeing that it was being development without her knowledge. She explained how she would gladly pay any back taxes, and that she never would have been delinquent in taxes. The tax invoices and assessments stopped coming to her, but she didn't realize that since they had always been included with her duplex property.

Owen, for his part, said that he couldn't understand how this could have happened, but he was going to get to the bottom of it, that this sort of thing should not have happened to Kye. He was hoping it would be amicably resolved, but if need be, "he would fight it to the highest court to see that Mrs. Davis got her beloved husband's property back."

Chapter 3

Drew Chambers graduated from college with a degree in accounting and joined a small accounting firm in Columbus, Ohio. By taking night classes, he had recently completed his Master's Degree and planned to take the CPA exam later in the summer. The son of Danny and Sally Chambers, Drew had grown up in Bekbourg, but at his parents' urging had taken an accounting job in Columbus. He liked his job, but when he got the opportunity a few months ago to return to Bekbourg, he did so.

"How's the job going?" Danny asked Drew as they sat at the dinner table enjoying his mother's strawberry short cake.

Drew laughed. "Better than I had expected. Owen can be a trip to work for, but that guy is brilliant. He really knows his stuff. Once I get past my CPA exams, he plans to have me help him on some things. I think, because it's just the two of us, I'll get to do a greater variety of things quicker than I would have if I'd stayed at the firm in Columbus."

Sally said, "I'm glad things worked out the way they did. You know, me and your dad didn't really want you to stay around here because of all the drug problems, but with the big drug bust and Sean becoming the interim sheriff, we hope things are turning around here."

"I know, Mom. I couldn't believe it when Mary called and asked me to lunch. She told me she knew you and Dad and that she had been Jeff Thompson's wife. She said that she wanted to try and make up to the community here for all the bad things that he did. She knew I had gotten my accounting degree and wanted to know if I was interested in coming back here to handle her foundation's work."

"She is such a nice woman," Sally said. "I felt so bad for her. She has tried to make things right. I don't blame her one bit for taking back her family's name, Zimmstein. The people around here seem to have accepted her. She is spending more and more time in Bekbourg."

"Yeah, I think she is. It sure worked out for me with Owen starting to think about retiring and with me being able to bring in Mary's work. After she asked me to handle the accounting for her foundation, I knew that Owen had handled your and Dad's accounting matters for years. I took a chance and called him, and he agreed to meet with me."

Danny said, "You know my concern was whether you would have enough to do. I didn't want you to give up that job in Columbus and then this not work out here. Is there enough work?"

"Dad, yeah, there's going to be plenty. Right now, the extra time I have when I'm not working on the foundation matters, I can spend preparing for the CPA exam. Owen is spending a lot of time on something. Once I have the exam behind me, I know that there'll be plenty of work. That reminds me, one of your high school English teachers came in to see him about a tax matter. I don't know how she knew I was your son, but she did, and she told me to tell you and Mom hello."

Danny chuckled. "That has to be Kye Davis."

"Yeah, that's her."

"It's no surprise she knew who you were. She knows everything about everyone around town. Being a high school teacher all those years, she has her ways of keeping up. She's not a gossip, she just cares about people. She was sure a great teacher."

Several years ago, Danny bought a neglected 1959 Eldorado Biarritz Cadillac convertible. He planned to restore it one day, but never had gotten around to it. Sean and Danny had practically grown up together but had lost touch during the twenty years that Sean was away in the Marines. Danny was glad when Sean returned to Bekbourg. The first time that Sean visited Danny's warehouse, Sean saw the old tail fin peeking out from under a large tarp. Danny showed him the Cadillac. After that, Danny had taken a renewed interest in restoring the old car.

Danny towed the old Cadillac convertible to the county vocational school—where high school students could learn trade skills and get certificates in various occupations. Art Myers was the auto shop instructor at the trade school. Danny told Art that the students could learn how to inventory needed parts for these types of restorations. Over the summer, Danny would acquire the necessary parts and in the fall when classes resumed, restoring the Cadillac could be a year-long project. Danny offered to assist Art as needed. Once the car was restored, Danny knew that he could sell it, because car enthusiasts were always looking for a 1959 Eldorado Biarritz Cadillac convertible.

Danny was watching Art work with the students to identify the parts they would need. Danny had already determined that the car wasn't in too bad shape. Beneath the paint-brushed gray primer that covered the original candy red, the exterior was in fairly decent shape. The convertible top and interior leather seats would have to be replaced, but that wasn't insurmountable.

Two of the boys, Rudy and Felipe, were going to be seniors next year and were excited about restoring the old car. Rudy was a skinny kid with sandy hair. He crawled in the back to see what it would take to recover the back-seat cushions. When he pulled the back-seat cushions, something caught his eye.

"Hey Teach, there's something weird about this back," he said as he got out of the back seat.

"Let me see," said Felipe crawling into the back. Art and Danny watched as Felipe had a look. When he got out, "Yep, Rudy's right. There is a plywood panel there."

"Let's have a look in the trunk," suggested Danny as he walked around. Art and the other students followed him to watch. He opened the trunk and looked up where the back seat was. He got into the big trunk space and probed, finding to his surprise a false back. "You're right, there is something here." Danny began pulling and finally managed to pry it loose. "There's a box in here." Danny pulled out the heavy box and sat it on the concrete floor. Other students had now gathered around, curious about the box.

"Looks like you need a bolt cutter, Danny," said Art. "Rudy, get that cutter off the wall over there."

Danny used the large cutter to cut open the lock. The students and Art all moved closer to get a look. Under stacks of old papers and things that looked like junk, Danny saw a dark piece of fabric. He pulled it back. There was a gasp from the students followed by a chorus of varying exclamations, "Holy shit," "Wow," "Where'd those come from?" "Are those real?" Danny and Art were astounded, looking from the box to each other.

"What are you going to do with all those coins, Danny?" asked Art, still in disbelieve.

"Well, I guess I'm going to take 'em home."

Harvey Bennett, President of Bekbourg Enterprises, didn't wait until the next morning. He called Nickolas Garrison, a County Commissioner, as soon as he saw the TV report. "Nickolas, did you see Kye Davis and Owen Donaldson on the news tonight about the Lake Meadows development?"

"Yeah, I saw it."

"I don't have to tell you that this negative publicity is not good."

"No, it's not. What makes it worse is that it's Kye Davis. She probably taught half the people in Bekbourg over the thirty-five years she was a teacher at the high school. She's thought highly of around here. That's bad enough, but having Donaldson representing her is going to be a pain in our asses."

"Do you know exactly where her property is in our development?" Harvey asked.

"It's not on the outskirts where we could simply drop it, but I would have to look at a map to know exactly where the parcel is. I know this much, we can't carve it out."

"I can't believe this."

"Look, Harvey. We'll fight it. Once she knows that we're not going to roll over on this, she's not going to want to incur those legal expenses. She probably can't afford the costs. She's an old lady. Even if she could afford it, she's not going to want the stress. Let's play hardball. It'll go away soon enough."

"I didn't expect this controversy. It's not good for the project. If we have to, we can settle with her and make the claim go away. Donaldson can't fight it if his client's not willing to."

After Danny took the coins home, he called Sean to stop by. Sean stood beside Danny looking at the coins. "You know, Danny, I think these may be the coins that Roger Burkhart had before he and his family were killed. There were rumors that he had coins, but no trace of them ever showed up. Roger had a Cadillac. I bet that was his car and these are the coins. He bragged that the coins were valued around $250,000."

Roger Burkhart had been an unscrupulous businessman who owned a car dealership, pawn shop and fireworks stand in Bekbourg. Most viewers cringed when his television commercials aired, urging, in his booming, fast-talking, down-home accent, his audience to visit his dealership for their "Drrreeeaaammmm" car. On July 4, 1980, Roger and his family were killed and their home burned to the ground. Before his death, Roger had been heard around town boasting about some valuable coins he had, but those coins never surfaced after his death, and their mystery faded with time.

Danny whistled, "$250,000? What should I do with them?"

"I think you should put them in a safe place until all this can be sorted out."

"I'll do that, but Sean, why don't you take the papers that were in the box? They might mean something to you."

Danny and Sally inventoried the coins and took pictures. An old leather bag held some really old ones. Old U.S. gold coins were contained in a canvas bag, and silver dollars were in a deteriorating cigar box. The rest of the coins were loose.

Meanwhile, except for one piece of paper, Sean locked everything that Danny had given him in his office safe. Roger Burkhart and his family had been murdered in the wee hours following the July 4, 1980, celebration. At the time, most people thought he had been killed because of the coins.

Recently, that myth had been shattered when his murderers were discovered. Sean didn't know if Roger had owned the coins, if he was a middleman in a transaction, or what the situation was, but knowing Roger, there was a good possibility that at least some of the coins were stolen.

The auto shop students told their friends and parents, and the story of Danny finding the coins spread like wildfire. The following day, Sally's customers were asking her about them. Danny was asked by several people. That evening, Noel Fischner stopped by their home to give Sally some campaign brochures and said, "Hey, Danny, what's this I hear about you finding a pot of gold?"

Danny laughed, "Well, I don't know much about them yet."

"Do you know where they came from?"

"Well, they may be the ones that Roger Burkhart was talking about before he died. He had a Cadillac then, so that's why we think that, but we're trying to find out for sure."

"Wow, that's really something. It's sure created a buzz around here. Lucky for Sally in her campaign that she now has money she can use. I sure wish I'd come into money like that to win against Riley Barnes in the Commissioner's race."

Peggy Thornton walked into the kitchen carrying a couple of grocery bags. Byron yelled from his favorite chair in the small living room, "Did you get me some cigarettes?"

"Yes, Hon." She pulled them out of one of the bags, opened the box, and carried two packs to him.

"Get me another beer."

She returned to the kitchen, and as she walked back in with a can, she said, "There was some excitement today at Sally's." Peggy worked two jobs. She was a full-time stylist at Sally Chambers' beauty salon and worked part-time three or four evenings a week at the Shopper's Pavilion, a box department store.

Byron was uninterested and ignored her as he lit a cigarette. She popped the top on the beer and moved some cans out of the way to make room for the can on the side table.

"Sally's husband, Danny, found a bunch of old coins worth a lot of money."

"Good for him. Here, make yourself useful and put this movie in the player. When will supper be ready?"

"About forty-five minutes. I have to be at the Pavilion by seven o'clock."

"Hmm."

As Peggy inserted the movie, she rattled on, "The coins were found in a car that people think used to belong to someone you did work for."

Byron was taking a drink from the beer waiting for the movie to boot up, "Yeah, who's that?"

"That man that used to own the car dealership here in town, you know the one who burned up with his family about twenty years ago."

Byron yanked up the remote and clamped down on the pause button, "What are you talkin' about?"

Peggy didn't want to agitate him. "Here, your movie is ready. I'll get dinner on so we can eat."

"Wait! What's this about? You talkin' about Roger? Roger Burkhart?"

"Yeah, that's him. Didn't you do work for him?"

"How did Chambers find those coins?"

"Well, a few years back, he bought an old Cadillac, thinking he would restore it. You know he works on old cars. He had it in his warehouse and loaned it to the school for the boys to get some experience on restoration. They found a hidden compartment that had a box of coins. Rumors are that the car used to belong to Mr. Burkhart. Anyways," Peggy was laughing, "Danny is shy, but the newspaper and TV station wanted to talk to him. People all day were coming into the shop talking about it. There's talk that the coins could be worth $250,000."

Byron squeezed the beer can so hard, beer spewed on the chair and on his shirt.

Peggy was alarmed, but she couldn't understand why the story would anger him. "What's wrong, Hon? Let me get you another beer."

"Shit! Now after all this time, they were in that car. That's not right that Chambers found them."

Byron slammed the beer down on the table causing more beer to spew out the top. For a fleeting moment, Peggy was afraid he might hit her. Instead, he charged out the front door. She heard his truck roar to life, and the tires screech as he burned rubber going to wherever he was headed.

Danny and Sean researched the history of the 1959 Cadillac through the state's motor vehicles records and by talking to previous owners. They learned that Roger had purchased the car a few years before his murder. It had been parked in the garage behind Roger's house and had not been damaged by the fire. As part of the probate proceeding, Roger's nephew had inherited it, and he sold the car to someone who had driven it for a few years. It broke down, and the owner was not interested in repairing such an old car. It sat in his back yard for a while when a man who worked on the railroad heard about the car. He wanted an old car to drive to work, and he liked big old Cadillacs. He bought the car, repaired it, and painted a primer on it, thinking to have it repainted at some point. He never got around to repainting the car. He eventually retired and parked the car in his garage. He got sick and didn't drive the car during the last years of his life. When his widow wanted to get rid of it, the husband of a friend told her about Danny. She was happy that Danny was willing to buy it.

Sean said, "Well, Danny, now that we know about the car, we need to find out what we can about the coins. We need to know if any of them were stolen, what their value is, and who owns them. I think we should talk to an attorney to figure out how to get started."

"Yeah, Sean, that makes sense to me. Owen Donaldson has always taken care of Sally and my accounting affairs. He's also a lawyer. We could go to him and see what he has to say. I'll call him and set up a time."

The local TV station and newspaper were pressing Danny for an interview. Danny told Sally he'd rather have a "root canal." She laughed, knowing his shyness made it difficult. However, she also knew that the rumors flying around Bekbourg about the coins were getting more exaggerated and needed to be put to rest. At her prompting, he finally met with the local media.

He explained that he had bought the car a number of years ago, but he didn't know the car's history until the title had been researched after the coins were discovered. He explained that he and Art thought it would be a good project for the shop class to restore the car the next school year. He told about the students discovering the panel in the car's trunk. When asked if there was anything else in the box with the coins, Danny laughed, "Well, there were some papers, but I couldn't tell much about what they were. There was even a large envelope with a stamp from Vienna. The papers inside were written in German. At least that's what Sally said, because I didn't know what language they were in."

"What are you planning to do with the coins?"

"Well, I guess we first need to understand what we have. I talked to Sheriff Neumann, and he thinks we need to find out if any of them were stolen and try to find out where they came from. We're going to get an expert to look at them."

"Rumor is that they are worth somewhere around $250,000. Are you and Sally planning a vacation?" Seth Trotter, owner of the *Bekbourg Tribune*, asked with a grin.

Danny smiled, "Well, we haven't gotten that far, that's for sure. Again, we don't have any idea how much they're worth. It could be a whole lot less than that."

"Any idea how Roger Burkhart ended up with the coins?"

"No, we really don't know anything about their history."

"Some of the boys said they saw some gold coins in the box."

"Well, there's quite a variety, but I don't know much about them. I plan to get them to an expert and go from there."

Chapter 4

Not surprising, the Treasurer's office had not provided Owen with any of the information that he requested, despite the fact that it was supposed to be public information. The Clerk of Court's office had files for the Sheriff's Sales, where the tax foreclosure properties were auctioned, but those files only contained the information specifically needed for the forfeiture and auction, not older invoices or assessments. He needed additional information, but the way the Treasurer's Office usually drug its feet, he didn't know when or if he would get the property information.

Time was of the essence, because if Bekbourg Enterprises sold Kye's property, the chances of her getting her property back would drop to about zero, and it was pretty close to that point now. He had to seek a restraining order to prevent Bekbourg Enterprises from moving forward with selling Kye's property until the ownership issues could be decided.

Owen prepared two filings. One for the restraining order and one requesting that the court order the county to produce the records he needed to adequately represent Kye. As soon as he filed those, he personally hand carried copies to the *Bekbourg Tribune* and the local TV station. Part of his strategy was to garner public opinion in favor of

Kye, and since most people knew her, he hoped public sentiment would rise up in support of Kye.

Sean and Danny were sitting in Owen's office explaining about the coins. Sean said, "Owen, when I talked to Jack Rhodes last year, I asked him if he knew anything about the coins that were rumored to have been in Roger's home the night he and his family were killed. He told me that Roger had been bragging about having some coins, but rumor was that Roger was just a middleman in selling the coins."

"Did anyone ever come forward claiming the coins?" asked Owen.

"No one ever raised it after Roger was killed."

Owen huffed, "I wouldn't be the least bit surprised if they were stolen. No sane person would mention them and incriminate themselves. With Roger, it was no telling which end was up. That's a lot of treasure if what Roger was claiming was right, but he was a con man. Who the hell knows whether he was telling the truth?"

Sean spied a half-empty Canadian Club whiskey bottle sitting on a file cabinet. Early afternoon to Owen was just as good as any to enjoy a couple of shots.

Sean figured when Owen laid the pencil that he had been tapping on a stack of papers, that they were about to hear Owen's thoughts on how best to proceed. His hunch was right. "Okay. Here's what we'll do. I know a coin dealer in Cincinnati. I trust him." Sean thought if Owen trusted him, he was good as gold. "He's been around a long time. I'll call him and tell him that we need for him to look at the coins and let us know what they're worth. I'll also ask if he can find out whether any are stolen. I'll let you know if he can help us."

Sally closed up her beauty shop and drove home. When she arrived, she saw the back door latch broken and the door partially open. She jumped back in her car and drove to the road and called Danny.

Sean walked through the house. "Sean, I put the box on the shelf in the utility room. Even though I didn't think someone would break in and steal the coins, I put some other things in front of the box. I guess I didn't hide them well enough. No one's ever broken into our house before."

"Is anything else missing, Danny?"

"Not that I know of. I did a quick look before I called you, but everything else seems okay—not that we have much that anyone would want. I'm sure glad that Sally and Drew weren't here."

Things weren't damaged, but some drawers and closet doors were left open. A couple of things from closets had been pulled out in the room. The kitchen and living room looked undisturbed except for the pantry door being open.

Danny and Sally lived in a modest three bedroom brick house on about five acres. The nearest house was not visible from their home. Sean suspected they could afford a larger home, but they both were frugal. The grass and hedges were neatly trimmed, and potted flowers were on the walk and front porch. Family pictures lined the mantel on the brick fireplace, and vibrant violets filled a window box above the kitchen sink. Since Sally was running for City Council, her picture was shown with other Reform Party candidates on the brochure materials laying on the kitchen cabinet.

Arlo Lopez, a new deputy on the force, knocked on the front door, and Sean walked out to see what he had learned. “Sheriff, I talked to the neighbors on both sides, but no one saw anything. I guess with their house being isolated like this, it was easy for whoever did this. I told the neighbors if they heard of anything to let me know.”

“Okay. Thanks, Arlo.” Sean nodded toward two deputies standing in the front yard. “Darrell and Syd looked around the outside of the house and out back, but they didn’t see anything unusual. Forensics is checking things. Hopefully, we’ll get a break.”

“I’ll be around, Chief, if you need me to do anything else,” Arlo assured Sean.

A forensics technician came out carrying a small plastic bag. “Sheriff Neumann, we found these heavy dust particles on the carpet in the guest bedroom closet. Looks like specks of sawdust, but we’ll know more once the lab analyzes them. I asked Mr. and Mrs. Chambers about them. They both said they don’t know why these would be there. She said that she vacuumed there two days ago when she cleaned the house, and no one has been in that room since then. Whoever did this pulled some boxes out of the closet. We checked closely in the utility room and found a few particles on the floor next to the shelf where the box of coins was taken. Just a theory, but they could have come from clothing or crevices in shoes."

"Good to know," said Sean.

Danny spoke up, "You know, Sean. Sally and I have an inventory and pictures of all the coins. They are in my truck. I took them with me when we went to talk to Owen in case he needed to see any of them."

"That's good, Danny. If they start to show up at pawn shops or with collectors, we might be able to find who stole them. The coin expert that Owen knows might be able to tell us something about them from the pictures. I don't know if that will help, but it's worth a try."

The slip of paper that Sean had kept with him from the box of coins was a small receipt with the name, "Ernie's Pawn Shop" printed at the top. Hand written were the names, "Leo Davis; Byron Thornton. June 19, 1980," and a signature by Leo Davis below a hand printed notation, "coins."

Mike Adams had been the Sheriff in Bekbourg when Sean returned from his service in the Marines. They had been best friends during their youth and had been a dreaded combination by their high school football opponents: Sean, the quarterback, and Mike, wide receiver. They went undefeated their senior year and won their Division's State Championship. Both had received scholarship offers, but Mike didn't want to leave Bekbourg and, instead, attended the Police

Academy. Mike had been gravely injured last year and retired on disability, leading to Sean becoming the interim Sheriff. Sean thought if anyone would know about the names on the slip of paper it would be Mike.

As much as Mike meant to Sean, it was awkward knowing that he was now the Sheriff and that Mike had left the Department under a cloud. But, it was good to see him and Geri, his wife. Geri seemed to be doing fine. She told him that she really enjoyed working for the foundation recently founded by Mary Zimmstein, "Bekbourg Gives." She especially enjoyed working with Dusty and his friend Carla. Sean laughed and agreed that Dusty was one-of-a-kind.

Sean said, "Mike, I guess you heard about Danny finding those coins."

"Yeah, that's incredible. Leave it to Danny to find something like that. I also heard that someone broke into his and Sally's home and stole them."

"Fortunately, no one was home. He gave me some papers that were in the box with the coins to see if I might be able to find anything out about them. One piece of paper had some names, 'Byron Thornton, Leo Davis, and Ernie's Pawn Shop.' Do you recognize any of those names?"

"Well, Leo Davis was from here, but he left town several years ago. As far as I know, he's never been back. Byron Thornton, now there's a piece of work. He used to work for the county until he got injured. They gave him a partial disability. He's never worked since, but his wife works two jobs. He's been trying to get a full disability."

"Has he been in trouble?"

"Just the usual: DUI, fights. A couple of times we were called by his wife when he slapped her around, but she wouldn't press charges."

Geri had been listening to their conversation. "You know Sean, Sophia Martin—well Bergmann when we were in high school. Anyway, if you want to find out more about Leo, you might talk to her."

Sean was surprised. "Why would Sophia know about Leo?"

Mike was surprised for a different reason, "How do you know Leo?"

She laughed, "I really didn't know Leo. He was a topic though among us girls. See, there was a rumor going around that Sophia and Leo were an item. He was about eight years older than us, but when the rumors started spinning that Sophia was dating him, we got up to speed real fast on him." She was grinning. "The girls were unanimous that he was super handsome, sexy and a 'bad boy'."

Sean and Mike eyed each other, shaking their heads. Geri's eyes sparkled with amusement.

"Leo and Sophia were dating?" asked Sean.

"Yeah. It had to have started after she went off to college, because she wasn't dating him when she left for college. Rumors were she had been seen with Leo that spring when I was expecting Matt."

"Gosh, that is a surprise. I'll talk to her. Can either of you think of anyone else?"

Geri and Mike looked at each other, with Geri shaking her head, "no." Mike turned back to Sean. "There is a guy who might know something. When Thornton was working for the county, he worked alongside a man named Roy Mynatt. When Thornton got hurt, I talked to Mynatt about what happened. Other than that, no one comes to mind. If we think of anyone else, Sean, I'll give you a call."

Their successful businesses assured that Danny and Sally were known by many around Bekbourg. When word fanned out that the coins had been stolen from their home, several of their customers stopped by to express concern and disbelief. Sally told Danny about how everyone was uneasy about the break-in at their house. "I never dreamed that we would be the topic of so much talk around town."

"I know what you mean. Several of my customers mentioned it today. Otis Mueller was having his car serviced. He doesn't talk much since his boy died of that drug overdose last year, but even he was asking me about it and making sure we were all okay."

"Well, I know Sean will figure it out."

"Yeah, he will."

Ever since Peggy had told Byron about Danny finding the coins, she had felt uneasy. He didn't return until the early morning hours after she told him, and he was so drunk, he passed out in his chair in the living room. He had been angry now for several days. Although Byron had not hit her since

Sheriff Adams had threatened him with prosecution for domestic violence, she still tried to steer clear of him during his foul moods.

Her anxiety was thrown into overdrive when she arrived at Sally's in the morning and learned that someone had broken into their home and stolen the coins. Thank God, no one was at home and got hurt, but she feared that Byron may have been the culprit. She was nervous and worried throughout the day, so much so that Sally asked her if she was okay. She pled a headache but didn't leave until closing time—despite Sally asking her if she wanted to leave early. She didn't want to forego the income by not working on her last three customers.

Having worked the day before, she didn't know if Byron had left the house, but he was home when set got there like he usually was, smoking, drinking and watching movies. As she entered the house this evening, she greeted him like always and started dinner. She had stopped and picked up fried chicken, which she knew he liked, and then supplemented it with her own cooking. As they were eating, she casually asked him if he had gone out the last couple of days. When he asked her why she was asking, she told him, "No real reason. Just wondering what your days were like."

His only reply was that his days "sucked." She wasn't about to push him further for an answer.

Sean pulled into the gravel driveway where Byron Thornton lived. The torn or missing window screens and gray and black smudges on the white exterior spoke of years of neglect on the small cinder block house. The random woody boxwoods were orphaned except for the weed-filled yard, which was sorely in need of mowing.

As Sean approached the front door, he heard the TV blaring with some type of action movie. He knocked on the door. Someone walked up to the front window and looked out. In no hurry to open the door, Byron must have lit the cigarette in his mouth before opening the door. He was unshaven, and his hairline was receding. He was heavy with a large beer belly, and he was wearing a white, stained, sleeveless underwear t-shirt and frayed looking jeans.

"Yeah?" was the greeting.

"Are you Byron Thornton?"

"I guess you know I live here. What do you want?"

"Sir, I'm Sheriff Neumann. I'd like to talk to you about Roger Burkhart and Leo Davis."

Blowing smoke upward, "Roger and Leo? Those are names I haven't heard in years. What about them?"

"You mind if I come in?"

Byron stepped back to let Sean enter.

Two empty beer cans and a full ashtray were sitting on the table beside a worn recliner that had a deep indention where the seat had long given way to his weight. Byron made no move to turn down the TV volume.

Sitting in his chair, he blew another smoke ring, "Have a seat," he said while looking at the TV.

Sean decided on a small upholstered chair that slightly tilted when he sat. "Roger died over twenty years ago, but you say you've heard nothing about Leo in a long time?"

Still watching the TV and blowing smoke from his Camel, "Yeah, that's right."

"Do you know where I can find Leo?"

This got Byron's attention. "Huh? He's been gone from here over twenty years. Why'd you want to talk to him?"

"Where is he?"

"Last I heard, he was movin' to Texas." Byron had already turned back to the movie.

"What was your relationship with Roger Burkhart?"

Byron sat there for a minute watching the TV. "Why are you askin' about Roger?"

"I take it you and Leo had some dealings with Roger?"

"Where'd you hear that?"

"Mr. Thornton, I'd like for you to answer my questions."

"Look, I don't know what this is about. I haven't seen Leo in twenty years, and Roger's been dead that long."

"Does 'Ernie's Pawn Shop' mean anything to you?"

"Ernie's?"

"Yes, Ernie's Pawn Shop?"

"I'm not sure." The cigarette was about half smoked, but Thornton picked up his pack and shook out another one and held it ready to light.

"Did you do anything with Roger and Leo in June or early July 1980?"

"Like I said, Sheriff, I can't help you."

"Well, tell me what you know about some missing coins that were found recently."

Looking up to blow another smoke ring but never taking his eyes off the television, "I don't know nothin' 'bout no coins."

"Where were you two days ago?"

Byron jerked his focus to Sean, "What? What's this all about?"

"Mr. Thornton, what were you doing day before yesterday?"

"'Bout what I'm doing now."

"Can anyone vouch for you?"

"Well, my old lady worked all day and got home around five o'clock." Byron was looking suspiciously at Sean.

"So, no one can account for you being here during the day?"

"Look, Sheriff. I don't know what this is all about, but I ain't done nothin'." He ground out the cigarette and lit the next one.

Sean wasn't satisfied with Thornton's answers. He would be back once he got more information. He was going to ask a deputy to check with Byron's neighbors to see if any of them remembered seeing his truck or him during the day that the coins were stolen. His department had already put word out to the state police, pawn shops and coin dealers to be on alert for coins.

Chapter 5

Kye sat at the counsel table beside Owen. She had never been a party to a lawsuit, but from what she could tell, she didn't think that she was going to win. Not because Owen wasn't doing a good job arguing her case—just the opposite. He was having none of the dismissive claims argued by the County Attorney, Claude Atwood, or Bekbourg Enterprises' attorney, Zack Norcross. It was because Judge Bergmann didn't seem impressed with Owen's legal position. That was not real surprising. Owen warned Kye that they were fighting an uphill battle before they entered the courthouse to argue for the temporary restraining order and to force the county to turn over the property records. He said that Judge Bergmann was "hard-nosed and biased in favor of the county," but he also tried to be reassuring when he told her the judge "didn't throw the law books out the door when he decided cases."

"Your Honor," argued Zack Norcross, "the law was followed here. The plaintiff didn't pay the property taxes on the thirty acres in question. The county sent the required notices. The tax foreclosure procedures were followed. Notice was published in the *Bekbourg Tribune* as required, and the Sheriff's sale of this property was conducted in accordance with the law. There is nothing untoward. There is no dispute about the county following the law. My client has invested a lot of time and money and is ready to move forward with Lake Meadows. Every day that the project is delayed is harmful to Bekbourg Enterprises."

Owen responded, "He's wrong, Judge. There is a lot to dispute here. First, Mrs. Davis couldn't pay her taxes if she never received an invoice. The county pulled a stunt when they stopped sending the invoices together. She thought she was paying for both properties. Why did they do that? The County Treasurer's office won't supply me any information—which is public information by the way—to be able to present all the facts to the Court to show that Mrs. Davis was wrongfully deprived of her property. What few files are in possession of the Clerk of Court show that the county was at fault, not Mrs. Davis. Those documents show the county, without any knowledge or consent by Mrs. Davis, changed their practice and started sending the tax invoices to the address at the property where she didn't live. She couldn't pay taxes if she didn't have an invoice. She actually thought she was paying them, because that was the way it had been handled until the county changed its practice for her property.

"The harm to Mrs. Davis will be much greater than to this big profitable company, because she will lose her property if it is sold to a third party. Something happened here, Judge, and I need to get to the bottom of it. The county is dragging its feet on giving me records that are public and ought to have already been made available."

Claude, on behalf of the county, argued that Owen had all the information he needed from the Clerk of Court's files, which Owen disputed and again reiterated that the records from the Treasurer's Office were supposed to be public anyway.

At the conclusion of the hearing, Judge Bergmann told the parties he would make his ruling on the temporary restraining order in two days.

"Owen, what do you think is going on?" asked Kye as they were walking out of the courtroom.

"I'll be damned if I know. The challenge we have, Kye, is that Bekbourg Enterprises bought your property at the Sheriff's Sales. They have been proceding with the development plans with the assumption they own it. Like I said before, we've got about as good a chance as it snowing in August. We'll just have to see. In the meantime, I'll keep working on it."

Sean was busy with paperwork when Kim buzzed him, "Sheriff, someone is here who would like to talk to you."

Something in her tone told him that something was up. "Who is it?"

"Cooper Townsend."

That didn't mean anything to Sean, but he figured he was about to be educated. "Tell him I'll be there shortly."

Sean pulled up on the computer "Cooper Townsend," and saw that he had gone to prison six years ago on drug possession.

Sean walked to the reception area. Townsend was sitting in one of the plastic chairs. "Mr. Townsend, I'm Sheriff Neumann. What can I do for you?"

"I'd like to talk to you, Sheriff."

"Sure, let's step in here." Sean pushed open a door to a small conference room. "What's this about, Mr. Townsend?"

Cooper was a tall, lanky man. His cheeks were sunken into his face. His nose looked like it had been broken. His long stringy hair was pushed behind his ears. "I just got out on parole, but I never should have been convicted. I was set up."

Sean had met many people over his years in law enforcement who claimed innocence despite their guilt, so he was immediately skeptical. "I wasn't here, Mr. Townsend. I'm not familiar with your case. Who do you think set you up?"

"Thompson."

This immediately got Sean's attention. "Which Thompson—Jeff or Randall?"

"I don't know which one. I just know it's one or maybe both of them."

"Why would they have set you up?"

"How the hell would I know? That's just the way they are."

"You know they both are dead?"

"Yeah, I heard that. Good riddance."

Obviously no love loss, Sean thought. "How did you know the Thompsons?"

"Biggest mistake I ever made going to work at that bar."

"Which bar?"

"Koot's."

"What did you do there?"

"I was one of the bartenders."

"How long did you work at Koot's?"

"I worked there for four years. Then they planted drugs in my car. That damn lawyer, hell, he was a drunk. He didn't do shit for me. I served six years of my life, screwed."

"You don't know why the Thompsons planted drugs in your car?" *They were both dead, so it was easy to blame them for framing him since they couldn't defend themselves. On the other hand, it would not be beneath either Thompson to frame someone, but if they did, there had to be a reason.*

"No idea."

"You don't know why they framed you?" Cooper shook his head. "Who was your attorney?"

"That drunk, Owen Donaldson."

"Mr. Townsend, why are you here? What do you want me to do?"

"Look at my case. You'll see that I'm innocent. I want my record cleared."

"I'll look at the file, Mr. Townsend, but you were convicted. I don't think I can do anything."

"I shouldn't have been convicted. That's the point. I was set up, and I had a drunk for a lawyer."

Sean didn't want to debate the matter with Cooper. He was bitter and agitated. "Okay, I'll look over the file. Where can I reach you?"

"I'm staying at my mother's place."

Sean's mother, Helen, instructed him to put up the badminton net before the kids arrived. "Mom, don't you think they're a little young to be playing badminton?" Sean's mother had invited the family to grill hamburgers and make home-made ice cream to celebrate Father's Day. It was a beautiful day, and Cheryl had helped Helen set the large picnic table in the back yard and set out the chairs and coolers for the afternoon. With their tasks complete, they were sitting on the front porch watching Sean wrestling with the strings and poles as he attempted to right the net.

"Not at all." Cheryl and Helen laughed as they watched him struggle with keeping the pole straight as he drove in the peg.

Sean soon finished and was standing in the front yard when a beige van pulled into the driveway. Linda slung open the van door, jumped out and ran straight into Sean's arms. They both were hugging and laughing. "Hi, Big Brother. Glad it's all set up. Ready for me to stomp your butt?"

Linda Neumann was an attorney who specialized in wills and estate planning. Her firm was smaller and focused on family law, such as divorce, custody cases, and custodial proceedings. Chris Delaney, her husband, practiced corporate law in a large diversified law firm.

Sean laughed. Even though his sister's family lived only two hours away in Cincinnati, he had only seen them a couple of times since returning to Bekbourg. Cheryl joined them, and

Linda gave her an exuberant hug, "So, Sean, I see she is still putting up with you."

Linda's husband walked over with their two children. It was a happy occasion for all. Chris extended his hand, "It's great to see you again, Sean," and gave Cheryl a hug.

Cheryl said, "Olivia and Ethan have grown since the last time we saw them."

Sean gave them both a hug, "I've got more stories to tell you about your mother."

Both kids eagerly responded, "Yes!"

Linda said, "Don't believe a word he tells you—unless it's good."

Buddy was weaving in and out between everyone—his thick tail wagging as fast as it would go. The kids took off running with him happily galloping in their wake. The adults walked to the back yard to help get things ready for dinner.

After everyone settled in, Jim put the burgers on the grill. Soon, the smell of grilling burgers had everyone starving. Helen, Cheryl and Linda saw to it that there were baked beans, sliced watermelon, deviled eggs, slaw and chips. They sat on the long benches enjoying the summertime feast. Holding up the hamburger before she took another bite, Linda said, "Dad, these are delicious. Too bad you had to cook on Father's Day."

"Wouldn't have it any other way," he said while chewing a bite.

Linda asked Jim how things were going at the milk plant. Sean's dad had worked there over forty years and had been planning to retire when it closed, but it now seemed to have new life.

Bekbourg Springs Milk Company has been in Bekbourg since the 1890's. Schriever High School was named after the milk company's founder, Harry Schriever. Jim worked for the plant when he graduated from high school, and then when he returned from the Marines, he went back to them as a shift manager. He'd been the plant manager for the last several years.

Jim said, "It's been busy, but things seem to be falling into place. T.J. Schriever," Jim looked at Cheryl not sure if she knew the plant's history, "he was the recent owner. He died a few months ago. Five years before he died, he drew up a contract so that after his death, the employees would take ownership of the plant. He wanted to keep the people employed and help the economy of Bekbourg. We recently hired an outside consultant to help develop a business plan to produce and market organic milk. Organic dairy products are growing in popularity, and the employee transition team believes that is the right direction for the company to move."

"Dad, who is on the transition team?"

"Well, it consists of the executive team and some of the managers. I'm part of it. I'm glad that we have the opportunity to keep the company operating. I'm cautiously optimistic that we can turn things around with this new business direction. Last year, I wasn't sure it would stay afloat."

After dinner, Sean cranked the ice cream maker while the adults talked, and the children chased Buddy. When it was ready, Helen scooped generous portions into bowls. Before the daylight started to fade, they moved to the front yard where Cheryl, Sean, Linda and Chris sat on the porch watching Jim and Helen playing badminton with the children. Buddy frolicked around them causing yells mixed with laughter for him to watch out as he tried to catch the birdie.

Linda said, "I hate what went down here last year, especially for you Sean, because I know what good friends you all were growing up."

"Well, it was both surprising and disappointing. I never knew when I returned that something like that was going on here."

"I'm glad you decided to run for sheriff. You have so much experience as a criminal investigator with the Marines. The county can certainly use someone with your knowledge and expertise."

"Well, hopefully, we won't have anything else like what was going on."

"I hope you're right, but there may be other shenanigans around here," Linda added.

This got Sean and Cheryl's attention. "What do you mean?" asked Sean.

"I don't know anything specific, but a couple of years ago, Chris and I were having dinner with a couple of attorneys who were in town on business from Columbus. When one of them heard I was from Bekbourg, she told me that she thought there may have been some shady dealings on forfeiture tax sales and tax auctions."

"Mmmmm," said Sean, thinking that was interesting.

"I have to say, Big Brother, I'm glad you came back."

"Well, you should be. I can help keep an eye on mom and dad."

Linda laughed, "Just don't tell them you plan to keep an eye on them."

They all laughed. Sean looked out at his niece and nephew. Olivia at seven reminded him so much of Linda when she was young, and Ethan who was eight was going to be a tall man like his father. There were lots of teasing, joking, laughter and fun.

That evening when they were walking Buddy, Cheryl told Sean about the tax problem that Kye was having. "When Linda mentioned what that attorney said about tax forfeiture matters here in Bekbourg, I thought of Kye."

"Mmmm. Have you heard anymore from her about where it stands?"

"No, but the next time I see her, I'm going to ask. I feel so bad for her. I hope that Owen can help her with this."

"The county might just jump through hoops to fix this so they don't have to deal with Owen. He makes their lives miserable. I guess the tricky part is that it's part of that new planned development."

"Yes, that's what has me concerned. Kye will be very disappointed if she can't get her property back."

Chapter 6

Cheryl had given much thought to Kye's situation. Then, at the Father's Day gathering, Linda had mentioned hearing about something flakey on tax forfeitures in Bekbourg. She couldn't shake the feeling that something was amiss. Prior corrupt activities by some local Commissioners gave reason to be suspicious. She called Linda and explained about Kye and told her that she would like to talk with the attorney and learn what she knew. Cheryl was now driving back from Columbus thinking about what she had learned.

Megan Tillery, the attorney in Columbus, told Cheryl that her client had grown up in Bekbourg. After retiring, he moved to Florida but still owned property in Bekbourg. He had been gone about ten years and realized that he had not received a property tax invoice for a few years. When he called the County Treasurer's office, he learned that no taxes had been paid, and the property had sold at a tax sale.

"At first, he was upset and called me, because I had helped him out years before on another matter. I contacted the Treasurer's department in Bekbourg. They told me that they would have to look into the case and that it would take some time to find the documents given the time that had passed. My client told me that he remembered when he first moved to Florida that he had received tax invoices, because he gave the county his mailing address for property notices. He said that he guessed he didn't get a tax invoice one year and probably just forgot about it after that. We don't know what happened.

"In the end, my client decided that he didn't want to spend the time or money dealing with the property since it wasn't worth much. Another factor was that he had been living in Florida for so long, and he didn't plan to return to Bekbourg. I can understand him not wanting to look into it further, but it's a shame that he didn't get anything for his property."

The case of the stolen coins took a strange turn. Sean was called to Danny's home to find that the box that had contained the coins had been returned to the back step. After Forensics dusted for finger prints, Danny opened the box. The mystery deepened when Danny and Sally determined that the leather pouch and its very old coins were the only coins that weren't returned. The check by Forensics didn't produce any evidence that pointed to a suspect, but Ronnie Vin had information on the sawdust particles that had been gathered when the coins were stolen.

"Sean, it's Lindenwood."

"I've never heard of it."

"You may know it by another name, Basswood. It's a good wood for making furniture. Because it's a softer wood, it's often used for carving. The fact that we found sawdust, it probably came from someone who uses it for one of these purposes."

"Is it a common wood around here?"

"Yes, it's all around the eastern part of the U.S."

"I appreciate you getting back on this so quickly. I'll check with Danny, but I don't think anyone in his family is a carver or makes furniture. Thanks, Ronnie."

"Anytime, Sean."

Kye hadn't slept well the last two nights, worrying about what the Judge would do. Now, feeling anxious, she sat beside Owen in the courtroom. Owen had told her this morning before they walked over to the courthouse that even if the judge ruled against them on the temporary restraining order, he was working on a lawsuit against Bekbourg Enterprises and the county to try to get her property back. "Once that lawsuit is filed, the county can't ignore my request for the documents. It will still be like pulling teeth, but they can't just sit on their butts and not provide anything. It'd be great if the judge grants the temporary restraining order to make sure they don't sell your property in the meantime, but we have to play the cards we're dealt."

Judge Bergmann presided like a captain over his ship. "I'm ready to make my ruling, but I've got a couple of questions for Counsel before I do." Kye's heart was racing. She was fearful she was getting ready to lose Cecil's birthright.

"Claude, you've seen the list of information that Owen wants. It's not unreasonable. How long will it take the Treasurer and Auditor's offices to produce that?"

"I'm not sure, Judge. Some of it is in a warehouse. Again, Judge, he has the information from the Clerk of Court's files. This is just another fishing trip, Judge. There's nothing there to support whatever it is that he's claiming. It's just another one of his harassments—"

"Counsel, I heard all the arguments the other day," the judge interrupted. "I'm not asking to hear them again. The records Owen is wanting are supposed to be open to the public. He has a right to see them even without litigation. Had he had access to them, I might know more about his position and be assured of my decision. This is a difficult case because Zack's client thought he had legal claim to the property. But, if what Owen alleged the other day is true that Mr. Bennett is part of a conspiracy to wrongfully take Mrs. Davis' property, then that's something entirely different. That seems far-fetched to me. Mr. Bennett has a long list of successful developments in Ohio, including Lake Shore here in Bekbourg."

"Oh, dear," thought Kye. "He's getting ready to rule against me." She started fanning herself with a tissue.

Owen had not noticed, but Judge Bergmann looked at her, "Mrs. Davis, are you okay?"

Owen quickly turned to her and then poured her a glass of water that was sitting on their Counsel table. She took a sip. “I’m so sorry, Your Honor. I’m not used to this type of thing.”

“No, I guess you’re not, Kye. Here’s what I’m going to rule. Claude, I’m going to grant Owen’s request for the information he has listed. Since you don’t know how long it will take to get Owen the information he wants, I’m going to give him five days after you supply him the information to amend his pleading. Owen, I’m not going to have games here. That’s your list, and that’s what I’m talking about. Zack, you said that Mr. Bennett is still doing preliminary work, so I reckon a few more days won’t hurt his project. I’m going to grant the restraining order until I see Owen’s supplemental filing, and the replies, which will be due five days after Owen files. I will then decide if I will issue an injunction to prevent Mrs. Davis’ property from being sold until a ruling in Owen’s lawsuit that he is going to file.”

Zack Norcross stood, “Judge, with all due respect, this uncertainty is doing harm to my client’s development. We can have our response to Owen’s filing filed within three days.”

“Fine. Then you and Claude have three days after Owen files his supplemental pleading to answer, Owen two days for rebuttal, and then I’ll rule.”

“Owen, I take it that the judge’s ruling wasn’t as bad as it could have been?” Kye asked. She and Owen were sitting on a bench outside the Courtroom.

“Kye, are you okay? You didn’t look well in there.”

"I'm feeling better now. I don't know what happened. I think the worry is starting to get to me. I've had some trouble sleeping, and then sitting there thinking the judge was getting ready to rule against us was unsettling."

"Well, I wish I could tell you to let me worry for you, but I know that won't help. Getting back to your question, either he's keeping an open mind, or he just wants to make sure there's a complete record before he rules against us."

"Oh, I didn't think about that."

"Well, in the meantime, Kye, I'm working on this and the bigger lawsuit that gets to the point that they wrongfully took your property."

Charlotte groaned to herself when Owen entered. Claude had given Pauline the list of information that Judge Bergmann ordered to be produced for Owen, and they were working on gathering the records. Charlotte was surprised that Pauline wanted it done quickly, because she usually slow-walked producing anything.

"Hi, Mr. Donaldson. Can I help you with something?"

Owen said before he got to the counter, "Let me guess. You haven't got the information I requested on the Davis property."

She could smell the liquor on his breath, "That's right. We're still working on it. Mr. Atwood told us to give it to him as soon as it was ready, and we will do that."

"Well, I've written down some more information that I need. It's not a secret what I'm going to do. With or without the judge's final ruling on the restraining order, I'm going to sue the county's you-know-what for wrongfully taking Kye Davis' property. That poor woman is under a lot of stress because of all this stuff the county is putting her through. I thought she was going to pass out during the hearing. Judge Bergmann wasn't too happy that you all had not given me the first round of documents I requested. So, I suggest you get your butts in gear and give me this additional information for my next lawsuit. It's here on the list."

Charlotte hesitated and picked up the sheet of paper, squinting. "You know, it would sure make it easier for us to help you if you typed these requests. Don't you have a computer?"

"Hell, no. No way am I going to use something like that. I don't believe in that crap. Besides, my secretary has got better things to do than make your life easier. There's not a darn thing wrong with my handwriting. You're just dragging your feet."

"I'll call you when it's ready."

"Yeah, like when hell freezes over. I'm not going to give up," Owen bellowed as he headed toward the door.

Sean's grandpa, Clarence Neumann, worked for the railroad for fifty years. He had helped Sean get a job as a brakeman when he graduated from high school. Although Sean wasn't cut out for life on the railroad, he cherished his time working there, because it gave him something in common with his grandpa. They had spent a lot of time sharing stories about the railroad and the entertaining characters who worked for it. Since returning to Bekbourg, Sean had reacquainted himself with some of the railroaders. Since Cheryl was late returning from Columbus, he decided to have dinner at Frau's Diner. Every time he walked in, Sean felt nostalgic. Frau's decor had been frozen in time with the jukebox and the plastic-covered seats on tarnished stainless steel bar stools and chair frames. It had been serving German favorites as well as traditional country food for breakfast, lunch and dinner since it opened in the late 1940's. He heard someone yell his name—Mule Head was waving for him to join him.

"Hey, Mule Head." For many of the railroaders, their nickname transcended their jobs. Sean ordered the chicken fried steak special at Mule Head's recommendation. Mule Head retired several years ago from the railroad on a disability from a job injury. He worked part-time for the Bekbourg auto dealership parking cars and delivering cars to and from the service department.

As they ate, Mule Head told Sean that he was back working. Becky Werner was running the dealership, "I wasn't sure if I wanted to continue working there after what all happened, but Mrs. Werner called me herself and asked me to come back. You know, I only work part-time, but she called me. She is a hard worker. I thought the dealership might be sold or even closed, but she seems to be doing a good job. It looks like she's getting that foreign car franchise."

Mule Head had thick, bushy eyebrows. He was a short, stocky man who had endured considerable pain from his injured arm. When he walked, he frequently anchored his damaged arm with his good hand to minimize jolts.

"That's good to know, Mule Head. I hope it works out for you and all the people there."

"Say, have you talked to Dusty recently?"

"No, why?"

"He was talking the other day. He's afraid something's getting ready to happen with the railroad. He's wondering if they might shut everything down here."

"Mmm, I hope it doesn't come to that. Businesses here still rely on the railroad."

"Yeah, I hope it doesn't happen. Say, did you hear about C.P. Traylor moving back here?"

"I saw something about him in the paper, but I never knew him or worked with him."

"Well, he's a big shot railroad man from Bekbourg. He retired from the railroad and went to Washington to work in some important job. Anyhows, I guess C.P.'s retired now from his D.C. job and has decided to move back here. I haven't seen him though."

Sean and Buddy were on the porch waiting for Cheryl. It was just getting dark when she pulled in. "Hey, beautiful," Sean said as he took Cheryl into his arms. "How was your trip to Columbus?"

"Very interesting," she said as she gave him a long passionate kiss. "Have you eaten?"

"Yes, I wasn't sure when you would be back, so I grabbed a bite at Frau's. I brought you a Cobb Salad. I'll sit with you and get caught up."

"Oh, that is music to my ears, because I am so hungry. Thank you." Cheryl loved to tease Sean. As they walked to the kitchen, she pretended to be serious. "I thought you might be campaigning tonight."

Sean rolled his eyes, and she couldn't help but laugh. Sean had been a deputy for less than six months when a horrible murder occurred. He had handled the investigation, and with assistance from state and federal authorities, solved the murders and brought down a major drug operation. With Mike Adams stepping aside as Sheriff, several members of the community urged Sean to become interim sheriff and run for the job in the November election. While Sean liked being sheriff, he did not relish the job's political side—especially campaigning. The good news for him was that no one was running against him.

Cheryl told him about her meeting in Columbus. "What's your next step?" he asked.

"I thought about that on the drive back. No one knows their way around the tax matters here better than Owen Donaldson. That's who Kye went to. I'm going to see him and get his thoughts on things."

As she munched on her salad and talked with Sean, she watched his 6'4" frame as he leaned back in the kitchen chair sipping coffee, Buddy lying by his chair. He was one of the most handsome men she knew with his rugged look and the square jaw and alert brown eyes. Gray peppered his sandy, medium-length hair. Being quarterback on the high school state championship team made him a celebrity around Bekbourg. People loved to reminisce with him about football. He still had an athletic body. Sean had suffered serious wounds in a traumatic blast that killed his best friend on his last military assignment in Kuwait. When Cheryl first met him, he was enduring pain in his leg from shrapnel still in his body and gut-wrenching nightmares from that horrific episode. Fortunately, the nightmares were less frequent, and his jogging and regular work-outs seemed to lessen the pain from the physical wounds. After Cheryl put away the dishes, she walked over to Sean and began to unbutton his shirt.

"Mmmmm, my thoughts exactly," he said as he got out of his chair and pulled her toward the bedroom. They were laughing as they shut the bedroom door—leaving Buddy standing in the hall.

Chapter 7

Nickolas Garrison was a county commissioner. He was in his office when the clerk popped her head in his office and told him that his guests had arrived early for the luncheon meeting.

"I don't have a lunch meeting," he responded, not sure why she thought he did.

She looked confused, "Two men are waiting out front here. They said there was a meeting. They're from out-of-town—Las Vegas."

His shirt went damp from the gush of cold perspiration.

"Commissioner, are you okay?" The clerk asked—alarmed at his sudden clammy pallor.

Nickolas pulled out a handkerchief and wiped his brow. He had avoided their phone calls knowing that his answer would not be satisfactory. Now, they had come to him. "Yeah, I'm fine. I remember now. Ask them to have a seat, and I'll be out shortly. Tell them I am finishing up a call."

The clerk looked uncertain, because he hadn't been on the phone when she came in. She nodded and closed his door when she left.

Since it was an early hour for lunch, Nickolas and his two guests had privacy as they sat at a table in the GilHaus.

Waiving around a fork—pierced with a chunk of bloody steak—above his plate, the man reminded Nickolas of a grizzly bear with a human head. "Mr. Garrison, you don't seem to like to talk about this on the phone, so we thought we'd pay you a visit. You've always been a good customer, but Mr. Lucchesi is losing patience on the money you owe him. You told us six months ago that you would pay this, but yet you haven't returned our calls."

"You know I'm good for this. We had some unexpected things happen here. My partner in the fracking venture was killed, and it delayed the final permits from the state. It's back on track, and as soon as the state issues the permits, the fracking company is ready to go. If my partner hadn't been killed, Mr. Lucchesi would already have his money. Once the operation starts, I'll have more than enough to cover the debt. I just need a little more time, but Mr. Lucchesi is going to get his money."

"That's not good enough, Mr. Garrison. That's not how it works. We don't care about any fracking deal. We want the money, and we want it now." Grizzly pierced another bloody steak chunk.

"I'm good for the money. Mr. Lucchesi knows that. The commission here approved the permits. The state is going to approve them. It's good for the state revenues and the economy. They are approving fracking permits all over the region. It's all sealed and delivered."

Even though he didn't want to signal discomfort, Nickolas wiped his brow. Oak Tree with a human head asked, “Something not good about your food?”

“It’s fine—just a little early for lunch for me.”

Oak Tree wasn’t waving around bloody beef mounds, but his bulging vest buttons looked suffocating. Oak Tree took another bite, “I never have that problem.”

Trying to mask his anxiety, Nickolas took a bite.

Grizzly licked his lips after draining his wine, “Okay, we’ll give you six weeks, but you better have it. If we have to come back, we won’t be quite so friendly.”

Oak Tree and Grizzly dropped their napkins on their plates and sauntered toward the door. Nickolas’ heart was racing. His muzzy appearance and a plate of mostly-uneaten food propelled the waitress to probe if everything was okay—could she get him anything. He absently ordered a double double Wild Turkey neat. As he sipped his drink, he cursed Owen Donaldson for having filed a protest with the state against the fracking permit application.

Kye was sitting in Owen’s office looking at the empty dog bed in the corner. “Where’s your dog today, Owen?”

“Oh, some days, he likes to stay home where he has more freedom to roam around. I’ll go home for lunch, and he may come back to the office then. Thanks for coming in. I’m still waiting on Claude to get me the information to support an injunction. I talked with him yesterday, and he told me I should have it within the next couple of days. I'll believe it when I see it, but since Harvey can't do anything with your property in the meantime, that's okay. I've made some progress. You know this, but that thirty acres you and Cecil own is located up in the area east of the large golf and residential development called Lake Shore. After that went in, I would have thought the assessed value of your property would have gone up, but—the damnest thing—it went down and never went up. I saw that in the copies of the property tax assessments you gave me before they stopped sending those to you.

Property valuations are handled by Joanne Fairhurst, the County Auditor. I asked her why the tax assessment went down. She was about as helpful as a pig in a poke. She said she just followed the Commission's order to lower taxes on rural property. She didn't remember if they lowered taxes across the entire county or just in certain areas. She'd have to check. I'm sure not holding my breath to hear back from her. I'll have to get that information as part of the lawsuit we file.

"Also, we're going to need more information about Bekbourg Enterprises. I'm sure Bennett won't voluntarily give me those documents, but we'll be able to get them in the discovery once we file the lawsuit. One of the things I'll be looking for are connections between Bekbourg Enterprises and county officials. For example, the president is Harvey Bennett. The two other officers of his company, the Secretary and Treasurer, were Jeff and Randall Thompson, who are dead. One was a Commissioner and the other a former Commissioner. I don't know why new officers haven't been named, but if a county commissioner was an officer, there may be other connections with county officials. I'm going to have to find just what the relationship is there. You know the saying, 'you scratch my back; I'll scratch yours.'

"Kye, I'll keep going on this, but it's costly. Also, it's an uphill battle, a steep hill. Do you still want me to work on this?"

"I appreciate all that you're doing, Owen. Yes, for now, I want to stay on this. I feel I've let Cecil down, and I just can't let go yet."

"That's fine, Kye. I'll keep you posted. I'm planning to file the lawsuit soon."

Chapter 8

Many of the railroaders dined at Frau's Diner before starting their night shift—as well as eating breakfast after clocking out from their night run. It wasn't unusual for Sean to run into one or more, and they always invited him to join them. This evening, it happened to be Chaw. Nicknamed for always chewing tobacco, Chaw was a conductor, nearing retirement. He had known Sean's grandpa and had shared stories with him about their time together on the railroad.

"Have a seat, Sean. Burgers are good today. How's it going?"

"Doing fine. How about you?"

"Good. Counting down 'til I can retire. Say, there's a story I thought of." Sean knew he was getting ready to hear a railroad story. These railroad guys sure knew a lot of stories. "Do you remember Pinky Luttrell?"

"Yeah, I remember him."

"Well, we'd take the train over to Wheeling, West Virginia, and of course we'd have to spend the night. Sometimes, we'd not be called back 'til late that evening. Anyways, there was a diner there that a lot of us railroaders would eat at—because it was cheap. They liked seeing us coming 'cause we were good business. But they didn't really like seeing ole Pinky comin' 'cause they lost money on him."

"Why's that?"

"Well, you see, you paid one price for their buffet, and then you got to eat all you wanted. Well, what Pinky would do was go in there for breakfast and pay the breakfast price, but if he didn't have to leave to head back, he'd just sit there and drink coffee, and when time came for lunch, he'd fill up on the lunch buffet. Sometimes, they pointed out that the all-you-can-eat buffet was for one meal, but he'd say that as long as he sat there and drank coffee, his price included the lunch buffet." Chaw chuckled. "For all I know, there may have been times he stayed through dinner. They sure lost money on him."

Sean laughed. "I bet. I never heard that story, but there's probably a lot I've not heard."

Chaw grinned, "There is Sean. There's a lot. Say, I heard that one of the big dogs is moving back here. C.P Traylor."

"I heard that. Did you know him?"

"I remember him."

"What do you know about him?"

"Well, I never worked with him. I know a few things though. He went to Schriever High School here and played football. One of the men graduated with him, I think it was in 1960. His grandfather worked on the railroad and got him a job as a clerk in the yard here in Bekbourg. People who worked with him said he was a hard worker. You know that a clerk had to check all the cars manually, and prepare the bills of lading and other reports and give those to the conductors before the train could leave the station. Some of those clerks were slow as molasses, but Traylor always got the paperwork to the conductors on time. He built up a little seniority while he worked here, and then was able to transfer to Cincinnati in the fall of 1961 to go to college. Since he was working, he could only go to school part-time. He worked as a clerk on the third shift. He was working on a business degree at the University of Cincinnati. Anyway, since he wasn't a full-time student, he got drafted. After he came back to the railroad, he moved into management and worked all over the system."

"Well, I look forward to meeting him. He has accomplished a lot in his career with the railroad, topping it off with a big job in D.C."

The next day, Sean returned to Cincinnati to talk to the coin expert Owen had recommended. This was the second time he had visited Cohen's Collectible Coins, which was located in an older part of downtown. There had been rumors that developers wanted to gentrify the area, but so far, not much had happened. The buildings dated back to the 1840's. Sean smiled to himself as he stood at the door waiting to be buzzed in. Uri Cohen, owner of Cohen's Collectible Coins, was at least in his 80's. Uri's back was slightly bowed—causing him to almost come to Sean's chest. He moved slowly because of his age, but Sean would put his sharpness up against any person half Uri's age. He reminded Sean of one of Santa's elves—without the pointed hat.

During his first visit, when Sean opened the box of coins and showed him the pictures of the stolen coins, Uri's eyes sparkled with interest. He had called Sean and told him he had some information about the coins.

"What have you got for me, Uri?"

"Well, there was a large assortment of coins. Some were not worth more than the value of the coin itself. Others were worth more. Let me start with these coins," he said pointing to about ten coins lying on felt on his counter. "These were the most valuable. They are twenty-dollar gold pieces, 'Gaudens Double Eagles.' Depending on their condition and the mint, they can be worth from a thousand dollars to over a million dollars."

Uri then moved to a series of other coins. "There are many old silver coins, like silver dollars, dimes, half-dollars, and quarters. Again, the value of each coin depends on mint marks and conditions. Here are several Indian head pennies." Pointing out more coins, he continued, "There were some Liberty Head Double Eagle gold pieces."

Pointing to one coin, Uri said, "There was only one of these. It's a ten-dollar gold piece, an Indian Head Gold Eagle minted in early 1900's. Here's an assortment of Morgan silver dollars. Now, this is something that could be priceless," he said pointing to pictures of about ten coins. "These are the ones you said were stolen from your friend. It's hard to be precise with just a list and pictures. I need to research them. They appear to be old Roman coins. Once I know more about them, I'll call you.

"Looking at what's here, I don't think Roger Burkhart really knew what he had. It's like he just collected from wherever he could get coins—possibly from pawn shops. These twenty-dollar gold pieces, the Gaudens Double Eagles, may have come from a collector, since they were all in the one bag, but that's a guess. It's possible some of these were stolen. If the police have reports, it might be possible to track them down. You told me Burkhart was bragging about all these being worth around $250,000. I'm not sure these add up to that, but it's possible he had a buyer who was looking for one certain coin to complete a collection and was willing to pay that much.

"You know, Sean, back in the 1970's when they deregulated gold and silver, the market for gold and silver exploded. People with old jewelry, like class rings, necklaces and things like that, all of a sudden had a valuable asset in their drawers, and a market sprung up to buy gold and silver from the average person. Back then, silver coins were quite common—even though the government had started taking silver out of coins in the 1960's.

"Pawn shops were in the forefront of buying these things. The result was that people's coins and old jewelry became targets for thieves. Add to this the exploding drug epidemic, and thieves had a field day stealing gold and silver. Once melted down, there was no way to trace it. People in the coin collecting business and even legitimate pawn brokers were appalled by what was happening. But I must admit, many of them were lured by the prospect of high profits and adopted a policy of looking the other way and not asking where things came from. Often the pawn shops would resell the stuff to dealers out of the area—who were set up to melt things into ingots. Unfortunately, a lot of rare coins were lost as a result."

"This is very helpful. I am glad to have your expertise, Uri. What do you know about Ernie's Pawn Shop?"

"Well, if it's the one I'm thinking of, they were known as one of the worst offenders of buying gold and silver—no questions asked."

"I'm a little curious about why Roger Burkhart didn't melt the coins into ingots."

"It's hard to say—other than he had a buyer of the coins. As I said, I don't think Roger knew much about coins. He was probably just thinking that he was going to pick up a quick profit."

"I really appreciate your help, Uri. If you ever head to Bekbourg, be sure and look me up."

Sean wanted to see what he could learn at Ernie's Pawn Shop. When he walked in, he noticed a large collection of electronics and cameras and a case containing miscellaneous jewelry and watches. A man in his early 50's sat behind the counter watching Sean. Walking up, Sean introduced himself and asked if he had worked there during the early 1980's.

"No, I wasn't working here then."

"What's your name?"

"Ernie Foltz. I go by 'Junior.'"

"I'm investigating the ownership of several coins that were found in an old case. From what I have found so far, it appears that your shop here may have sold these coins to a man named Roger Burkhart. I am trying to find out just what the story was with these coins."

"When did this happen?"

"Summer of 1980."

"I don't know anything about it. I wasn't here then."

"Who owned the shop then?"

"My father owned and ran it."

"Can I talk to him?"

"Well, he's not here."

Sean knew he was trying to appear cooperative but playing a rope-a-dope game. "Well, this is really important. I need to talk to him and find out what he knows."

"I don't know if that is going to be possible. My father is a very old man. He's not really involved in the business anymore and probably can't help you."

"Well, do you have any records from those years?"

"I really don't know. I really can't answer."

"Mmm, I guess I'll have to come back with a search warrant and go through all your records. If I need to, I can bring someone back with the state who can do a complete audit of your books."

Junior's eyes widened. "Whoa, whoa. No need to do anything like that."

Sean gave him a stern look, "This is a serious matter, Mr. Foltz, and I want you to take this seriously."

"Can you come back tomorrow?"

"Yes, I guess I could, but I don't want to come back and not be able to see some records. I'd like to talk to your father, too. I could go to his house if that would be more convenient."

"I'll make sure he's here, but I don't know if he can help you much."

"Let me be the judge of that."

The following day, Sean returned to Cincinnati. The old man, Ernie Foltz, Sr., was there—with his son standing behind him. He was in a wheel chair, but he looked in better shape than his son had led Sean to believe. He had a ledger on his lap. "Mr. Foltz, I'm Sean Neumann, Sheriff in Bekbourg County, and I'm hoping you can help me with a mystery," Sean began.

"My son told me what you were looking for and the year you mentioned, and I pulled the ledger out. If I have anything, it will be in the ledger."

Sean thought, *He knows what I'm looking for*. "Mr. Foltz, I want to know about a possible transaction between you and Roger Burkhart. June of 1980. It involved the purchase of an unknown quantity of gold and silver coins. Possibly some other things, but it's the coins I'm interested in."

"I remember Burkhart. Wasn't he murdered around that time?"

"Yes, that's the man."

"Does this have something to do with his murder?"

"No, it's nothing like that. We know who killed him. This has to do with the coins he purchased a short while before he died."

"Well, that's good. I don't know anything about the murder, but I do remember selling him an assortment of un-catalogued coins that I had accumulated over the previous year, maybe longer. I'm not a coin dealer, and I really didn't want to go that route with coins. Frankly, I just wanted to sell them and recover the money I had in them. I don't remember the number of coins, but there weren't a lot. If there were lots of coins, he must have gotten them from other places."

"Where did you get the coins?"

The old man paused and seemed to weigh his words. "Well, in those days, gold and silver had been deregulated, and people were bringing in gold and silver. At the time, I thought it was a good business to be in. Finally, though, I decided I didn't want to be in it because there were a lot of shady characters. I decided once I sold the coins to Burkhart, I was getting out of the coin business."

"I see you have a ledger there. Do you have any records of this transaction?"

"We'll have to look through this to see what I got. I haven't had time to look through it."

Sean thought that was a lie. Sean asked to see the ledger, and the old man found the pages that covered the timeframe. Sean looked through the ledger, which had hand-written entries by date of short transaction descriptions. He found an entry, "assorted coins, Burkhart, June 19, 1980, $4,000."

He read it out loud to Ernie. Sean said, "That's a lot of money to be paid for uncertified and unvalued coins."

"Well, Burkhart was willing to pay that, and I gave him everything I had."

"Did he buy anything else?"

"No, this time he only wanted coins. He'd bought other things in the past, but just the coins this time. Took every one I had."

Glancing again at the page, Sean saw a note, "Leo Davis and Byron Thornton, pick up June 19."

"Tell me about Davis and Thornton."

"Oh, those were two punks he would send to pick up things he bought from me. They brought the money, and I turned the coins over to them."

"Can I borrow this ledger? It's evidence for my investigation."

He looked at Sean uneasily, "I'd prefer not to turn it over."

"Well, I can get a warrant and take anything in your shop I need for this investigation."

"Well, when can I get it back?"

"In due time."

As he walked to his cruiser, Sean mused that this was a break-through, although he wasn't sure what it all meant. It also confirmed his initial impression that Byron Thornton had not been as forthcoming as he could have, but he couldn't imagine that Thornton would have returned any of the coins to Danny. *Why would someone return all but the few old coins?* He needed to find who had worked with Basswood.

Chapter 9

Nelson Predit was the owner of Predit Drilling, which was headquartered in Pittsburgh, Pennsylvania. His company conducted fracking operations to extract oil and natural gas. He was a newer player in the fracking operations and was hungry for opportunities. He had ongoing operations already in West Virginia, Ohio and Pennsylvania, when two county commissioners, Jeff Thompson and Nickolas Garrison, contacted him for a meeting. They had heard about fracking and were looking at buying some property if it had potential. Nelson's geologist analyzed the prospect, which was on a hundred acres on the far eastern side of Bekbourg County. The geologist determined the play was promising, so Jeff and Nickolas purchased the acreage.

Predit started work. Once everything was in place, he filed an application for a permit with the Bekbourg County Commission, which sailed right through their review process. With the county permit in hand, Predit Drilling applied with the state for a permit. He was waiting on the state's approval, which was the last hurdle.

Nickolas and Predit were having lunch at the GilHaus. Nickolas was anxious for the state to sign off on the project so the drilling could start. He needed money in the worst way coming in from the drilling revenues. Even though it had only been a few days since Mr. Lucchesi's muscle had paid him a visit, he was getting phone calls from Mr. Lucchesi's office. Giving him six weeks didn't mean they were backing off applying pressure.

Nickolas's frustration was on full display, "You told us going in that the state has a favorable track record on approving these fracking applications. You said that if the county approved it, and I quote, 'it'll be a cakewalk.' Well, we did approve it, and now it's held up at the state. What's going on? When is the state going to approve it?"

"Nickolas, I'm not happy about the situation either. Like I told you on the phone, our problem is that the group of landowners around here filed that protest to my application at the state. They weren't heard at the county level, because they didn't file a protest there. That's one of the issues Owen Donaldson is raising. He's claiming there wasn't fair notice at the county for them to participate in the proceeding. Your county attorney is involved, but this is all taking time."

"Well, we did what you asked and filed in support of the project, pointing out the benefits to the county and even the state. I don't understand this, Nelson. You guaranteed us you'd get the approvals. I need for you to get going on this."

"I've spent the last two days in Columbus with my lawyer and talking to everyone I could about this. Donaldson has thrown a monkey wrench into the works—big time."

"Nelson, you told us that it was going to be rubberstamped by the state. You told us that protests were not unusual in these fracking applications with these 'NIMBY' protesters. Donaldson is always filing frivolous lawsuits trying to gum up the works. Your lawyers need to get this done."

"See here, Nickolas. I want this as much as you do—probably more. I've been outbid too many times in the past two years, and I need this project. What about you? Why don't you try to settle with the landowners? Get them to withdraw their protest. What do they want—money?" Nelson paused to lower the temperature. "Look, my attorneys are pushing as much as they can, but there is only so much they can do. The state has to address the protest, but they are used to these landowner protests. The fracking operations are good for the counties and the state. They know that. I don't think it will be too much longer."

Nickolas came off his high horse, "Well, one thing your lawyers might do is look up Owen's history. He's always filing against the county about this or that. If they can show the state that he has a history of filing frivolous lawsuits, maybe that will help."

"I'll tell them. I can assure you that I am working this as hard as I can."

Sean called his friend, Harold Greene, the chief of the state police for southeast Ohio, who he had worked with on the Pinkston murders the previous summer. Sean described about finding the coins in Roger Burkhart's old Cadillac.

"So, that mystery is solved?"

"Yeah," Sean chuckled, "but it opened another one. Someone broke in and stole the coins from Danny, but then the box of coins showed up on Danny's back porch, except for a bag of about ten coins."

"Someone returned all the coins but ten?"

"Yeah. Odd, isn't it? So, I'm trying to find out what I can about the coins that Danny found to see if they were stolen back when Roger Burkhart had them, and I'm trying to learn more about the old ones that are missing from the box. Uri Cohen, a coin dealer in Cincinnati, is helping me, but we need to see what we can find about whether any of the coins are stolen. I can email a list to you."

"Sure Sean. I'll get someone on it, and I'll blast out Uri's list to all the states to check their files. I'll also get the list to Lucky to see if the FBI has any information. I'll get back to you when I have something."

Cheryl had never met Owen Donaldson, but his reputation preceded him. He handled tax matters for Bri and Max, who owned the B&B and bistro. They felt no one was better at what he did, but he was "not for the faint of heart," as Bri had put it. They thought of him as an unconventional uncle and loved him as such.

His office was in a compact 1920's two-story brick house in the old downtown. The white sign protruding from the post supporting the entrance overhang stated in black letters, "Donaldson Tax and Legal Services." The engaging entryway was unexpected. The floors were a dark hardwood, and dark baseboard and crown molding outlined light beige walls. A rich floral runner centered the staircase straight ahead—likely leading to a couple of small rooms. The hall extended forward alongside the stairway, and the previous parlor hosted a cozy reception room. Two open doors down the hall hinted at offices. A large oil landscape encased in an ornate gold leaf frame commanded attention, and a vase of fresh flowers sat on a foyer table.

The secretary's desk was sitting to the right in the former dining room. Cheryl knew that Drew Chambers worked for Owen, so she suspected the movie-star looking young man standing beside the secretary's desk holding a thick journal was Drew. Both he and the older woman looked up when Cheryl entered.

The secretary warmly greeted Cheryl, "You must be Ms. Seton. I'm Martha Bolton. This is Drew Chambers."

Cheryl walked over to shake their hands. "It's very nice to meet you both. Drew, you look just like your dad. I'm glad to finally meet you."

Before anyone else could comment, Cheryl heard the curmudgeon enter behind her.

"Ms. Seton. Come on back. Martha can get you something to drink."

Martha and Drew didn't move a muscle until Cheryl followed Owen down the hall. "Any idea why Owen would be so friendly to Ms. Seton?" Drew whispered to Martha.

"No idea. I have more fingers on one hand than the number of times he has come out here to greet a client. Maybe it's because of what happened to her grandfather. I don't know, but I'd better get Ms. Seton some coffee."

Cheryl entered a large cluttered office that reminded her of her editor's at *The Presenter* in Cleveland, except there were more filing cabinets here. A large oak bookcase held books and binders. Stacks of documents and folders at least a foot high covered the desk's surface except for about a two-foot square area right in front of Owen's chair. Fortunately, there were no ash trays or stale cigarette smoke odor, but unlike Keith, Owen obviously didn't hide his whiskey in a drawer. A bottle of Canadian Club sat in plain sight on a filing cabinet near his desk. Another difference from Keith's office was that lying on the floor in the corner was a dog bed.

Not wasting time, "Have a seat. You said you were friends with Kye and you thought there was something suspicious about her case and some other tax foreclosures here in Bekbourg."

Just then, Martha brought in two cups of coffee, handing one to Cheryl and picking up an empty cup on Owen's desk and replacing it with another cup. "This better not be that damn tasteless mud water you try to push on me."

Martha efficiently turned to leave, casting a quick smile and wink at Cheryl.

Drew popped his head in from an adjoining office that had a connecting door, "Owen, I'm going to close this door so I won't disturb you and Ms. Seton. I need to make some calls about the foundation."

Owen murmured something about all the distractions but ignored Drew and cringed when he took a drink of the coffee that Martha had brought. "That woman lords over me like I'm an idiot. After I've had six cups of the real stuff, she starts pushing this on me. Now, what's this all about?"

Cheryl assumed he was talking about why she was there rather than the decaf coffee he was scowling at. "Kye told me about what happened with her property and that you're handling the case for her. It seems odd to me that something like that would happen. Do you know of anything like this happening before, where someone has claimed their land had been sold due to some tax forfeiture and claimed some type of impropriety by the county?"

Owen sat for a long minute looking at Cheryl, tapping a pencil on his desk. Finally, he said, "I've been watching these land sales for years around here. There have been several sales of property for tax forfeiture. Some people just abandon the property. It's rural, and maybe they inherit it and don't want it. Maybe they move and don't think it will sell. Prices have been depressed around here for years. I'm suspicious by nature and especially of the county, but I'm not aware of anyone ever contesting a tax sale after the land sold at a Sheriff's Sale."

"Will you explain to me how a tax forfeiture proceeding works?"

"Yeah. I won't bore you with the technical details and deadlines about taxpayers' ability to get their property back during the foreclosure process. Joanne Fairhurst is Bekbourg's County Auditor. She is supposed to determine the property values, which is usually done every six years. Those property values then are used to determine the property taxes. The whiskey-nose bitch is our County Treasurer." Cheryl struggled to suppress a smile. Obviously, the Treasurer wasn't on his favorite person's list. "The Treasurer's office sends out the tax bills. If the property owner fails to pay the tax invoice, then after tax forfeiture notices and procedures, that property will be sold at a Sheriff's Sale. Some people call these tax auctions. They're essentially the same thing. Here in Bekbourg, the property that is up for sale is supposed to be listed in the *Bekbourg Tribune* along with the notice of the Sheriff's Sale. The Sheriff's Sale is public and is like a public auction. The tax deeds are sold in a bundle at a Sheriff's Sale. This is the way the tax foreclosure process is supposed to work here, but with these yahoos in the county office, I don't know if they take shortcuts in some cases."

"Thank you, Owen. What can you tell me about Bekbourg Enterprises Corp.?"

"Bekbourg Enterprises bought property over time and developed it into that gated residential community up north of here as well as the golf course—named the Lake Shore development. It also is the purchaser of Kye's property, and that's part of the new development, which is called Lake Meadows. Harvey Bennett is the President. I'm not telling you something you don't know, but the two other officers are Jeff and Randall Thompson, both dead." Owen dryly added, "Don't know how they can still be officers."

Cheryl couldn't contain a laugh at his dry sense of humor, "Yes, I saw that. Do you happen to know who the shareholders are?"

"No, I don't know that. Most corporations don't publicly disclose their shareholders. It's hard to learn that information."

"All this development is near the large lake. I suppose that makes it desirable for development."

"Well, there may be more to it. The Army Corps of Engineers built Lake Peatmont years ago. Back in the 60's and early 70's around Ohio, the state was developing state parks with conference centers and overnight rental accommodations. There was a plan for the state to add conference facilities and lodge and cabin rentals in Peatmont State Park. When the downturn in the economy happened in the 70's, the state put those plans in deep freeze. I don't know if the state is now thinking about dusting them off."

"I see. I'm going to go to the county and see what their records show, but before I do, I wanted to learn something about the history. You've been very helpful. I appreciate your time."

"Good luck on getting any information from them. That information is supposed to be public, but they guard it like it's the nuclear code. Hell, they won't even give me information for Kye, and she's my client. If you have any problems, let me know. I might have some ideas for you."

"Thank you."

As she started to stand, he said, "Ms. Seton, give Milton Grant my regards."

Stunned, Cheryl asked, "Do you know him?"

Cheryl figured it was the closest Owen ever came to smiling. "I'll let him tell you."

Cheryl indicated toward the dog bed, "What kind of dog do you have?"

"He's a Beagle. Name's Skip. He sometimes comes to the office with me, but today, he wanted to stay home. He likes it there better, because he has the run of the house and a dog door where he can go outside. Here, Martha makes him stay in my office."

Chapter 10

The oral argument before Judge Bergmann didn't go well. Sure, there was a question about why the mailing address for the tax invoices and assessments had been changed, but the judge was receptive to Zack's argument that Kye should have looked closer. She was the taxpayer and had some responsibility. Also, she hadn't checked on the property in several years. Had she done so, she would have noticed the work being done on the property. Also, economic harm would accrue to Bekbourg Enterprises if the project was delayed.

The judge lifted the temporary restraining order, which closed the door on an injunction being in place while Owen's lawsuit made its way through the trial process. He admonished Claude that the county needed to be timely in providing public records and that he wouldn't be patient if Owen sought a court order to force the production of documents that should already be accessible to the public.

Back in his office, Owen explained, "Kye, unfortunately, this is not a surprise."

"Since there isn't a restraining order or an injunction, does that mean Bekbourg Enterprises can sell my property?"

"Yeah, but try not to worry, Kye. Harvey and the county are on notice that I am planning to file the lawsuit on a wrongful taking of your property. Also, now, with the judge's warning to Claude, he'll tell them to give me the documents I need. He won't want to go back before the judge on that. The county will still try to drag their feet, but they will only push so far. I'm working on the suit, and I'll get it filed soon. It's important that I have as many facts as I can when it's filed."

"You told me that, if the judge wouldn't issue the injunction, that means he feels we probably won't win the lawsuit."

"That's the prevailing wisdom, Kye, but don't lose hope. In my experience, you never know what the facts might show."

"Thanks for all you are doing, Owen. If you need anything from me, let me know."

Charlotte seemed nervous when Cheryl told her that she was a reporter for *The Cleveland Presenter*.

"How can I help you, Ms. Seton?"

"There are property records and tax information for Bekbourg County that I would like to review. Is there a computer that is available to the public where I can view those records?"

"Mmm. What are you asking?"

"Do you maintain that type of information electronically and make it available to the public?"

About that time, a tall, wiry woman walked out of an office. "Is there something that I can help you with? I'm Pauline Kaufmann, the County Treasurer."

The "*whiskey-nose bitch*," so named by Owen, Cheryl thought. "Thank you, Ms. Kaufmann. I was just telling her that I am looking for some property records and tax information. I was asking if that information has been computerized and available to the public. By the way, I'm Cheryl Seton, a reporter for *The Cleveland Presenter*."

"I know who you are, Ms. Seton." Cheryl smelled cigarette smoke when she walked up. Pauline's raspy voice was probably a product of years of smoking and drinking. "No, we don't have the resources like the larger counties to computerize our records. I wish we did, but that's just the way it is. We also are very short-staffed, so you have to be more specific so we don't waste time. You need to make a written request so that we know exactly what you are looking for. I might then be able to tell you how long it will take."

Cheryl deliberated whether to tell her, but knew that she'd never get the information without telling them.

"I would like to see the tax assessments, invoices and notices as well as the documents in the proceedings for tax sales going back at least twenty years. How long would that take?"

Pauline's eyebrows arched, "Just out of curiosity, why are you asking for this information?"

"I'd prefer not to go into that. How long do you think this will take to get this information?"

"Well, of course, I need to know what properties."

Charlotte had edged away from the conversation as soon as Pauline walked up and was standing off to the other side looking through a stack of papers. Cheryl suspected she was listening to every word.

"This information is all public. I don't need to have specific properties."

"Well, that goes back much farther than I realized. You are looking at a lot of information. I can't give you a definitive time. You will need to put your request in writing before we can proceed with finding the documents."

Nickolas Garrison, Harvey Bennett, Pauline Kaufmann and Charles Martin were sitting in a conference room in Harvey's office building. All the employees had left for the day.

"We escaped that injunction request, but Donaldson's made clear he's moving forward with filing a lawsuit against the county. You told us that you had handled things and that nothing looked out of place or could be traced to us. You better be right, because Donaldson will turn over every stone. If you screwed up, he'll find it."

Nickolas' whining was wearing thin on Pauline, "Get over it, Nickolas. He's not going to find anything. We are certainly not going to give him anything. He can dig all he wants to. You and Randall were the ones who insisted that we push up the schedule. If not for that, I wouldn't have had to be creative with Kye Davis's parcel."

"That remains to be seen," groused Nickolas.

Harvey Bennett intervened, “This is getting us nowhere. We don’t need to panic. It sounds like Donaldson can look all he wants, but he’ll keep running into dead ends. We just need to be firm that we feel sorry for Mrs. Davis, but she didn’t pay the tax bills, and procedures were properly followed and the property sold at the Sheriff’s Sale, all in accordance with the law. She’s an old lady. She’s not going to want to keep fighting this.”

Charles Martin, president of the local bank, asked, “What about that reporter’s request for information on tax sales going back years?”

“Well, she’s not going to get that either. There’s no reason to think anything will come about on any of this,” Pauline assured them.

“Then why is a reporter asking about it?” Nickolas growled.

Harvey thought to himself, *This is like a bunch of kids fighting. There’s no way this would be happening if Jeff Thompson was still around.* He tried to sound reassuring, “I don’t know, and I don’t care. I’m not worried about it. We just need to not overreact.”

“I agree we shouldn’t panic.” Pauline was confident. “There were only a few properties over the years I had to get creative with. There’s no way that anyone can find anything.”

“I hope you’re right.” grumbled Nickolas. “We’ve got too much at stake and too much to lose if this falls apart.”

Chapter 11

After reviewing Cooper's file, Sean thought there might be something to his claim. The first hint was that Ben Clark had been the arresting officer. Ben had a history of doing the bidding of the Thompsons.

Cooper was driving home after getting off from his job at Koot's. Ben claimed that Cooper was speeding, and when he pulled Cooper over, he smelled pot when he approached the car. He cuffed Cooper and then searched the car and found ten grams in the trunk of his car. Sean noted that the report showed that a 9mm gun was found in the glove compartment. There were no witnesses to the arrest. Cooper persistently denied having drugs in his car and smoking pot there. Since Ben was dead, Sean couldn't question him, but Kyle Ramsey had frequently patrolled with Ben, so Sean decided to ask Kyle.

"Sheriff, you wanted to see me?"

"Have a seat, Kyle. Cooper Townsend is out on parole. He came by the station and insisted that he was framed with the drugs found in his car. I've reviewed the file. Ben was the arresting officer. Do you know anything about the case?"

Kyle looked at his hands where he was picking at the cuticle on his right thumb. "Well, I wasn't with Ben that night. I remember it though, 'cause I didn't know why Ben told me he'd work alone, but he did that sometimes, so I guess it wasn't too unusual. You know how Ben was when he drank too much. We were at Knuck's that night when the jury convicted Coop. Ben was saying somethin' like, 'Yeah, that shithead messed with the wrong men.' Ben had a mean laugh. He laughed and said, 'Yep, hope you enjoy prison life, Coop,' raising his glass like a toast. I never knew when to believe what Ben was sayin', so I never said nothin', 'cause I didn't know."

"He didn't mention anyone when he said that Cooper messed with the wrong men?"

"Nope. He didn't say no names."

"Let me know if you think of anything else about the case, Kyle."

"I will, Sheriff, but that's all I can remember now."

Cheryl was talking on the phone with Keith Jamison, editor for *The Cleveland Presenter*, and Milton Grant, a highly-respected reporter for the newspaper as well as her mentor. Her recent articles on the state's efforts to combat the illegal drug trade and its focus on drug treatment funding had garnered much interest. She advised them, "I'm working on a story concerning tax forfeitures here in Bekbourg. I have a feeling that some questionable conduct may have taken place." She told them about Kye's situation and what she had learned in Columbus. "None of the tax documents or property information has been computerized. I went to the Treasurer's office to request information going back twenty years. The County Treasurer, Pauline Kaufmann, came out of her office to talk to me. She is one cool cookie. She said that they would get started on my request, but I doubt that. Kye's attorney said that it's virtually impossible getting information from them even though it's public."

"Sounds like you would have more luck getting into Fort Knox," Keith said.

"It certainly raises red flags with me," Milton chimed in.

"Bekbourg Enterprises Corp. developed Lake Shore and is planning to develop Lake Meadows. Kye's property is part of the Lake Meadows project. Harvey Bennett is the President. What's interesting is that both Jeff and Randall Thompson were the other two officers. Even though they both are dead, they haven't been removed from the officer slate. I'm going to see what I can find out about land sales around here. Milton, can you see what you can find out about Bekbourg Enterprises Corp.?"

"I'll get on it."

"One thing Kye's attorney told me is that years ago, the state had a plan to develop the state park in that area with a lodge and cabins, but they didn't follow through because of the economy. He wasn't sure if Harvey knows something about the state looking again at that project, but it could be a possibility. That state park lies on the west and north sides of the lake. The planned Lake Meadows is on the northeastern side of Lake Peatmont beside the state park, and Lake Shore was on the southern and southeastern sides of the lake."

Keith said, "So, Bekbourg Enterprises had two phases."

"Yes. I want to see if any property, either for the Lake Shore golfing development or for this planned Lake Meadows community, was acquired through a tax forfeiture sale. That's why I need access to the property records."

"Cheryl, you might check the County Recorder. You may not have much luck there, but they might have computerized the existing owners of property. At least you can find out who owns the property now, see what Bekbourg Enterprises owns."

"That is a great idea, Keith."

"Are you and Davis' attorney looking at the same things?"

"I don't think so. He seems focused on Kye's property situation. He would like to be able to have access to the public information from the county, but I didn't pick up that he is looking at a possible scheme going back years. He didn't seem aware of anything like what the Columbus attorney told me. I really want to look at a wide-scale picture to see if something wasn't kosher with the first development and also possibly with this new development that Kye's property got swept up in."

"Yeah, that makes sense."

"Oh Milton, I saved the best for last. The local tax expert, who is Kye Davis's attorney, is

Owen Donaldson. He told me to give you his regards."

There was a brief pause on the phone line before she heard, "Owen? Well I'll be. I don't believe it."

Cheryl laughed. "I take it you and he know each other?"

"We sure do. Years ago, there was a company located in Cleveland, Packard Oil. It was a huge distributor throughout the state of fuel oil and propane. What its customers didn't know was that their measurement instruments had been altered. Their customers were small, and they relied on the quantities measured by Packard and paid based on those volumes."

Keith spoke up, "Cheryl, this happened many years before you started work with us. Milton broke the story. It was a huge story at the time. Our circulation almost doubled all during the breaking of the story and the aftermath—which included the trials and appeals."

Cheryl said, "Oh, yeah, I do remembering hearing something about that story when I started work at *The Presenter*. Milton, you were a legend at the newspaper for that story." *The Cleveland Presenter* was a small evening newspaper with a respected reputation for its in-depth investigative reporting.

"He sure was," agreed Keith.

Milton laughed "Well, I don't know about that, but it was a big story at the time. Anyway, the tip I got from Owen got me started on that trail. He was representing a small company in Tapsaw

County, the county bordering Bekbourg to the east. His client had become suspicious that Packard's measurements and charges were not correct. They hired Owen to look into things. Once he realized what was happening, his client didn't want to be named. They were afraid of reprisals from Packard, but they hoped that Owen would find a way to expose the scheme.

"With the supplier having its main office in Cleveland, Owen decided to contact our paper—me in particular—because of a couple of in-depth stories I had written. He gave me all the evidence he had, and then I was able to identify another small customer who I thought might be willing to work with me. Sure enough, they were a victim of Packard's deception, too. After I broke the story, the FBI got involved. Packard ended up paying heavy fines and being sued in civil courts. I can't believe you're working with Owen. He's a little cantankerous, but he's a good man. I might have to make a trip to Bekbourg to see that old coot."

Cheryl laughed. "One of his fans calls him a 'sour puss.'"

Chucking, Milton agreed, "Yeah, I guess that sounds right. Can't imagine what he's called by those not fond of him."

They all appreciated the humor.

"One more thing. I've done a little research about Harvey Bennett and learned that he lived for a while in Cleveland. Frank and Eve Bennett are his parents. Do either of you know anything about him?"

She could hear Keith and Milton talking together. Milton was the one who spoke, "We don't know much about them, but I know someone who might be able to give you some information. Let me see what I can arrange for you."

Sean and Cheryl stopped by his parents' house after dinner. After visiting with his parents and enjoying Helen's freshly baked cobbler, Sean asked Jim if they could walk to his work shop. "Sure, Son. I'm working on a chair I'd like to show you."

A few years back, Jim had built a work shop and started a hobby of building furniture. Over the years, he had honed his skills. "Dad, you are really good at this. When you do decide to retire from the milk plant, you're ready for a second career."

Jim laughed, "Well, I don't know about that. It's really just a hobby, but I enjoy building furniture. Linda really likes the two end tables I made for their den."

"Say, Dad. The forensics techs found some sawdust at Danny's house when the coins were stolen. It's Basswood. Some people call it Lindenwood. It's used for making furniture and carving. Do you use that wood?"

"No, I don't, but there are two big wood suppliers in the area. One is J.D. Strong's Lumber and Supply in Athens and another place is in Jasper—Draker Farm Supplies. It's known for its farm supplies, but it carries a good supply of lumber and a variety of woods. That's where I buy the wood I work with. Rusty Draker mostly runs it now. It's a family business. It's been around a long time."

"That's good to know. I'll check out both places."

"Yeah, and they might know some other places. That's the two that I am familiar with."

"Do you know of anyone locally who's into making furniture or wood carving?"

"Mmmm. I don't know if I can be of much help there, son. Noel Fischner does some carving. He sells them in his shop, but that's all I can think of."

Chapter 12

Owen filed the lawsuit on behalf of Kye naming two defendants—Bekbourg Enterprises and the county, including individually named county officials—alleging that Kye's property was wrongfully taken from her. For its part, he claimed the county wrongfully changed the mailing address for the tax invoices and foreclosure documents. He delivered copies to the *Bekbourg Tribune* and the local TV station as well as to Cheryl. The *Tribune* interviewed Owen and published a front page article about the lawsuit.

Nickolas Garrison and Harvey Bennett sat at a back corner table at the GilHaus sipping Scotch. "Harvey, I've been thinking. Kye Davis is well known around Bekbourg. I've looked, and Kye's property is right along the road almost in the center of the development. The main road is going to cut right up beside what was her property. It would really chop up the development if we didn't have it. Now, people around here are happy with our first development. It's brought the county a nice stream of property tax revenue, and it's been good for the area. They support this new development and see it as a boost for the area. There's no injunction in place that stops us from selling the property she owned. Is there any way that we could somehow go ahead and put up some lots for sale, including on what Kye owned? If you could sell at least one lot on her property, then I can't imagine any jury would rule against us."

"I've had similar thoughts. You're right about the planned main road leading into the subdivision, but the surveyor is still plotting out the lots and even the roads back in there. I've asked them to speed up, but it's still probably a month or so away until that work is complete. One thing though that I can do is to go ahead and put up 'For Sale' signs and start talking to potential buyers. Our model and drawings show the planned layout and individual plots, so it would be easy enough to discuss with prospective buyers."

"That'll work. That way, when all the surveying is done, you can begin selling the lots. If Kye won't drop the suit or settle with us, by the time the trial starts, hopefully, some of the lots would have sold."

"It's worth a try, Nickolas. There might be some buyers who, if they are aware of the lawsuit, won't take the risk, but we might as well try. I'll talk to my lawyer. I might even be able to sell the lots and include a clause that the sale is subject to a final survey. That way, we can move even faster on selling the lots."

"Hey, I like that."

"Well, I'll see what I can do. We'll make a public announcement that we're ready to move forward with selling lots. I've already had a few inquiries from interested buyers, so this probably makes sense regardless of the Davis situation, but I agree with you that we need to move fast to help our chances in court."

Each year, the Garden Club of Bekbourg hosted a fundraiser gala to support area charities. This year, the Garden Club had added Mary's foundation to the recipients' list for proceeds raised from their fundraiser efforts. Mary Zimmstein's foundation, Bekbourg Gives, was established to educate and support people facing difficult circumstances. It helped domestic violence victims, funded Dusty and Carla's program to fight drug addictions, supported Bri and Max's program to help at-risk women get back on their feet, and provided college scholarships to children of parents who had drug addiction histories.

During the pre-dinner cocktail reception, Sophia Martin, a high school classmate, walked up to Sean, "Hi, Sean. I don't know if you remember me, but we graduated from high school together. I am Sophia Martin. My last name during high school was Bergmann.

"I remember you, Sophia. It's nice to see you again. This is Cheryl Seton, my fiancée."

"It's very nice to meet you, Cheryl. I enjoyed reading your stories about what happened here last year. The *Tribune* does a good job, but we just don't get the detailed reporting that your articles had."

"It's nice to meet you too, Sophia, and that is very kind of you."

Sophia smiled, "I am glad that you are back in Bekbourg, Sean. I feel you are a shoo-in to win the Sheriff's race."

They all laughed since he was running unopposed.

Sophia was beautiful and refined and moved with grace that came from years of private ballet instruction. Sean remembered her from high school. Even though her dad was the judge and they lived in a large home with domestic help, she was never a snob. She was kind to everyone. Because he hung around with the athletes, Sean didn't know her very well, but they spoke to each other when they passed in the hall and had been in some of the same classes.

Sophia's husband, Charles Martin, walked up to the group. Charles ran Bekbourg's largest bank, the First Guaranty Bank of Bekbourg. Charles was polite in greeting Sean and Cheryl, but excused himself and Sophia to join others at their table. Because Charles was several years ahead in school, Sean didn't know him very well.

Noel Fischner came over to Sean and Cheryl. Noel owned an outfitter's shop toward the end of the town. He and Sean had also graduated together from high school.

"How's your campaign going, Noel?"

He smiled. "I wish I could say as well as yours."

That brought a chuckle from the group. After the scandal involving Jeff and Randall Thompson, several community members decided enough with the one-party political system in

Bekbourg. For as long as anyone could remember, the Thompsons had run the county, and all the politicians had been hand-picked. No one dared run against those chosen by the Thompsons. After the deaths of Jeff and Randall, Riley Barnes had been appointed as interim County Commissioner to replace Jeff. Noel had decided to run against Riley in the November election as part of a newly formed Reform Party. The Reform Party candidates included Bri Sanderson, owner of the B&B, who was running for Mayor of the City of Bekbourg. Sally Chambers, Danny's wife, and Boone Carter were running for city council seats.

Noel said, "The current commissioners still have a lot of sway with people and deep roots in the community. I'm afraid that it is going to be hard to unseat them. While those running on the Reform ticket have some general recognition with people here, it'd be great to have people on the ticket who are well known throughout the county. Sean, I wish your dad had decided to run. He has been an outspoken opponent of this one-party political system we have here. I can understand him deciding not to retire from the milk plant, but he would have been a great candidate for our new party. We need new blood, new ideas. I don't mean to complain, because I appreciate his support on my campaign, but he would be a great Reform candidate."

Cheryl said, "I think what happened here last year opened people's eyes. I feel that the tide is turning here, Noel. I think all of you on the Reform ticket have a good shot."

"I sure hope you're right. There are deep pockets funding my opponent and others running against the Reform Party. I wish I had more funds. Even if I do get elected, I'll probably be at odds with the other two Commissioners, Nickolas Garrison and Lance Pruitt. We may not see the change we want right away, but hopefully, things will improve."

"Yeah, and if changes occur at the city level with the mayor and city council, that may help you as well."

"That's right. Jeff Thompson not only controlled the county, he controlled the city leaders. It's about time the city of Bekbourg asserts itself in county politics."

"I saw in the silent auction room the beautiful carving you did. I'm sure the Garden Club was thrilled for your donation," Cheryl said.

"Thanks. Yeah, Mom asked me if I'd donate one."

"Well, the eagle will be a big hit."

"You sell your work, too, don't you?" Sean asked.

"Yeah, I sell them in my outfitter's shop. I started carving small things as a kid and just kept going with it."

"I'd like to drop by and see them sometime," said Sean.

"Sure, anytime."

"I haven't seen your father this evening."

"He wasn't feeling well, so he stayed home."

"I'm sorry to hear that," Cheryl said. "We hope he starts to feel better soon."

"Thanks. I guess it's an age thing. He's slowed down over the last year. Mom's been trying to get him to go to the doctor, but he won't hear of it."

Jennifer Fischner, the chairwoman for this year's gala and who also happened to be Noel's mother, saw Hans Mueller walk into the room. Even though they lived quiet lives, he and his wife, Hilda, were known by many around Bekbourg—Hilda, because of her seamstress skills, and Hans, because of the beautiful Cuckoo clocks he made. Over the years, Hilda had outfitted many brides and bridal parties, as well as made prom and specialty dresses. For his part, Hans had built a successful business shipping his Cuckoo clocks throughout the U.S. Each year, Hans donated one of his clocks to the gala fundraiser.

Jennifer went to welcome him, "Mr. Mueller, it is so wonderful to see you, and as always, we are thrilled to have one of your beautiful Cuckoo clocks to auction."

In the past, Hans was accompanied by his son, Otis, and daughter-in-law. Hilda shied away from most public events and had never attended the gala. Jennifer was not surprised, however, that Otis and his wife weren't attending with Hans this year, because their teenage son had recently died of a drug overdose, and he and his wife had been slow to get back out into the community

Hans was a tall, thin man who looked twenty years younger than his age, which was in the mid 80's. Despite having been in the United States for over fifty years, he still spoke with a heavy German accent.

He responded to Jennifer in his customary way, "It is my pleasure to do so. My wife and I support what you do to help the people here."

"Well, I want you to know how much we appreciate your donation. Your clocks always raise a lot of money for our causes. Dinner is about to be announced. You are sitting at my table. Let's make our way over there."

At the conclusion of the dinner program, Sophia and Nickolas Garrison's wife excused themselves to attend the auction events, and Judge Bergmann left to speak to his former law partners. Remaining at their table were Pauline, Nickolas, Harvey Bennett and Charles Martin.

The server had just finished pouring the after-dinner drinks when Owen wandered over to their table. He was in his usual state of inebriation, "Gentlemen, Madam. Enjoying your evening, I presume. Well, that's good, since it's just a matter of time until your backsides get put on full display, and I'm going to be leading the charge. Your days of raping the town and bullying the citizens are numbered." They sat staring at him as he looked around their table. "Now, you have a nice evening."

Owen faked the tip of a nonexistent hat and teetered toward the bar. Nickolas was the first to speak, "He is a royal pain. Why is he here anyway?"

"He is one of the donors," Pauline said. "Actually, has been for years. Fairly generous."

Harvey spoke in a hushed tone so not to be overheard outside the circle, "Well, he still is a jerk. But, unfortunately, because of all the publicity about Kye Davis' property, he is echoing a growing chorus of people. I've been receiving mail and getting calls from people accusing me of running roughshod over Davis. Some feel our developments are hurting the way of life here and only benefit the rich. We didn't experience any of this sentiment when we did our first development. Somehow, we need to change that perception, or we're going to start running into headwinds."

"It's that darn Reform Party group," growled Nickolas. "They're spreading that bullshit. I agree that we need to do a better job of showing how everyone is benefiting from these developments and the great job we've done in growing businesses and jobs around here. That needs to be our message, loud and clear."

"That unfortunate business with the Thompsons gave the whole local government a black eye," said Pauline. "That opened the door for those who have been opposed to the strangle hold Jeff had on the county and city leadership. Now, that Reform Party has gained a lot of traction in their platform to make the city council stronger."

"You're right, Pauline, and that's a real problem," agreed Nickolas.

"We need to focus in the campaign on that point, Nickolas, and convince people that what the Reform candidates are for will lead to more gridlock. That should be easy enough, because if the city and county are at loggerheads, nothing will get done, and that hurts growth and job creation."

"I agree with what Pauline just said." Harvey continued, "I'm going to get the *Tribune* to run some advertisements that talk up how our developments here help the local economy. In the campaign, you can reinforce that point, but also emphasize the fact that the county government has been responsible for the prosperity when other rust belt economies are in shambles."

"Yeah, the last thing we need is a city council to question every blasted thing we want to do. Donaldson's a drunk, but he's got a lot of support around here. You can bet he will do just what he said and be a pain in our ass on the Lake Meadows development and in the election." Nickolas brooded as he took a drink.

After the dinner and speaker, a band started playing. People were mixing and talking. Jennifer and a distinguished-looking man came up to Mary, "Mary, I'd like to introduce a son of Bekbourg who has recently returned after a most illustrious career. He has made a very generous donation tonight. This is C.P. Traylor."

Across the room, Sean and Cheryl approached a circle that included Jim and Helen. Jim said, "You know, this is the first year that the paper company has not been a sponsor of the gala. Same with the Bekbourg dealership."

"Hopefully, they'll both be back next year," Sean said. "I talked to someone the other day who told me that Becky seems to be turning things around at the dealership. I understand that she may have secured a foreign car franchise."

"That business sure took a hit. I was wondering if it would make it. Thank goodness the governor got involved in saving the paper factory. It if had gone under, that would have been devastating to the folks and economy around here. It was bad enough with it shut down for a while."

On their way home, Cheryl commented on seeing Pauline at the gala. She told Sean about her experience with Pauline when she went to the county office seeking documents. Sean said, "She's an interesting person to say the least. She can be charming." A groan interrupted him. He grinned. "I was going to say, she can be charming, which has enabled her to be extremely successful in real estate, but she can also be pure acid."

"Unhuh."

He laughed. She had obviously not seen Pauline's charming side.

He thought for a minute, "You know, Sweetie. I might be able to help you. We have files for all the Sheriff Sales. Those are public documents. Since those would include all the documents used to support the foreclosures, such as notices of delinquency and the foreclosure filings, you may be able to find a lot of what you're looking for. Drop by and see Kim. She can help you."

"That's a wonderful idea. I may just have to reward you with a big kiss when we get home."

He smiled, thinking that sounded really good.

Chapter 13

Mary Zimmstein had moved with her young daughter back to Columbus last year after the horrific fiasco, but she sometimes wondered if she had been too hasty. Mary came from an affluent family in Columbus. Her grandfather was Theodore Zimmstein, who ran the state house for thirty years. He founded a law firm, which her father joined, Zimmstein & Zimmstein, that grew to prominence throughout the state.

Jeff knew her husband from law school, and when he perished in a plane crash, Jeff reached out to Mary to offer support to her and her young daughter. As time went on, they grew close and married. They had been married a little over two years when Jeff was killed. After what happened last year, she felt compelled to start the foundation, Bekbourg Gives, to try and atone for Jeff's crimes, and to her surprise, she had been supported with open arms. Her mother and father took care of Rachel when she was in Bekbourg. She now found herself spending three days a week in Bekbourg and occasionally more when necessary.

When Mary decided to start the foundation, she purchased a small two-story building just down from Max's bistro. Otis Mueller designed the remodel, and Karl Fischner, Noel's dad, did the construction work. Mary wanted the interior to be bright and uplifting. The paint colors and contemporary furnishings were vibrant yellows, oranges, greens and blues. As was Hans Mueller, Karl was of German descent. Karl spoke in a heavy accent when he commented to Mary, "I first not sure about bright colors, but I like result."

She loved the remodel. The renovation project was unique from others she had undertaken.

Geri was working on some promotional materials when Mary arrived at the foundation. "How was your trip to Montana?" Mary asked.

"It was great. We had a wonderful time seeing the children. Matt loves working for the Park Service, and Mike and I were so glad that it worked out that Miranda was able to join us there. We went hiking in Glacier National Park. The views were spectacular. I fell in love with the beautiful little town of Kalispell. Mike and I are thinking that we might make this an annual trip to spend with both the kids as long as it works out with their schedule."

"I am really happy that you and Mike had such a special time with Matt and Miranda. How is he doing?"

"He is continuing to improve. He's working out at the high school and walks each day. I'm glad he's thinking about the future. It was hard at first. He's even thinking about coaching Youth Football this fall."

"I'm glad to hear about his progress. He's been through a lot."

"How was the gala?"

"I thoroughly enjoyed it. Jennifer was very pleased. She had been concerned that donations would be down since the paper company and the dealership were not sponsoring tables, but the Garden Club met its goal."

"Oh, that is great news."

"Yes, it is. Someone who grew up in Bekbourg and only recently returned here gave quite a generous donation. Jennifer introduced me to him. His name is C.P. Traylor. Do you know him?"

Geri smiled, "No, I don't, but he called yesterday and asked to speak to you. I told him that you were out of the office. I have his phone number on your desk."

"Mmm. I wonder what he is calling about."

"I asked if I could assist him, but he asked that I give you his message when you returned."

"I'll return his call this afternoon after my luncheon appointment."

"I arranged a meeting with Hillsrock Community College next week. They would like to talk with you about the foundation funding a scholarship. I'll get you the file I started about that."

Sean said, "Alex, I need you to go to Athens to J.D. Strong's Lumber and Supply. Find out if they sell Lindenwood or Basswood to anyone here in Bekbourg. It's the same wood, but has two different names. I need to know the names and the quantities and when the sales were made."

Although Alex was young, Sean was impressed with his abilities. He was a graduate from the police academy and had two years of college from the local community college. Mack, Mike's assistant, had never impressed Sean, so when Sean became the interim sheriff, he gave Alex more responsibilities and delegated more of the paperwork to Mack.

"How far back do you need the information, Chief?"

"Let's go back five years. Some people might buy a large supply to last for a while. Also, ask them if they know of any other business in the region that sells this wood. I'm going to run over to Jasper and check out the Draker store."

"I'll let you know what I find out, Chief."

Mary had mixed feelings about her luncheon appointment. She had arrived early at Max's bistro and sat at the table sipping iced tea. Margaret Thompson was her former mother-in-law, Jeff's mother. Mary liked her and had empathy for her. She had lost so much. Mary understood all of that. However, she was not looking forward to seeing Margaret for the simple reason that it brought back her life with Jeff, something that she wished she could expunge from her mind.

As Max showed her to the table, Mary observed that Margaret was still a striking woman, but she had aged and now walked with a cane. Mary stood, and they hugged, "Hello, Margaret."

"Hello, Mary."

Max helped Margaret into her seat. They exchanged pleasantries until he brought her a glass of white wine. They both ordered the lobster bisque.

Margaret looked at Mary, "How are you and Rachel?"

"We've been fine. Rachel is enjoying her summer break. She likes her school. It's where she was enrolled before we moved to Bekbourg."

"I'm surprised you are not in Europe with her this summer."

"It's later than we usually go, but we are leaving in a few days. How are you doing?"

"It's been difficult, Mary. Learning about Randall and Jeff has been crushing. It's worse than any nightmare I thought imaginable. The torture has been my knowing what they inflicted on others. I admire you. I know that you suffered horribly, but you didn't cower. You came back, which I know wasn't easy, and established the foundation to help the community and those directly hurt by Jeff and Randall. Anyway, I now have to deal with all the thorny issues of Randall's estate. I've decided to move back here, at least temporarily, to be closer to my attorneys so I can deal with the issues. I am so glad to see you. I was concerned you had already left for Europe. I'm returning to Florida for a short time. Then I'll be back here.

"The main reason I wanted to see you today is to tell you that Randall had a brother, Eddie, who was much younger. I only met him once or twice. He left Bekbourg many years ago. Well, with Randall's death, he is back in Bekbourg. From what my attorneys have told me, Randall and Eddie's father left a will stating that certain properties were jointly inherited by them, and if one died, then the other one inherited the property in its entirety. Eddie is making claims on those properties."

"I never heard about him. Where has he been all these years?" Mary asked.

"That's a good question. From what I understand, he has been living in Colorado, at least in recent years. Randall never talked about him, but I once overheard him and his dad talking about Eddie. Randall's dad set up his affairs to send Eddie a monthly allowance, and when he passed away, Randall continued to send Eddie those monthly funds. I don't know the reason he left here, but I gather that his father wanted to make sure that he was financially taken care of—even though he wasn't here running things."

"Do you think this affects my affairs with Jeff's estate?"

"I don't know. I know that the house that you and Jeff lived in was Jeff's, because that was all Randall's. But, I'm not sure about the acreage that is adjacent to the house. I also know that Randall and Eddie were joint owners in that disgusting Koot's."

"What is that?"

"It is an old run-down biker bar in the eastern part of the county. Randall's father opened it sometime during Prohibition. He used it to keep control on the sale of liquor in the county. Thank God I'm not involved in that property. I don't want anything to do with it. Eddie's already claimed ownership of that. Another thing is the older part of that trailer park, Acorn Knoll. Randall's father bought that property during the Depression. It's about thirty acres, and it was used to house people he employed. That property was jointly owned by Randall and Eddie. Jeff tried to transfer it to the corporation that was part of the paper plant. Well, he didn't have the legal title to do that, so my attorneys said that property belongs to Eddie. I'm fine with that, too. I don't know what to expect on the other properties, but I wanted you to be aware of this."

"Who is your attorney?"

"I've hired an attorney who Judge Bergmann practiced with before he was elected to the bench. He's been around a long time and knows the county."

A server brought their soup and refreshed their drinks.

"Well, my father's firm is handling the legal things as well as Boone Carter here locally. They haven't mentioned anything to me about Eddie, but I will tell them."

"Well, I am going to have to deal with Eddie. I've found a small house to rent in the downtown area. Once everything is settled with Randall's estate, including issues with the federal authorities, I would like to make a donation to your foundation."

Mary smiled, "I would be grateful for your contribution, Margaret. When the time comes, we will work out those details."

Chapter 14

"Sheriff Neumann, this is Uri Cohen. I've got some information on those Roman coins."

"Hi, Uri. What have you got?"

"I was suspicious when I first saw the picture of them, but I didn't want to speculate until I knew more. It's taken a lot of research and tracking down people who knew. Back in the 1930's, a photograph of these coins was taken for insurance purposes by a Jewish man as part of his private collection, because they were rare. When the Jewish people were being taken away from their homes, they sewed such things as coins and jewelry in the lining of their clothes. They hoped such valuables wouldn't be found, and they would have something of value to live on.

I believe Salomon Matzner was the owner of these coins. He was sent to a concentration camp in northern Germany. The German guards there took his coat. His coins were never found. It is a blessing that he survived that atrocity. After he was liberated by the British, Mr. Matzner tried to find his family—but to no avail. After a while, he started to put his life back together. He had been a successful middle-class business owner in Berlin and had much of his valuables insured. He eventually located an insurance agent for the company with which he had taken some of his policies. The agent was willing to help, and after a long time, he found copies of a few of the policies—including those of the coins which are shown on those pictures. Mr. Matzner tried numerous times to get payment for those polices but was not successful.

"Over time, there were organizations that were founded to help the Holocaust victims with restitution for property lost to them, and countries created their own efforts to help these victims. In the late 1970's here in the U.S., an organization was started to help those victims that had relocated here. Catalogues and more recently databases were compiled of personal property that had not been located. I eventually found the picture of these coins. I closely examined the insurance picture I found of Mr. Matzner's coins. Sean, I can't be one-hundred percent certain, because I'm only looking at pictures, but I think these are the same coins."

"Uri, if those are the same coins, how do you think they ended up here in Bekbourg?"

"It's hard to know. When the War was over, some of our soldiers may have brought them back. They could have found them, or loot was passed around among them. The coins may have been found or stolen at some point after the War and somehow made their way over here to collectors. Another possibility is that a Nazi escaped with them to the U.S. or another country, and the coins were sold or stolen, maybe a combination of all of this. Somehow the coins made their way to the area. Roger may have bought or stole them from a pawn shop or private owner. There are many possibilities."

Danny and Sally were happy to be sitting on the porch enjoying the evening with Drew. "How's the studying going?" Sally asked.

"It's going fine, Mom. I'm doing everything I can to prepare. I talked to Mary, and she is fine with me taking off a couple of weeks before the exam so I can devote all my time to studying. I'll just be glad when it's over with."

"That's so nice of her. Is Owen okay with it?"

Drew laughed. "I told him that Mary was okay with it and asked if he would mind if I took off. He mumbled that I might as well do what I wanted, since he wasn't the boss anyway."

Sally looked shocked, "What on earth made him say that?"

Drew laughed more. "Martha had just given him a cup of decaf coffee."

They all laughed.

"That reminds me, Dad. Mrs. Davis stopped by the other day again to see Owen. She told me to remind you of that car that belonged to her husband. She'd like for you to stop by some time to look at it. She told me that it originally belonged to her husband's dad, so it must be pretty old."

"Yeah, I've been meaning to do that. She mentioned it to me last year, but I was working on another car. I'll give her a call."

"Mom, how is your campaign going?"

Sally laughed, "I can't believe I did this. I never thought I'd run for an office of any sort. After all that happened last year, I had been so concerned about the kids here and all the drugs. I just wanted to do something. It's going fine, I guess. Noel and Bri are helping me a lot. I'm going with them to meet people. It's going to get hectic after Labor Day, but I guess I'm ready for it."

Danny said, "Yeah, Drew, we'll have to call your mom, 'Madam Council Woman.'"

They all laughed. "No joking though, Sally, you'll be great at it. Also, you know a lot of people because of the beauty shop. I think people around here are ready for a change."

Opal Crowley was the County Recorder. Opal was around forty and heavy-set. She wore large, navy rimmed glasses, and wore her medium-length hair pulled back in a cloth headband. She overheard Cheryl asking Charlotte if she could speak with her and walked out of her office.

"I'm Opal Crowley. How can I help you?"

"Ms. Crowley, is there a place we can talk? I'm Cheryl Seton, a reporter from *The Cleveland Presenter*. I'm working on a story about land deals and related matters."

Opal said, "I guess. There's a conference room down the hall. I don't think it's in use."

Cheryl followed Opal into the small conference room. "What's this about, Ms. Seton?"

"You oversee all the land records here in Bekbourg, is that right?"

"Yes, that's true—deeds, mortgages, surveys, things like that."

"I would like to look up the names of current property owners. Has that information been computerized?"

"Yes, it has. We also have computerized the mortgages, liens, even the surveys. If you want to view that, we have a computer the public can use."

"When did your office start to computerize this information?"

"Well, shortly after I took over. It is convenient for realtors, banks, lending institutions and others needing information about a particular property to be able to access that information."

"Why did you decide to do that?"

"I went to college in northern Ohio, but I had to work my way through. I was a single mom. It took me about eight years to get my degree. While I was taking classes, I worked part time at a small title company. I couldn't believe when I came to the County Recorder's office that this information wasn't computerized. After I became Recorder, I talked to Pauline and Joanne and others, and they saw the value of having that information accessible on computer. I wrote up a proposal, and the Commission approved it."

"How do you know the mailing address for the particular property?"

"Well, we're pretty informal around here. If I have a question, I just ask someone here, but usually, there is a file on each property that shows the owner and the mailing address. If I got something in the mail from an owner to change an address, I'd tell Charlotte, and let her tell everyone and put it in the file."

"So there isn't a procedure for a request for a change in address coming from the landowner?"

"No, not really."

"Are you involved if a delinquent tax notice is sent to a landowner and in foreclosure notices?"

"No, that would be Pauline's area."

"So, your department is the only one that has computerized records?"

"Yes, that's right."

"Why are the tax information and assessments not part of the computerized data?"

"I really don't know."

"Are you involved with assessing property for tax purposes?"

"That's not my department either."

"How did you end up with this job?"

Opal smiled. "I was lucky, pure and simple. I was a clerk, and the Recorder had a heart attack. Since I had experience with a title company, they asked me to fill in for him until he returned. Unfortunately, his illness lasted about a year, and then he died. Commissioner Thompson asked me if I would act as Interim Recorder until the next election. I worked hard, and I guess I did an okay job, because they asked me to run for the Recorder's office. No one was running against me, or I might not have run, because I'm too shy for that. I've been here since, almost ten years."

"I appreciate your time. If you don't mind showing me the computer where I can look up current property owners, I'd appreciate it."

"Sean, this is Danny."

"Hey, Danny. How are things going?"

"Fine, Sean. It's great having Drew back in Bekbourg. He really likes his work with Mary's foundation, and believe it or not, he likes working with Owen."

Sean laughed. "Yeah, he's not so bad if he likes you."

"Say, Kye Davis stopped in to see Owen the other day and told Drew to remind me that she'd like me to take a look at that old car that her husband stored before he died. I called, and she told me to drop by and get the key to the storage garage. I was wondering if you wanted to go with me to see what she has."

"Sure. I'm off tomorrow if that's good for you."

"That works. I'll swing by your place and get the key from Kye around noon."

"Sounds fine. Say, Danny, maybe you'll find another box of coins." They both laughed.

The next day, they drove to the storage unit. Danny unlocked the storage garage door. After their eyes adjusted to the unlit unit, Sean and Danny slowly peeled back the tarp that covered the car. Danny smiled as he circled it, "Look at this beauty. Can you believe it's a DeSoto?"

"This is really something to see one of these. I always said that those old railroaders were car enthusiasts. Many of the cars they had were real treasures."

Fortunately, the key was in the ignition like Kye had hoped. Danny put the key in his pocket and Sean helped him pull the car onto his tow truck. When they arrived at the duplex, Sean knocked on Kye's door to see if she wanted to see the car before Danny took it to his warehouse.

"My, my, so that's what Cecil was so proud of." Tears came to her eyes. "I never saw the car. It belonged to Cecil's dad. It was parked in the old tobacco barn when he died. I guess it must have sat there for years. Although it wasn't close, the barn was visible from the house and a gravel path led back to it. After Leo left for Texas, Cecil became concerned the barn might fall down on it or it could be vandalized, so he had the car towed and stored closer to here. He thought that someday he would get around to working on it. Unfortunately, he was already in poor health and never got around to it. I don't think he ever went back to the garage again."

Sean put his arm around her shoulders. "Kye, Danny's going to take it to his warehouse and see what he thinks can be done with it. After that, we can all sit down and talk about whether you should sell it as is or what would be involved in restoring it."

Chapter 15

The 1954 four-door Desoto was a classic. Someone not schooled in these old cars might think it was ready for the car graveyard, but he knew better. Many times, Danny had transformed old heaps to their original grandeur. Granted, it was painstaking work and required patience as he tracked down authentic parts to keep the car in original form, but he marveled at the end results. Looking it over, he knew it would dazzle both car enthusiasts and common admirers. The body needed work, and the engine would have to be overhauled and parts replaced. Restoring the seats to their original design should be no problem for the upholstery specialist he used in the nearby city of Athens. After close inspection of the interior gadgets and fixtures, he saw no real obstacles.

He put the key in the lock and turned. Danny was relieved when he felt the catch on the trunk lid click. He slowly pushed it open. The heavy trunk lid's hinges held it open, giving him full access to the spaciousness offered by these older model cars. The musty smell wasn't surprising—given that the car had been undisturbed for close to four decades. Off to the side was a dark-olive metal fishing tackle box and fishing rod, and an old duffle was pushed to the back of the trunk. Something lay concealed under the frayed wool blanket strewn across the trunk bed. He paused. He took hold of the blanket's edge and slowly started to peel it away, rationalizing that his restrained movement was to minimize stirring more dust. *Oh, God*, he thought as his mind fought against the image emerging from under the time-worn blanket. Unsure if he should continue, hesitancy gave way to curiosity as the dark secret was laid bare. *No box of coins this time.*

The state's coroner, Dennis Douglass, "DD" as he was called, had taken custody of the remains found in the trunk of the car. Ronnie Vin, the state forensics leader, had sent techs to the garage where the car had been stored. She towed the car back to Columbus to examine it.

The clothes on the skeletal form were deteriorated to the point of not being recognizable. The leather shoes were dry-rotted. The duffle was packed with clothes and remnants of personal items.

While the Forensics and the coroner were investigating the car and its contents, Danny worked on one of his cars. After they left, Sean came over to him, "Danny, what is it with you and these cars? Every one you touch turns into a mystery."

"Yeah, I'm getting gun shy about opening their trunks. I just wish this had been another box of coins."

"Roger that," said Sean. "Well, I'm heading out."

"I'll walk you out. Sally is home and ready to hear all about my day."

Kye was sitting on the front porch with Buddy lying beside her when Sean arrived.

Buddy jumped up to get patted by Sean and then laid back down beside Kye as Sean sat down. "Kye, are you doing okay?" News traveled fast around Bekbourg, so Sean figured Kye had heard.

"Yes, but I cannot imagine how a body got there. I hope whoever it was—they were dead before they were put there."

"The coroner will be able to tell us more once he has completed his examination. He couldn't begin to guess how long it's been there. I take it you don't have any ideas about who it might be?"

"No, Sean. I have no idea. Do you think it was put there after Cecil stored the car in the storage garage?"

"Well, the Techs don't think so. The storage door lock worked with the key you gave us, and they didn't think anyone had tampered with it. They are going to look closer at the lock, but that's their preliminary thoughts."

Sean was concerned about Kye. She was worried about the property situation and now this. "Kye, we'll get to the bottom of this. There's not much we can do until we hear back from the Coroner. The starting point is seeing if he can identify the body. It's starting to get late, and the air is damp. Let me walk you inside."

She smiled, "Always so gallant. Cheryl's got a good one."

He smiled.

"Mary, I'm glad that you were able to join me for lunch."

"Thank you for asking me. You mentioned at the gala that you were looking for a place to live. Have you had any luck?"

C.P. responded, "Not yet. Harvey Bennett showed me around his Lake Shore development. It's in a nice area near the lake and golf course, but I'm more interested in the area near the downtown. I've looked at a couple of other places. I'm not in a hurry. I'm staying at the B&B. Bri Sanderson knows how to pamper guests. I find myself exercising longer each day just so I can enjoy the delicious pastries she serves."

Mary smiled. "She is such a special person. Not only is she terrific in running the B&B, but she and her husband contribute so much to Bekbourg, especially assisting at-risk women."

"Yes. She told me that your foundation has enhanced what she and others around the area have been able to do. That is one of the reasons that I wanted to have lunch with you. I support what you are doing here in Bekbourg, and I would like to make a contribution."

Mary was surprised, "Jennifer told me that you made a very generous contribution at the gala's fundraising event. My foundation receives funds from that. I will be receiving some of those funds you contributed."

"I realize that, but I would like to also contribute directly, if that is okay with you?"

Mary was delighted. She and C.P. talked about her goals for the foundation and agreed to meet again once she and Rachel returned from their yearly summer trip to Europe.

Sean entered Max's bistro for a cup of coffee and walked over to speak to Max.

"Hey, Sean, it's always good to see you in here. Keeps the crime down."

Sean chuckled. "Well, your discounting the coffee for me and my deputies is a way to ensure our presence." Max laughed. Just then, Sean heard a Cuckoo clock strike two. He looked up and saw a beautiful clock. "That's some clock, Max. The design and colors are really something."

"Yeah, Bri is thinking of getting one for the B&B. Otis' father makes them. They are a work of art." As Max handed Sean the coffee, he said, "Bri is working hard on the election. She said it will really get cooking after Labor Day. She envies you not having someone running against you."

Sean laughed. "I have to say, I'm sure glad about that. I wouldn't look forward to campaigning."

"I hear you."

Mary and C.P. walked up.

"Hi, Mary," said Sean. "How have you been doing?"

"Thank you, Sean, for asking. I have been well. Sean, do you know C.P. Traylor?"

"No, we haven't met."

"Sheriff Neumann, it's nice to meet you," C.P. said as the men shook hands.

"It's nice to meet you. You may have worked with my grandpa on the railroad. His name was Clarence Neumann."

C.P. thought before answering, "I think I do remember him. He was a conductor, wasn't he?"

"Yes, that's him."

"It's a small world."

"Yes. I even worked for a couple of years as a brakeman before I joined the Marines."

"I didn't know that either. I always enjoy talking about the railroad. I'll give you a call sometime for lunch, Sean."

"That'd be great."

Chapter 16

Buddy loved to ride, so Sean stopped by and picked him up for the ride to Jasper. He sat in the back seat with his head looking out the window letting his ears flop in the air. Sean pulled into the parking lot at Draker's. A man of medium height and wiry build had just finished loading some equipment into a customer's pickup. He saw Sean's cruiser pull in and walked over after saying "bye" to the customer. Sean guessed he was in his 50's. He was dressed in jeans and a short sleeve blue chambray shirt with "Draker's" written in red. He looked at Buddy in the back seat, "What'd you pick him up for?"

Sean laughed. "This is Buddy. He likes to ride."

The man patted Buddy on the head and said, "That's a nice-looking dog. A Lab?"

"Yeah. I'm Sean Neumann, sheriff in Bekbourg." Sean extended his hand to shake.

When the man returned his hand shake, he looked at Sean with some recognition. "Sean Neumann? Are you the Neumann who was the quarterback who won the championship?"

Sean smiled, "Yep, guilty as charged."

The man said, "Well, isn't this something? I'm Rusty Draker. What brings you out here?"

"I'm investigating something and need some information. My dad, Jim, buys his wood supplies from you. I need to know if you sell any Lindenwood or Basswood to individuals or businesses in Bekbourg."

"I thought when you said 'Neumann' you might be some relation to Jim. Sure thing, Sheriff. Let's go in, and I'll pull the paperwork. You can bring Buddy with you if you want. People bring their dogs in all the time."

Sean and Buddy walked up and down the aisles while Rusty gathered the information. "Sheriff, here is a list."

Sean glanced over the list. "This is very helpful. Thank you for doing this for me."

"Any time. You and Buddy have a nice drive back."

Nine names were listed. A couple of men who worked for the county were on the list. A woman who worked in Sally's salon was listed. Otis Mueller and Noel Fischner were on the list, and the other four individuals Sean didn't recognize.

Alex had a list waiting for Sean when he arrived at the precinct the following morning. The area trade school was on his list along with seventeen other names. Sean and Alex split up the list to talk to the people.

Milton called Cheryl and told her that Sloan Lander was willing to talk to her about Harvey Bennett. Through her research, she learned that Harvey was born in Cleveland to Frank and Eve Bennett. Frank owned an upscale nightclub that had been opened by Harvey's grandfather, Luca Benito. Cheryl was confused about the names, because she ran across the name "Francesco Benito." She was hoping that Sloan could clear up her confusion.

Sloan Lander had come up through the ranks of a police department in the Cleveland area and served as the chief of police for seventeen years before retiring in the mid 90's.

"Thank you, Chief Lander, for seeing me."

"When my old buddy Milton called and said that you had some questions about the Bennetts, it raised my curiosity. What is it you want to know?"

Cheryl described how Harvey Bennett had developed the golf course and residential community in Bekbourg. She explained that Harvey's company had announced another large development. She was looking into the matter because of what had happened to her neighbor and close friend. She also mentioned the corruption with Jeff Thompson and his father Randall, and that Jeff had brought Harvey into Bekbourg to develop the property. "There seems to be a lot of connecting dots, Chief Lander, and I'm trying to run down rabbit trails and see if something pops up."

"I understand. Well, I don't know anything about Bekbourg and local happenings there, but I do know a little about the Bennett family, actually the Benito family. Law enforcement never could lay a hand on him, but Luca Benito ran the rackets. That's Harvey's grandfather. He was into liquor sales during prohibition, gambling and prostitution. He was part of a powerful organized crime family in Cleveland. His nightclub opened in Cleveland in the 1930's, and that's where he ran his businesses from. Luca expanded his operations into Newport, Kentucky. He was ruthless and unfortunately had police, judges and politicians on his payroll who did his biding. His club in Cleveland and the one in Newport were never raided. Heck, he was untouchable. It was all planned. His son Francesco was going to follow in his old man's footsteps.

"The problem was that Luca got on the wrong side of a local nightclub owner in Newport who had his own side businesses in alcohol, gambling and prostitution. His name was Lefty Finnigan. Lefty wasn't greedy. He played nice as long as others played nice with him. He just wanted to run a small-time operation from a club on Monmouth Street. He didn't sell the smooth Canadian booze like they did in New York. His was that 'rotgut' alcohol, but it sold just fine." Cheryl and Sloan chuckled.

"Because the Monmouth Street location was considered premium, Luca wanted to horn in on Lefty's enterprise and used some strong-arm tactics, like hassling customers who were entering and leaving Lefty's. He even had some of his goons rob a couple of Lefty's employees. Things like that. Luca was a cocky SOB—pardon the language—and he severely underestimated Lefty. That was part of Lefty's strategy. He acted easy-going, even like a pushover, but he was anything but. He got word around that he didn't want any trouble with the Cleveland bosses. Sent word to Luca he was ready to deal.

"Luca thought it was all worked out. He walked into Lefty's club all cocky with his two body guards and mistress. Everything looked like business as usual. Lefty greeted Luca like a long-lost brother and welcomed Luca and his entourage into his office. Everyone got comfortably seated. During the conversation, I was told that Lefty said to Luca, 'Newport is a big enough place for us both to have some fun. What do you say, Luca? Let's be friends.' Luca rejected that proposal. Lefty said, 'Okay, okay. I don't want no hard feelins'. My daddy had a sayin', Luca, 'pigs get fat, hogs get slaughtered.' Those were the last words Luca ever heard.

"What Luca didn't know was that there were hollow walls on two sides, and men had been set up to fire on the signal. Hundreds of bullets left them all four unrecognizable from what I was told. Their bodies were never found. With the mighty Ohio River close by, that may have been their final resting place, but I don't know. The cops never showed up at Lefty's place that night. I don't know if it was because they weren't called, or if they had been told to stay away.

"When Francesco realized that his father wasn't coming back, he worked a deal with the Cleveland boss to take over Luca's business, but Francesco would continue to own the nightclub. With the mob starting to move the operations to Vegas, they didn't care about the club, so Francesco kept it. He changed his name to Frank Bennett.

"Over time, people lost interest in that sort of thing, and Frank closed the nightclub. Frank and his wife had two kids, Harvey and a daughter. He eventually moved his family to Florida. I lost contact after that, so I don't know what happened after the Bennetts moved to Florida. When Milton called me, I checked, and Frank Bennett stills lives there."

"Milton said you were a gold mine of information. How did you know all this about Lefty?"

"One of the guys who worked at Lefty's club was a busboy. He heard it through the grapevine. It wasn't like people who worked at the club were afraid to talk in front of employees there, because everyone who worked there knew what happened at Lefty's stayed at Lefty's. The busboy eventually moved up here and, believe it or not, joined the police force. One night, when he and I were on a stakeout, he was a rookie, and I guess he wanted to impress me. He told me the story. I told him he best not ever breath another word about it to anyone. All those old players like Lefty and Luca are long dead, so I don't see a problem with telling you, but it's not something I want to see in print."

"No, of course not. I appreciate the background."

"Well, from what you told me, I figure the apple doesn't fall too far from the tree in the Bennett family. There are also deep pockets if Harvey ever needed money from Frank."

Before Harvey Bennett relocated to Bekbourg, he was an investor in a residential community on the eastern side of Columbus. Cheryl also found a picture where Harvey and four other men were attending a ribbon-cutting ceremony where he was the developer in an upscale golfing community in northeastern Columbus. From what she learned, he sold his interest in both projects before he moved to Bekbourg. The *Bekbourg Tribune* interviewed Harvey soon after he announced the Lake Shore development. He told how he and Jeff Thompson had met during college, and they stayed in touch. Jeff contacted Harvey when the local business leaders wanted to bring in someone who had the experience and expertise to develop an upscale residential community. After visiting Bekbourg and exploring the opportunities, Harvey decided Bekbourg offered the ideal conditions for the desired development.

Cheryl decided it was time to talk with Harvey.

Chapter 17

"Sean, we looked through all the police reports in the state and asked the authorities in the other states for their help. Lucky Brennan also checked the FBI files. We asked to look for stolen coins going back decades. There were no reports that included the coins Uri inventoried as being stolen."

"Mmmm." Sean thought about what Harold had just told him.

"You know, Sean. It's possible that some of these were stolen, but the owner didn't report them to the authorities. It may be that people sold them to those pawn shops that Burkhart bought from. Heck, Burkhart may have bought directly from individuals. It's hard to know where all those coins came from, but the bottom line is that we can't find any reports of them being stolen."

When Sean didn't say anything, Harold asked, "I heard about the body that was found in the trunk of the car. How's that going?"

"Ronnie Vin is nervous about how many ballistics she's going to have to check."

Harold laughed, remembering all the bullets she had tested a year ago for Sean. "I lost count of all the bullets you sent up to her."

Sean laughed, "It was something. Anyway, solving a twenty-year old murder is a challenge. I just keep turning over stones."

"Yeah, I hear you. Well, let me know if I can help."

"Thanks, Harold, and I appreciate your checking on the coins."

Sean stopped by to see Kye, who was on the porch, knitting. "Kye, you got a minute?"

"Always—for a handsome lawman."

Sean grinned. She was keeping her sense of humor despite everything. "The Coroner found something that might be a way to identify the body. He's also trying to check dental records."

"There wasn't a wallet?"

"No."

"Sean, could he tell what happened?"

"Yes, Kye, he determined the cause of death. The victim had been shot."

"Oh no. Sean, this seems impossible. I don't know what to think."

"I was wondering if you would look at something DD found on the body and see if you recognize it?"

"Of course."

Sean pulled out an evidence bag. Inside was a watch. The leather band was in pretty bad shape, but the watch was not damaged.

Kye gasped. "Oh, Sean. Oh no."

"Are you okay, Kye?" She looked drained. "Don't get up. I'm going to get you some water."

When he returned, she told him, "I'm okay, but I cannot believe it. I know that watch. It's Leo's. It was Cecil's dad's railroad watch, a Ball. He had to wear that watch at all times when he was working, even had to get it set by the railroad time keeper once a month. That's how engineers stayed on the same time with dispatch. That white face and large black numbers made it easy to see in the dark. Cecil had his own, so when his dad died, Lester got his, and then Leo got it when Lester died. There is no doubt in my mind that's Leo's watch, but Leo told us he was going to Texas. That can't be Leo, can it? How could this happen? Do you think he gave someone the watch? Why would it happen?"

"I'll tell DD, and he can check dental records, and that way, we can know for sure. What can you tell me about Leo?"

"Leo's mother died when he was eleven years old. Lester did the best he could to raise Leo. Cecil and I helped when we could. Lester was injured and he was unemployed for a while. Cecil bought his interest in the property, but Lester and Leo continued to live there. Cecil never charged them anything. After Lester passed away, Leo continued living in the old home place. We didn't see him often. He'd drop by on Christmas, and once in a while he'd come around at dinner time because he knew I'd always have plenty."

"You thought he moved to Texas. Do you know what was going on with him at the time?"

"I don't mean to speak ill of him, Sean, but I know you need to know as much as you can to find out what happened. Leo was an unsettled young man. When Leo was a teenager, Lester told Cecil that he was concerned about Leo. He ran around with a rough crowd. Not violent, that's not what I mean, but I got the impression that they stole things and knew how to make money from those things. He never had a steady girlfriend that I knew of, but he was a handsome young man. He was likeable. I always thought he would make a good salesman. It was easy enough to fall for something he was telling, but I was always a little hesitant to believe what he told us. Cecil offered to help him get on at the railroad several times, but he had no interest in working a steady job.

"Then, one evening, he came by. I remember it so clearly. It was July Fourth. I thought he had come by because it was a holiday. We weren't expecting him, but I had fried some extra chicken and sides. We had a nice dinner. He seemed different. He had gotten a haircut and was dressed better than I had ever seen him. He said that he was leaving the next day, moving to Texas. He had found a job working on an oil rig. It was the first time he didn't seem restless. I actually remember commenting to Cecil after he left that he seemed content, that maybe he finally was maturing. We never saw him or heard from him after that. We had no idea how to contact him, and I guess we thought that one day, he'd just show up for dinner."

"Do you know who his friends were? Did he work for anyone?"

"He was very private, or at least he never talked about things like that around us. The only person I know who was his friend was Byron Thornton."

When Sophia and Charles married, they moved into the house previously occupied by his grandparents. She was repulsed by the towering dark-red brick structure with its domineering gables looming with judgmental presence. The interior was similarly cast with oversized dark woods and heavy upholsteries. She never cared enough to redecorate a place that filtered out sunlight. Now, with Michelle away at school, she felt it leached out emotion.

The exception was the small sun room. The sunlight warmed the room with its radiance. Surrounded by her favorite accessories, she was comforted. She loved how it offered a view of the garden through the large windows. This was her refuge where she now spent most of her days.

"Good morning, Mrs. Martin. I'll bring your coffee right in."

"Thank you, Blaire."

Sophia glided to gaze out the window that overlooked the flower garden. She and Michelle each spring would go to the nursery and buy whatever flowers struck their fancy with no rhyme or reason other than being their favorites. They would work over the next week or so planting the flowers. Each day, they would stroll through their flower garden admiring the bright colors and varying textures. She had loved the variety and the way the flowers competed and complimented each other. No professional gardener would have ever made such selections and arrangements, but Sophia and Michelle loved their creations.

After Michelle went to college five years ago, Sophia lost interest in working in the garden. She now hired a gardener each year to do the planting. As she peered out over the grounds, the flowers looked foreign, planted perfectly as an expert would do. Her passion for their beauty had given way to indifference. Like so many other things, indifference had become the bane of her existence, except for her daughter. Michelle had brought tremendous joy and fulfillment to her life and made her feel complete. She and Michelle were still extremely close, but being a first-year medical student more than consumed her life. Sophia was very happy for her and proud of the successful life she was making for herself. But, as Michelle's life had expanded since going off to college, Sophia had experienced a corresponding contraction in her life.

Blaire entered with the tray, interrupting Sophia's thoughts. "Here you go, Mrs. Martin." As she poured a cup of coffee, she said, "There's an interesting article in today's *Tribune.* They identified the body found in that car trunk. He may have been dead for over twenty years."

"Mmmmm."

"Do you expect Mr. Martin back this evening for dinner?"

"No, he called last night and said that he would be in New York for one more day. I don't know what my plans are for dinner tonight, but don't worry. I'll make something if I stay in."

"I'll make a chicken salad and put it in the refrigerator if you decide to eat here."

"That will be fine. Thank you."

After Blaire left, Sophia sipped her coffee and nibbled at the scone. She really didn't have much of an appetite. The pills that she was increasingly relying on left her detached from most things, including food. She picked up the paper and unfolded it to find the headline story, the one Blaine had mentioned. She started reading and suddenly the cup slipped in her hand, spilling coffee on her slacks. Blood drained from her face and she felt faint. "Oh, my God!" she gasped.

Sophia sped up the circular driveway, bringing the car to a screeching stop. She bolted from the car, not bothering to close its door. She charged up the steps, but before she could get to the door, her dad's housekeeper opened the door. "Hi, Mrs. Martin. How are you doing?"

"Not very good, Joanie. I need to see my dad. Is he here?"

"Yes, in his office."

"Thank you."

Sophia barged into her dad's office without knocking. He was sitting behind his desk working on something. He put down his pen and leaned casually back in his chair when he saw her.

"Hello, Sophia. It's nice of you to stop by. Did you drop something on your slacks?"

Sophia pushed the door shut. She started crying. "How could you?" she angrily demanded.

"How could I do what?"

"You know what I mean." Sophia felt like she was coming apart. "How could you kill him?"

"Calm down, Sophia," Pierce Bergmann responded in his controlled voice. "Why do you think I would have done that?"

He had seen the *Tribune* and knew the history between Leo Davis and Sophia.

"You never liked me seeing Leo. I remember very clearly that night. You were gone until after midnight. I never saw or heard from him again. He's dead," she shrieked. "They found the body." Sophia was sobbing uncontrollably.

"I saw the article this morning, and it came as a surprise to me, Sophia. I did not kill him."

"Then you had him killed."

"No, I didn't," the judge watched Sophia with his impassive stare.

"You're not going to get by with this. I'm going to tell Sean Neumann. He's not like the other flunkies in this town. He can't be bought."

"No, Sophia, you're not going to do that. You love Michelle too much to cause her the turmoil your irresponsible action will bring. And it would be irresponsible, because, while I certainly did not approve of that man, I had nothing to do with his death."

At the mention of Michelle, Sophia ceased her tirade. Her dad was right on that score. She would never want to do anything to cause distress to her daughter. Sophia glared at her dad. "I don't believe you for a minute, and I will never forgive you," she hissed as she spun to leave.

Chapter 18

Nothing much had changed since Sean last visited Byron Thornton—his clothes, the beer cans sitting on the side table, a cigarette lodged between his lips, and a violent action movie blaring across the room, "I take it you haven't heard the news about Leo?"

Still focused on the TV, "What news?"

"We found Leo's body in the trunk of a car."

Thornton jerked to face Sean and pulled the remaining cigarette butt from his mouth. "Huh? Leo in a trunk? What car? What was he doing in a car?" He ground out the cigarette.

"That's what I was hoping you could tell me."

Thornton looked surprised. "How the hell would I know?"

Thornton turned back to his movie, but wasn't tuned in.

Knucklepin's Tavern was the beer joint of choice for many around Bekbourg. It had been there long before Sean was born. From its limited menu, food was served at the few wall booths and at the round, dark oak tables bearing scars from years of use. Sunlight escaping into the bar when the door opened noticeably lit the otherwise dim area. Bar stools bolted to the floor lined the long plain bar. A couple of neon beer signs adorned the walls along with a plastic-faced clock with a beer logo that was centered on the wall behind the bar. It seemed little had changed during the twenty years that Sean was away.

Sean had talked to the owner of Knuck's, who remembered Leo and Byron. They were frequent customers. Then, one day, Leo just stopped coming in. The owner finally asked Byron about Leo. He told him that Leo had left town, moved out west somewhere.

"I understand that you and Leo were good friends. What can you tell me about him?"

Byron's petulance waned, "Well, he wasn't the type to want any obligations. He liked his beer. Did odd jobs."

"Did he take drugs?"

"No, not really. He may have smoked a little weed when we were in high school. Maybe a little after we got out, but that wasn't his thing. He liked beer, but he never really drank enough to get shit-faced."

"Who else did he hang out with?"

Thornton smiled. "Well, women threw themselves at him. He was eye-candy to them. We had some fun with the ladies."

"I didn't mean that. What about friends?"

"He was something of a loner when it came to friends. I was about the only one he hung out with."

"What about enemies?"

"He pissed off people from time to time, but no one I'd call an enemy."

"You were friends, and then you just don't see him anymore, and that didn't raise questions to you?"

Byron's temper flashed, "I don't like what you're implying, Sheriff. Leo told me he was leaving Bekbourg. Said he was going west. It didn't really surprise me. He had become bored. I don't know what was going on in his head." Thornton shook out another cigarette and held it.

"Had he been acting strange before he left?"

"No, same ole Leo."

"Byron, do you do wood carving or work with wood, like making furniture?"

Thornton was incredulous, "Huh? I ain't got time for shit like that."

"Do you know anyone who does?"

He lit the Camel, "Do I look like an encyclopedia? What's making furniture got to do with Leo being found?"

"Just answer the question, Byron."

"No, I don't know anyone that does that."

"Well, if you think of anything else, I'd appreciate you contacting me." Byron returned to his movie, so Sean laid another card on the coffee table, which got swallowed in the jumble of other things.

"Hi, Sean. This is Ronnie Vin."

"Hey, Ronnie. How are you?"

"Doing fine. I've got some information on the bullet that was found in the Leo Davis case. DD probably told you he found it in his chest region, probably the heart. There was a blood stain in the trunk. There was no sign that Mr. Davis was conscious after he was put in the trunk—based on the way his remains were found. Since there is no tissue to analyze, there is no way to know whether someone struggled to place him in the trunk. The bullet was from a 38. I don't guess you have a gun for me to test?"

Sean laughed. "Not likely. You know this happened a little over twenty years ago."

"Yes, that is what DD told me. What is it with Bekbourg and these murders?"

"Well, let me make it a little more interesting for you," Sean said. "You remember the murders of Roger Burkhart when you ran the ballistics for me?"

"Yes, the ones that occurred back in 1980?"

"Yep. This murder occurred that same night."

At first, Sean couldn't even hear Ronnie breathing. "Oh, God."

Sean laughed. "I'll call you if more bodies show up."

"You do that, Sean."

Sean was smiling as he hung up. Ronnie had helped him last year solve a complicated web of murders.

Sean was shown into the sunroom. Sophia stood to greet him and offered him something to drink. She wore a tailored light blue summer pant suit. Her perfectly manicured nails clicked as she gently entwined the long string of pearls.

"Hi, Sophia."

"Hi, Sean. You said on the phone that you needed to talk to me about some official business?"

"Yes, that's right."

"Well, like I said on the phone, I cannot imagine about what."

"Sophia, what can you tell me about Leo Davis?"

Sophia flinched, "Leo? I don't understand, Sean."

"Leo was shot, Sophia. I'm trying to find out who knew him."

Her eyes widened, "You surely don't suspect me?"

"Right now, I don't have any suspects. I'm just trying to find out who knew Leo. Your name came up. I need for you to tell me what you know about him."

Sophia hesitated, "Yes, I knew him, but that was a long time ago."

Sophia's hand was trembling as she picked up a cup of tea. She returned it to its saucer without taking a sip. She continued to look at the cup.

"Tell me about Leo. How well did you know him?"

She remained focused on the tea cup. "Not all that well."

"How did you know him?"

She lifted her eyes to look at Sean. "I came in for winter break from college during my sophomore year. I met him at the Christmas parade. There were a lot of young people, my age, gathered at the end of the parade route. We were all laughing and having a good time. You probably remember that was the tradition to be at the end of the parade route. I don't even know why that practice got started. There was this tall candy cane on one of the floats, and a gust of wind caused it to fall. It was falling right toward me, and someone pushed me out of the way. But when we fell, he broke my fall, so he hit the ground with me on top." She started twisting her pearls again. "It was Leo. Of course, I didn't know him at the time, but I was so thankful that I invited him to join me at the GilHaus for a cup of hot chocolate afterwards."

Sean thought about the specificity of Sophia's recollection. It was like she relived it every day.

"Did you see him after that?"

"Yes, but I had to return to school in January, so not too much."

"Did you see him when you came back for spring break?"

Sean saw her guard go up. "Yes, but spring break is so short."

"Stop holding back on me, Sophia. I'm trying to find out who killed Leo. I know it was twenty years ago, but anything you can remember will be helpful."

Sophia slightly shook her head. "I have no idea who killed him, Sean, none. I thought he just left Bekbourg. I didn't know anything about who his friends were or who he was close to. I don't know how I can help you."

"Did he ever mention Byron Thornton?"

She paused, "Well, now that you mention him, yes, they were friends. Byron lived at Leo's place."

"When was the last time you saw Leo?"

Sophia's voice had a slight quiver, "When I came home for the summer, I saw him then." She whispered, "Then, he was gone."

"Did he tell you he was leaving Bekbourg?"

"Sean, I can't help you."

Sophia pushed back her chair and left the room. As he let himself out, Sean knew there was more to the story than she had been willing to share.

Blaire finished serving the dinner and left Sophia and Charles alone. Sophia was pushing the food around while Charles was enjoying the lobster salad. "I heard that Sean Neumann was here. What did he want?"

She didn't look up from her plate, "Spying on me, Charles?"

"Don't try to change the subject, Sophia. Why was the Sheriff here?"

"He is raising money for the sheriff's department, something about a police vest." Sophia put down her fork and laid her napkin on the table. "Now, if you'll excuse me," she said as she stood to leave the room.

"Wait, Sophia," but she had already disappeared down the hall.

Chapter 19

When Sean and Cheryl walked into the GilHaus, Mike was standing beside Geri in the bar area, smiling.

"Happy Birthday, Geri!" She was surprised but beamed. Sean kissed her on the cheek, and Cheryl gave her a warm hug.

Mike put his arm around her shoulders. "What a wonderful birthday gift. Mike didn't tell me that you were joining us. My day just keeps getting better."

Mike leaned over and kissed the side of her head. "I think they are ready for us," he said with a smile.

Just then, Otis Mueller walked in with his wife, Candice, and his parents. Otis walked over to where the four were standing and greeted them. His parents were still standing off to the side with Candice. "It's Mom's birthday. She's eighty-four. Dad just turned eighty-five two months ago. Mom and dad never go out to eat, but Candy and I convinced them to celebrate her birthday."

Geri said, "Oh, my gosh! She and I share birthdays."

"Well, Happy Birthday to you," Otis said. "Come over, and I'll tell Mom it's also your birthday."

Hans and Hilda made a handsome couple. Hilda was about five-and-a-half feet tall and stout in structure. She had beautiful white hair and a deeply lined face. Hans was a foot taller and lean. Hilda was a stoic woman, but cordial. In broken English, she thanked them for their birthday wishes and returned like wishes to Geri.

After being seated at their table, "How wonderful seeing Otis's parents," Geri said.

"It's good to see Candy and Otis out," Mike was in agreement.

Cheryl smiled, "Yes, it is. God, I can't imagine what they went through losing their son like that. I ran into Otis the other day at Bri's. He brought over one of those beautiful Cuckoo clocks his dad makes to hang for her."

Cheryl changed the subject, "How are Matt and Miranda?"

"Oh, they are wonderful. Matt loves Montana and his job."

Mike added, "Well there may be another reason he's so happy there."

Geri smiled, "Mike's right. When we were there recently, he brought someone to dinner one night."

"Oh, what do you know about that?" Cheryl was intrigued.

"Not much yet, but you can bet Geri is staying on top of the news there."

They all laughed.

"I can't believe that Miranda just finished her sophomore year. It's flying by. She's now thinking about maybe going to medical school."

"That's great that she's into the sciences. I'm really glad to see women going into those fields."

"I know what you mean, Cheryl." Geri turned to Sean, "You know, Sean, Sophia Martin's daughter, Michelle, is in her first year of med school."

"I didn't know that. I didn't know that she had a child that age," said Sean.

"Yeah, she was born a few months after Matt. Michelle was a year behind him in school."

"Sophia must have quit college."

"Yes, she did, and then married Charles around the first of August. I remember, because I was huge with Matt, and the heat was hard on me. With her being the judge's daughter, we were expecting a huge fairy-tale wedding, but she and Charles eloped. His parents hosted a reception and dinner when they returned."

Sean asked, "Were you friends with her in high school?"

"No, not really. I always liked Sophia, but I never got to know her that much. She never really seemed to have any close friends in high school. Then, she went away to that private college and wasn't around here much. You probably remember her mom died that summer before our senior year. God, that was so awful. Sophia was devastated. It really affected her. Anyway, that June when I was expecting Matt, I ran into her at the drug store. She seemed upset, looked like she had been crying. I was surprised to see her. She told me she was home for the summer. I was concerned about her. I asked her if something was wrong. She said she really missed her mom."

"That's sad," Cheryl said.

"Yes. I worked on some PTA activities with her. She was very dedicated to Michelle. She wanted the school to have enrichment opportunities beyond just classes, so she helped with fundraisers and chaperoned field trips, participated on parents' committees, things like that. With her being Charles' wife, you'd think that she would be active with the wives in the social circles here, but she really never was a participant as far as I knew. I never heard of her working on the charities or the Garden Club." Geri looked at Cheryl. "During high school, she always was dressed in the most up-to-date clothes—nothing flashy, just very classy. None of the other girls ever dressed anywhere close to the way Sophia dressed."

"I don't remember much about her. Who were her friends?" Sean asked.

"Well, that's what's odd. You would think that with her being the judge's daughter, she'd be the most popular girl in our class, but she was more like a wall flower. Sophia didn't participate much in extracurricular activities at school. She took private lessons, like in ballet, violin and piano. Her mother even signed her up for private painting classes. Sophia never really seemed to have close friends.

"I know that you and Mike never paid any attention, but during high school, there were basically four cliques. One was the athletes, which we were all a part of; one was the popular kids, mostly the kids of the rich and powerful families;

then there were the hoods; and then everyone else. Sophia could easily have been in the popular group, but she kind of was in a group of her own. At lunch, she sometimes sat with people from the 'everyone else' crowd, and occasionally with the popular kids. I don't remember her going to many events at any of the kids' houses.

"But that all changed after her mother died the summer before our senior year. It was like a lid was taken off Sophia. She started wearing torn jeans and t-shirts and sweat shirts. Some days, I wasn't sure if she had even brushed her hair. The first time I saw her smoking in the smoking area near the gym, I was shocked. One thing though that she always wore, even with the sweat shirts and t-shirts, was a heart-shaped sapphire pendent. It was beautiful. I never saw her without it back then."

Sean said, "I never knew about her changing like that. I remember something about her mother dying, but none of this."

"Yeah, Sophia even started hanging out with one of the wildest girls in the twelfth grade, Angie Albrecht. They were inseparable."

Mike started laughing, "Sweetheart, you do know that Angie is now a Department Head at Hillsrock Community College?"

Geri smiled, "Of course I do."

They all laughed.

Mike said, "It's funny the turns life takes."

"Yeah. Angie met her husband at Michigan while she was working on her PhD. He was in med school. After they completed their education, they moved here. Sean, he's the doctor that took care of Mike at the hospital."

"I had no idea."

They went on talking and laughing and enjoying the happy occasion of Geri's birthday. Sean was happy that things were working out for Mike and Geri.

Harvey Bennett agreed to meet Cheryl at the GilHaus. During her interview, Cheryl said, "I find it interesting that you ended up in Bekbourg—given that your family is from Cleveland. What brought you to Bekbourg?"

"I had gone to college with Jeff Thompson, and we stayed in touch. Several years ago, he and I were at a meeting in Columbus. I had developed a golfing community there. We got to talking, and he mentioned that there was a nice area on the north side of Bekbourg that I should look at. I came down and spent some time and realized the potential. The county commissioners were trying to grow Bekbourg and also promote tourism, which I thought made a lot of sense given the proximity to the large lake northwest of town and the nearby national forest and state park. Also, being close to Cincinnati and Columbus and the college town of Athens were other pluses. The local leaders were willing to invest their own money. One thing led to another, and we moved forward with the Lake Shore development. It's been great for Bekbourg and the surrounding area. Tourism has increased, revenues have increased, and more and more businesses are looking at this area."

"How many acres were included in the Lake Shore development?"

"Oh, about eight hundred."

"That's a pretty good size. How long did it take to acquire that property?"

"Well, I don't know how long it took. Most of the land was purchased before I got involved."

"Your company is also developing the new development, Lake Meadows. How long was that in the planning stages?"

"Well, actually from the beginning. I couldn't bite off too much, so I started with the first development. The second one was going to be different, because it is tailored more toward weekend and vacation homes."

"Years ago, the state started building lodges, conference facilities, vacation cabins, things like that at some of the state parks, but a downturn in the economy forced them to stop. Do you know if the state plans to do anything with the Peatmont State Park?"

"Mmmm. I guess the state can always dust off plans like that."

"Do you know if there were any landowners who didn't want to sell to your company?"

"No, I don't know."

"What about Mrs. Davis's claim that she never knew her property was taken for tax foreclose. It's now part of Lake Meadows. Any comment on that?"

"No, I really don't know, Ms. Seton. What I do know though is how successful our Lake Shore development has been for Bekbourg, and our new

Lake Meadows project will bring even more vibrancy and revenues to our county."

"You are President of Bekbourg Enterprises Corp. I looked up the company on the state records. It shows that Jeff and Randall Thompson are the other two officers. The state records have not been updated to show the officers who replaced them. Who are the officers for Bekbourg Enterprises?"

"Oh, I guess I overlooked updating those records."

"But who replaced them?"

"No one has, Ms. Seton. I guess with everything, I haven't focused on replacing them."

"What about your shareholders?"

"What about them?

"Is it possible that some of them might fill the officer positions?"

"Like I said, I haven't thought about it, so I don't know."

"Who are your shareholders?"

"Our corporation doesn't disclose that information, but if a shareholder wants to disclose that about themselves, they are free to do that. I'm proud of what we've been able to do in Bekbourg. Unfortunately, I have another commitment that I am running late for. I hope that I have answered all your questions." He stood, signaling the end of the interview.

"Your assistant told me you have a full schedule today. I appreciate you seeing me, Judge."

"What can I do for you, Sheriff?"

"I'm investigating Leo Davis' death. He was shot to death and put in a trunk of a car. You probably read about it or saw it on the news. Anyway, people who knew him thought he had left town to take a job out west."

"Yes, I read about it."

"From what I have discovered, he and Sophia were very close before he disappeared."

Judge Bergmann looked at Sean with his steely eyes. No way to read his thoughts or emotions. "Judge, what were your thoughts about Sophia dating Leo?"

"I don't know if I would say they were dating, but any normal father would object if their daughter was seeing a punk like Davis."

"Did Sophia know you objected to her seeing Leo?"

"Sophia would have known my thoughts."

"Did you know Leo?"

"He appeared in my court a couple of times, so I knew about him. I knew he hung out at Burkhart's place of business some. Any side kick of Burkhart's was a con man just like him."

"She was your only child, Judge. She was a beautiful young woman with so much ahead of her. Were your objections strong enough that you would have taken action to get Leo Davis out of her life?"

The judge stared hard at Sean. "I guess you have to investigate his death. I'll be perfectly clear. I didn't kill Davis, and I didn't hire someone to kill him. I had nothing to do with his death. Now Sheriff, do you have any further questions?"

"That's all I have for now, Judge."

Sean tracked down Roy Mynatt at Knucklepin's. After Sean asked, the bartender nodded toward a table, where three county workers were sitting. When Sean walked up to the table, they all stopped talking and looked at Sean. Sean nodded. "Roy, I'd like to talk to you."

The other two men gladly got up and left the table.

"Mind if I join you?" Sean said as he sat down.

Roy was in his 30's, a stocky man with a beer belly. The ball cap covered dark, shortly trimmed hair. He still had on his work clothes, which consisted of an orange t-shirt with the county name, a pair of jeans and work boots.

Roy looked around to see if others were watching, which they were. Sean looked around, and they turned their heads.

"Sheriff, what can I do for you?"

"I'm investigating the murder of a man who has been dead about twenty years. You may have heard. His name is Leo Davis."

Roy immediately looked relieved and picked up his beer, but realizing the sheriff was sitting there, he put it back down without taking a drink.

"I heard about that, but I didn't know him."

"Had you ever heard of Leo Davis?"

"No, never heard of him."

"What about Byron Thornton?"

"Byron? What about him?"

"Do you know him?"

“Sure, he and I used to work together. We were on the same crew. He got hurt and went on disability. He doesn’t work for the county no more.”

“Do you ever talk to him?”

“Well, not regular. I sometimes see him here, but we don’t hang out if that’s what you mean.”

“Did he ever mention Leo Davis to you?”

Roy thought for a minute, “No, I don’t remember him ever mentioning that name.”

“What was Byron like?”

“What do you mean?”

“Tell me what he was like.”

“Well, I didn’t know him real well. We worked together like I said. Sometimes after work, we’d come here and get a beer. It usually wasn’t just us two, there’d be some others. He was kind of lazy. Didn’t work too fast, and if it involved somethin’ that just one person needed to do, I’d have to do it, He’d stand there watchin’. He didn’t miss work, though. He just didn’t like it and would take the easy way out when he could. He was friendly enough, but he was more of a loner. I’d try to talk about things, and sometimes he’d talk and other times, he wouldn’t.”

“What did he like to talk about?”

“Oh, you know, cars, huntin’, things like that. He never was into sports much.”

“Did he hunt?”

“I guess some. I know this isn’t really huntin’, but he kept a gun in his car—had a nice car—and if he’d see somethin’ along the road, like a possum or rabbit, he’d shoot at it. He’d brag about it if he hit it. It wasn't always an animal. He'd shoot at a tire or somethin' that might be lyin' beside the road."

"What kind of gun did he have?"

"I don't really know. It was a pistol, but I never saw the gun up close."

"Anything else you can think of, Roy?"

"No."

"Well, if you do, give me a call. Here's my card. I probably don't need to tell you, but you need to keep quiet about what we've talked about."

"Okay, Sheriff."

Sean knocked three times before Byron came to the door. "Byron, I need to talk to you," Sean said after Byron opened the screen door.

"What is it this time, Sheriff?" he asked—a cigarette hanging out the side of his mouth.

"Can I come in?"

He grunted and headed back to his chair with Sean following.

A violent fight scene where someone was getting pummeled with a metal pipe had Byron's rapt attention.

"Turn off the TV now." Byron huffed, but turned it off. Sean asked, "What guns do you have, Byron?"

"That's none of your business."

"Yeah, Byron, it is. Now, you can answer my questions here, or we can go to the station."

Byron looked as Sean, "I don't know why you keep hasslin' me, but I had nothin' to do with Leo dyin'."

"Tell me about what kind of guns you have."

"I have a couple of huntin' rifles."

"What about a hand gun? What kind of those do you have?"

"I don't have none."

"You don't have a hand gun?"

"No, I used to, but it got stolen out of my car, and I never bothered to replace it."

"Did you report it stolen?"

"Are you kiddin' me? Why would I have done that? Cops wouldn't have done nothing but hassle me on why I had a gun."

"What kind of gun was it?"

"I don't remember."

"You didn't level with me, Byron, when I asked you about Ernie's pawn shop."

"What's that supposed to mean?"

"Ernie's books show that you and Leo picked up some coins from his pawn shop in June 1980. What do you know about those coins?"

"It was no big deal. Look, man. Leo and I drove over there and picked up the coins for Roger. I never looked inside the bag to see what was in there. Leo put the bag in the trunk, and we drove to Roger's pawn shop and dropped them off with Roger."

"What type of bag?"

"Just some brown paper bag like you'd get at a grocery store, but heavier. The top was folded down and stapled across the top. We didn't tear it open to look inside."

"What about picking up coins for Roger from other places?"

"I don't remember all that shit. Leo and I helped Roger out with things. He'd tell us to go here and there to pick up things. We didn't always know what we were pickin' up. He paid us, and that's all I cared about."

Sean looked at him, and Byron turned back toward the TV wanting to turn it on to watch the movie. "I want you to try and remember, Byron, what kind of gun you had. I will be back."

As he drove back to the station, Sean reflected on Thornton. There was still something Thornton wasn't telling. He was going to see if Byron's gun was registered, but he suspected it wasn't.

Perusing twenty-years-worth of Sheriff Sales files was a laborious task, and since there wasn't any way to know which file involved a property sale under tax forfeiture, Cheryl had to review every file. Kim provided a vacant office, and as Cheryl worked her way through a stack, she returned those to Kim, who then brought in the next batch. Cheryl developed a computer spreadsheet. For each parcel, she logged the property's location, the size of the parcel, the date of the notice, and the purchaser. She looked at the mailing address to see if the legal notices and tax invoices were mailed to the address of the property itself or to a different address. It was a long, tedious process, but worth the effort. The end result was that she had at her fingertips the data she needed. She was particularly focused on property around the large development up north and property near Kye's.

For the property bought by Bekbourg Enterprises for the Lake Shore community, she identified the properties sold at tax sales where the legal notices were mailed to an address that was the same as the property itself. She tracked down most of those owners. Some lived there or didn't bother updating their mailing address for lack of interest. A couple of the original owners couldn't be located. She identified the property that the attorney from Columbus had told her about. The owner's name was Dex Chance. Her research led her to find two parcels that had a similar story to that of Dex's. She tracked down the parties who had owned those two properties, both of which became part of the Lake Shore development. They had lived out of town for years. Didn't really know whatever happened to their property. They had received tax invoices for some years and didn't really focus on the fact that the invoices stopped coming. At the time, they didn't think the property was worth much, and they had moved on with their lives.

Through the County Recorder's computerized records, the only property department that had computerized records, Cheryl confirmed that Bekbourg Enterprises had acquired around four-hundred acres for the Lake Meadows plan. She researched the Sheriff Sales files to see if any of that property had been acquired by Bekbourg Enterprises through a tax sale other than Kye's property. Cheryl was surprised when she discovered that a large 200-acre parcel owned by Adam

Steinsen had been purchased through a tax lien process several years ago. She consulted her map and saw that the Steinsen property was joined on the west side by the Peatmont State Park and on the east side by the other two-hundred acres now part of the Lake Meadows plan.

Chapter 20

Both were the same height, same dark hair and blue eyes, and dressed in tailored navy business suits. The only difference was that the woman wore a skirt. Both were immaculately groomed down to their Italian leather shoes. Despite their expensive dress, Celeste and Collin Steinsen were not put off in the least by their surly attorney or his disheveled office. Even the smell of dog and Skip's occasional grunt as he lay sleeping on his bed in the corner did nothing to distract them from their business at hand.

"Mr. Donaldson, we appreciate you seeing us on such short notice. I'll get right to the point." Celeste Steinsen was accustomed to being direct. "Our grandfather, Adam Steinsen, owned a farm here—two-hundred acres. Dad grew up here on that property but moved to Cincinnati after graduating from college. When we were young, Dad used to bring us here to visit Grandfather. Grandfather came to live with our family in Cincinnati several years ago after Grandmother died, and he began having health problems. For a few years after he moved in with us, he leased the property to some dairy farmers, but that stopped when they sold their dairy cows.

"When Grandfather died, Dad was supposed to have inherited the farm. Even though Dad never wanted to return here to live, it was his intent that the farm pass to us. Collin and I had discussed possibly building a weekend retreat here on the property, but we are very busy with our careers and never got serious about that notion until Dad recently died. The will, which was updated three years ago, explicitly listed this farm. We recently read about the new Lake Meadows development and drove here to see where it was in relation to our property. We were shocked to see a graded roadway and stakes on our property."

Collin picked up the conversation, "The county offices were closed, it being a weekend, so we returned to Cincinnati. We both had meetings on Monday, but I called Monday morning. At first, I talked with a clerk, Charlotte Mooney. She told me that she couldn't help and said that the Treasurer, a Ms. Kaufmann, would return my call. I had to call back several times the next day before Ms. Kaufmann finally took my call. She told me our family farm had been purchased several years ago at an auction due to a tax foreclosure. Beyond that, Ms. Kaufmann wasn't helpful.

"Celeste and I went through Dad's ledgers. Grandfather was independent and handled his affairs. His health gradually deteriorated, and he began having memory issues. Dad then took over Grandfather's affairs but only for a short time, because he died suddenly last year. Mr. Donaldson, Dad was a chief financial officer for a corporation. He was organized and a meticulous record-keeper. Grandfather didn't know this property sold at a tax auction, and Dad didn't have enough time with Grandfather's affairs to discover this.

"We have with us," Collin touched a briefcase sitting beside his chair, "all the files that we could find in Dad's records pertaining to this matter. Max Bryant and Bri Sanderson gave us your name. Something is not right about this whole matter. We don't have the time ourselves to check into this. Your assistant gave us your billing rates. We are fine with those. Tell us what you need from us. We want to hire you to get to the bottom of this."

As Celeste and Collin spelled out the facts, Owen sat reclined in his chair, tapping his pencil on the desk's edge. He suspected they were twins. He didn't know their occupations, but they appeared to be successful business-types. "Okay, I'll tell you what I'll do. I'll look into things, but something you should know is that this property was being used as a landing strip for an illegal drug trade that was busted last year. I don't know the status of the property, so that's something that I'll have to check on. It must be cleared by the Feds since Lake Meadows has it, but that could make things more complicated."

They both had been well schooled in hiding their reactions, even when presented with such an unusual circumstance. Celeste spoke first, "An illegal drug trade on Grandfather's farm? This is preposterous."

"I also can't promise how this will turn out." Owen continued, "This property was sold several years ago. Bekbourg Enterprises has owned it since then. I don't want you to get your hopes up. This is beyond being a long shot. It may be impossible to get this property back. I want to be clear on that."

"We don't know what is going on here, Mr. Donaldson, but we are not going to be deprived of our birthright. Please keep me and my sister posted on your progress. No stone should be left unturned on getting to the bottom of this."

Owen reviewed the documents the Steinsens had brought. Interestingly, the fact pattern was similar to what he found happened in Kye's case. Their records showed that the tax invoices had initially been mailed to their grandfather in Cincinnati. After a while, there was no record of their grandfather receiving any further tax invoices. Celeste and Collin's grandfather must not have picked up on the fact that the tax invoices were not being sent by the county, and there were no tax foreclosure notices, which most certainly would have raised a red flag. However, with their dad's unexpected demise, he didn't have the opportunity to discover the matter. Owen thought it noteworthy that the Steinsen records showed that the tax value on the assessments was lowered before the tax sale.

Owen went to the Clerk of Court and obtained copies of the legal documents used to foreclose on the property. He found where all the legal documents, including the tax invoices and tax forfeiture notices, were sent to the property address itself, not to the Cincinnati address. For some reason, the mailing address was changed from Cincinnati. If the tax bills weren't sent to Cincinnati and the owner wasn't paying attention, the taxes would not get paid. He saw in the courthouse files a copy of the newspaper notice of the Sheriff's Sale. The property's description posted in the *Bekbourg Tribune* was vague.

The Steinsen property was a prime piece of property that bordered Peatmont State Park and included the top of a ridge. The top of the ridge had been used as a landing strip for illegal drug operations. Upon Owen's further review, he learned that the authorities never found drugs on the property, and they didn't have enough evidence to confiscate it. This meant that Bekbourg Enterprises was the owner of the property.

"Of all the days for Charlotte to be out sick," thought Kathy Isaac, as she saw Owen walk in. Kathy was a clerk who typically worked in the Clerk of Court's Office.

"Where's the other clerk?"

"Sir, she's not here today. Is there something that I can help you with?"

"I sure wish to hell someone around here would. I've written down another list of documents that I want." He plunked down a sheet of notebook paper with a hand written list scribbled down the page. "It's all listed here, but it's the same type of information that I requested for Kye Davis' property, but this is for another property. Rightful owner was Adam Steinsen, now his grandchildren, Collin and Celeste Steinsen."

Owen was talking so loudly, Kathy unconsciously took a step back. "Mr. Donaldson, I mostly work in Ida's department, so I don't think I can help much on this, but as soon as Charlotte gets back, I'll be sure and give her your list."

This triggered Owen, "There's some other people sitting on their asses back in those offices that damn well know how to get this information. I'll be back on Friday, and it better be ready."

He walked out and headed back toward his office. That had gone about as he expected and hoped. He had the proof that they weren't providing public documents. That refusal would be a basis for his next lawsuit. They weren't going to know what hit them. He knew something was rotten, and by God, he was going to get to the bottom of it.

Sean visited Noel's outfitter's shop and looked at his carvings. Noel was glad to talk about them. Sean asked what type of wood he used. "I find Basswood is the easiest wood to work with. I take a block of wood and carve the figures from the block. I also use wood shavings to add texture and dimension. As you can see, except for eyes and highlights like on the feathers or legs or something, I don't use colored paints. I just use stains."

"Your subjects are always animals?"

"Mostly, but I do other things. In September, I start carving Santas for the holidays. I enjoy it, but unfortunately, with getting involved in the campaign, I haven't carved much in a few months."

"What about the eagle you donated to the Garden Club for the fundraiser?"

Noel laughed, "I did that in the winter along with lots of other carvings. I was already thinking about running for the Commission and knew I needed to get a supply. I knew Mom would want something for her gala."

"These are skillfully done. Where is your workshop?"

"Oh, in the back here. Sometimes when it's not busy, I work on the carvings. I have an alarm that lets me know when someone enters the shop."

"Mind if I see it?"

"No, not at all."

Noel opened the door. "You see, we have to walk though my storage room to get to this room." He turned on the lights.

Sean looked around. "This is quite a collection of tools, Noel. You've got a nice area here."

Everything about the room was organized and clean and well lit. There was a door out the back of the building with a large window. "I see you've got a window. Was that always here?"

"No, I can't work in a room without windows. Dad put that in for me when I bought the place."

"Does your dad carve?"

"Sure. He's who taught me."

"Does he use the same type of wood that you use?"

"Yeah, I always buy extra and take it to him. Saves him a trip."

"Well, thanks for showing me around."

"Sure, Sean."

Chapter 21

Nickolas, Harvey, Pauline and Charles sat in a private room upstairs at the GilHaus.

"What the hell? Now Donaldson is asking about the Steinsen property? That was taken care of years ago. Old man Steinsen moved to Cincinnati. Why's he asking about that property?"

Pauline responded, "Nickolas, look. We bought that property several years ago. They didn't pay the taxes. The time requirement ran out, and we foreclosed. It's done."

"I agree with Nickolas. It's odd that these are coming up now," said Charles Martin.

Pauline replied to Charles, "You weren't involved when we did the Lake Shore project, but your father was. There were a couple of those properties where the landowners had long been gone from Bekbourg. It worked out then, and it will be fine here. We're going to keep stringing Owen along. The Steinsen property sold long ago. I don't know how Owen came up with it. I recently receive a call from someone checking on the property, claiming to be an heir. Maybe they contacted Owen, but they lived in Cincinnati."

"I tend to agree with Pauline," Harvey said. "I can't imagine that they're going to keep pushing this. The surveyor is about finished with the work.

As soon as I can, I'm going to announce that lots are for sale. I want to move forward as quickly as possible."

Nickolas complained, "Well, if it wasn't Owen, I might agree with you, but he's like a damn bulldog. Another thing: that blasted Reform Party has momentum because of that scandal last year. We can't afford this shit storm. You can bet that Noel Fischner is going to be using this."

"The election isn't until November. This is all going to die down," Harvey said. "You need to be campaigning on how this new development is going to help the county. Talk up the success of Lake Shore and the benefits of our new development project. Fischner doesn't have any successes like that to point to."

"That's right," Pauline agreed. "Nickolas, you worry too much. We have done a good job on the economy here. Fischner doesn't have any type of track record. It's the same with the rest of that Reform Party. We just need to keep reminding people of that. It will turn out fine."

All of them had a financial stake in the outcome of the Lake Meadows litigation. However, Nickolas felt they weren't showing a similar level of interest about the election. That was probably because he could be uniquely affected by the November election. Pauline didn't have to worry, because as Treasurer, as long as the commission was satisfied with her, she was good, and he doubted if the other two commissioners would ever try to look over her shoulder. Harvey had never had any trouble getting what he wanted out of the commission. But, if Noel defeated Riley and got a seat on the commission, if he was persuasive with Lance Pruitt, the third commissioner, they could make things difficult for Nickolas. Jeff Thompson had ruled the commission with an iron fist, and what he said went. Nickolas had tried to exert control, but Lance sometimes pushed back. Noel was making noises about being against development because of environmental issues. If Owen brought up the fracking permit and Noel was on the commission, he might try to take another look at it. What if Noel and Lance tried to pull it back from the state for a further review? He was going to have to make sure they kept their eye on the election ball.

Sean saw Dusty in Frau's Diner and joined him at a table. Dusty was looking gloomy, "Yeah, I heard all about it, Dusty."

"I'm not sure I know what I'm going to do. They completely closed the yard in Bekbourg, so all the businesses in Bekbourg are now being served by the main line trains out of Cincinnati."

"What are you going to do?"

"I'm going to have to drive into Cincinnati and work out of there. I'm not old enough to retire, so I'll have to work out of Cincinnati."

"Any chance you'll move back there?"

"No, no chance of that. I'll just have to drive. I guess you heard. That was the last straw for Chaw. He put in his papers. He's retiring."

"What about Duke Winters? Isn't he getting close to retirement?"

"No, he needs five more years. He's going to have to get qualified back on the road and work out of Cincinnati as well. You know, Sean, I think this is just the beginning of the end. I think they're going to shut down the whole railroad running through Bekbourg. They're just giving businesses time to make other arrangements. I've noticed that they haven't been doing much to maintain the rails. Most of the trains have been diverted to the lines just south of here going up the Ohio River."

"You could be right. The railroads all over the country have consolidated and moved their operations to the most economical routes."

"Yeah, local railroad business is a thing of the past."

Sean said, "It's a shame, because for some of these companies, the only way they can stay in business is to have rail service. I wonder what is going to happen to them."

"That's a good question."

Cheryl said, "I would have been glad to come to Cincinnati to meet with you."

"Bri's delicious crumb cake has grown on us." Celeste was getting ready to take another bite.

Collin said, "Yes, you offered that, but we want to spend more time here. Finding Bri and Max here was a bonus. Bri and Max have done a nice job with the B&B and bistro. The business model is a perfect fit for an area like Bekbourg that is promoting tourism and is surrounded with the many outdoor opportunities. We regret that we lost contact with them but we've re-established that connection."

Cheryl smiled, "Bri and Max are definitely good ambassadors for Bekbourg. Bri told me that you were friends when they lived in Cincinnati. I agree with you about how friendly people here are. It's a great place."

"Owen Donaldson suggested that we call you." Celeste was ready to talk business. "He is handling a property matter for us. He thought you might be working on a story about some property dealings here in Bekbourg and would be interested in hearing about our situation."

They described to Cheryl what had happened to their grandfather's property.

"Sheriff, I hate to bother you at home, but I thought you should know what's happened."

The sun had just set, and Sean and Cheryl were returning from walking Buddy when his phone rang. "What's going on, Arlo?"

"Owen Donaldson had just left his office and was walking home when a man came up to him and started yelling. They didn't get into a fight, but the yelling between him and Mr. Donaldson was so loud, the neighbors were watching and calling dispatch."

"What happened?"

"Cooper Townsend was waiting outside his office, and when Mr. Donaldson walked out, Townsend started yelling at him. I guess that Mr. Donaldson isn't the type to walk away. He was giving as good as he got for a man his age. The witnesses said that Mr. Townsend was yelling things like, 'You let me go to hell, and you're going to hell, you SOB.' Mr. Donaldson was yelling for him to get out of there. Mr. Townsend was yelling that if Mr. Donaldson hadn't been drunk, he would have done his job and gotten him off. Mr. Donaldson said that he was fooling himself, that 'God Almighty couldn't have gotten him off.' Mr. Townsend said that was 'bullshit.' That's the type of things being said until I got there and told Mr. Townsend that he needed to move on, that he didn't want an arrest. As he started to leave, he told Mr. Donaldson that 'he'd get his.' I could smell alcohol on Mr. Donaldson. I suggested he go on home. He was cussing a streak as he walked on to his home."

"Arlo, I'm glad you called me. Who's on call with you tonight?"

"Darrell."

"Ask him to hang around there near Donaldson's home and keep an eye out. I don't think Townsend will come back tonight, but let's watch."

"I'll wait until he gets here before I leave."

"Thanks, Arlo. You handled the situation well."

The following morning, Sean knocked on the door of the double wide trailer. An older woman dressed in a duster and house shoes cracked open the door. Her short heavily peppered gray-brown hair was in disarray. "What do you want?"

"Ma'am, I understand that your son, Cooper, lives here. I need to talk to him."

"My boy ain't done nothin'. You people pinned things on him and sent him to prison."

"Ma'am, I just need to talk to him. I can take him into the station, but I would prefer to talk to him here."

She told Sean she would get him and closed the door. After a while, Cooper opened the door. It looked like he had just rolled out of bed. "Cooper, I need to talk to you. Can you step out here so we won't bother your mother?"

Reluctantly, he stepped out on the small concrete porch with a dilapidated redwood railing.

"Cooper, when you were arrested for the drug possession, the police report showed that you were in possession of a hand gun. Where is that gun?"

"Huh? How should I know? I never seen it after then."

"You never got it back?"

"Hell no."

"You don't know what happened to it?"

"No. Why're you askin' about that?"

"Look, Cooper. I understand there were some problems yesterday evening outside of Owen Donaldson's office. I'm not going to give you another warning. You go near Owen's office or home, and I'll have you arrested. You'll find yourself back in prison if you're not careful."

"With the Thompsons dead, who's pulling your strings, Sheriff? This whole place is corrupt. I thought you might be different, but you're protectin' that shit excuse of a lawyer. He's the one that should be in prison. He doesn't do his job, and people like me end off in that hell hole for somethin' I didn't do."

"Cooper, you need to pay attention here. I am looking into your case, but I won't tolerate you causing problems here or harassing Owen. Do you understand, Cooper?"

"Yeah, I understand just fine."

Skip was lying on his bed and raised his head, looking toward Martha and Sean when they entered Owen's office. He got out of bed and wagged his tail. Martha said, "Alright, come on. I'll take you outside and give you a treat."

Sean watched Skip slowly wag his tail as he lumbered after Martha down the hall.

"I thought you might show up after what happened last night. You want a drink, Sheriff?" Owen asked--pointing toward a Canadian Club bottle. Owen had obviously gotten an early start as the glass in his hand showed.

"No, Owen, but I would like for you to tell me what that was all about."

"Ah, hell. I probably should never have taken the case, but Townsend needed a lawyer and couldn't pay. I volunteered to take his case. He maintained from the beginning that he was set up. I kept asking him why he thought someone would frame him, but he claimed there wasn't a reason. He probably was set up, but if he wouldn't tell me by whom and why, I couldn't defend that. There was no record of him using or selling drugs, and that damn Ben Clark was the arresting officer. No witnesses. The prosecutor took Ben's word and charged him. Defending him was like trying to fight with both hands tied behind my back and my legs shackled. I did my best, Sean, but it was damn impossible."

"Any idea who might have planted drugs or why?"

"No. He worked at Koot's. He was sleeping with a woman, but I never heard of any reason she would have had it done. She even seemed upset at the trial when they found him guilty. My guess—and it's only that—is that it had something to do with goings-on's at Koot's. The Thompsons owned it, and I don't have to tell you what they were capable of."

"Thanks, Owen. I talked with Townsend. Hopefully, he won't come near you again, but be on alert."

"I appreciate that, but I've never cowered to anyone, and I'm not going to start now."

"Just take care, Owen. A lot of people depend on you."

Owen poured another shot of whiskey after Sean left.

Chapter 22

Cheryl called Milton to update him. "Milton, in my research, I found that a large two-hundred acre property, known as the Steinsen farm, was sold at a tax sale to Bekbourg Enterprises Corp. several years ago. It was the property used as a landing strip for illegal drugs, but it wasn't confiscated. Anyway, I met with the grandchildren of the original owner. Their names are Celeste and Collin Steinsen. Owen suggested they call me. He told them I was working on a story and thought I might be interested in what happened to their family farm. As it turns out, what happened to their grandfather and father is very similar to what happened to Kye."

"All this is interesting, Cheryl. For Owen to send them to you, I wonder if he's thinking of a repeat."

"A repeat?"

"Remember what I told you about Owen telling me about a client who was being cheated by Packard Oil?"

"Yes, the energy supplier. That's where you investigated and broke the story."

"That's right."

"Oh, I see. He might be hoping I can discover what's going on and publish a story."

"My guess. It sounds like you're well on your way. I've been digging. Randall Thompson started Bekbourg Enterprises, but once Harvey decided he wanted in, he bought control. I couldn't find the terms of the sale or anything about the shareholders and the ownership percentages. Harvey became the President.

"I've also found some old newspaper articles about the Lake Shore community. Since Harvey was involved in similar developments in Columbus, I looked at old newspaper articles there, too. I'll send them to you, but I thought you should know. Pauline Kaufmann's realty company was the only realty company that sold the lots in Lake Shore. She wasn't the only local that got an exclusive. From all the stuff I've been able to dig up, Nickolas Garrison was the builder of all the homes there. It also seems that First City Bank of Bekbourg arranged financing for most of the home constructions. The bank president at that time was Jeremy Martin. Harvey was quoted in one of the articles:

> *'We're excited about this new, luxury development. We're building a first-class golf course, and many amenities for families that include a swimming pool and play ground. The club house will have a pro shop and restaurant that will sell snacks and also serve lunch and dinner. Bekbourg is a*

growing area. It's ideally located near Wayne National Forest, Peatmont State Park and the Scioto River. Beautiful Peatmont Lake is close by with a boat launch and boat storage. It's convenient to Columbus, Athens, and Chillicothe, and Cincinnati is only two hours west. To make it seamless to folks wanting to join our beautiful community, we've put together a one-stop service. Pauline Kaufmann is the foremost authority in real estate around Bekbourg. Her team will expertly handle all real estate matters. Nickolas Garrison is synonymous with quality building in Bekbourg. His business has been constructing buildings and beautiful homes for over thirty years. He is a custom builder and already has home designs with the latest in offerings, but he will gladly work with customers to make sure their dream home is built to

> *their satisfaction. And, of course, First City Bank of Bekbourg brings its expertise for financing for those who want a local bank. Jeremy Martin, the bank president, is standing ready to welcome you.'"*

"Milton, things are starting to click about how the participants each benefited. Of course, Jeff and Randall were officers in the company, so they stood to gain. Pauline and Nickolas benefited by those exclusive arrangements. Even though the bank was not the sole means of financing, it didn't hurt that Harvey was promoting it."

"Yep. If we could find a list of the shareholders, I would bet my bottom dollar that would include the officers as well as Nickolas and Pauline. Heck, you never know, Martin might even have been a shareholder then. Jeremy Martin died a few years back; his son, Charles, is the bank's president now."

"It will be interesting to see if Pauline and Nickolas get exclusives for Lake Meadows."

"Yep. I wonder if Charles Martin is involved."

"I don't know. I'll keep you posted, Milton. I really appreciate all that you've done. This is a major step forward."

Martha and Drew had already left for the day when she called. She told him that she had some information that she thought he would be interested in. She wanted to meet where they would not be seen together, away from Bekbourg, so Owen suggested a small family-style diner about twenty miles from Bekbourg heading toward Athens.

"Okay. What's this all about?" Owen said to the woman sitting in front of him.

"I know you are trying to help those landowners. I don't want you to ever use my name about any of this, because I cannot afford to lose my job. I'm helping my daughter raise her two children."

Owen didn't trust many people, and he sure didn't trust anyone from the county. When she called him, he was skeptical, but he didn't think it would hurt to meet. Even if it was some kind of trick or a waste of time, he might learn something useful.

"Look. I can't promise you anything. I don't even know why you called me."

She seemed wary when he said he couldn't assure her that he would stay quiet about the fact that she had talked to him, but she felt she had no choice. "I don't have any specific evidence, but I think that Pauline changed the addresses for people's property for those developments. Years ago, when an attorney called from Columbus, I told her that she would need to talk to Pauline. Pauline seemed uptight at first, but when the attorney never called back, it just died. I figured that if the property owner didn't care, then maybe it was not important to them. Mrs. Kaufmann runs the Treasurer's office like a dictator. No one wants to get on her wrong side. She's never been too bad to me, but I just try to keep my head down."

"You never saw her change Mrs. Davis's address or that of the Steinsens?"

"No."

"Did she ever tell you to change them?"

"No, but it had to be her. I don't know who else could have done it."

Owen leaned back in his chair, taking a drink of coffee. He didn't see how this was helpful. He also was suspicious.

"Why would you tell me this? You've worked for the county for years."

She had been a little unsure when she and Owen sat down, but she was now nervous.

"When I heard that Mrs. Davis had lost her property that belonged to her husband's family, I just couldn't sit back anymore. Mrs. Davis helped my daughter when she was going through a tough time during high school."

Owen looked at her.

"I don't have much money to pay you, but if I hire you as my attorney, will you keep my name secret?"

"I'm going to be blunt. I don't know the significance of what you just told me about Pauline. I'm still going to be doing depositions and document discovery as part of my lawsuit."

She could tell he was getting impatient. "There's more. There are more than people losing their property. I needed someone to turn to, and I know that the people who hire you trust you. My daughter said she heard good things about you. I'm scared."

Owen was still skeptical, but he was listening. "Go on."

"My job is good paying. There wasn't anything else like it for me in Bekbourg. So I kept working there. Some of the people there are good people, but to be honest, I feel like it's a snake pit. I try to keep my head down and do my job, but I was afraid that they might try to frame me. I may just be paranoid, but I don't trust them. So, I made copies of some things in case it ever got discovered. I didn't want them pinning me with anything." She hesitated and took a sip of coffee—the cup unsteady in her trembling hand. Owen took another drink, watching her. She set the cup down.

"Are you telling me that you have evidence that someone or some people have been doing something illegal?"

"Well, I think it could be illegal."

"And why would you come forward now?"

"You've stirred up a hornet's nest. People around there aren't trying to show it in public, but I can tell they are worried. Like I told you, I'm afraid that if they feel they could be discovered, they will look for a scapegoat. I don't trust them, and I don't want to be blamed for anything."

"You are going to have to decide for yourself. I can only promise to do what I can to keep your name out of things."

She was clearly torn. Owen sat watching her, waiting. Finally, "I didn't bring the copies with me, but I can give those to you. Here's what they show."

By the time she finished telling Owen everything, he thought, "I've finally got those sons-of-bitches."

Claiming they were wrongfully denied of their property, Owen's lawsuits against Bekbourg Enterprises and Bekbourg County on behalf of the Steinsens made allegations similar to those in Kye's lawsuit. He emphasized the similarity in the two cases—the change in mailing addresses without consent or notice of not only the tax invoices and assessments, but also all of the foreclosure notices and pleadings. "The Plaintiffs didn't stand a chance to pay their taxes or defend against foreclosure, because they were never notified." Based on the similarities, Owen also requested an injunction until there was a decision on the lawsuit. "If the defendant, Bekbourg Enterprises, sells any of the property covered by these two cases, the Steinsens and Mrs. Davis will be irreparably harmed."

He also filed a separate petition with the state to compel the county to computerize all property records. The basis for his petition was that the property information was public, but the county had a history of not providing documents when requested. He argued the need for transparency, that the County Recorder had already computerized information related to property owners, mortgages, liens, and surveys. He also showed that many Ohio counties had already computerized their files or were moving in that direction.

Owen hand carried copies of his filings to Cheryl. "In case you're working on a story, here."

Cheryl glanced at the large envelope.

"That's just my first salvo. That greedy, grabbing bitch, she just thinks she can control property records like it's her own personal kingdom. This is small potatoes to what's coming. Stay tuned. See you."

He turned to leave. She didn't know what he meant but was interested in what she found in the envelope.

Owen also delivered a copy to the *Bekbourg Tribune* and the local TV station.

The Steinsen twins presented a stark contrast—dressed in their tailored dark business suits sitting beside Owen at the Counselor's table. Their presence brought a more formal air to the courtroom than the usual individuals, including the area attorneys. Even Judge Bergmann seemed to be sitting straighter.

"Your Honor, the facts for my clients are very similar to what happened to Kye Davis. There was no basis whatsoever for the mailing address for the tax invoices to be changed back to the original property. Everything, invoices and assessments, was being mailed to my clients' grandfather, Adam Steinsen, the property owner, to the Cincinnati address he had specified to the county. Then how 'bout this? The county abruptly starts mailing the documents to the property address itself, where it happens that no one lives. The property gets foreclosed on and—wa-la—ends up owned by

Bekbourg Enterprises to be part of a very lucrative land development. There's a pattern here, Judge, and it's not right. In fact, it down right stinks!"

"Your Honor, this is ridiculous!" interrupted Zack Norcross. "Mr. Donaldson is pulling things out of thin air. My client bought this property several years ago at a tax foreclosure sale, all done in accordance with the law. Now, wanting to undo something where the law was properly followed is without merit, but on top of this, is several years too late. There is no basis to halt my client's Lake Meadows project. He has spent a tremendous amount of time and money to develop this project. Indeed, he will be irreparably harmed if this injunction is granted."

Owen started to interrupt, but Judge Bergmann told both lawyers to sit down. "Mr. Norcross, I now have two cases before me where the mailing addresses for the tax invoices were changed. Both plaintiffs claim they never authorized this change. The county is going to have to address this in Mr. Donaldson's lawsuits, but it is troublesome that both of the properties are part of the Lake Meadows project. It's going to get more complex if this property is sold. I can fast track Owen's lawsuits. Of course, that will depend on how quickly Claude can get the county to produce the necessary documents, which, despite my admonishments last time, apparently hasn't happened."

Claude Atwood, the county's attorney, jumped up to protest, but the Judge waived him to sit. "Claude, I've looked at the list of documents that Owen is wanting. It's a lot of information, but nothing looks unreasonable to me."

Judge Bergmann looked at some papers, while not another sound could be heard in the courtroom except for the whirling old fan. The Judge looked up. "I'm going to grant Owen's injunction. He's renewed the request to also include an injunction on Mrs. Davis' property in light of the new facts here. I'm granting that as well."

Both Zack and Claude jumped up to object, but the Judge was having none of it. "Sit down, Counselors! Now, I've reviewed Owen's discovery requests for documents and depositions. None of those are unreasonable. I'll set a trial date on both the Davis case and this case quickly—after the full discovery is complete. Claude and Zack, that means the quicker you comply with the document production and depositions, the quicker the trials and the final resolutions. The injunctions are granted. We're adjourned."

Cheryl and reporters from both the *Tribune* and local TV station were observers in the courtroom. The story made headlines around Bekbourg.

The four participants were not happy with the injunction being granted. This stopped Harvey from proceeding with the development pending the outcome of Owen's lawsuits. Nickolas, in particular, was in a foul mood. Harvey took a seat after putting the whiskey bottle on the conference table. "I can't believe Bergmann ruled for those injunctions," Nickolas fumed.

"Not only that, but Owen's filing with the state could bring a spotlight from the state, if they decide to examine the issues he raised," offered Charles.

"This is a huge mess. I've invested a lot of money," Nickolas took a drink from his whiskey.

"We all have, Nickolas," said Harvey. "Look, I talked to my attorney. Pauline, you need to get the county moving on producing the documents. We both need to get the discovery to Owen as quickly as we can."

Nickolas said pointedly, "Pauline, I sure hope you're right that we don't have to worry about anything in the county records."

Pauline bristled. "I don't see you doing anything, Nickolas, but wringing your hands. Maybe we should rethink the scope of the development. Without the Steinsen and Davis properties, we still have one-hundred seventy acres. It wouldn't adjoin the state park property, but it would be close enough."

"No way are we going to do that!" bellowed Nickolas.

"Look, we're in too deep to turn around now." Harvey tried to calm the waters. "We can't get the trial done until we produce the documents. We can't complete the surveys and roads and finalize the development to start the sales until the jury rules in our favor."

"*IF* the jury rules in our favor," interjected Nickolas. "Charles, the judge is your father-in-law. Think you can be persuasive with him?"

"I don't know about that. I might find the opportunity to say something, but I don't think we should count on that to solve this dilemma. You know how Pierce is."

"I think was should reach out to Kye and the Steinsens and try to settle with them," Harvey offered.

Nickolas wasn't convinced. "Hell, did you see the Steinsens? They don't look like they need the money. They've got us over a barrel. Even Kye does. I don't like it. If we offer to settle, they might think we're running scared—afraid we've got the losing side. That blasted Owen."

"Well, Pauline might be on to something," Harvey said. "If Kye will sell, that would give us a two-hundred acre plot. Maybe we then give more thought to what Pauline suggested."

They left the meeting without reaching a consensus. Harvey was frustrated. He didn't like having his hands tied. With the injunction in place, he couldn't do a darn thing on the project, which was costing him. He had contractors and employees to pay, and no revenue was coming in. Since everything was on hold until the trial, he wasn't sure when he might start seeing a return on his investment. He had invested substantial time and money in the Lake Meadows project.

His lawyer, Zack Norcross, didn't think much of trying to sell the lots. It was highly unlikely that a customer would be willing to enter into an agreement to buy a lot with the uncertainty hanging over the purchase, but on top of that, Judge

Bergmann had issued an injunction. Also, if Harvey was to lose, the whole project would falter. Zack said, “Harvey, you don’t have anything to lose by making an offer to settle with Kye and the Steinsens. My suggestion is, that if this is the route you want to take, I would make the offer a serious one—one that would be hard for them to turn down. The sooner you can get those lawsuits dropped, the better for you. I’ll call Owen and tell him that you are going to approach his clients with a settlement offer.”

“Okay, do that, but I don’t want the others in the lawsuit told that I’m making the offers.”

Owen alerted both Kye and the Steinsens that Harvey was going to contact them about a potential settlement and advised them not to accept any offer until he had a chance to discuss the advisability of settling on Harvey’s terms.

Chapter 23

Kye answered the door and invited Harvey into her home. She had coffee and croissants waiting.

After exchanging pleasantries, Harvey said, "Mrs. Davis, first let me say that I deeply regret this most unfortunate situation in which both you and I find ourselves. I'm not here to talk about why or how it happened or who is to blame. That's for the lawyers. I wanted to talk to you and see how we might resolve this. I've heard what your lawyer, Mr. Donaldson, had to say in the courtroom, but I'd like to hear from you. Will you tell me your feelings?"

"Mr. Bennett, this property has been in my deceased husband's family for over a hundred years. It was his childhood home and his birth right. He would have never sold it for your development. I feel that I have let him down. I have been so upset that I am afraid it is taking a toll on me. I appreciate you coming here to talk to me, but, to be honest, I just don't think I can let it go like this."

"Well, neither of us knows how the trial will turn out," said Harvey. "Your attorney is probably telling you that you have a good chance to win, and my attorney is telling me the same. If we can come to an agreement on a win-win for both of us, there doesn't have to be a winner and loser."

Kye took a sip of coffee as she thought that over. "Well, you've come here, Mr. Bennett. Please go ahead and tell me what you have in mind."

Harvey was glad he asked Kye about her feelings, because he thought of something else other than the monetary offer he was prepared to make that might entice her to settle. "I don't know what your plans were for the property, Mrs. Davis, but given that it was in your husband's family for such a long time, it would seem a lasting tribute in his family's name would be a good thing. The Lake Meadow development will be there indefinitely, a place where people come to share good times with family and friends. I could name the main road through the development 'Davis Boulevard,' and the recreational area with the playground and other game courts will be, could be called 'Davis Park'."

Kye felt the monetary proposal was generous, but she was particularly persuaded by his offer to memorialized Cecil's family name. But, following Owen's advice, she wasn't going to accept anything until she discussed it with Owen. She thanked Harvey and told him that she needed to discuss it with Owen and give it some thought.

"I understand, Mrs. Davis. I'm hoping to hear back from you soon."

Harvey drove to Cincinnati and met with Collin and Celeste at their offices. He was impressed with the view of the Ohio River from their thirtieth floor lavish office suite that included a large conference room, an exquisite round walnut meeting table and an antique Turkish rug.

The brother and sister were not into chit-chat. He offered them the prime twenty-acres of the two-hundred acres on the top of the ridge that bordered the state park. Seeing their swanky offices, he offered more money than he had intended, because he figured he had one shot with them. They thanked him for coming and told him that he would be contacted with their response.

The settlement offer weighted heavily on Kye's mind. *What was she going to do with the property anyway? Having Cecil's name on the main road in the development and on the park would be a nice lasting legacy to his family's namesake.* When she met with Owen, she told him about the offer and that she thought she might accept it.

"Kye, Harvey wants to settle this case in the worst way. My bet is he'll be willing to settle on those terms or maybe even better the closer we get to trial. There's no rush on your part. I'm looking into something. If it turns out to be true, it will turn things upside down for those yahoos. Let me finish looking into this. Don't agree to anything with him right now."

"Okay, Owen."

Celeste and Collin knew that, given the nature of the lawsuit, a win meant they would get their property back, and a loss would mean they got nothing. Of course, there was the appeals process for whoever lost at the trial level. Twenty acres would allow them each to build a house and have room to start a vineyard—even though it wouldn't be as large as they were thinking.

When they met with Owen, they told him they were seriously considering accepting Harvey's offer. Owen told them what he had told Kye, which sounded reasonable to the Steinsens. They told him they didn't want to sit on the offer too long, because if something happened in the case before the trial started, it could swing the leverage away from them, and then Harvey might withdraw his offer.

Owen was on his way to the county building and happened upon Pauline and Nickolas talking on the sidewalk. They saw him just before he reached them. "Well, if it isn't the esteemed Ms. Kaufmann and Mr. Garrison. How might you be doing today?"

Neither Pauline nor Nickolas wanted to spend time with Owen. Both mumbled something back, like, "Fine" or "Fine, Owen," but quickly started to move on. Owen was having none of being summarily dismissed, "That's okay. Go on with your day. Enjoy your freedom while you can."

Pauline glanced at him, "What are you talking about now, Owen?"

He smirked, "You're going to find out very soon. You won't know what hit you. I'm going to blow your scheme sky high. Think about that."

He sauntered toward the county building.

Nickolas whispered, "What do you think that was all about?"

"I have no idea, and I don't think Owen does either. You know how he is—always spouting off. Don't worry about Owen, Nickolas."

Chapter 24

Sean sat in front of Angie Albrecht's desk. "I didn't have trouble finding your office. I just looked for the nameplate, 'Dr. Albrecht,'" he said smiling.

Angie laughed, "I don't know why they can't just put our first name and leave it at that." Her medium length hair sprung like thick honeysuckle vines, and her red-rimmed glasses took up a third of her face.

He chuckled, "I guess they figure their professors have earned that. I understand you are Department Head. You've done well."

"Not bad for one of the wild kids, huh?" she said laughing.

Sean liked her energetic and jovial personality. "We all were once teenagers." They both were laughing. "What are your studies?"

"I teach English and Communications. In recent years, I've moved more into the latter field with the digital and the public relations side of things. It's a dynamic field, but I still love to teach an English class now and then. I heard you were back in Bekbourg. How do you like it?"

"It wasn't my choice at first. I suffered a serious injury that made it impossible to continue with the Marine investigative unit I had been with.

I didn't want a desk job, so I retired. I came here to heal and get my life back together. I didn't plan to stay, but I've made a life here. I'm engaged to get married and enjoy being in law enforcement."

"Congratulations. I'm glad for you, Sean. Speaking of law enforcement, I assume this isn't purely a social call?"

"Yeah, that's right. What can you tell me about Sophia Martin?"

Angie looked surprised. "Sophia?"

"Yes."

"What do you want to know?"

"Tell me about your friendship with her."

Angie laughed. "It was a snapshot in time. Our friendship blasted off, orbited our senior year, and then crashed at the end of the school year.

"Sophia and I barely knew each other existed from kindergarten through eleventh grade. The first week of senior year, she came up to me and my friends during lunch and asked if she could join us. Surprised the heck out of me! I remember we looked at each other, and I said, 'Sure, why not.' She sure didn't look like the judge's daughter that day. She had on ripped jeans and some type of t-shirt. I had heard that her mom died, but I couldn't compute the transformation in the way Sophia was dressed. Anyway, she and I just kind of clicked that day. We started hanging out, and within a week, we were best friends."

Angie laughed, "Sean, after my daughter was born, I prayed that she didn't turn out to be wild like me. I still feel for my poor mother. I was part of party central during high school. Maybe that's what Sophia was looking for, because she embraced the party life. She hung out with me outside the gym area where we smoked during breaks. We hung out after school and partied with other kids over the weekends. We drank our fair share and smoked a little pot, but not too much."

They both laughed.

"What about boys?"

"There were some in our group, but I never saw Sophia get close with any of them. Neither of us had a boyfriend back then. We just hung out to have something to do."

"What was Sophia like?"

"Well, I don't know what she was like before she joined our group, but she fit in. She could be sarcastic, cuss like the best of us, but there was still something classy about her. Looking back, I think Sophia was confused about who she was and was trying to figure it out like many teenagers do. Her dad sure didn't approve."

"What do you mean?"

"I never met him, and I'm glad I didn't. Sophia was over at my house all the time. My mother worked, so we had a lot of time to ourselves. My mom was the greatest. Sophia seemed to like her. Sophia slept over a lot of weekend nights. Now, we weren't angels, Sean. We got caught hanging out behind the football stadium drinking. Once the police found out who Sophia was, they took the alcohol and drove us home. Sophia got pulled over for speeding some, but her dad got her off.

"What blew my mom away was when he called her and demanded that she quit letting me hang out with Sophia. He said he didn't think it was good for either one of us. Told her that if we got in trouble, he wasn't sure there was anything he could do to help. Mom thanked him for calling. She didn't tell me about that phone call until years later. She wasn't going to interfere in what she thought was a normal teenage phase, especially when she felt for Sophia, losing her mother. When she finally told me about the judge calling her, she said that she lost some sleep, because she was concerned that he was implying that he could cause trouble for me. He didn't come out and say that, and he never did anything, but that's how she felt.

"Anyway, Sophia and I spent a lot of time together during the school year, but two days after graduation, she and her grandparents went to Europe for the summer. She came back a couple of weeks before she left for college. I saw her once or twice, but then she left for college, and I never talked to her after that. I wrote a couple of times, but when she didn't respond, I figured she had moved on." Angie paused. Seeming more somber, "Sophia never really talked about personal things, but I think she missed her mother terribly. I never saw her without a heart-shaped sapphire necklace that her mother gave her for her tenth birthday. It's kind of sad to think about."

"Was there anyone that she was close to?"

"Mmmm. I don't know about friends before she and I started hanging out. I don't think she was close to her dad. I think she was close to the housekeeper. She talked about her a few times. She had been with the family for a long time."

"You wouldn't happen to know her name?"

"No, Sean. I'm sorry, but I can't remember."

Sean thought about his conversation with Angie. Sophia was more complex than he knew.

The first time Sean saw Kim Connor, she was talking on the phone behind the desk at the police station. He knew then she was a gold mine for the department, and his initial impression had proven right. Not only was she a dedicated and hard-working employee, but she was a people person and was liked by others. She was forever taking food to homes to help out. She kept Mike and Geri's home supplied with homemade dinners for several weeks after Mike was wounded. Chances were that if she didn't know a person, she knew someone who would.

"Hi, Chief. All the paperwork is done. I've registered Darrell for a training course." The department had lost two deputies with the death of Ben Clark and with Wade Frisch taking a police job in Cincinnati. Since becoming Sheriff, Sean had hired two deputies, Sydney Johnson and Arlo Lopez. He was trying to better educate his deputies by arranging for them to attend training courses. Given the drug and domestic abuse problems in the county, he particularly wanted them to have better training in these two areas.

"Great, Kim. Thanks for taking care of all that."

"Sure thing, Boss."

"Say, I am trying to find out the name of the housekeeper for Judge Bergmann. Would you happen to know?"

"Yes. I don't know her last name, but Joanie is her first name. She's been with the judge for about ten years."

"Who was there before then?"

"Oh, that would be Evie Klein. She was with the judge for years. She retired. That's when Joanie started with him."

"Do you know how I can get in touch with Evie?"

Kim smiled. She entered something on her computer and wrote down Evie's phone number and address.

Chapter 25

Sean stopped by the duplex to have lunch with Cheryl. He was surprised to see her and Kye sitting on the front porch with C.P. Traylor. Buddy rushed to welcome him. As he walked up on the porch, he said, "Hi, Kye, C.P. How are you?"

"We're enjoying this beautiful day," Kye replied. "C.P. dropped by to get some information about Cecil's service during the War."

"When I was in D.C., I volunteered to work with some Veteran's groups who were trying to get memorials set up in their home towns. I talked with the Commissioners here, and they are in favor of setting up a memorial in Bekbourg. We're going to start with a memorial for our World War II veterans. I mentioned the Library of Congress' initiative to get videos of these veterans, and Cheryl has volunteered to help with that."

"I'm going to talk to Annalee, but I think this would be a great opportunity for Lilly to participate in videotaping the Vets." added Cheryl.

"This all sounds real good," Sean said.

"Yeah, everyone I have talked to is enthusiastic about this project. I've already met some Vets who had some interesting stories about their time in the War. I didn't know about Cecil's experience until just now when Kye told us."

"Kye, I don't believe I have ever heard about Cecil's service," said Sean. "What did he do?"

"He was in the Army. He served in Europe, but what I didn't know until the late 1990's is that Cecil was on the SS Leopoldville. What happened was basically a secret until the early 90's. After he could talk about it, he told me the story."

This piqued Sean's interest. "I've never heard of the Leopoldville. What happened?"

"The Leopoldville was a huge ship used to transport troops. Cecil boarded it along with over two-thousand other American soldiers in Southampton, England, en route to Cherbourg, France, to join the Battle of the Bulge. They were about five miles out from Cherbourg when a torpedo shot from a German U-boat hit the Leopoldville. It was Christmas Eve, 1944. It was a disaster. So many men were killed by the blast. What made it more tragic—according to Cecil—was that there weren't enough ships to come to the rescue. Many of the men drowned. Cecil was one of the lucky ones. A British destroyer came along before the Leopoldville sank and tried to rescue as many as it could. Cecil jumped on it, but it couldn't hold everyone. Some men got rescued by some other boats that arrived, but over seven-hundred men died from the attack on the Leopoldville."

"That's an incredible story, Kye."

"Yes, it is. I never heard him talk about it after that one time when he told me. I think it haunted Cecil knowing so many men had died."

C.P. said, "I want to capture these things for our veterans, their families and the community before it's too late. This is what the Library of Congress's project is all about. Well, I know Cheryl was waiting for you to join her for lunch. I won't keep you any longer. Kye, thanks for the information about Cecil. I'll keep you posted on the progress on getting the WWII Memorial for our veterans. I'll see you all later."

Cheryl and Sean convinced Kye to join them for lunch. As they were starting to eat, Sean said, "I had no idea about Cecil's experience during the War. I'm glad that C.P. has undertaken this project. Those men have been reluctant to talk about their war-time experiences. If they are willing to open up, it's going to be interesting to hear their stories."

"I agree, Sean. I don't think I've ever told Cecil's story until now. I never had a reason to, but I'm glad that I was able to. I don't know if you know this, but we have a couple of men living here in Bekbourg that fought for the Germans during War World II. I imagine they have some interesting stories, although I've never heard that they talked about their experiences."

Both Sean and Cheryl were surprised. "Who are they?" Sean asked at the same time that Cheryl said, "They were German soldiers? How would people know that?"

"Well, Dears, no one did know until, let me see, it was the mid 70's. Karl Fischner and Hans Mueller had lived here for several years. I don't remember when they each actually moved in. Karl worked for a while with a contractor and eventually started working by himself doing small construction jobs. As time went on, he grew his business to what it is today. Hans and Hilda also made a good life here, but they have always lived a pretty quiet life—especially Hilda. Hans has that successful Cuckoo clock business, and Hilda is the most talented seamstress I have ever known. She makes beautiful wedding and prom dresses, those types of dresses.

"Anyway, it was odd, and I don't remember the details, but a couple of federal agents showed up one day in Bekbourg. I don't know if they were with the FBI or Immigration or just who, but they were checking to verify who Hans was and also Karl. They wanted to confirm that they were not Nazi Party members during the War. From what I learned, both men were just German soldiers. The Federal agents must have concluded they weren't part of the Nazi regime, because they left and nothing ever came of it. It really caused a stir at first, but after they left, people around here just forgot about it."

They each poured a glass from the Scotch Harvey set on the table. They liked meeting at his office, because there weren't people around to see them together or overhear their conversation. "That lawsuit crap and publicity is all over the county. It raises more suspicions, reminding people of county corruption. Plays right into the hands of that Reform Party," complained Nickolas.

Harvey said, "One thing I've been meaning to mention. When I talked to that reporter, she questioned why Jeff and Randall are still listed on the state records as being officers of my company. We need to change that. Who should we put in as officers?"

"What difference does it make?" Nickolas barked. He paused, and then added, "That does raise a point. With them being dead, there's no reason why they should benefit by our new development. Take them off as officers and drop them as shareholders. Their widows will never know."

Charles spoke up. "I'm not sure it's that easy, Nickolas."

"Why not? I don't see how they would ever find out they were shareholders. If they ever raise it, we'll just tell them they sold their interest to us."

"Let's all think about this. We can discuss it next time," Harvey suggested, hoping to avoid Nickolas digging in his heels.

Nickolas was ready to move on. "Pauline and I ran into Owen, and he was sword rattling again. He said something to the effect that he knew something that was going to blow up in our faces."

Harvey asked, "Any idea what he was talking about?"

Pauline spoke up, "No, and I told Nickolas that I didn't think Owen knew what he was talking about. He's just trying to spook us. We can't let him get to us."

Each left the impromptu meeting feeling somewhat uneasy about what might happen. There had never been any hiccups with the Lake Shore project. The eight-hundred acres had been acquired over time, most of it purchased from landowners only too willing to sell. Some parcels had been abandoned, and the legal process was followed in selling at the tax auctions. There had been only a couple of instances where the tax lien process had been skirted, but it had worked. Bekbourg Enterprises ended up buying all the property through those tax sales it needed for the Lake Shore development.

They had planned a phase-two development that would consist of about four-hundred acres. Adam Steinsen had refused to sell his property, and it was the anchor parcel for the entire development. They used the tax auction, and after a few years, thought they were free and clear. In the meantime, they bought what they could from willing sellers. Randall Thompson learned that the state was going to push forward with the state park lodge and conference facility that had been on the books for fifty years. He, Jeff and Nickolas thought they should move forward with Lake Meadows to capitalize on the opportunities arising from the state's plans. There was rural, undeveloped land near the state park. Randall thought it best to strike while the iron was hot and stake out their development in case competitors might have similar ideas on that underdeveloped property.

Now, with Owen Donaldson poking around, there was a concern that he would find the tax foreclosure improprieties. Nickolas waited behind as Harvey locked up. Nickolas said, "Owen is going scorched earth on all the information he is trying to get in this lawsuit and the people he is wanting to interview. He's going back twenty years. We've got to pay close attention."

"I know," agreed Harvey.

Max, Bri and Noel were sitting in the small court yard off the back of the B&B enjoying strawberry scones and coffee. "You've got the Commissioners riled about your proposal for the city to get a fire department. I saw Nickolas's retort in the *Tribune* yesterday," Max said to Noel.

"Yeah, I know. No surprise. He's supporting Riley Barnes. That group has tightly controlled this county for so long. What's amazing to me is that they pushed for bringing in tourism-related businesses, and of course, the Lake Shore community, and other business in that area have grown. You'd think they would support a city fire department. We wouldn't have to rely on volunteers."

"I agree, Noel, but I think it's what they see happening with the Reform Party that's got them bothered. It's a threat to their control. Riley opposes it because it wasn't his idea, and it would bring more infra-structure to the city. The county commissioners don't want an independent city mayor and city council. They see that as the first step to eroding their influence and power. Of course, it doesn't have to be that way. It'd be great if the two government entities would work together. The people running on the Reform ticket want the best for the residents. Starting a city fire department is a good first step."

"Yeah, and the city council should have its own planning commission for attracting businesses and input on zoning considerations and redevelopment initiatives."

Bri said, "Noel, if the Reform candidates are successful, hopefully Nickolas Garrison and Lance Pruitt will work with us to get mutually agreeable decisions. I hope those two won't just be road blocks to everything."

Noel said, "Well, Lance might, but I can't imagine Nickolas ever becoming a team player. He joined the county commission when Randall Thompson was on the Commission. He's as old school as it gets with the way things are run. His dad and Randall's dad were friends."

Max asked, "Have you heard anything about Jason Worley running for the County Treasurer's job?"

"No, not really. He'd indicated some interest, so when I saw him at the last meeting, I asked. He said he was still thinking about it. He feels it will be hard to unseat Pauline."

"He seems qualified if he decides to run," Bri said.

"Noel, you are to be commended for pushing this initiative to form the Reform Party. We've got some good people running this time around, and I think the slate of possible candidates will only grow for future elections."

"You know, I grew up here. I've seen what a strangle-hold the one-party system has created on the county and city. Jim Neumann has been raising concerns about it for a while now. After what happened last year, I finally understand what Jim's point was. It's not just in the way the local governments are run. It goes deeper than that. Jason Worley tried to break into real estate when he returned from Columbus, but Pauline had such a grip on it, Jason had to start a marketing and public relations business. Fortunately for him, his brother-in-law owned the dealership and threw business his way. I think that Pauline's position as County Treasurer has enabled her to control the real estate business around here. My dad has felt for years that Nickolas Garrison got advance notice about construction projects and had a leg up when it came to bidding and winning the construction projects around here. Fortunately, Dad's very good at what he does, and people know that. He's been able to make a living with his construction business, but Mom working full time was a necessity."

"I know that Mary was very happy with the renovations he made to the building she bought for the foundation. With Otis' design and your dad's construction, it turned out really nice. They sure did a great job on remodeling the B&B and the bistro for us."

"Thanks, Bri. They've made a good team over the years, especially on some of the downtown revitalization initiatives."

Chapter 26

After talking briefly with Jennifer Fischner, Sean asked if Karl was home.

"Yes, he is in the kitchen. Please come in."

She poured Karl and Sean a cup of coffee and then excused herself to make a couple of phone calls.

Sean could see that Karl was less robust than when Sean had returned to Bekbourg, but he still oversaw his construction company. His younger son, Cole, was picking up the mantle of running the business. Noel had never had an interest in construction. Karl Fischner was in his mid 80's and had moved to Bekbourg over fifty years ago. He had met Jennifer after moving to Bekbourg. She was twenty years his junior, but that didn't matter to either of them. They got married and had been part of the Bekbourg social scene for many years.

"Karl, I understand that in the mid 70's, some Federal agents came to Bekbourg looking for men who had been members of the Nazi regime during the War. Your name came up as one of the men they were interested in."

Karl suddenly had a coughing spell, and Jennifer rushed into the room and got him a glass of water. Once the coughing began to subside, she gave him some medicine. After Karl assured her he was fine, she left the room. Karl looked warily at Sean. "The American agents asked about this and found nothing." Despite having lived in the United States for over fifty years, he still had a thick accent. "I'm American citizen for many years."

"Roger Burkhart had some documents that were found in the box of coins. Those documents were from Vienna, written in German." Sean noticed anger flare in Karl's eyes. "It seems strange to me that Burkhart would have something like that. Do you know why he would have those documents?"

Karl's face turned red, and he banged his fist on the table. "Burkhart a der Arsch." Sean knew enough German to know the reference to "Ass."

Another coughing fit brought Jennifer rushing into the room. As she went to comfort Karl, she looked questioningly at Sean. She got Karl to drink some water. He finally got the coughing under control, but looked drained. He started to stand, and both Jennifer and Sean helped him to his feet. "I'm sorry, Sheriff, but I must rest."

Sean drove to Hans and Hilda's home. It was a small house in the rural part of the county. He could see a work shop out back. He rang the doorbell. After a couple of minutes, Hans opened the door. "Mr. Mueller, I'd like to talk to you, Sir. Mind if I come in?"

Hilda was standing in the middle of the room in a blue small-print dress and a white apron. Hans asked Sean if he would like anything to drink. When Sean declined, Hans spoke something in

German to Hilda, and she nodded to Sean and left them alone.

In his heavy German accent, "Sheriff Neumann, how can I help you?"

"I saw one of your clocks at the coffee bistro. It is quite a work of art. You ship your clocks all over the U.S., I understand. Does Otis help you, Mr. Mueller, with your business? Does he help carve or put them together or pack them for shipping?"

"Yes, he help me on occasion. He a good son."

"Did you know Roger Burkhart?"

Though stoic, Sean saw a grimace.

"The man who died long ago in the fire?"

"Yes."

"I did not know him well. He had the car place."

"Did you ever buy a car from him?"

"Nein."

"Why's that?"

"On the picture box, I not like the way he was. Did not trust him."

Sean could well relate to that. He never liked Roger's TV commercials.

"He had some documents that were written in German in the box of coins that Danny Chambers found." Sean watched closely, but Hans' stoic mask was firmly in place. "They were from Vienna and were from the organization that looked for Nazi war criminals."

Hans sat still, waiting for Sean to continue.

"I was told that in the mid 70's, some Federal agents came to Bekbourg looking for men who may have been in the Nazi regime. Do you know anything about that, Hans?"

"Ja. They talked to me, but they found no evidence of that to be the case. They also talked to Karl Fischner. Had they found us a Nazi, things would be different for us, but they left. I'm curious why you ask me this thing, Sheriff."

"I was wondering if you might know why Burkhart would have these documents from an organization that has as its mission to locate and bring to justice former Nazis."

"It is too bad that he is not alive for you to ask him, Sheriff, but I cannot help you."

"Ms. Kaufmann, I'd like to ask you a few questions about the lawsuit that Owen Donaldson filed against the county that included the County Treasurer."

"I'm sorry, but I don't comment on litigation matters."

Pauline was walking swiftly from her office in the county building to her car. Cheryl continued to follow.

"Can you tell me why some property that was sold for the proposed Lake Meadows project for failure to pay taxes was purchased by Bekbourg Enterprises Corp.?"

No response by Pauline, still quickly walking to avoid Cheryl.

"Why would tax values be reduced before the property was acquired by Bekbourg Enterprises?"

Pauline was a hard-looking woman with deep creases in her face, and at the moment, her contempt was obvious. "That's a frivolous lawsuit and so is his complaint at the state. I don't know why he filed them. He's wasting the taxpayers' money as well as his clients.' I don't know where you've gotten your facts, but it sounds like ramblings of Owen."

"I have some questions that I would like to ask you, because this investigation is far from over."

"I really don't have time to talk to you, Cheryl. We are working on Owen's request for information. We have followed procedures. Beyond that, I have nothing to say."

"Are you a shareholder in Bekbourg Enterprises Corp.?"

"I don't comment on my private affairs."

"Is it true that you got exclusive rights to sell the lots in Lake Shore developed by Bekbourg Enterprises Corp.? Will you get an exclusive right for Lake Meadow?" Cheryl was walking quickly alongside Pauline hoping that she would be enticed into responding.

Pauline reached her car. "Whatever you are getting at, I have done nothing wrong. Now, please excuse me."

"Can you explain why the county changed the mailing address for tax invoices without the landowner's request? If people don't receive tax bills, they don't know to pay taxes."

"I don't know the specifics that you are referring to, but I suspect that someone moved or died and we were not properly informed. Whatever the case, we have to follow proper procedures."

Cheryl watched her get in her car with an air of authority. Without a doubt, she was a formidable foe.

Chapter 27

Despite being around 70, Evie Klein was robust. She lived in a modest home just on the outskirts of downtown. She told Sean that the pictures he was looking at were her three children and eight grandchildren. Her husband had passed away a couple of years after she retired. "That's why I retired when I did. My husband's diabetes was starting to cause him a lot of problems, and I wanted to be there to help him. I just made some coffee. How does a cup sound while we sit and talk?"

"I'd appreciate some coffee. Thank you."

"Let's sit at the kitchen table if you don't mind." While she poured the coffee, Sean could see why she had suggested the kitchen. It was stocked and designed for someone who loved cooking. This was probably her favorite room. "Okay, Sheriff, what can I do for you?"

"I am investigating the murder of Leo Davis. You may have heard about it. He was killed a little over twenty years ago, but his body was only recently discovered. I'm talking to people who may have known Leo or who knew people who knew him. I understand that you worked for Judge

Bergmann's household. How long were you employed?"

"I worked for them for twenty-five years. I retired ten years ago."

"I understand that Sophia knew Leo Davis. You were working for them in 1980. Did you know that she knew him?"

Evie hesitated, "Sheriff, I don't mean to be disrespectful here, but I don't feel comfortable talking about the family that I worked for."

"I know how you feel, Mrs. Klein. Unfortunately, this is a murder investigation, and I need your help. You really have to talk to me about this."

She took a sip of coffee, considering what Sean had said. Finally, she answered, "Yes, she knew him. I don't think they knew each other for long though. I gathered that she must have met him when she was home for Christmas break from college. That was during her sophomore year. She saw him during her spring break that year and then when she came home that summer. Then, I never heard his name again. I never asked, so I didn't know what happened."

"How do you know all this?"

"I was there, Sheriff, working. I never intentionally eavesdropped, but there were some things that I couldn't miss. The judge did not want her seeing Mr. Davis, but she was having none of that. They got in some rolls over that."

"Did he ever come to their home?"

"Not that I know of. I don't think Sophia was that brave to bring him around the judge. I never met him."

"Why do you think the judge objected to Sophia seeing Leo?"

"From what I heard, he thought he was a con man. He thought he was taking advantage of Sophia because of who the judge was. He said that she was too good for him. He wasn't even working—at least not doing things that were legal."

"What did Sophia have to say?"

"She said that he didn't know Mr. Davis. That he wasn't like anything that her dad claimed he was. She told the judge she loved him and that he loved her."

"What happened?"

"Well, nothing that I know of. It seemed like a standoff. She kept seeing him, but then suddenly, I never heard his name. It seemed that Sophia was no longer seeing him."

"How was Sophia after that?"

"She was very upset. Would hardly come out of her room. Finally one day, she came out and seemed to be back to herself. She started seeing Mr. Martin. Next thing I knew, they had eloped."

"Did that surprise you?"

"Well, it did in a way, just because she had said she was in love with Mr. Davis. But, Mr. Martin had been pursuing Sophia since she graduated from high school. Their families knew each other, and he started calling that summer after she got back from Europe. He always made a point to see her when she was in on breaks and went up to see her a few times at college if there was a special event or dance."

"What did the judge think about the elopement?"

"He seemed happy enough. I think he wanted Sophia to marry Mr. Martin. He always was glad to see him. Once when they were arguing about Mr. Davis, he said something like she should just accept that she was to marry Mr. Martin. She said that wasn't going to happen, but then it did."

"When there was a disagreement between the judge and Sophia, did they yell at each other? What was it like around their house?"

"The judge never raised his voice. I think that is one reason Sophia would get so mad. She tried not to yell, but she would get so frustrated, she would start crying and run out of the room or leave the house."

"I understand that another time the judge wasn't happy with her was during her senior year."

"That's right. He didn't at all like the things she was doing. His parents took Sophia to Europe for the summer. I never knew for sure, but I think he asked them to take her."

"Other than Leo Davis and her husband, do you know if Sophia ever dated anyone else?"

"Not that I know of."

"How did Sophia feel about her mother's death?"

"Oh, that was the most terrible time. She and her mother were very close. Mrs. Bergmann loved that girl, and she loved her mother. She cried the rest of the summer. I always thought that was why

Sophia changed so much during her senior year—she was missing her mother so much."

Sean's deputies talked to people around town, but no one knew much about Leo Davis. Although he had spent twenty-eight years of his life in Bekbourg, he had been a loner. Except for his association with Roger Burkhart, who was deceased, and Byron Thornton, hardly any one remembered him except for being classmates. They also reviewed Leo's police records, but nothing in those gave them any leads.

"Hey, Boss."

"Hi, Kim. Anything I need to know about?"

"Nope, not really. The same old, same old. Well, except for one thing. Arlo's on the scene. It's okay now, but a dog killed another dog."

Sean arched his brows. "A dog killed a dog?"

"Yes, it was a revenge killing or trespass killing or something like that."

Sean patiently waited for the story.

"It began about a year or year and a half ago when Mr. Fredricks and his German Shepherd, Prince, were walking down the road. By the way, he loves that dog. Claims it comes from a real German pedigree. The only thing, he's always telling people what a chicken Prince is. Back to the story, there's a big Setter in the neighborhood, acts like the king of the hill. All the dogs are scared of him. That dog saw Prince and took after him. Prince tried to run away, but he caught him and nearly killed poor

Prince. The vet got him patched up, and thankfully, he was okay. Prince wouldn't go near where that Setter lived. Well, today, that dog came into Mr. Fredricks's yard. Prince went after the Setter and killed it. Arlo said that Mr. Fredricks was crowing about Prince, how he took on that bully dog."

"Who owned the Setter?"

"Ian O'Brien."

"How did he react?"

"Ian isn't very happy, but there isn't much he can say, because his dog was on Fredricks's property."

"Mmm. Well, I'm glad Arlo handled it. Things like that can get out of hand. Say, do you remember much about the accident when Judge Bergmann's wife was killed?"

"I sure do. That was big news around here. Well, by big news, it was with people talking about it. There wasn't much in the paper about it. The Judge wasn't there at their house that evening. He was having dinner with some people. She left their home and was going somewhere and ran off the road. Hit a tree. She died at the scene. A driver came by and saw the tail lights. They didn't have a public memorial or anything—just the family."

"Will you get me the police report on it?"

"Sure thing. Oh, after you asked me about Evie the other day, I started thinking. Mrs. Bergmann had a close friend from high school, Jane Thatcher. She and her husband live near here. I wrote her contact information on this in case you wanted it."

Sean looked at the note, "I don't know what we would do without you. Thanks."

There wasn't much in the police report on Bonnie Bergmann's death. Like Kim had said, a motorist saw the car and ran down to see if he could help. He saw her leaning back in the driver's seat with blood on her face. He yelled for his wife to flag down a car and finally got into the car from the rear door. He realized she was dead. The police arrived, and Jack Rhodes, the sheriff at the time, came to the scene. In the meantime, someone had driven to the GilHaus where the judge was having dinner and drove him to the scene. Her body was taken directly to the morgue. No alcohol or drug tests were run.

Kim had also found a copy of the only article written about the accident by the *Bekbourg Tribune*. There wasn't much to the article. Sean suspected the judge wouldn't talk to the reporter, and people who were close to the family probably didn't want to comment. The reporter had interviewed the husband and wife who arrived at the scene, but that part was basically the same information Sean learned from the police report.

Sean paid Karl Fischner another visit.

"Karl, I need for you to tell me about Burkhart. He had those papers. Did he accuse you of being a Nazi?"

Karl's face got red. "I spit in his face and told him never to come near me or my family."

"Did Roger threaten you or your family?"

Karl's water glass was almost empty. Sean got up and refilled the glass. Karl didn't answer, so Sean tried again. "Karl, I need to know what Roger did."

Karl continued to stare out the window. "Karl, I'm not here to check on your citizenship, but I do need to know about what Burkhart was up to." Sean tried another tactic. "Some of the coins stolen from Danny Chambers were old coins. They have been traced back to a Jewish man who survived a concentration camp. The coins disappeared when his coat was taken from him by the Nazis when he arrived at the camp. He had sewn them into the lining and thought they would be safe, but they took the coat. I think whoever stole the coins from Danny may have known the coins' history. Do you know about the coins, Karl?"

Karl relented. "I know nothing about the coins."

"Do you know why Roger had the documents?"

"He said I was Nazi. Said he had proof from Vienna. I spit in his face. I told him I kill him if he came near me or my family."

"Did he ever bring it back up to you?"

"Nein." Karl responded angrily.

"Do you know if he told anyone?"

"Nein, I don't know."

"No one ever said anything to you about it after that?"

"Nein. You the only one."

"So, he said this to you after the Federal agents had come to Bekbourg and talked to you?"

"Ja."

"Do you know if Burkhart ever talked to Hans Mueller about any of this?"

"Nein. I not talk to Hans or anyone."

"Karl, I know this may be painful, but would you tell me about what your role was in the German army?"

Kart sat quietly for a long while, taking a couple of drinks from his water glass. Sean gave him time. Finally, Karl nodded that he would answer Sean's question.

Karl was conscripted into the German army when he was eighteen years old. After being stationed around Berlin for a couple of years, he was sent to the Russian front in 1943, but was not part of the invasion. He became seriously ill from a foot infection and was sent back to Germany—where he almost died. He recovered enough so that when the German military started preparing for the Ardennes Counteroffensive, Karl was assigned to the infantry that accompanied the Panzer units that were going to cross into France and Belgium. By then he had reached the rank of "Gefreiter," meaning he was a more experienced soldier, no longer tasked with the more menial jobs.

The weather was cold and rainy, and he knew that the end was near. Even if they were successful in this mission, the Allies would soon win the War. All would be lost in Germany. His tank now rolled along with over a thousand tanks, numerous artillery vehicles and hundreds of thousands of soldiers heading toward Antwerp, Belgium. They were heading to the fuel depot controlled by the Allies that the Germans needed to reach before advancing to Antwerp. He didn't hold any delusions. It would take a miracle for them to reach the fuel depot because they were running short on fuel. Sure enough, their offensive faltered as the tanks and trucks rolled to stops when the fuel gauges hit zero.

The German soldiers found themselves unable to advance and soon were surrounded by Ally forces. The reality was stark: either surrender or die at the hands of the Allie. The Germans knew it was a lost cause, and most threw down their weapons and walked away. Karl was eventually taken to the prisoner of war camp in Virginia. When he was released, he got lucky and was allowed to stay in the U. S. due to his skills as a stone mason.

"Hi, Sean. Thanks for meeting me here. A client wanted my ideas on how it might be refurbished, and I'm trying to get a portfolio prepared."

"No problem, Otis. Looks like a nice building."

"It's got great character and potential. A lot can be done with it. What can I do for you?"

"I understand that you buy Lindenwood. Care to tell me what you do with it?"

Otis looked surprised. "You want to know why I buy wood?"

"Yes, it's for carving or making furniture. At least that's what most people use it for."

"Well, I don't do anything with it."

"Then, why do you buy it?"

"Dad's too old to drive very far. I buy it for him. He uses it for the Cuckoo clocks he makes."

"Do you ever help him with his clock business, other than buy wood?"

"Well, I don't carve—if that's what you mean. I help him with buying materials, like paints and packing materials. Things like that. When I have time, I also help pack the clocks for shipping, and I also deliver them around here if someone needs my help in hanging it."

"So you go to his shop?"

"Oh, sure. It's there behind their house."

"Do you know if your dad knew Roger Burkhart?"

Otis looked confused. "You mean the car dealer?"

Sean nodded.

"No, Sean. I don't know. He's been dead for years. I don't know where Dad bought his cars, but he hasn't bought many over the years, because he drives them for years, and Mom never learned to drive. He has his business van. Wouldn't trade or sell it either until it was pretty much on its last wheels," Otis and Sean smiled at the attempted joke.

Chapter 28

"Ms. Fairhurst, do you have a few minutes for some questions?" Joanne Fairhurst was the County Auditor responsible for property valuations.

"Aren't you the reporter who is engaged to Sheriff Neumann?"

"Yes, I'm Cheryl Seton. I'm a reporter for *The Presenter* in Cleveland. I'd like to talk to you about the two lawsuits filed by Owen Donaldson against the county. Your department was named."

"I'm sorry, but I really don't think I can help you. I'm not at liberty to comment on litigation matters."

Joanne was in her early sixties and had been the County Auditor for thirty years. She was medium build with a little extra weight around her middle. She had short, wavy blond hair with brown roots. She was an engaging woman, but also guarded, at least when talking to a reporter.

"As the Auditor, you are responsible for assessing property values. Why has that information not been computerized? That's public information."

Joanne stopped in the parking lot. "Ms. Seton, is that right?"

"Yes."

"We are a small county, a rural county, and we don't have a lot of money like Cleveland. There has never been a reason here to put that information on a computer. If someone wants to know what their taxes are, they can call us. People around here aren't nosey about other people's property. If people thought it was important, they would have raised the issue, but I haven't ever heard anyone raise it but you and Mr. Donaldson. Now, I must be on my way."

Cheryl asked as she started to walk away, "Are you a shareholder in Bekbourg Enterprises Corp.?"

"I don't know why you're asking me these questions. I'm sure the County Attorney is who you need to be talking to. Now, please excuse me."

Jane and John Thatcher lived three streets over from Kye. John had worked forty years for the railroad, while Jane had raised their three children. After John retired, they sold their home and moved into this smaller home in the downtown.

"Come in, Sheriff. Jane just brewed a fresh pot of coffee. I've got a dentist appointment, but I'm glad I got a chance to say hello. I wanted to tell you how much I liked your grandpa. He was a conductor a long time."

"It's nice to meet you, Mr. Thatcher. Yeah, he was with the railroad for fifty years."

"Yeah, that's right. You worked for it, too, didn't you?"

"For two years; then I left to join the Marines."

"I remember watching you play football during high school. That game where you won the championship was something. I hated you got hurt. We all thought we'd be watching you play in the Pros one day."

Jane brought in a tray with two coffee cups and sugar and cream. "Sheriff, how do you like your coffee?"

"Black is fine, thank you."

"Well, I better take off, or I'm going to be late. Hate going to the dentist, but that's the way it is. It was nice talking to you, Sheriff."

"Same here, Mr. Thatcher."

After he had left, Sean said, "I appreciate you talking with me. As I said on the phone, I'm investigating the death of Leo Davis, and I'm trying to find out about him. It seems that Sophia Martin briefly knew him. I got your name from someone who said you knew Sophia's mother, Bonnie."

"Yes, God rest her soul. She and I were best friends from the time we were in elementary school."

"What can you tell me about Bonnie?"

"She and I both came from poor families, real poor. Her father did odd jobs whenever he could find them to support the family, mostly at planting and harvesting time. She had two younger brothers. Her mother sewed all their clothes and canned food for them to eat. They lived like my family in a small two-bedroom box house. Bonnie was special. Even though she was from a poor family, there was something dignified about her, the way she talked and acted. Another thing, she was beautiful. She had long blond hair, and her smile would light up a room. I loved her dimple when she smiled. I always kidded her that she was really a princess who had been kidnapped and left in Bekbourg.

"Anyway, she was working as a waitress at the GilHaus the summer before her senior year—at only seventeen years old. The judge had just finished law school and came back here to join his dad's law firm. He was rich for sure, but Bonnie fell in love with him because he was so much more mature than the other boys and he was a serious person. She liked to tease him. She had never dated anyone, so she was floating on air, thinking she had found her Prince Charming. She got pregnant, and they eloped.

"At first, they seemed happy together, but the big thing they had going against them was that the judge's parents felt Bonnie was beneath them and had trapped Pierce. Also, because they didn't approve of her, their circle of friends never accepted her. She used to talk to me about everything. She had thought that over time, they would accept her and everything would work out. It broke my heart, because Bonnie was such a good person and really wanted to be a good wife and mother. Pierce was spending more and more time away from home because of his job, and other than me, Bonnie didn't really have any friends. The few times she was at something where the other wives were, she felt they were whispering behind her back or snubbing her.

"Anyway, she told me that she never wanted Sophia to go through what she went through, so she made sure she had the best of everything in clothes, music lessons, going to Columbus to see the art museums, everything.

"Finally, as Sophia got older, Pierce's parents started to get more involved with Bonnie and Sophia, but by then, Bonnie was pretty much cut off from the social circles around here. Pierce had become the judge, and his world was different from Bonnie's. He didn't want to be bothered by her insecurities. Unfortunately, Bonnie started drinking about the time that Sophia started high school. I tried to get her to stop, but I think the pressure was too much for her.

"I loved her, Sheriff, like she was a sister." Jane had tears in her eyes. "I wish things had turned out better for her."

"What do you know about the relationship between Sophia and the judge? Did he spend much time with her? Did they do much as a family?"

"Well, I personally don't think he ever gave Sophia much of a thought. He knew that Bonnie was a good mother. He saw that, and he gave her all the money she ever asked for. He paid for Sophia's lessons and clothes and never complained. He just wasn't around that much. He was busy with his own career, and Bonnie didn't want to attend those social functions with him. After Bonnie's death, I lost touch, so I never knew much after that."

Jane got up and poured them some more coffee. Sean could tell something was on her mind. After she sat back down, he finally asked, "Mrs. Thatcher, is there anything else that you think I should know?"

She paused before continuing, "I don't know that this matters, but there was something else. When the judge moved them into that big house where he still lives, he hired a housekeeper, Mrs. Klein, whom Bonnie loved. She was great at helping both Bonnie and Sophia. When Bonnie did go out, she took great care of Sophia. I think she gave Bonnie the support she needed to manage as long as she did. Anyway, as Pierce got busier and busier, he couldn't keep up with all the business side of running the household, and for whatever reason, he never asked Bonnie to handle it. He hired a woman, Faith Powell, as a bookkeeper and manager, like if the cars needed servicing, or landscaping was needed, or paying Mrs. Klein, those types of things. She and Bonnie got along okay, I guess.

"Faith suddenly quit. Bonnie didn't know why. Pierce just told her one night at dinner that Faith was no longer with them, that she had moved out of town to take a new job. He told her that he was going to ask his assistant at work to pick up with what Faith had been doing. I could tell that there was something about Faith and her leaving that puzzled Bonnie.

"A couple of years later, which was about a year before Bonnie died, she and I were sitting on her patio looking out over the rose garden, which she loved. Something was on her mind. Finally, she told me that she needed to find out what something had cost for one of Sophia's private lessons. She never went into the judge's office there at the house, but she knew where he kept his check records. She found an entry for a check to "FP" for a lot of money. She then looked back and saw another one for the month before. The check book records only went back to the start of the calendar year, but that entry was the same amount for every month. She wondered if "FP" was a reference to Faith Powell. I asked her why she thought he might be writing checks to Faith, but she had no idea. I told her not to jump to conclusions, because he could be referring to anything. He was in various business arrangements, so it could be anything. I think I got her calmed down, and I have no idea that the checks were made out to Faith, but Bonnie had suspicions, and I have always wondered."

Chapter 29

Before she left for the evening, Martha brought in a box delivered earlier in the day. Owen had finished for the evening and poured another shot of his Canadian Club. He figured he might as well open it. Sometimes, his sister would send him a bottle of wine from her high falutin' vineyard in Napa. He found a letter opener tucked back in a drawer. When he reached in, he could tell all the wrapping was securing a bottle. When he unwrapped the bottle, he chuckled, "Well, what do you know?"

He held up the prize and looked at the label. Bushmills—Milton Grant's favorite Irish whiskey. He didn't need to look for a card. He doubted there even was one. Only his old friend would send him this. He got up and got a clean glass off the top of the file cabinet and poured a shot. He leaned back in his chair and savored the taste. He didn't think Martha or Drew would mess with his whiskey, but he was going to keep this in his desk drawer out of sight. Before he left, he pulled out some files from the drawer, and stashed his Bushmills for tomorrow.

Nickolas Garrison met Cheryl at the GilHaus. It was late afternoon, so they sat in the bar area. Cheryl had a cup of coffee, and Nickolas drank a tall whiskey sour. "Ms. Seton, you sure have made a name for yourself reporting on things here in Bekbourg."

"Does the county have any plans to computerize the property records?"

"Well, I assume you are talking about the lawsuits filed by Mr. Donaldson. If that's why you wanted to talk to me, I'm afraid you wasted your time. I'm not going to comment on ongoing litigation."

"Are you a shareholder in Bekbourg Enterprises Corp?"

He smiled and took a sip of his whiskey and looked around the bar area. "I don't make it a practice of commenting on my private affairs, Ms. Seton."

"I understand that you were the only contractor who built houses in the Lake Shore community. Care to comment on that?"

His smile didn't reach his eyes. "Are you against progress, Ms. Seton? You haven't been here long, but for people who are from here, they can attest to the quality of homes and buildings I have built. I have worked my entire career to build my reputation as a quality builder. I am proud of my accomplishments. If you ask people in Lake Shore, I'm sure you will hear how satisfied they are."

"Will you be the exclusive builder in the Lake Meadows development?"

"I don't want to get ahead of any arrangements that Mr. Bennett might be planning. I understand that you've been asking our hard-working county public employees about land stuff, but you're barking up the wrong tree. Yeah, sure, you broke that story about the Thompsons. I'm glad all that was discovered and stopped. We don't need corruption here, and I don't know of any. So, whatever you're trying to imply, it's not there."

"Did you know that both Jeff Thompson and his dad, Randall, were officers of Bekbourg Enterprises Corp.?"

He paused. "Well, they had their fingers in a lot of pies."

He had just put money on the bar and was starting to walk away. She asked, "What about the fact that some of that property has been bought at a tax sale by Bekbourg Enterprises?"

He looked at her like she was naïve. "What of it? Tax sales happen all over. Oh, tell Sean that I'm still supporting him for sheriff," he said as he left the bar.

Cheryl stared as he walked away. Was he threatening Sean's run for sheriff?

"Babe, don't worry about it. For one thing, no one is running against me. That gives me a leg up." The worried creases in Cheryl's forehead disappeared, and she couldn't help but smile. Sean was grinning. "Second, there's not the faintest hint anywhere that someone might run against me."

"What if he starts to give you a hard time? He can do that. He can cut your funding and publicly criticize you. There are several things he might try."

"Look, sweetheart," he said getting out of the chair and pulling Cheryl up into his arms. "If he does, I will handle it. What I think you should be thinking about is that Nickolas is trying to side track you. That tells me that there must be a reason. Do your job and don't worry about me. Okay?" He pulled her tighter. "Let me see if I'm better at side tracking you from your investigation."

Cheryl started giggling, because his intention was clear. They both started laughing, because Buddy was trying to wiggle in between them. "No, Buddy, we're not going to play ball now. So much for a mood killer!"

Cheryl was laughing, and Sean stood there smiling, "I'm going to close the bedroom door tonight." Cheryl laughed out loud as Sean tried to keep from laughing.

"I better get dinner on the table since we have plans tonight sans Buddy."

Clay had been the bartender at Koot's since before Sean left to join the Marines. He was wiping glasses when Sean walked in. Although a couple of customers were sitting at a table drinking beer, it was early for most of the regulars, "Hey, Clay."

"Hi, Sheriff. I'd offer you a drink, but I think you'd probably say 'no.'"

"Thanks, Clay, but you're right. I need to talk to you."

"Sure. Let's move over here. I can still watch the room, but we'll have a little privacy."

"What can you tell me about Cooper Townsend?"

"Oh, wow. I heard he's out. I haven't seen him though. What do you want to know?"

"I heard he was a bartender here?"

"Yeah, that's right. He worked during the day and sometimes helped out when we knew it'd be extra busy. He worked my night-off, too. Worked about four or five years—until he was arrested."

"Did it surprise you that he was arrested for drug possession?"

"Yeah, it did. I never knew him to do drugs. He never even talked about them like he was using or selling. I never got any idea here that he was selling to anyone."

"Do you know if he got on the wrong side of someone here?"

Clay looked around the room. He lowered his voice, "I have a good relationship with our suppliers. One day when Coop had the day off, I was helping our beer delivery unload the boxes. He asked me what was going on. I didn't know what he was talking about. He told me that Jeff Thompson had called him and said that his dad, Randall, wanted copies of the inventories that his company had for deliveries. Randall ran the place. Jeff wasn't ever involved, but the old man must have called Jeff to get those lists since he was living in Florida. Coop wasn't the brightest bulb around. If he was taking off the top against the Thompsons, that wasn't a smart move.

"After the trial, Randall stopped by while he was in town. He told me that I was the only one to ever take deliveries from any of our suppliers from then on. After that, I was here when deliveries were made. Our cigarette supplier told me he was glad about the change. He thought Coop might have been skimming, but he had no proof."

No wonder, Sean thought after he left Koot's, *Townsend didn't tell Owen why he may have been framed. He didn't want to admit that he was stealing from the Thompsons*. With them being dead, he was free to blame Owen with impunity. It was easier to blame Owen than reflect on how he had brought the whole problem on himself. Clay didn't know anything about Cooper owning a gun. Of course, if he was framed, which it increasingly looked to be the case, Sean still needed to try and clear him.

Sean ran into Dusty, Carla and Mule Head at Frau's.

"How is it working out driving to Cincinnati, Dusty?"

"It's not. It is almost impossible to keep doing it, but I'm too young to retire. We got a letter recently, because the Union set a meeting up. Most of the guys who work here don't want to move to Cincinnati. They're working in West Virginia and all up and down the road. The company has offered a buyout for us, and I'm seriously thinking about taking it. Morale's been bad. Before the company offered the buyout, Curly showed up for work and had completely shaved off the whole left side of his beard. Weirdest thing I've ever seen. Duke asked him why he'd done it. Curly said all the driving made him confused."

Sean fought hard to not laugh. "It's a wonder he didn't shave off his hair."

"Oh, he doesn't have any hair. He's bald as a light bulb. That's why they call him 'Curly.'"

Dusty was grinning while the other three were rolling with laugher.

Mule Head, who had a clear view of the front door, stopped laughing. Sean heard him mutter, "Here comes trouble."

Dusty must have heard because he glanced in the same direction, "Oh, no. Not that guy."

Sean, whose back was to the front door, wasn't kept in suspense long.

"Gentlemen, Madam," the man said as he shook his head, "what a sorry crew this is. They must have been scraping the bottom of the emergency board when they called you guys out." He looked at Carla, "The fair lady is excluded, of course."

"Good evening to you, too, Jules," said Dusty. "I guess you remember Sean here and Mule Head?"

"Well, you had me going for a while, Dusty. I was called out tonight. I thought this was my crew for tonight. How are you, Sean? I've not seen you in a while."

"I'm doing good, Jules. If you're getting ready to go out, you might try the meatloaf. It'll hold you all night long."

Standing ramrod straight like always, Jules Leroux curled his upper lip as he glanced at the meatloaf, "I think I will pass on the meatloaf. My fair Renee has prepared me a very tasty dinner. Well, gentlemen and dear madam, I just came in here to get a cup of coffee before I head over to the railroad. It's good seeing all of you—especially you, Sean. I really had some good times with your grandfather back in the day." With the faintest of repugnance, he asked, "You don't smoke those cigars, do you?"

"No, never took that up."

After everyone bid goodbye and Jules was out of earshot, "Dusty said, "As prissy as he may be, he is one dang good engineer."

Carla asked, "What do you mean, 'prissy'?"

"Well, for one thing, the first thing he does once he gets on the engine cab, is sweep it out. Then, he wipes everything down with a disinfectant he brings from home—especially the controls and his seat. He then washes all the windows on the inside and the one in front if he can reach it. If it's cold and the windows have to stay closed, he'll spray air freshener in the engine cab and definitely do that in the toilet compartment—although that is usually a lost cause. He then covers all the surfaces with paper towels. He sets down his grip and gets out his personal equipment: his gloves, hand cleaner, things like that. He also makes it very clear that you are not allowed on the engine if you are going to track in any kind of mud or dirt."

Mule Head had been nodding his head in agreement as Dusty talked. "Everything Dusty just said is the truth. I remember all that when I worked with him. He sure likes things clean."

Chapter 30

Hilda served Hans and Sean coffee and then left them alone.

"A few weeks ago, someone broke into Danny Chambers' home and stole some coins that had been missing since Roger Burkhart—along with his family—was killed in July, 1980. When Danny found them, before they were stolen, he took pictures of them and inventoried them. There were some coins that were not returned to Danny. A coin expert believes he knows where those coins came from." Sean was watching closely for any type of reaction—nothing. "Those coins, we believe, had been sewed into the coat lining of a Jewish man, Salomon Matzner, who was taken to a concentration camp in northern Germany. Those coins disappeared, but years before, Mr. Matzner had those coins insured and pictures were taken. The coin dealer helping us found a copy of those pictures. He is pretty certain that Mr. Matzner's stolen coins are the same ones stolen from Danny. Seems the dates are identical, and the coins look identical."

Hans sat stoic. Sean continued, "There's something else. There was some sawdust found at Danny's house. The forensic tests showed that the wood was Lindenwood, also known as Basswood. I've done some research and found that wood is the type that woodcarvers use. It can also be used in making furniture. Cuckoo clocks are frequently made from this type of wood. Mr. Mueller, I have seen a few of the beautiful Cuckoo clocks you make. I found records that Otis bought Lindenwood from a nearby store. He bought the wood for you to use?"

"Ja."

"Will you tell me what happened? Was Burkhart blackmailing you?"

"I know nothing."

"What about Otis? Does he know?"

"There is nothing for him to know."

"Mr. Mueller, did you take the coins?"

Hans continued to sit there silently.

Arlo had talked to a person living next to Danny's property. She was walking down her driveway to the mailbox when she saw the work van owned by Hans drive by on the day the coins were returned. She positively identified it, because he had his business name on the side. When Kye told the story that Karl and Hans were German soldiers during the War, Sean felt that was a break in the case. Arlo checked, and Otis was meeting with a client that day. When Sean asked Hans if he was on the road where Danny and Sally lived on the day the coins were returned, Hans refused to answer.

"Mr. Mueller, I need for you and Mrs. Mueller to go with me to the station. I'll call Otis to join us there."

"Why she go with us?"

"I don't want to leave her here by herself. I will see that she is taken care of."

Hans sat there for a minute, and stood and called for Hilda. She looked at him and was alarmed as she looked between the two men. He walked over and took her hand, which had begun to tremble. He spoke in German to her. She nodded but was shaken.

Sean told Hans he needed to make sure they had no weapons. Hans nodded and again said something in German to Hilda. She looked stoic and nodded. After checking them for weapons, he helped them into the back of his cruiser. He contacted Alex and asked him to bring Otis to the station.

Once they were at the station, Otis's wife came and took Hilda home with her. After conferring with his father, Otis called Boone Carter. Sean called the County Prosecutor, Tyler Forquet, and told him about the situation. Sean obtained a search warrant. Arlo and Darrell found the missing coins hidden in Hans's workshop.

Chapter 31

Except for the entryway and hall lights, Owen turned off the lights in the other parts of the office and sat down in his chair. He smiled as he pulled out the drawer and lifted the bottle of Bushmills. He poured a generous glass of whiskey and leaned back. He nursed his drink, thinking a salute to Milton. Skip was lying in his bed, knowing that soon, they would be going home. Having drained the glass, Owen thought he'd have another one. He poured another generous portion and twisted the cap on the bottle. He didn't put it away since he might just help himself to one more. He looked over at Skip, "Yeah, old buddy, it's been a long day. I'll finish real soon, and then we'll head home." He sipped his drink and had his eyes closed when he heard the front door open. He looked up and listened, thinking Drew would come down the hall. *Drew must have returned for a file or something.*

At first, it was quiet. Then he heard a creak in the hall's wood flooring. Owen began to think it wasn't Drew, but he knew Martha wouldn't be returning to the office this late. He set the glass on his desk and started to say something when an intruder slipped to the doorway.

"What the hell are you doing here?" Owen demanded.

Before Owen could react, the intruder shot twice. Owen fell back in his chair.

Skip yelped and flopped down on his bed, shivering. The intruder looked down at the dog then turned and walked out.

A dispatcher knocked on Sean's door, "Sheriff, we've got a call that Owen Donaldson's secretary just found him in his office. Looks like he's been shot." As he rushed out, he told Kim to have Alex, Arlo and Syd meet him at Owen's office.

When Sean arrived at the scene, he found Martha and Drew sitting on the porch with Skip. Drew was trying to comfort Martha. The EMT's were already inside. Sean walked to where they were sitting. Drew said, "Sheriff, I think he's dead."

"Stay here with Martha. I need to check things out."

Sean looked around as he was walking to the back office where he could see the EMT's. "What have you got?"

"He's dead. Looks like he was shot twice. I'd guess he's been dead about twelve hours or so. You're probably going to want to bring in Forensics. The dog was here when he was found by his secretary. She called 911 from her office and took the dog outside with her. We haven't touched anything. We were waiting here for you."

"Yeah, let's clear out until the Forensics team can check things out."

His three deputies had arrived and were standing in the front yard. He asked Alex and Syd to start questioning people in the neighborhood to see if they had heard or seen anything. He asked Arlo to keep people at a distance. He called Ronnie and DD.

Martha was softly crying, and Drew was sitting beside her with his chair pulled close where he could hold her hand.

"Either of you need some water?" Sean asked. They both shook their head no.

He needed to separately question Drew and Martha. He asked Drew to walk with him toward the street. Once out of hearing range, he asked Drew, "Tell me about when you last saw Owen."

"I left a little early yesterday afternoon. I wanted to go home and study for the CPA exam. Owen was in his office."

"You didn't come back here for any reason after you left?'

"No, Sheriff. I was at home with Mom and Dad the rest of the evening—until I left this morning to come back here."

"How did he seem to you when you left? Anything out of the ordinary?"

"Just the same as he always was."

Can you think of anything, Drew, that might be helpful here?"

"Well, there was something that he was working on. I don't know what it was, but I came into the office one morning, and Owen was already there. That was unusual. In fact, it had never happened before. It was a first for Owen being in a good mood, especially in the morning. He was actually joking. He said something like, 'I've finally got those SOBs. Their asses are grasses,' and he laughed. I asked him what he was talking about, but he just said that I'd know soon."

"You don't know what he was referring to?"

"No clue."

During Sean's interview with Martha, she told him that she "left about four o'clock. That's the time I usually leave. There wasn't anything unusual. Owen had walked home for a late lunch and brought Skip back with him. He said he needed to work on something. He didn't have any appointments. I checked in on him as I was leaving."

"Was he expecting anyone after you left?"

"No. At least not that I knew of."

"Anything that he was working on that might have caused someone to do this?"

Martha said, "He was working on three big cases. One was for the milk company. With the employees taking over the ownership, he was working through all the tax matters relating to that corporate transition. There was nothing that I know of that was controversial about that. The second big case was the two lawsuits he had filed against the county regarding the properties that were foreclosed on for the Lake Meadows project and the request to computerize all property information here in the county. The third case, he was representing some landowners on the eastern side of the county. They didn't want the state to approve fracking. The county had approved the permit. It was for one of the Commissioner's property. The neighbors didn't want the noise and all, and they were afraid that the fracking company might want to eventually try to get on their properties. He also handles tax matters for several of the businesses around town, but I don't know of anything that was going on right now with those."

"Which Commissioner's property is the one involved in the fracking?"

"Nickolas Garrison."

"Drew mentioned that he was working on something that had him energized. Was that one of these cases?"

"Oh. I know what Drew was talking about. I remember that morning. He was even whistling from his office. We both commented on his good mood. But Sean, I don't know what it was. I thought he was working on something, but he didn't ask me to open a file or type anything."

"Any idea if there might be a file or papers anywhere?"

"I can check his office."

"Okay, once it's clear to go in there, I'd appreciate your checking. Also, let me know if anything looks disturbed or unusual or missing."

Nothing looked disturbed at Owen's house, so the murderer must not have searched it. DD and Ronnie each sent their techs. After all their analyses came back, they concluded that someone shot Owen twice. There was no indication he had tried to move before being shot, so they speculated that he was either caught by surprise or knew his killer. It was determined that the bullets came from a 9mm.

Once the scene was cleared out, Martha looked through the files. Nothing seemed to have been removed from the office. Arlo and Syd's interviews with neighbors didn't turn up much. A couple of the elderly people in the neighborhood thought they had heard firecrackers going off but didn't get up to look out. No one saw anyone who looked new or strange in the neighborhood. Pauline Kaufmann had been seen earlier, but that wasn't unusual, because she had two listings on the street.

Sean decided he would pull Alex and Syd off their regular duties and use them to assist with the investigation. He held a meeting with them that afternoon to map out how he was going to proceed with the investigation. He knew how critical the first few days were in solving a murder. His main criteria in identifying persons of interest was to find out who benefited from his death and those who held a strong grudge against him that could lead to murder.

He already had the start of a list of persons of interest that he personally intended to interview. At the top of that list was Cooper. He also listed the county officials who were individually named in the lawsuits as well as Harvey Bennett. Another name on his list was the president of the fracking company. He needed information about the whereabouts of all these individuals, and any possible motive. He wanted to know if any of these people had registered guns. Background information was needed on the fracking company.

He discussed with Alex and Syd the other people that he wanted them to interview, including certain county employees in the Treasurer's and Auditor's offices. They also needed more information about the case Owen had filed opposing the fracking permit at the state. Even though he had no reason to suspect Kye or the Steinsens, he wanted Alex and Syd to see if they might know something. One of Sean's goals was to use this as a training opportunity to teach Alex and Syd how to conduct an investigation and to interview witnesses.

After Sean had finished discussing the assignments, Alex said, "Chief, you mentioned that you are planning to interview Commissioner Garrison. I don't know if this has anything to do with the case, but a while back, Alice and I were at the GilHaus. We sometimes stop there after work. A friend of hers works there, and we talk to her if she has some spare time.

"She was laughing when she told us. She said that she thought she was in the middle of a Hollywood casting. Commissioner Garrison was having lunch with two men that she had never seen before. They were both big men, dressed in suits—but no ties. The Commissioner hardly touched his food, but the men ate their lunch. He just sat there for about fifteen minutes after they left. She was concerned, because he looked pale. She asked him if he was okay. She was afraid there was something wrong with his food. He mumbled he was fine, but he had her bring him a double, double Wild Turkey."

"Alex, talk to her again, and see if she remembers anything else about that."

Alex and Syd brought Cooper in for questioning that very afternoon. He was fuming, and when Sean entered the room, he let go, "What is this all about? I'm going to hire a lawyer to sue you for harassment."

Sean indicated for Alex and Syd to remain. He sat down across from Cooper. "Where were you last night?"

"What is this about?"

"Just answer the question, Townsend."

"I don't have to tell you shit."

He looked at the wall, trying to ignore the officers.

Sean said, "Owen Donaldson was killed last night."

Cooper whipped around to face Sean. "Well, I'll be," he smirked.

"Where were you last evening?"

He suddenly sobered up. "What? You think I killed him?" Sean continued to look at him. "Wait a minute. You're accusin' me of killin' him? No damn way are you goin' to pin something on me again. I didn't kill that SOB, even though I'm not sad he's dead."

"Cooper, where were you yesterday evening?"

He now was looking anxious. "I was home."

"Was anyone with you?"

"Naw. Ma is at her sister's for a few days up in Chillicothe, but I didn't kill him. No way. I've not seen him since I went to his office that one time. You told me I better not if I wanted to stay out of trouble, and I ain't gone near him."

Alex drove Cooper back home. Sean asked Syd to see if any guns were registered to his mother.

"Sheriff, you don't think we should arrest him?"

"No one saw him in the area, but that doesn't mean anything. Check with the folks near where he lives and see if they saw him. Also, see if you can find out if he's got any friends or if he's hanging out somewhere. See what you can find out about him."

"Will do, Sheriff."

Chapter 32

Martha had given Sean the McClain's names as parties to the lawsuit trying to stop the state from approving the fracking permit. Sean had met them last year when he was investigating the Pinkston murders. The McClains lived on the eastern side of Bekbourg County in an area known as Possum Gap. When he arrived, they were sitting on the front porch—Mr. McClain in his ladder-back chair and Mrs. McClain in her wood rocking chair. Their old dog raised his head enough to watch Sean and Syd walk up the steps and then laid it back down on his small carpet.

"Mr. and Mrs. McClain, it's good to see you again. This is Deputy Johnson."

Mrs. McClain said, "You too, Sheriff. Ms. Johnson. We ain't heard of no more killin's 'round here. Hope that's not what brought you here."

Sean smiled, "No ma'am. Not close by anyway, but unfortunately, it does involve a murder. I want to talk to you about one of the cases that Owen Donaldson was working on. You and some other landowners around here were his clients. Can you tell us about that case?"

Mr. and Mrs. McClain were both hardy people—despite being elderly. She was dressed in a loose, cotton floral dress. Mr. McClain was dressed in a pair of jeans and flannel shirt despite it being a hot summer day.

Mr. McClain said, "Sure, Sheriff. You all have a seat. Let me make my smoke, and I'll tell you all 'bout those bastards." He slowly poured some loose tobacco in a piece of cigarette paper. Mrs. McClain kept rocking, watching him roll his cigarette. He rolled the paper around the tobacco and licked the edge of the paper. He put the cigarette between his lips and pulled out a match book from his shirt pocket, lit the cigarette, and put the spent match in a tin can sitting beside his chair.

"Yeah, we can tell you 'bout it. We've lived here all our lives, Sheriff. This property belonged to my dad and his dad and even further back. I told Bess here when those politicians bought the old Henning place they were up to somethin', that they were lookin' to pad their pockets somehow. They're all corrupt. Anyhow, us and our neighbors all talked 'bout it. We all have suspicions. We didn't know it, but last spring, that group of county commissioners approved the frackin'. We only found out when one of the neighbor's kids who works for the state's environmental office told him that the frackin' company was tryin' to get the state's okay. That's when we found out those bastards had given the frackin' company a permit.

"We were all upset. That's when we joined together to hire Owen. He's good. We knew he wouldn't let those jackasses get by with nothin'. We all hate to spend our money on this nonsense, but we ain't goin' to let them ruin our property. When that one Commissioner got killed last year, I thought maybe that other Commissioner would drop his plans, at least that's what we hoped would happen. But he ain't. That's 'bout the way of it."

"Was any of your group upset with Owen about the case?"

"Heck no. He was givin' 'em fits. That Commissioner came around to each of us seein' if we would settle, but we told him where he could go. Owen was doin' a great job. We hated that he was killed. We've got to find another attorney now."

Mrs. McClain said, "Owen's secretary—her name is Martha. She is so nice. I could tell that she was tore up about Owen when she called. Anyhow, she told us that a Mr. Boone Carter would be a good attorney for us to use. She said she'd send all the papers to him if that was okay with all of us. We told her to go ahead. If she trusts him, that was good enough for us."

"Well, if you can think of anything, here is my card. I appreciate your time."

Mrs. McClain said as Sean and Syd stood to leave, "Sheriff, we sure hope you find who killed Owen. He's one of the few 'round here who stood up for us common folk. He was a good man."

"I will, Mrs. McClain. Thank you both."

Syd visited the other landowners who were part of the McClain lawsuit group, and they told her about the same thing the McClains had told them.

Alex researched the fracking company, Predit Drilling. The owner's name was Nelson Predit. At first, nothing seemed out of the ordinary with the fracking company. No negative reports or complaints had been filed against the company with governmental authorities except for filings opposing certain fracking operations. After drilling a little deeper, he found the company was in financial trouble and badly needed this project. Its state corporate filings seemed to be in order. With respect to the property—the Henning place—it was purchased by Jeff Thompson and Nickolas Garrison. There were about a hundred acres. It was a cash transaction. The seller lived in Tapsaw County, next door to Bekbourg County. He told Alex that they approached him about buying it. He thought it was worthless, and when they offered the money, he jumped at it.

Alex added, "I called Ms. Zimmstein, Commissioner Thompson's widow, about what was happening with his interest in the property. She told me to call Boone Carter, because she didn't know. Well, I called Boone, and he told me that he didn't even know that Thompson owned that property. He was going to look into it."

"Good work, Alex." Sean was thinking that Nickolas probably had no intention of telling anyone that Jeff was a part owner. Sean decided it was time to pay Nickolas Garrison a visit.

"How are you doing, Commissioner."

"Just fine, Sean. What's this about?"

"I'm investigating Owen Donaldson's death."

"Oh, sure. I hated to hear that. Can't say I was a fan of Donaldson. He could sure be a thorn, but that shouldn't happen to anyone."

"I understand that Owen was the attorney for some landowners here that opposed the state granting approvals for fracking on the land that you own, the old Henning place."

"Yeah, he was."

"If the state approves the fracking request, there's probably a lot of money to be made by you?"

Nickolas looked hard a Sean. "I can't say that I appreciate what you're implying, Sean. But, yeah, it would bring me some extra cash. I don't have any reason to think they won't eventually approve it. They've approved fracking in other places around the state. It's good business for the state. I own the property. Donaldson's lawsuit is just a nuisance, just a delay."

"I understand that Jeff Thompson was also an owner in the property."

"Well, yeah, that's true. I've been meaning to talk to Mary about that, but she's in Columbus a lot. Been hard to catch up with her." Sean thought: *Jeff's been dead about a year. You've not tried very hard to contact Mary.*

"Yeah, I'm sure she would be interested to hear from you. She is pouring all the money from Jeff's interests into the foundation. Sounds like this could be a big boost to the foundation."

"Well, I'm not sure that Mary would want to fool with this property. We'll probably work out a deal where I buy Jeff's interest."

"Mary is here about three days a week, but if you can't reach her, Boone Carter is handling these types of affairs for her."

"Oh, good to know. I might give him a call."

"What about the lawsuit Owen was handling about the tax information?"

"What about it?"

"He was asking that all of the county's property information be computerized and made more accessible to the public. He was also asking for information to be turned over to him about the Davis and Steinsen properties."

"It's a nuisance, Sean. I think the cases will be dropped. No attorney worth his salt will pursue that nonsense."

"Are you saying that now that Owen is dead, the case will be dropped?"

"I think it will be. It certainly should be."

"So, your group will benefit now that Owen is dead?"

"Now wait a minute. We didn't like what Owen was doing, but I didn't kill him, and I don't believe any of them would have. Anyway, he would have lost in court and with the state on the permit."

"You're a big contractor around the area. Didn't you build the houses in that Lake Shore development near the golf course?"

"Yeah. I'm proud of that." Nickolas was tiring of the conversation. "It's nice for the area. Good for Bekbourg."

"Are you going to build all the houses in this new development?"

"I have submitted a plan for its development."

"You know of any improprieties with that development or with the way the Davis or Steinsen properties were acquired?"

"Look, I don't know of anything. I think you're barking up the wrong tree, Sheriff, if you're trying to find Owen's killer."

"I'm talking to a lot of people, Nickolas. Where do you think I should be looking?"

"Well, I sure don't know. That's your job, but I know it's not because the fracking or land stuff you've been asking me about."

"Well, I really appreciate your time, Commissioner. One other thing: I need to know where you were when Owen was killed."

Harvey Bennett's office was located along the Bekbourg Highway near the Lake Shore development. Sean and Alex pulled into the large parking lot. The old C&W Feed and Supply Store had been transformed from a dilapidated wood siding structure into a light-gray brick front with large, grid-less windows. The reception area was spacious and well-lit with a plush sitting area off to one side. Off to the other side were two glass-enclosed small conference rooms. Photos of various phases of the Lake Shore development hung on the walls. An attractive woman was sitting behind a counter. She greeted Sean and Alex. "Mr. Bennett is on a phone call, but he is expecting you. May I offer you something to drink?"

"Thank you, but I'm fine."

"Okay, please make yourself comfortable. He'll be with you shortly."

Sean was looking around at the photos when he heard, "Hello, Sean. Good to see you."

Sean turned around and shook his hand. "Hi, Harvey. This is Deputy Ogle. You've done a nice job fixing up the old C&W."

"Thanks. It's amazing how a building can be remade. Nickolas' company handled the renovations for me. Let's step back to my office. You sure we can't get you something to drink?" They both declined.

Harvey's office was large, with a glass top desk and a round matching conference table. The black lacquer shelving behind his desk displayed awards for his developments and various ground-breaking and construction photographs.

"Let's sit at the table. It's more comfortable. Now, what can I do for you?"

"We're investigating Owen's murder. How well did you know Owen?"

"I ran into him around town, but I can't say I knew him. I was sorry to hear about his death. I know that a lot of people around the county thought a lot of him."

"Your company is a defendant in his lawsuits. He claimed that Bekbourg Enterprises wrongfully acquired through tax sales, properties belonging to Kye Davis and Adam Steinsen and his heirs. What can you tell me about Owen's claims?"

"Well, not much, Sean. First thing, I hired an attorney to represent my company, and he has advised me not to discuss the lawsuits with anyone, so I'm not able to talk about that."

"Owen wanted information going back several years. Your company bought property for the Lake Shore development. Do you know of any reason why Owen may have wanted to see county records that far back?"

"No, I don't"

"Harvey, how worried were you about Owen's lawsuits?"

"Not at all."

"Your entire development, which I'm sure you have spent substantial money and time on, could fail to go forward if you lose. You're not concerned?"

"No, Sean, I'm not. For one thing, my attorney told me that he doesn't think the plaintiffs will win, but I don't think it will ever go to court. I've offered to settle with both Kye and the Steinsens. I think it'll settle."

"Do you know anyone who wanted Owen dead?"

"No."

Harvey didn't have an alibi for the time Owen was murdered. He had driven to Columbus late that evening for a breakfast meeting the next morning. He said that he went home after work, packed a bag and left. There was no one who could verify his time, and he didn't use a credit card on the drive up. The motel where he stayed didn't show him checking in until around ten o'clock. No guns were registered to Harvey, and he claimed he didn't own one.

"Sheriff, I've got some information about Cooper Townsend."

"Have a seat, Syd. What have you learned?"

"Well, first. His mother doesn't have any guns registered to her. The report filed by Ben Clark when he arrested Cooper on the drug charge said the gun Cooper had was a 9mm. I've asked around the precinct, and no one knows what happened to that gun."

"Okay. What else do you have?"

"He's been hanging out at that dive just past the trailer park. People are not very cooperative talking to the police, but there were a couple of people who were willing to talk to me when I told them I was looking into Owen's murder. Seems Owen helped them out years ago. They said that Townsend is a big mouth. Talks too much. Always complaining about one thing or another. Anyway, before Owen was killed, Townsend was shooting his mouth off a couple of times talking about Owen. They said he blamed Owen for his going to prison. Said that Owen had his coming, called him a SOB, things like that. I'm still looking for any people he might be hanging out with."

"Syd, get a warrant for us to search his mother's place and the vehicle he drives. When the judge issues it, let me know. You and I will drive out to his place."

Sean knocked on the door a third time. An old Ford was sitting in the driveway. Cooper finally opened the door. He only had on a pair of jeans. It looked like he had been asleep—even though it was almost noon.

"Mr. Townsend, we have a warrant to search your place."

"What for?" he demanded.

"We're looking for a gun."

"What? I ain't got a gun."

"When you were arrested for having drugs, you had a 9mm. What happened to that?"

"I already told you. I don't know."

"It's not here?"

"No."

"Okay, then. We need to come in."

Syd and Sean went through the trailer, but didn't find any guns or anything incriminating. Nothing of interest was in the car.

Cooper fumed the entire time, cursing them and vowing that they weren't going to frame him like before. Sean assured him that they were not there to frame him, but they needed to investigate, because he had been heard threatening Owen and saying incriminating things.

"Well, I ain't got no love lost for him, that's for sure, and I ain't made no secret of my feelin's for him. But you won't find nothin' that ties me to his death. I ain't goin' back to prison."

"What's your mother's sister's name, the one you said she was staying with—in Chillicothe?"

"This is pure harassment. That's none of your business."

"Cooper, I'm thinking about arresting you for Owen's murder. How you cooperate right now is going to influence whether I go ahead and do it."

After Sean and Syd left Cooper's home, Sean asked Syd to drive up to Chillicothe and talk to his mother. "Be sure to see what you can find out about what happened to that gun he used to have."

"Pauline, this is Sean Neumann. I need to talk to you. I'd like to stop by when you're in your office, unless there is a more convenient place to meet."

When Sean and Syd walked into Pauline's office, Pauline was smoking a cigarette. Exhaling smoke, she asked, "To what do I owe this honor, Sheriff?" Sean introduced Syd, but Pauline just nodded her head.

"We're trying to track all leads in Owen's murder, and I am wondering what you know about Owen's investigation in the land deals. We've been looking for a motive in his murder, and this might very well be why he was killed."

"I was blindsided by his lawsuits. We were trying to get him the information. I can tell you we followed the law and procedures on all tax foreclosures. Anyway, I don't see how his lawsuits could possibly have anything to do with his death."

"Well, Owen didn't think procedures were being followed from what I gathered and was trying to find out how this all came down with the Steinsens and Kye Davis."

"Well, like I said, we were trying to cooperate with him, but Owen was always impulsive, and he'd come in here demanding this and that. We'd ask him what he was working on so we could get him the information he needed, and he wouldn't tell us. We were left in the dark many times with what he was really wanting. I think that was because he wasn't sure what he was after. He must have tried to impress his clients, so he filed these lawsuits, which I must add have no merit."

"I understand that you were seen in Owen's neighborhood around the time he was killed."

She looked aghast. "Surely you don't suspect me?" When Sean just sat there looking at her, she said in a dismissive tone tapping ashes in the tray, "Well, I have two listings on that street, and I was checking on those houses. I've been working with several clients." Alex had already checked with the owners of those two houses. The houses were both empty. Neither of the owners was aware of any interest shown in the houses in months.

"Did you meet with anyone at one of those houses?"

"No, I was just checking on a few things."

"Do you own a gun?"

Pauline took a long drawl. "Yes. I used to carry one, being in the real estate business, but I don't bother anymore."

"What kind of gun?"

"Oh, I don't know that. Just a gun."

"You don't keep it with you?"

"There's no reason, Sean. I'm not even sure where it may be."

"I need to know if anyone can vouch for you that evening."

Pauline watched them walk out of her office, blowing smoke from a long inhale.

Chapter 33

Cheryl's story ran in *The Cleveland Presenter* and was picked up in the *Bekbourg Tribune.*

Bekbourg County Treasurer and Auditor Sued for Improper Property Forfeitures

Before his death, attorney Owen Donaldson filed a series of lawsuits in the Bekbourg County court alleging that the county improperly seized certain properties under the tax forfeiture process. These properties were purchased by Bekbourg Enterprises, also a named defendant, at the Sheriff Sales and became part of the recently announced Lake Meadows development. Because the Treasurer and Auditor did not produce the land records relevant to these sales, he petitioned the

Court to compel the county to produce these documents. (These documents are all public records and should be available to the public when requested.)

Mr. Donaldson also petitioned the state to force Bekbourg County to computerize all its land documents so that they are easily accessible to the public. He stated that many counties had either already computerized their data or were moving to do so.

When asked to comment on the lack of transparency, the County Treasurer, Pauline Kaufmann, told us they did not comment on any pending litigation, but she denied any wrongdoing in response to the "frivolous lawsuit" and stated that her department was working on Mr. Donaldson's request for information.

In the course of our investigation, we were able to uncover a disturbing process in the handling of delinquent taxes in certain properties acquired for both the Lake Shore and Lake Meadows developments. Without the owner's knowledge or consent, tax bills were sent to the property's address, even if no one lived there. Of course, the tax bills were returned to the County. After the requisite time period expired for paying delinquent taxes, notices were sent to the same address that warned of pending tax forfeiture proceedings. Each of these warnings, as well as the announcements of tax auctions, was returned to the County. Obscure notices of the tax auctions would then be posted in the Bekbourg Tribune, and the auction was held where Bekbourg Enterprises would buy the land.

It must also be pointed out that the Lake Shore development has been a source of pride for Bekbourg County and has attracted many new people to the community. It must be noted, however, that most of the work on developing the project was given exclusively to a rather small group of people. County Commissioner, Nickolas Garrison, had the exclusive rights to build all the homes in the Lake Shore development, and Pauline Kaufmann, the County Treasurer, had exclusive rights to all the real estate transactions. The First City Bank of Bekbourg handled the majority of the mortgage business. When asked if he would be the exclusive builder in the Lake Meadows development, County Commissioner Nickolas Garrison said, "I don't want to get ahead of any arrangements that Mr. Bennett might be planning."

One further point that was uncovered during our investigation is that the state has dusted off their plans to develop the Peatmont State Park and

> *plan to build a lodge and conference center along with vacation cabins on Lake Peatmont near the new Lake Meadows development. Finally, it must be noted that in the course of the investigation, we also found that as of the date we published, the current list of corporate officers in Bekbourg Enterprises includes Harvey Bennett, President, Randall Thompson, Treasurer, and Jeff Thompson, Secretary.*

"What's that blasted reporter trying to do?" Nickolas roared. "She is really becoming a problem."

Charles Martin responded, "She was already a problem. She's the one who wrote all those stories about what happened here last year."

"I know all that. What is this all about? Why's she doing this? She's even reported on the state's plans to develop that big lodge and all. How does she get all this information?"

"First, it's not like the state was hiding that. Randall just happened upon it. Anyone could have found out about it, so I'm not surprised she found out."

Nickolas interrupted Pauline, "That's not the point. Why's she even investigating all this? Why look at what the state is planning? What's her point?"

"She's just blowing smoke. Look, just like Owen, there is nothing for her to find." Pauline's impatience with Nickolas was evident. "This will die down. People around here don't care. Most rural property hasn't been worth much in years. The county benefited from the Lake Shore project. We need to talk up the benefits of these development projects and deny any wrongdoing without saying negative things about Kye or the Steinsens. We just say that they didn't pay their taxes, and we followed the law."

Harvey tried to calm the tension, "I agree. We cannot overreact."

Ignoring Harvey, Nickolas aimed his fire at Pauline. "It's easy for you to say that. You're the one who brought all this on. All this crap about 'no one will notice; it will be fine.'"

Her volume trumped his, "I don't remember you raising any objections as you counted your money."

The last thing Harvey wanted was for anyone to do something stupid. They were clearly rattled. While Jeff and Randall Thompson were alive, no one dared argue with either one of them. Now, Harvey often found himself acting as mediator. "This is getting us nowhere. Look at it this way. The reporter isn't the one who brought the lawsuit. Her stuff is just an article with not much to go on as I read it. With Owen dead, I don't see how those two lawsuits will go anywhere. I don't think Kye or the Steinsens will bother now. Even if they call another attorney, he won't take the case because it's so ludicrous.

"We should be proactive. We should come out publicly and say that we deny these allegations, that the Commission will set up a committee to look at the feasibility of computerizing property data; that progress is important for Bekbourg, and that's why it's not struggling like so many other midwestern towns. The Lake Shore development was a good thing, and the Lake Meadows development is going to be great for the area.

"Let's make it all about politics. We need to put the Reform Party on the defense. Let's make them look like the anti-progress party. Use Owen's lawsuits and that reporter's articles to drive that point home. Make people believe that their efforts are political, and that if the anti-progress, anti-development Reform Party gets in control, it will ruin the economy and jobs around here. It will also make it look like we don't fear the lawsuits or have anything to hide."

Pauline disagreed with Harvey, "I'm not sure that's a good idea. I think we ought to let the lawyer handle the case and just deny any wrongdoing. The more we say, the more we escalate the matter. We want the citizens to forget it."

Nickolas jumped on Harvey's bandwagon, "That's what we should do, Harvey. I also think we add to this that those Reform yahoos, if elected to the city council, will try and stop the county, which is working hard to bring in jobs and new businesses. That gridlock will slow down progress and hurt people in Bekbourg."

"There's something else," Harvey said. "Another way to diffuse what that reporter said is to tell people that it was the Thompsons that set up the structure. People know they ran things around the county. We'll make them look responsible. I could tell them that I'm not setting things up the way they did. No one company is going to have an exclusive on construction or real estate sales."

While the other two were pondering Harvey's idea, Charles spoke up, "I think that's a good idea. Nickolas and Pauline already have a head start over anyone else who might try to wedge themselves in, because they know all about the project and they have the history of Phase One."

Pauline agreed, but Nickolas wasn't on board, "Yeah, that's easy for both of you to agree to, because there's no other real estate broker in the county, and Charles' bank is the largest here. I'm the one who loses out. That Fischner group will certainly be vying for building the homes."

"Okay," said Harvey. "It was just a thought. That can be an arrow in our quiver down the road if we need it."

Pauline again voiced her hesitancy in pushing so hard on the political front, but the other three were in favor. After the meeting broke up, Nickolas and Harvey walked out together. When they were out of earshot of the others, Nickolas said, "She's never been a team player. I sure don't trust her. Randall Thompson's the one who brought her in at the beginning."

"She is a battle axe, but she knows more about property and the county records around here than anyone. Pauline's okay. The first development wouldn't have gone as smoothly without her."

Learning that Nelson's company was encountering financial strains, Sean wanted to question him. Sean and Alex drove to Pittsburgh to meet with Nelson. He told them that he wasn't concerned about the permit being granted by the state. He told them that he frequently encountered opposition on his fracking projects, especially by landowners.

"You must have spent a lot of time and money on this prospect, Mr. Predit. You have employees on your staff as well as contractors that you use. There is a substantial upfront cost that goes into a project like this. If the state doesn't approve your permit application, won't that be a financial setback to you?"

"I've got other drilling projects and prospects. I've weathered other storms. Like they say, 'win some, lose some.' It's just part of doing business, but like I said, I think the state will come through on this."

Sean asked him if Commissioner Garrison was concerned about the permit being approved. "He's not happy about the delay. Told me that Donaldson was always meddling in things. I told him it wasn't unusual. Lots of people are opposed to fracking. But, the state is favorably disposed to approve fracking applications, because they bring in revenues and oil and gas. The Bekbourg commission approved it. I think it won't be much longer."

Sean asked him where he was on the evening that Owen was murdered. For the first time since they sat down, Nelson seemed hesitant. "I don't see that it's necessary to go into that except to say I was here in Pittsburg. I didn't murder Mr. Donaldson—if that is what you're getting at."

"Do you have a hand gun, Mr. Predit?"

"Yes."

"What kind of gun do you have?"

"Do you have a warrant?"

"No."

"Then, I'm not going to talk about it."

After Alex and Sean got in the car to drive back, Alex said, "What he said about his company not struggling isn't consistent with what I learned."

"I know. I wanted to see how he responded to our questions."

"Why do you think he wouldn't answer about an alibi or about his gun? Do you think he shot Owen?"

"It's too early to say. Either he doesn't have an alibi or he was somewhere or with someone that he doesn't want us to know about. He may feel he wants to talk to a lawyer before he gives any answers. Dig some more and see if you can find anything else. We are certainly not dropping him off our list."

Syd was driving back from talking with Cooper's mother. Kim put her call through to Sean. "Hi, Syd. What'd you find out?"

"Not much, Sheriff. She didn't want to talk. She doesn't trust the police. I finally got her to talk to me though. She didn't even know that Mr. Donaldson was killed. Her sister is battling cancer, so she's up there helping out. She said she hasn't talked to Cooper since she got here. I asked her about the gun. She doesn't know what happened to it. Before Cooper was released, she went through the house to make sure that there were no weapons and didn't find anything. She said she doesn't own a gun."

"Okay, Syd. Thanks."

Chapter 34

Jason Worley sat down at the bar at the GilHaus. He ordered a beer. He turned to Pauline, "You wanted to talk to me?"

"Hello, Jason. It's nice to see you," she said as she leaned and rubbed her shoulder against his.

Her voice grated on him. Pauline was an irritant. He leaned away, "I don't have much time, Pauline. I'm on my way to a meeting."

He took a sip and waited.

"I've been hearing rumors that you are considering running for my position."

"You mean the County Treasurer?"

Pauline smiled, "Yes, Jason, Treasurer."

He took another sip. "I'm giving it some thought."

"You surely know you would have no chance of unseating me. In fact, this whole idea of this Reform Party is silly. They don't stand a chance."

"They wouldn't agree with you, Pauline."

Pauline took a drink from her Gin and Tonic. "Look, Jason. This whole notion is nonsense. Reform? They don't have any idea what it's like to run the county. We've brought jobs here, and tourism is doing well. If it hadn't been for our efforts, we'd be like many of the other rust-belt towns."

Jason continued to nurse his beer. "Pauline, let's not kid ourselves. What came down last year shows that corruption has run rampant. They want to root out that corruption and take the county in a new direction while building on its strong points."

"Ump, sounds like you've memorized their talking points. How is that supposed to help the area?"

"Well, for starters, it helps the people who haven't gained from this recent development while the local politicians line their pockets. People don't want that fracking in their back door, ruining their way of life and their property values. People are looking for new leadership. That's why you're scared, isn't it? You can feel this change coming. That's why you're trying to convince me not to run against you. Even if I don't run, Pauline, the gig is up for you and your cronies. At least some of these Reform Party candidates are going to win, and once the camel gets its nose under the tent, the spot light will shine on what's been going on here. It's all about to come down. Last year was just the start."

"Ha! You are such a hypocrite. You don't belong in this Reform movement any more than I do."

"Well, I've got to go."

Jason put his money on the bar and left. Pauline watched him walk away, thinking to herself, *I can't believe all this nonsense and distraction brought on by Owen and that Reform movement! I've worked too hard to see it crater.*

Hans was released on bail shortly after being charged for theft of the coins.

Tyler Forquet, the county prosecutor, called Sean to give him an update on the investigation. He told Sean that Hans would not talk. "Sean, he won't say a word. Won't say why he took those coins. I've asked him about Roger Burkhart, if he knew why Roger had the papers from Vienna, everything I can think of, but he wouldn't say anything. When I threatened him with jail time for stealing the coins, it didn't faze him. The federal agencies have looked into his past, but they can't find anything. He may be here under an alias, but there's no proof of that.

"The reason I wanted to talk to you is that Danny and Sally are refusing to press charges. The federal agencies can't find any evidence of him being a Nazi war criminal or anything like that. They aren't pursing it. I'm going to drop all charges against him."

"Well, thanks for the heads-up, Tyler. I guess it's one of those things we may never know the answer to."

"Yeah, seems that way."

Sean called Lucky, his friend with the FBI, to see what he could find out about the federal investigation into Hans. After looking into it, Lucky called Sean. "They couldn't find anything that led them to think he was anyone other than who he claims to be. He's too young to have been a commandant or any position of authority in the death camps. There's just no evidence. It's impossible to say how he came to possess those coins. Your theory that Roger Burkhart heard about the federal agents coming to town and decided to see if he could get information on Karl and Hans for being in the Nazi party may be right. Those documents from Vienna were general and told about how to find Nazis. Maybe he tried to mislead Karl into thinking he had compromising information and shake him down, but that didn't work, but maybe there was something to it with Hans. Maybe Hans believed Burkhart had some dirt and paid him with the coins to keep him quiet. Roger was killed not too long after that, and the coins disappeared. If all that is correct, when Hans heard about the coins reappearing, he panicked because he thought they might somehow lead back to him, which they did."

"Well, that's my theory, but it's hard to say. Unless Hans talks, we just don't know, and it appears that he has no intention of talking. Okay, Lucky. I appreciate your checking."

"Any time, Sean."

Monica was dating Cooper when he was arrested. She had since moved on with her life and married while he was in prison. She agreed to come in the next day to talk to Sean.

"You said this is about Coop?"

"Yes. I understand you were seeing him when he was arrested. He claims he is innocent, that he was set up. Did he ever mention anything like that to you?" asked Sean.

"Well, that's what he told me at the time. I believed him, because he wasn't into drugs. I mean he may have smoked a joint now and then, but nothing much. He was a bartender at Koot's. He liked his job."

Sean thought, *If he was skimming off the top from some of the suppliers, that was probably a nice income, so yeah, he probably didn't want to lose his job.*

"Did he ever mention who might have planted drugs in his car?"

"No, that was the odd thing. He never said who, even though I asked him."

"Did he ever say anything about his attorney, Owen Donaldson?"

"Well, he was bitter about him. He felt he didn't do a good job as his lawyer. He blamed him for being found guilty. That's the thing, Sheriff. I felt bad when he went to prison. I thought I loved him, but he changed. I went to see him a few times, but he was a different person. He was so angry and bitter. All he did was complain that he was innocent and that it was Mr. Donaldson's fault that he was in prison. Finally, the last time I went to see him, I told him that it was hard for Mr. Donaldson to help him if he didn't have an idea about who set him up. He exploded. Told me I was stupid. I never went back to see him. I sent him a letter and told him that it was over between us. He never wrote me, so I guess he didn't care. I heard he was out, but I don't want anything to do with him. I'm married and have a baby."

"Did you ever hear him threaten Owen Donaldson?"

She thought for a minute. "Well, he sure talked bad about him, but I don't remember ever hearing him threaten him."

"Did you ever see Cooper with a gun?"

"No, I never saw him with a gun. I don't even know if he had one."

"Did you ever see him violent? Did he ever hit anyone or fight?"

"No. He never did anything violent around me. He got mad easy and carried grudges, but he showed his anger by yelling and cussing, that sort of thing."

"Were there any people he hung out with?"

"No one comes to mind. Sheriff, I hope that you won't mention to him that I talked to you. I don't want him to think that I'm causing him any problems. I've got my husband and baby. I just don't want any problems."

"I understand, Monica. I appreciate you meeting with me. There's no reason for me to mention your name to him."

Sean drove to Mike's house to see what he knew of Cooper. Mike told him that he remembered that the arrest report mentioned a gun, but since it wasn't used in the commission of the crime, he never focused on it.

"It's possible that Ben took the gun, but if that was his intent, why did he list it on the arrest report?" Mike asked.

“Maybe he thought it would come in handy in the prosecution.”

“Could be. It’s hard to know what happened.”

“Cooper claims he was framed. Ben was the arresting officer. Did you have any reason to suspect that Ben planted drugs?”

“Well, I wondered if there was something to Townsend’s claim, but I couldn’t find any evidence that Ben planted the drugs. Thing is, Cooper claimed he was framed, but he never told who or why he was set up. Without more to go on, it was pretty much an open and shut case as far as the prosecutor was concerned.”

“Well, Townsend blames Owen for his conviction. He claims that Owen didn’t adequately represent him.”

“I don’t know anything about that, Sean, but if he didn’t give Owen any more information than he gave me to work with, I don’t see how Owen could have done much more.”

Chapter 35

Owen's wake was held on a Saturday morning. For someone who had a reputation of being so disagreeable, there were a surprisingly large number of people. After the service at the church, a reception immediately followed in the church's fellowship hall. Many of his former and existing clients were there, including the McClains. When he saw people from the county offices, Sean reasoned that people could put aside their personal feelings in death. Bri and Max catered the refreshments, and Carla and Sally stood behind the tables helping with the service.

Sean and Mike were standing off to the side watching the people. Mike took a drink from a plastic cup. "Any luck on finding Owen's killer?"

"No. Unfortunately, there is a long list of suspects."

Mike smiled. "Yep, sure doesn't help when the victim has agitated so many people—all that plus the Leo Davis case. You've been busy since you arrived in Bekbourg."

They both laughed. "Certainly not bored."

Mike pointed his cup toward a striking woman, "I heard that's Owen's sister in from California."

"Yeah, that's right. I met her at Bri's. That's where she's staying."

"Say, Sean, there's something I've been wanting to tell you. Geri and I have decided to move to Montana."

"What? When did you decide this?" Sean was not expecting this news.

"Well, we had been giving it some thought. We finally made the decision last week. Mary is returning from Europe soon, and Geri is going to tell her. We've already started to go through the house and decide what to get rid of."

"Wow, this is quick."

"Yeah, well, it's not the same for us, Sean. I think it would be a good thing to start over. Geri has enjoyed working with Mary and everything, but I need to move on."

"What are you going to do?"

"I'm going to try to find something with the state park service there—maybe a security guard. I'm going to have to do physical therapy for a long time, but I think this is for the best."

Cheryl looked around to see that Mike and Sean seemed to be in a private conversation, so she walked over to where Martha was flanked by Drew and Owen's sister, Delphia Beaumont. Affectionately nicknamed since childhood, Dillie was of medium height and well proportioned. She had platinum-colored hair that hung in wild curls down her back. She had large, gold-looped earrings and colorful bangles on her right arm. Her bright purple silk dress was belted with a gold chain that matched the gold stilettos. She was the opposite in personality from Owen. She appeared to have boosted Martha's spirits since arriving two days earlier.

There had been a steady stream of people coming through to greet them. During a brief lull, Cheryl asked if she could get them something to drink. Both Martha and Drew declined, but Dillie answered, "Thank you, Darling. I was just getting ready to partake of a glass of that delicious lemonade. I'll share with you what I just was telling Martha and Drew." Drew and Martha were smiling at Dillie's drama, "It's time for me to make a change. Bekbourg is calling to me. I was born here, of course, and lived here during my early years. Martha, Drew, you and that handsome hunk of yours, Bri and Max are my new best friends. This is where I belong. I'm going back to California and instruct my attorney to put things in order. I'm moving back to Bekbourg."

Cheryl was surprised that such a big decision could be made on the spur of the moment. "Well, that's great, Dillie."

"Yes, Darling, I was just telling Martha, who I love as a sister, and this handsome young man that I don't have a man in my life now. I just got divorced from my fifth husband. He was a dear, but well, I just didn't want to spend all that time in France. I recently moved back to my lovely place in California—got that from husband number four. He was a dear, too, but he died of a heart attack when we were in Rome." Her bangles sang with her animated arm motions. "Martha and Drew have promised to look for a place for me. I am coming home."

Cheryl humorously thought to herself, *Bekbourg may never be the same.*

Dillie's attention was redirected when she saw Bri. "Oh, please excuse me, Loves. I must tell darling Bri that I shall need to stay in her royal B&B until I find a *la maison* (house)."

Off she went, saying hello to everyone she passed.

Cheryl started to say something to Martha and Drew when she froze. They both followed her gaze. Cheryl said almost to herself, "I don't believe it. Oh, my gosh." She then remembered they were standing there, "Milton Grant just walked in the door. I'll be right back with him."

Milton was standing at the door looking around when he saw Cheryl nearing with her arms open. As she went to hug him, she said, "Oh Milton. I didn't know you were coming. It is wonderful to see you." Cheryl took stock at how nice he looked in pressed navy slacks and a blue and white striped button-up shirt, which was actually tucked in. His unruly white hair was combed, and he was clean-shaven. She owed her skills and success in a big way to him.

"Well, I wanted to come."

"Come with me. I want to introduce you to Martha, who was his secretary, and Drew."

Cheryl introduced Milton. Martha said, "Milton, this means so much that you are here. I know you drove a long way. I really appreciate it very much. Owen thought a lot of you and thought of you as a friend."

"He was one of the good guys, Martha."

Some other people walked up, and Cheryl and Milton stepped back to let them talk to Martha and Drew. Cheryl said, "Milton, when are you planning to go back? I've got something I would like to talk to you about."

"How about we meet tomorrow for breakfast?"

"That's perfect. I'll drop by and pick you up. You need to experience Frau's Diner."

"Always ready for a new experience." He told her he was staying in a motel near the Shopper's Pavilion.

After the guests finished paying their respects and walked away, Martha said, "Milton, please, if you don't mind, Drew and I would appreciate you standing here with us. I know Owen would want you here."

Milton turned pink but nodded that he would and moved in beside Martha.

Martha and Milton were talking, so Drew used it as an opportunity. "Hey, Cheryl, do you have a minute?"

"Of course."

"You know about those lawsuits Owen filed, but Cheryl, he was also working on something else. He never told us what, but he had recently discovered something. One morning, he arrived in a really good mood. Even kidded me about my bright orange polo shirt—said he needed sunglasses in the office. Do you know anything about what he was working on?"

"Well, he didn't tell me, Drew, but I want you and Martha both to know that I'm not going to let the story about the land matters rest. There is no way to know for sure until Sean solves the case, but I have a feeling that his death has something to do with that case."

Bri and Dillie were still having a nice conversation when Bri realized she needed to put out more food. About that time, Celeste and Collin walked over. Dillie said, "Hi, Loves. I saw you last night at Darling Bri's. Are you staying there?"

"Yes, I'm Celeste Steinsen and this is my brother, Collin. Bri told us that Owen was your brother. We are very sorry for your loss."

"Thank you, Dear. How did you know my dear brother?"

"He was handling a land matter for us."

"I see. I take it since you are staying with Bri that you are not from here?"

"No, we're from Cincinnati. What about you?"

"Well, I currently live in Yountville, California."

"That is a beautiful area. We go there when visiting the Napa Region looking at the vineyards."

"Of course. I have a small vineyard there. My fourth husband, Dear Man, loved it so much. He taught me about vineyards. I fell in love with their beauty."

Collin spoke, "The reason that Celeste and I sought Owen's assistance is because we have inherited our grandfather's farm here. We won't bore you with the particulars, but we planned to build a couple of homes there and start a winery. We've been researching the topic, and from what we have learned, this area is conducive to raising nice grapes."

"Well, of course you should pursue that dream, Love. I made the decision last night that I am going to move back to Bekbourg. When I return here, let's plan to meet, and I can put you in touch with the wonderful people who work at my vineyard. They are very knowledgeable. They will be happy to assist."

"That is very generous of you."

"Think nothing of it. We'll plan on it. Now, if you will excuse me. I need to go see if Martha needs anything. She loved my brother. This has been very hard on her. Ta Ta, Loves."

Collin turned to Celeste, "We need to decide whether we are going to accept Harvey's offer. If we accept it, the scope of the winery we were planning will be drastically curtailed. The twenty acres may be too small."

"I know. Maybe we should accept his offer, because the part of the property he is proposing that we keep is a beautiful place for our haciendas, and there would be room to start our vineyard. If we determine we want to expand, we could look around Bekbourg for more acreage."

"I like that idea. Martha said that she is arranging a new counsel for us. We'll talk to him or her and get their feedback."

A short time later, Boone Carter walked up to Celeste and Collin and introduced himself. "Martha, Owen's secretary, pointed you out to me. She told me a little about the case Owen was handling for you. If you are interested in talking to me about it, I'd like to discuss the case."

Celeste and Collin both agreed, "Of course. We'd like to meet as soon as possible, because we need to return to Cincinnati."

"What about tomorrow morning?"

"That would be great." They set a time, and he told them where his office was.

Drew felt Martha was in capable hands with Milton, so he excused himself to get something to drink. He saw Kye sitting at one of the tables. He walked over and asked if she wanted something to eat or drink. "Dear, if they still have some of that delicious lemonade, I'd like that."

A few minutes later, Drew returned with lemonades for both of them. "You doing okay, Kye?"

"Yes, Dear. There's a lot of people here. I'm sad of course about Owen, but it's comforting to see so many people celebrating his life."

"Well, that's what both Martha and his sister, Dillie, wanted: a celebration. They felt he had accomplished a lot during his life and did a lot of good for people."

"I agree with all of that."

"Kye, it's probably not a good time to mention this, but I know how important that property is to you. Martha was going to call you, but we think Boone Carter is who Owen would want his legal clients to go to. He had a lot of respect for Boone, and Martha said that if he couldn't take a case for some reason, he would recommend Boone."

"I know Boone. He was one of my students. I'll call him tomorrow. Harvey Bennett made an offer to pay me for my property. Owen didn't want me to accept it just yet because of something he was working on. Now, with what's happened, I may just accept his offer."

"Don't do anything before you talk to Boone. There may be something in the file. Give him a chance to familiarize himself with your case, Kye, before you do anything."

"That's good advice, Drew. I'm just so unsure about what to do. I'll talk to Boone before I do anything. What about you, Drew? You gave up that good job in Columbus to come here and join Owen. You must feel unsure about your situation."

Drew sighed, "It's been a difficult time for us dealing with Owen's death, but Martha and I are trying to stay on top of the priority matters. She's already talked to some clients to get them to Boone to take care of things where there were deadlines. I've only been working on Mary Zimmstein's foundation's work. Once I took the CPA, Owen was going to get me involved in his tax work. I don't know how that's going to work, but I'm not going to worry about it right now. I'm getting ready to start my final two weeks all-in study for the CPA, and then once the test is over, I'll see what happens."

"Well, Owen had a lot of CPA business. I know the work is going to be there. It will all work out."

"Yes, it will."

Throughout the evening, Sean observed the people coming and going. One person, in particular, spurred his interest. When Charlotte Mooney entered, she looked around. Kathy Isaac, one of the clerks for the county, walked up to her and said something. Charlotte nodded but kept looking around the room. Kathy talked to her a couple more minutes, but Charlotte seemed distracted. Finally, Kathy told her that she was leaving. Charlotte then walked toward Martha and waited in line to speak with her and Dillie. Dillie gave her a big hug—like she had known her forever, and then Charlotte said something to Martha. They talked for a brief time. When she stepped away, she turned and saw Sean looking at her and quickly turned back. She left soon afterwards.

Sean needed to get back to the station, but Cheryl stayed along with several other people to help clean up and put things away. Dillie thought Owen would have been delighted with the wake. Many people attended and shared memorable stories of how he had helped them over the years. Jennifer Fischner paid tribute for his generous donations each year at the Garden Club gala. Cheryl walked with Kye and Martha to Martha's home where Kye was going to visit a while longer with Martha. Buddy greeted Cheryl with his usual exuberance when she returned home.

Sean left Owen's wake early to meet with his team to evaluate where the investigation stood. Other than Cooper, they didn't know if any of the persons of interest had a 9mm gun. Syd had checked and learned that Nickolas had refinanced his home a number of times and had a low credit score. Nelson Predit's fracking business was treading water. Nothing indicated that either Pauline or Harvey was experiencing financial difficulties, although Sean wondered just how overextended Harvey might be with the upfront expenses for the Lake Meadows development. Nelson had been unwilling to provide an alibi but said he had one. Cooper and the other four had not provided an alibi. Witnesses had seen Pauline in the area but couldn't pin down the precise time frame. Other than the one he served on Cooper, Sean didn't believe there was sufficient evidence to currently justify a warrant against any of the four. He asked Syd and Alex to double down on their efforts and provided a list of additional avenues to pursue. He also told them that they might need to widen their investigation beyond the five they were focused on.

Cheryl and Sean took Buddy for a walk. After they got to the park, Sean removed the leash, and they laughed watching Buddy bound after the tennis ball. Buddy never tired of his fetch game. He would bring the ball back and drop it at Sean's feet to be thrown again. After throwing another ball, Sean said, "Mike told me something that surprised me. He and Geri have decided to move to Montana."

"Whaaaat?"

"Yeah, that was my reaction. I've thought about it. You know, I guess it makes sense. Mike was the sheriff, and now he's not. I know that people probably associate him with Jeff. It has to be an uncomfortable thing for him and Geri. She's tried to get back out there, working for Mary's foundation, but Mike never really has. Of course, he's been recovering from nearly dying, but when he could have started doing something, I don't think he wanted to. He told me he's going to try to get on with the state at a park, or maybe a security guard somewhere."

"Well, I guess I understand their decision. They'll also be closer to their children, and that's important to both of them. I'm going to miss them."

"Yeah, me, too."

Cheryl said, "Hon, Drew mentioned something at the wake. He said that Owen was working on something. He wasn't sure what it was, but apparently it was significant. When Owen brought me a copy of the lawsuits that he filed, he said something like there was more to come, but I didn't think much about it until tonight."

"Any idea what it could be?"

"No, but do you think whatever it was, that was why he was killed?"

"I don't know. He was working on some other cases, but Owen also had a knack of getting under people's skin. It could have been personal. I don't want to prejudge anything. I can't afford to. I need to be objective."

"You're right. I just can't shake the feeling that this property tax case somehow has something to do with it."

"Were you surprised to see Milton tonight?"

"Oh, my gosh! I was thrilled. I know he and Owen had mutual professional respect for each other, but they were friends, too. I was glad he was there."

"Ready to take Buddy back home?"

"Sure thing, Sheriff."

Chapter 36

A few days earlier, Cheryl had received a call from Mattie Trotter, asking if she and her husband, Seth, could meet with her. They were the owners of the *Bekbourg Tribune*, which had been in their family for generations. Cheryl had been buzzing with a mixture of apprehension and excitement since that meeting. Neither of their sons wanted to return to Bekbourg to run the paper. They had been impressed with her reporting and professionalism. They wanted to sell the newspaper and retire, but they didn't want to sell it to someone who would use it as a political arm or kowtow to pressures. They assured her the transition would go at her pace, "We can do this over time and work with you on the financing. We can move out slowly or more quickly. We have a dedicated group of employees, Cheryl, and they will be happy that someone like you will take the reins. We are convinced this is a good move for the paper and for Bekbourg."

Cheryl was enthusiastic about possibly taking ownership of the *Tribune*, but it was also unsettling. It was a huge step from being a reporter to running a newspaper. She had talked to Sean about it, and he was supportive. He told her he didn't think there was anyone more qualified in Bekbourg. "Also, Honey, you've gained the confidence of people here. You have a steady following. You are a quick learner. I have no doubt you can get up to speed on the business aspects, and you'll have good people working there to rely on."

She picked up Milton and grinned to herself when they walked into Frau's Diner. He looked around, "My kind of place."

"I knew you would love this. Let's order."

He ordered the Railroader's Special—a large plate of bacon, sausage, eggs, toast and hash browns, with a side of Goetta.

"So, what's up? You said you had something you wanted to talk with me about."

When she told him about the opportunity with the *Tribune*, he sat back and gave a low whistle. He looked at Cheryl, "This is big. What are you thinking?"

"Several things are going through my mind. One is that I'd have to leave *The Presenter*. I love the people there. Keith has been so wonderful; so has everyone else. It's a great paper, but this could be such a great move for me. It's something that excites me. It seems like a wonderful opportunity. But, wow, it sure would take me out of my comfort zone. I don't know anything about running a business. I don't know what to do. Do you have any thoughts?"

"What do you know about their sales?"

"I asked them about that. I'll need to do a due diligence review, but I've been impressed with what I've seen. They have made it a priority to work with the local businesses and other institutions here, like the schools, hospital, churches and other community organizations. They told me that their circulation is solid and they have the support of the community through advertisements. It appears to be in a better condition than other small town papers."

Milton looked at her with those shrewd eyes. "Put aside your worry about not having the experience. Is this something you want to do?"

Cheryl took a sip of coffee. She looked at Milton. Her eyes sparkled, "I would love it, Milton. Oh my gosh, it's beyond a dream."

Milton nodded, "Then plow ahead."

"Really? You think I can do it?"

"No doubt, Cheryl. Listen, if you're interested, here's the thing. I've mentioned it to Keith, but I'm planning to retire at the end of the summer from *The Presenter*. It's time for me to do something new. I have no ties to Cleveland. What little I've seen of Bekbourg, I like it. You haven't asked, but if you want my help, I'll be glad to help."

Cheryl jumped up and went over and bent down and hugged him. Milton blushed. She returned to her seat. "Oh Milton, this is too good to be true. You really would move here?"

He grinned, "Yep. One thing, it's your business, but if you decide this is something you are serious about pursuing, you ought to tell Keith. If it doesn't happen, he'll be fine with that, but I think you ought to tell him."

"That's right. I don't want him hearing from anyone else. I owe it to him to let him know."

Milton said, "Now, let's talk about what needs to be done. You need an outside CPA to review the records. You also need to hire an attorney to handle your side of the transaction."

"That's all true, but I've also got to think about the financing side. They told me they would work with me, but that's still a huge hurdle."

"Cheryl, I have money. I can help finance this. We can talk about the best way to proceed after you talk to the Trotters, but I could buy a minority share to give you funds or even loan you money. Don't let that be a concern to you."

Cheryl was dumbfounded, "I don't know what to say, Milton. That is very generous."

"Look Cheryl. I never had kids. You are the closet I've ever had to a daughter. I want to help you. I can even be a reporter or editor or whatever if you need me."

Cheryl was overwhelmed with excitement and gratitude. "Milton, you've made the decision easy for me. I'm going to tell Seth and Mattie that I'm ready to move the ball forward."

The rest of the breakfast was energized, talking about everything that needed to be done.

Celeste and Collin sat in the conference room in the Boone Carter law office, "Thank you for meeting with us this morning."

"I'm glad it worked out. I'm trying to meet with Owen's clients as soon as I can. I know in addition to his death, they must be anxious about their legal matters. Now, what can I do for you?"

Celeste and Collin thoroughly described the situation. They also mentioned that Owen had them talk to Cheryl about their property matter. "You probably saw her article."

"Yes, I read it. I fully understand why Owen filed the lawsuits. I'm going to look into the matter further. I'll get up to speed and give you a call."

Celeste said, "We told Owen that we wanted every stone turned over. We wanted our grandfather's farm. However, Harvey Bennett made us an offer. We haven't responded to him, because Owen told us that he had learned something that might be a game changer in our favor. We've held off responding to Harvey, but we've been giving his offer serious consideration. We are thinking about accepting it."

Collin said, "Harvey called us after Owen died and pressed us to respond to his offer. We recognized his ploy for what it was—he knew our lawyer had died and thought we might feel insecure about our case. We're on to games like that, and we won't let his tactics influence our decision. If we think we should accept the offer, we will."

Boone advised, "Owen wasn't one to play games. He took his clients' interests very serious. I don't want you to do something prematurely. Let me go through his files and get up to speed. I'll be in a better position to advise you on whether to accept his settlement proposal."

"Fair enough."

"Kye, was that Harvey Bennett I saw here earlier?"

Cheryl and Kye were sitting on the duplex's front porch.

"Yes. He came by to see if I had thought about his settlement proposal."

"What did you tell him?"

"I told him that I had. That I thought his offer was fair, and I was probably going to accept it, but I wanted to talk to Boone about it first."

"What did he say?"

"He understood that I would want to talk to my new attorney, but he hoped that I would accept it. I called Boone and told him that I wanted to accept the offer. I asked him to call Harvey and tell him. What am I going to do with that property, even if we win the case? Harvey said he would name the park and the main road in Lake Meadows after Cecil. His family will have a lasting legacy on his family's homestead."

"What did Boone say?"

"He knew that Owen was looking into something that would help our case. He asked if he could look into that before he makes that call. I told him okay, but I've made up my mind."

Sean had decided to wait until after Owen's wake to stop by and talk with Martha. He called, and she told him that she was leaving the office a little early today. She asked if he would mind coming to her home.

"Hi, Sean. Please come in. I've got some coffee. Would you like some?"

"If it's not too much trouble."

"Not at all. Please have a seat. How do you take it?"

"Black."

Skip came up to Sean and sniffed. Sean reached down and petted his head, "Hey, Boy."

Sean had never seen a dog tail like Skip's. It was bent about half-way, forming an "L." It was unusual watching Skip wag it. He turned and waddled over to a large, cushioned dog bed and plopped down.

"Here you go, Sheriff."

"Has that dog's tail always been like that?"

She smiled, "Yes. When Owen got him as a puppy, it was like that. I think that's one of the reasons Owen chose him."

Martha lived in a small house about a mile from the law office, whereas Owen's house was just two doors down from the law office. Sean suspected her furniture was from the 70's. There was a slip-cover on the sofa, and the floral pattern on the two upholstered chairs was worn. An oak magazine rack filled with several magazines sat beside a rocking chair, and a book was lying on a small table beside the rocking chair. She had numerous what-nots in an oak curio cabinet, and white dollies were on all the small end tables. Pictures of her grown children and grandchildren were sitting on the mantel. The home was comfortable, clean and neat, just like he had found her area in the office.

She sat down in the rocking chair.

"You doing okay, Martha?"

"Yes, as well as can be expected. It's been a terrible shock, but there was a lot to do to get ready for the wake. Owen's sister, whom you met, was a big help."

"There were a lot of people at the wake."

"Yes, many of his past and present clients."

"I also saw the judge there and even Harvey Bennett."

"Yes," said Martha. "You know that was the first time I met Mr. Bennett. Owen referred to him as a 'bag of wind,' always trying to promote himself. It's funny. Owen went up in front of Judge Bergmann a lot over the years, and he usually gave Owen a hard time in court, but other than Owen calling him a 'SOB,' he never had much bad to say about him."

They both laughed.

"All three county commissioners were there—even though he has given them fits over the years. I saw Pauline Kaufmann there, too."

"Yes, that was nice that they came." She took a sip of coffee and continued, "Pauline was gracious. She told me that she knew that she and Owen had a combative history, but she knew he was dedicated to his causes."

"Whose idea was it to put those coolers in the back room of the church?" Sean asked grinning.

Martha laughed, "You saw those, huh?"

"Couldn't miss the trail of people making their way back there and coming out with plastic cups."

They both were laughing. "Well, that was Dillie's idea. She said Owen would have loved the idea, that he loved a good drink, and I agreed. Dillie hadn't been back to Bekbourg since she left for college a long time ago, but Owen visited her about every five or so years. He really liked it when she lived in California."

Sean asked, "What about the other county people? What did he think about them?"

"Well, he sure didn't care for Commissioner Garrison. He didn't trust him and thought he was out to 'pad his pockets,' as Owen put it. He really didn't mention the other two Commissioners much. Now, he didn't care at all for Jeff or Randall Thompson. As far as the people who worked at the county in the property division, he didn't have nice things to say about Pauline or Joanne. He thought Ida did a good job as Clerk of Court and Opal as the Recorder. One thing that surprised me was that Charlotte Mooney seemed upset about Owen's passing. I know she was on the receiving end of some of Owen's tirades. He gave those clerks, Kathy and Charlotte, a hard time, but he never said anything much bad about them. I think he felt they were just doing what they were told to."

"Do you know why Charlotte would have been upset?" Sean, too, had noticed that Charlotte seemed awkward.

"No, I don't."

"Were you ever able to think of what Owen may have been working on that was special?"

"No."

Sean changed the subject, "How are things going at the office?"

"Drew has been a tremendous help—even though I know he's about ready to take the CPA test. We've had to contact all the clients, and for the active cases, I've had to help the clients find a new attorney. I'm actually glad to have this to do. Helps keep my mind off what's happened."

"I'm sorry about what happened to Owen, Martha. I know he meant a lot to you."

Sean was watching Martha. She looked at Sean, and her eyes filled with tears. "Yes, he did."

They both sat in silence—Sean using the time to sip his coffee.

Finally, Martha said, "How did you find out?"

"I found a couple of things in the bedroom and the bath. It wasn't hard to put it together."

Martha shook her head. She wiped her eyes with a tissue. "I don't think anyone knew. I started work for him about twenty years ago after Tim died. I saw in the paper that he was looking for a secretary, and before Tim and I got married, I had been a secretary. No one could believe that I worked for Owen. You know his reputation. But, I fell in love with him. He didn't have any idea, but after a while, I guess he figured it out. Neither one of us wanted to get married." She laughed. "We were afraid being together all the time might not be good for our relationship. So, we kept living in our own homes and would see each other. I didn't kill him, Sheriff. I loved him, and I miss him so much."

Sean stood up and walked over to her and put his hand on hers. "I hope you understand that I had to ask."

She nodded. He took his cup to the kitchen. Looking toward Skip, "Who's gonna take care of the dog?"

She smiled, "I am. Skip and I are buddies."

Sean smiled and told her that if there was anything he could do, to let him know.

Chapter 37

It was well orchestrated. Commissioner Garrison and Harvey Bennett sat down with a reporter from the *Bekbourg Tribune*. Garrison mostly was quoted. He talked about how Bekbourg had not fallen victim to the rustbelt casualties the way so many other small towns had. He talked about the booming tourism business and credited a large part of its growth to the beautiful Lake Shore development. He explained that Lake Meadows would be an even larger boost to the economy, because it would promote, with its vacation and weekend homes, more people coming into the area, and when they spread the word about how wonderful Bekbourg was, even more people would visit.

> *The leaders of this county are bringing in jobs and opportunities. Our track record is clear. One thing people need to ask themselves, do they want leaders who want to stop the growth in our great county? The Reform Party is against growth and bringing jobs and revenues. If you look closely at what*

Mr. Donaldson's lawsuit is trying to do and those running against us, it's obvious they are just throwing up road blocks to Lake Meadows. We felt bad that people lost their property, but that's what happens if they don't pay the taxes. We followed the law. Nothing improper was done. We're sorry for them, but we can't hold everyone's hands and make sure they are staying on top of their business affairs. Same with that reporter, Ms. Seton's articles. She is just echoing Mr. Donaldson.

Bekbourg went through a difficult time last year when it was discovered that Randall and Jeff Thompson had breached the trust of Bekbourg's citizens and engaged in illegal activities. Those days are behind us, and Bekbourg is moving ahead. This Lake Meadows development is proof of how the leadership here is dedicated to promoting opportunities that make life better for our citizens. We adamantly deny the allegations of Mr. Donaldson's lawsuits. We have always been committed to fairness and transparency in the way our government works, and we are setting up a committee to study what it would take from a technology and monetary standpoint to computerize our property records. Once that report is prepared, we will share with our fine residents the recommendations of the committee. We can't let these nay-sayers stop progress. We've avoided the economic disasters felt by many Ohio small towns because we've had forward-looking people running the county. The people running on this supposed Reform Party are just using the actions of a couple of people as an excuse to try and take power and bring all progress to a halt. Another thing, the City

> *Council and County Commissioners have always worked together. If those Reform people get on the City Council, they will be at odds with our progress. That stalemate will surely hurt Bekbourg. The negative allegations are going to be found false, but in the meantime while the County fights these ridiculous allegations, we are going to support progress for our county and welcome this new Lake Meadows community.*

Sean called Cheryl to see if she had seen the article. "Yes, I did. What they are doing with the properties of Kye and the Steinsens is not right, Sean. Now, they're trying to justify their actions in the name of progress. I hope Bri and Noel and the others are ready to fight back. The truth is on their side."

"I was afraid you'd be down about all this, but Sweetie, you are a professional. You did your work and put it in the story. That's your job."

"I love you, Sweetie. Thanks for calling me. I'll see you tonight."

"I love you, too."

Cheryl was not surprised that Nickolas was using her story to turn sentiment against the Reform Party. She wanted to see Bri and talk to her. When she walked into the B&B, Bri and Noel were talking. Bri got up and gave Cheryl a hug. Cheryl said, "Guys, I assume you've seen the *Tribune's* article."

Bri said, "I've just made fresh iced tea. Let me get you some."

Cheryl looked at Noel, who did not look happy. "We have worked so hard on this Reform Party ticket and had so much momentum going for us with what all happened last year with the Thompsons. Now, your article has given them just the thing they needed to turn momentum against us. I've already had some calls asking why we are against progress and why we're against the new development. I have to say, this is bad, Cheryl."

Cheryl said, "Noel, the election is not until November. A lot can happen between now and then. Also, this doesn't change the Reform Party's goals. Corruption has been going on a long time, and the leaders here didn't do anything about it. New leadership is needed, and of course the Reform Party supports progress. It just doesn't want laws bent or broken in the process."

Bri walked into the room just as Noel responded, "Yeah, well, that's all good and noble, Cheryl, but what good does all that do for the Reform Party if we lose?"

Cheryl didn't like his inference that she had done something wrong. "You pick up the pieces and go after them next time. I am an investigative reporter. I go where the facts take me, and I report them so that people know the facts. Most times, people don't like what I report, but that's my job, Noel, and I'm going to continue to do it. Nothing I reported was incorrect. The people will decide what they want. Besides, this story is not finished."

"Noel," said Bri, "that's what we need here: someone who brings things to light. That's how the Reform movement got started. Thank goodness for bringing all those terrible things to light last year."

Noel looked at Cheryl and then stood and said, "I need to shove off. I'll see you all later."

Bri handed Cheryl the tea and sat down. "I'm sorry about that, Cheryl. Noel will get over it. We can't give up. We have to stay focused on what we're trying to accomplish in this election. This won't be the only thing that happens during this campaign. We just need to fight back."

Jeff Thompson and Harvey went back to their college days. It was Jeff who brought Harvey to Bekbourg to develop Lake Shore and then Lake Meadows. They were friends and understood each other. Ever since Jeff's death, Harvey was not impressed with what he had seen with the county commission. Nickolas was unpredictable and a hot-head, and Harvey didn't trust him. By happenstance if the scheme to change the mailing addresses was discovered, he wouldn't be the least bit surprised if Nickolas threw Pauline under the bus. Lance Pruitt went along with everything Jeff decided, but he was an unknown with Jeff gone. Harvey doubted that he would automatically bow to Nickolas. He agreed that Nickolas had a good point about the potential for gridlock if the county could no longer control the city.

Harvey needed someone on the commission who he could count on. Riley had been brought in as an interim commissioner by Nickolas and Lance, so he wasn't sure how reliable he would be. Maybe, if Harvey funded Noel's campaign, he would have a friend on the commission. If Noel expressed views favorable to Harvey during the campaign, it might drive a wedge between him and some of the other Reform candidates, weakening their chances of winning. Even if they did win the city council seats, if Noel was working with Harvey, it might not matter, because they may not be able to assert much influence. He wasn't going to tell the others, but he had decided to support Noel—if he could reach an understanding with him.

Harvey invited Noel to join him at the GilHaus for dinner. Their entrees had just been served when Harvey said to Noel, "I haven't decided who I'm going to throw my support behind for County Commissioner."

This surprised Noel, because he assumed that given how tight Harvey had been with the Thompsons and the existing commissioners, he was going to support Riley Barnes.

"No doubt Riley is pro-development and pro-growth, but he is viewed as part of the old guard. Of course, I wouldn't support anyone who isn't in favor of residential and commercial development. I wanted to hear first-hand from you what your views are and what your priorities would be as a Commissioner."

Noel had been concerned about how he could compete against Riley, because he had financial backing from people like Nickolas and Pauline and others. *Heck*, he thought, *if Harvey is willing to throw his support behind me, that would be a huge boost, and it might prompt others to do the same.*

"Well, Harvey, my thinking has always been that there is a right balance, a development like the Lake Meadows development will bring revenues to the county. Of course, I'd be in favor of growth like that. The Lake Shore development has been great for Bekbourg with the newcomers that it brought here as well as the property revenues. Having such a nice golf course is no doubt an asset. So, you don't have to worry about my willingness to support those types of projects as well as other growth initiatives that are beneficial to Bekbourg."

"Good, good to hear. I thought that's probably where you were, but I wanted to hear it from you. Another issue concerns this push to build up the city's power. The county has been successful in bringing jobs and opportunities to Bekbourg. The city and county have been aligned on matters. What we don't need here is gridlock. If the city gets a bunch of radicals who want to over analyze every detail or oppose developments or other business opportunities, that could end up hurting growth around here."

Harvey was closely watching Noel, because Noel has been an outspoken proponent of building the power base of the city council and mayor position. Noel took a bite of his food and looked as his plate while he chewed.

When he looked up, he said, "We're swimming in the same direction, Harvey. I don't want tension or gridlock between the two entities. That's not good for anybody. I think you'll find my position on the campaign trail consistent with yours."

"That's good, Noel. I'm glad. I don't know about others on the Reform ticket, but people on a ticket can have their own positions about what's best for the county, don't you agree?"

"Oh, sure. Not everyone on the same ticket can always see eye-to-eye on everything."

"You and I see things alike, Noel. I'm glad. I'm going to write your campaign a check, and as the campaign goes along, then we'll see where we go with more support."

"That's fair. You won't be disappointed."

Bri called and asked Cheryl if she could stop by the B&B. Cheryl knew instantly when she saw Bri something was wrong.

"Let's sit out back, Cheryl. I've got some fresh lemonade."

"Okay, Bri, I know something's going on. Might as well tell me what it is."

"All the candidates met this morning to talk about what's been going on. Well, Boone wasn't there, because of a prior commitment. It's bad, Cheryl. Noel says he feels we've lost a big part of our supporters. He is meeting with people to try to keep their support, but some have already told him that they just can't support us. Others that we thought we had are now saying they are on the fence. What's crazy is that Noel is even talking about actively supporting Harvey's projects. He thinks we need to come out and say we're not against those. He's talking about balancing competing interests but with a pro-business agenda. He even said that we should say that, since the county looks out for a bigger piece of the pie, that the city council should be amendable to the county's preferences. That will help prevent gridlock. Max told him that he sounded like the other side, but he said that he felt that's what the citizens want. Max told me after everyone left that we could end up having a split on policy issues among people on the Reform ticket."

"Oh," groaned Cheryl. "I thought knowing what the Thompsons did, that their eyes would be open and they would demand accountability by the county officials. What's happened to Celeste, Collin and Kye is not right."

"I haven't told you the rest."

Cheryl looked sharply at Bri, "Oh, what's that?"

"Sally was thinking of dropping out. She never thought running might cause customers to stop coming to her shop, but one woman called and told Sally that she can't come to her shop anymore since she's with the Reform Party. A couple of customers made snide comments. We talked her out of it. We told her that there may be people who take exception to her positions, but we explained that people trust her. They know she will do what she thinks is best for Bekbourg."

"I'm glad you convinced her to stay in. She will be a good city council member."

"Noel received a couple of nasty letters. Now, those could be from our opponents, but they could be from concerned voters."

"Yeah, I know about the letters. I've received some that say that I'm not from Bekbourg, even though that's not entirely true since I was born here, and that I have no business coming down from a big city and trying to hurt our town. They tell me to go back to Cleveland. As a reporter, I'm used to letters like that, but I sure don't want my friends to receive them. How about you, Bri? Are you getting any pushback?"

"No, but my business is mostly tourists, not like Sally's and Noel's."

"What about Max? Has he been the target of any of this backlash?"

"Well, if he has, he hasn't said anything. We are hoping it dies down. The campaign is still in the early stages. We are all thinking about how to fight back. We'll see how it goes."

That evening, Cheryl was sitting on the porch brushing Buddy when Sean got home. Buddy jumped off the porch and ran to him. Sean walked up and sat down beside Cheryl and could see that she was distracted. He reached over and took her hand, "Tell me what's going on. I can see something's wrong."

"I talked to Bri today. She said that people have called Noel telling him that they were withdrawing their support, and others are thinking about whether to continue to support their campaign. They talked Sally out of dropping out. Some of her customers were threatening to stop coming to her shop. Nickolas' interview with the *Tribune* really spooked people into believing that the Reform Party is for stopping growth, which will hurt jobs and development. A couple more letters arrived today telling me that I should go back to Cleveland, that I don't know what's best for Bekbourg. That I don't belong here."

Sean got up and pulled Cheryl into his arms. "Babe, none of that is true. You can't let that stuff get to you." He lightly kissed her and said, "Honey, I don't like to see you down like this. Let's take Buddy for a walk."

Chapter 38

The next day, a team of state auditors showed up at the Bekbourg County offices. They wanted to interview people and review records. When Sean learned of the state's audit, he figured the state had taken Owen's complaint seriously because of Bekbourg's past history.

It didn't take long for word to reach the *Bekbourg Tribune*. Its morning headline was, *State Auditors at County Offices.* The article explained how the state auditors were auditing the County Treasurer, Auditor and Recorder's offices. The article discussed how Owen had filed a complaint with the state. None of the county officials would comment.

Alex and Syd interviewed all the women in the county offices and continued to work the case, but there wasn't conclusive evidence pointing to any one suspect.

The Investigation into Leo's death was still on the front burner, but Owen's murder investigation had derailed those efforts. Sean had intended to talk with Faith Powell before now, but that had not been possible. Syd and Alex were continuing their investigation, so now was a good time to make the trip to Akron. Judge Bergmann had a motive for wanting Leo dead. Sean hoped that Faith might have some answers.

After Sean left that morning for Akron, Cheryl was sitting on their porch when her phone rang. No one said anything. She repeated, "Hello" a little louder. When no one answered, she thought it was one of the callers who had been giving her a hard time about her news story. She started to hang up when she heard a woman say, "Ms. Seton?"

"Yes, this is she."

There was a light cough. "Umm."

"Can I help you?"

"Ms. Seton. I'm afraid, but I just can't let this go on. I don't know who I can trust, except you. I read your article. I know you believed Mr. Donaldson."

Cheryl wasn't sure if this was a prank, but the caller's voice seemed strained, and she was taking deep breaths as she stammered through.

"I do believe that Owen was on to something. Is there something that you know about the story?"

"Ummm. I've got something, but I am so scared. I'm scared to not do anything, but I'm scared to do something. If I help you, can you guarantee me that you won't use my name?"

"Yes, I will not disclose you as a source. I can promise that."

"Mr. Donaldson was killed. I don't want that to happen to me."

"I don't want you to be afraid. Would you like for us to meet?"

"Yes, but it can't be where anyone would see us together. I know this is a long way, but there is a small café on the road to Athens about twenty miles from here. It's in a strip center. It's kinda loud, but I don't want anyone to overhear what I have to say."

"That sounds fine." They planned to meet that evening. Sean was in Akron, so she left a note on the kitchen counter. She didn't think this was some kind of set up, but she told Kye that she was going to a meeting and that if she wasn't back by midnight, to call Sean and tell him she had left a message on the kitchen counter. He was driving back from Akron and would be late returning. Kye was worried, but Cheryl told her she thought things would be fine, but it was a practice she had used for meetings when she had a question about the source.

Faith Powell had moved to Akron, Ohio, when she left Bekbourg nearly twenty-seven years ago. "Come in, Sheriff. Please have a seat. Can I get you something to drink?"

"No, thank you." Sean looked around the living room. It was nicely decorated with light beige walls and furniture made of brass and glass. Sitting on a table were some family photographs.

Faith was a slender woman—her hair cut short close to her head. She wore beige slacks and a short sleeve cotton sweater. She had an air of confidence and professionalism.

"I was surprised you want to talk with me. I've been gone for years. You've driven a long way. I don't know how I can be of help."

"Ms. Powell, I am investigating a death that occurred a little over twenty years ago. The victim was Leo Davis."

"I didn't live there then. I don't remember the man."

"I understand that you worked for the Bergmann family." Faith's eyes widened. "What did you do for them?"

"For the Bergmanns? I managed all the household's finances and took care of hiring any staff needed for the household."

"Did you work from their house?"

"Yes, I had an office at the back of the house."

"How long did you work for them?"

"About four years."

"Why did you leave?"

"To come here."

"Did you have a job when you left?"

Faith blinked, "No, but I wasn't worried about finding one. I had good experience in bookkeeping."

"When did you start work here?"

She didn't answer.

"Ms. Powell, let me answer the question for you. You didn't start work for about a year after you moved here. I checked the property records. You paid cash for this place soon after you moved here. There was a reference in Judge Bergmann's check book ledger for a generous monthly payment.

Those were still going on two years after you moved from Bekbourg."

Faith paled. "I don't know a Leo Davis. I don't know how any of this relates to my employment for the Bergmanns."

Sean had done his research. The young man in many of the photographs was her son, born six months after she moved to Akron. Sean noticed the similarity between the young man and Pierce Bergmann. It hadn't taken much imagination to put two-and-two together.

"He's a fine-looking young man."

Her voice caught, "Yes, he is."

"Faith, what were the monthly payments for?"

She took a deep breath, "Pierce didn't want anyone to know. He promised me he would generously support the baby and help me get a job. He knew someone here in a large tire manufacturing company. I didn't want to be an unwed mother in Bekbourg. So I took the payments. He kept his word. He paid for all of Cory's expenses, all through law school."

"Does Cory know?"

"Not who his father is. He hasn't pushed me on his identity."

"When was the last time you spoke to Judge Bergmann?"

"We had no contact after I left Bekbourg other than me telling him where to mail the checks. I called him when Cory was admitted into OSU, because I needed more money for his tuition. I also called him when he was admitted into law school.

He didn't ask anything about Cory. He wanted to get off the phone both times, but he told me he would send the money for the school expenses. The monthly checks were never late, and he paid all his school expenses."

"He never saw Cory or talked to him or asked about him?"

"No."

Cheryl arrived at the restaurant about thirty minutes early and parked off to the side where she could watch people. About five minutes 'til seven o'clock, an older model Pontiac pulled up close to the entrance door. For a couple of minutes, the person sat in the car. She slowly opened the door and moved to get out but was looking around. She had a large envelope in her hand. When she didn't see anyone, she got out of her car and walked into the restaurant. Cheryl knew the woman. It was Charlotte Mooney.

Cheryl looked around the parking lot one more time, exited her car and walked into the restaurant. There were mostly teenagers and young families. It was noisy. She saw Charlotte sitting in a booth looking her way, clearly anxious.

Once Cheryl sat down, the waitress took their drink orders and dropped off the dinner menus. "I'm too nervous to eat."

"That's okay. We'll just order something to drink."

"Okay."

"Charlotte, tell me what this is all about."

She was nervously twisting the napkin the waitress had laid down for the Coke she had ordered. "Did Owen tell you anything about me?"

"What do you mean?"

She looked around the room as if thinking someone might be there watching her. The waitress walked up with the drinks, and Charlotte jerked as if she'd been startled. The waitress looked at her and gave her another napkin and set the Coke on it. Cheryl had also ordered a Coke.

After the waitress walked away, Charlotte said, "I called Mr. Donaldson. I told him I had some information that might help him. At first, he thought it was a trick, but we met here. I told him what it was about. I didn't want him to use my name. I didn't have the documents with me, but after he heard what I had to say, he told me I needed to get that information to him.

"We were going to meet here again, but he died the day before we were supposed to meet. I was going to give him the copies," she said nodding to the envelope lying beside her in the booth. "I went to him, because I was afraid that I would be the scapegoat for what they have been doing. I am even more afraid of that now with the state auditors looking at things. I overhead Pauline telling one of the state investigators that she was just there part-time and couldn't possibly know everything that goes on there. I am so scared. I think Mr. Donaldson may have been killed because of his lawsuits, and that I'm going to be implicated in what they have been doing."

"Why did you contact me?"

"I don't know who else to trust. If the information that I have gets out there, maybe it will stop them from blaming me. I don't know, but I can't just sit back anymore. I'm becoming a nervous wreck."

"Okay. Why don't you tell me what you told Owen?"

She looked at the documents. "Those tell the story."

"Okay, let's start with those materials. What are they?"

"When they were doing the Lake Shore project, they took public funds out of different accounts over about a three year period and used them to build the golf course and roads and improvements."

Cheryl looked at her, "Who did this?"

"Well, Jeff Thompson and Nickolas Garrison were involved, and Pauline is the one who wrote the checks and handled the book-keeping for all this."

"Tell me how this worked."

"Well, I know that there is no way that the Bekbourg County funds were supposed to be used to build that golf course. It was a private course. Only people with a membership can play there—unless they are a guest. That entire development was built by Bekbourg Enterprises. We have to divide our county budget into individual accounts to show how the money is going to be spent. For example, we have a 'road repairs' account. There are many other accounts, such as 'drainage,' 'bridge repairs.' There are also service items, like 'waste collection,' 'sewage service,' 'water service.' During this three year period, Pauline told us that the Commission approved a budget increase in several of those categories, especially related to road and construction accounts. You will see from these copies that they are about three times more than they were for the year before and the year after the three-year period. There is no way that much money was spent around the county, and it wasn't. What happened, and it's all here in these papers, is that checks were written supposedly for these items, but some of the payments went to Commissioner Garrison's company. They never did our county's road work, but his company built the golf club house. Other payments went to a H.B. Construction. I looked it up. That was Harvey Bennett's company. I can't say for sure, but it may have made the roads in the Lake Shore Development."

"How much public money is it that we are talking about that was used for the development?"

"Around two million dollars."

Cheryl thought to herself, *Two million dollars!*

"How did you get this information?"

"I knew what they were doing wasn't right. I also didn't trust them. I was afraid since I worked there they might try to set me up, so I made copies of everything when Pauline was out of the office. I just made it look like I was doing something that Pauline had asked me to do. The others in the office had no idea what was going on since they didn't work on Treasury matters."

"What about Joanne Fairhurst, did she know?"

"I don't think so. I don't think anyone who works for the county knew except for Pauline and Mr. Garrison and Mr. Thompson."

"I need to show these papers to the Sheriff, but I will keep your name out of this."

"I understand."

When Sean returned home from Akron late that night, Cheryl was sitting at the kitchen table with papers spread in front of her. Buddy was lying beside her and leaped up to greet Sean. Sean looked at her while he rubbed Buddy's head.

"What's all this about? It's almost two o'clock in the morning."

"Honey, the coffee is still hot. I know you must be tired, but you need to hear this."

Cheryl told Sean. She pointed to several of the papers as she explained the details.

"So, Bekbourg Enterprises didn't have to spend money for the improvements for the golf course or club house. This scheme increased its profits. We have never found who the shareholders are to Bekbourg Enterprises, but they would have benefited from this arrangement."

Sean was amazed. "Does all this look authentic?"

"Well, these are copies, but it looks like the originals were authentic. There are invoices that show, for example, $500,000 for pot holes for one year, which is several times more than the year leading up to this. These are copies of the returned checks. They certainly look legitimate. They have the Bank's stamp on the back. The Commissioners approved a larger budget for a three-year period than before or after that. Best I can tell, Sean, these documents support the claim. My source is terrified. I said I would keep the identity confidential, but this person talked to Owen about all this and had planned to give him a copy of the documents, but he was killed before they could meet again. I believe this was the next grenade he was going to throw."

"More like a missile launcher. I need to give these to the state. Did your source think anyone knew that this was being looked into?"

"The person didn't think so but told me that the state is doing the audit. If this comes to light, my source is concerned that they will be made a scapegoat or worse, killed. They are concerned that Owen was killed because of his lawsuits. Owen knew of this before he was killed. Do you think he said something to someone or either they found out, and he was killed because of this?"

"I don't know."

"Well, I made a copy of everything. I figured you would want one. This is my copy. Your copy is in the envelope lying beside the stove. I'm going to talk to Keith and Milton, but I'm going to run a story about this development."

Chapter 39

Nelson Predit was irate. "Have you seen that letter that an attorney from Bekbourg, Boone Carter, sent?"

"What are you talking about?" Nickolas asked.

"A letter, damn it. It was addressed to both of us."

"No, I've not seen it. What does it say?"

"It says that he is representing Mary Zimmstein, the widow of Jeff Thompson. He attached a copy of the property records that shows that Jeff owned a half interest in the property that we are planning to drill. Since Mrs. Zimmstein is now the owner of Jeff's interest, he is demanding that we halt all drilling initiatives until it can be resolved between her and you about how the property will be handled."

"What?" Nickolas bellowed, but before he could say anything else, Nelson interrupted him, "Hold on a minute." Nickolas could hear him talking to someone. "I've got to call you back. I have to take this call," Nelson hung up.

Nickolas went through his inbox and found the letter. He couldn't believe what he was reading. This was disastrous. He didn't have the money to pay Lucchesi, and time was running out.

His phone rang. Nickolas picked up on the first ring. He didn't have a chance to say anything. Nelson's every word sputtered in controlled anger toward the crescendo. "That was my attorney in Columbus. Did you know that Jeff's widow is the granddaughter of Ted Zimmstein?" he demanded.

"What the hell has that got to do with anything?"

"Everything, Nickolas! Everything! Boone Carter filed with the state asking that it stop all reviews of my permit application until the landowner issues are resolved. The regulatory staff is preparing an order for the commission to issue that will do just that!" he yelled and slammed the phone down.

Nickolas felt chest pains as a damp perspiration blanketed his body.

Boone couldn't find anything in Owen's files that he had learned of something that tilted the lawsuits in their favor. He was puzzled, because he knew that Owen wasn't one to lead on his clients. Boone called Kye and the Steinsens to give them the update. Kye wanted to accept Harvey's offer, but the Steinsens wanted to make a counter offer on the price. Boone called Harvey's attorney, Zack Norcross, and told him. Knowing Harvey's wishes, Zack told Boone it was "a go." Boone volunteered to draft the documents, which would finalize the settlement terms and withdraw the litigation, both in the county and at the state.

Chapter 40

Sean had run into a wall in his investigation of Leo's death. Sean never believed that Byron Thornton had been completely forthcoming with him. It was time to pay him another visit and apply some pressure.

Byron reluctantly opened the door.

"I need to talk to you, Thornton. Your lying to me has not helped you. So, I'm giving you one more chance before I decide to arrest you."

The threat of being arrested shook Byron. He opened the screen door and stepped back. Sean followed him into the room. "I don't know what you're talking about. I ain't lied to you." He said as he lit a Camel.

"Well, maybe you just haven't told me everything, and I consider that lying. Now, let's go through what happened. I know that you and Leo were working for Roger Burkhart. You and he went around to pawn shops and collected coins and turned those in to Roger. He'd give you a fee for what you brought him. You didn't want to share that fee did you, Byron? You knew that Leo was planning to leave town. You killed him for his share. You knew about the old tobacco barn at the back of the property. You knew about the car. You put him in there and left him." Sean's voice grew more forceful and clipped, "Did you find something more valuable in your collection from the pawn shops? Was it more than just his cut from Roger? Did Leo catch you skimming and threaten to tell Roger? Was it wanting Leo's share or did you kill him to keep him quiet? Or was it for both reasons? Why was it, Thornton? Why did you kill Leo?" Sean was yelling.

Sweat was beading across Byron's forehead and running down the sides of his face. He shouted, "That's bullshit! I didn't kill Leo! No freaking way!"

Byron's gun was not registered, so Sean didn't know the make, but that didn't stop him. Sean lowered his voice and looked hard at Byron, leaning toward him, "After you shot him, you got rid of the weapon. That's why you don't have it. You got rid of the evidence, or maybe with a search warrant, I'll find it here. Which is it Byron? Did you get rid of it or is it hidden here?" Sean was shouting again. "Answer me!"

"Why are you looking at me?" Byron was yelling. "Ask that judge. He's the one that gave Leo money to leave town." Sean wasn't sure he meant to let this slip, but now Sean had something.

"What are you talking about, Thornton?"

Byron took a deep breath and picked up a beer and took a long drink. He wiped the sweat from his face. He took a long draw on his Camel. He was agitated. "Leo had been seeing his daughter. I came up there that night because I knew he and Sophia were planning to leave to go to Texas. I wanted to say bye to him. We had been friends for a long time. I never thought Leo would ever fall for a woman, but he fell for her. Her dad was raising hell with her about seeing Leo. They knew they would never have any peace, so they decided to leave. Leo was bragging that the judge had tried to bribe him. He'd called Leo to meet him that night at his chambers. Leo was laughing.

"He took the money, but he was still planning for him and Sophia to leave together. He said that the money was a nice nest egg for him and Sophia to start out with. The joke was on that arrogant SOB. Leo was mocking the way the judge talked, saying that the judge said that he knew about Leo and his daughter and that he was not going to allow it. He told Leo that he could do things the easy way or the hard way. He would give Leo $10,000 to pack up and leave Bekbourg for good, or the hard way. He even called Leo a pretty boy and said that he wouldn't like being in prison. Leo was supposed to leave town that night with the money or start a new day behind bars."

"You're lying, Byron." Sean believed him, but needed to see if he revealed more information.

"I'm tellin' the truth, man! There was a brown envelope layin' on his things. When Leo told me about the money, he pointed to the envelope. I don't know why he would have lied to me about it."

Sean asked, "Do you know if Sophia knew that her father tried to bribe Leo?"

"I don't see how. It happened the same night that they were supposed to leave, but she might have. I don't know."

"What else, Byron, aren't you telling me?"

"That's it, man. That's all I know. I didn't kill Leo."

The judge had paid Faith to leave town and now it looked like he had done the same with Leo. He wondered if the judge was willing to murder to get his way.

Pierce Bergmann was of medium height with a long, thin neck and a barrel chest. His thinning gray hair parted on the side. He was always clean shaven, but the most pronounced feature was his dark, cold eyes. When Sean entered his chambers, Pierce was leaning back in his leather chair, "Have a seat, Sheriff."

"Thank you, Judge. I have some questions about Leo Davis."

"Let's not beat around the bush, Sheriff. What did you come here to ask me this time?"

Sean got straight to the point, "For starters, did you give Leo Davis money to leave town and to stay away from Sophia?"

He looked at Sean, "I'm curious how you found that out, but I guess you won't tell." Sean just looked at the judge. "Yes, I gave him money. No way was I going to let my daughter be conned by a punk like him. My daughter was a young woman who didn't know what she wanted, but he sure was not it. I did what any responsible father would have done."

"What did you tell him?"

"I told him it was a one-time offer, and he was never to show his face around Bekbourg or Sophia again."

"What did he do?"

"He took it—like I knew he would. That's all he was after anyway."

"Did you kill him?"

"I answered that once before, Sheriff. The answer is still the same, no. Yes, I gave him the money. He told me he was leaving. Why would I kill him? I had what I wanted—him leaving town."

"Maybe you found out he planned to double cross you? That he was taking the money and leaving town with Sophia."

The judge would be a great poker play, thought Sean. *No hint at his thoughts*. "Maybe doesn't cut it, Neumann. I had solved the problem. He told me he was leaving that night. I gave him the money. I went home. I just wanted that punk away from Sophia."

"Did you find out that he planned to take the money and leave with Sophia anyway?"

The judge looked hard at him. "No, I never heard that, and I wouldn't have believed it. There was no reason for him to double cross me, and I think he knew better than to try a stunt like that."

"Why's that?"

The judge's eyes drilled into Sean, "Just because."

When he called and told her he needed to talk to her, Sophia had asked that Sean arrive around two o'clock. She looked stunning as always but had lost weight, and the makeup lost its battle against the dark circles beneath her eyes. She was gracious but edgy. She tried to appear in control, but both hands were trembling. She suggested they walk to a pond a good distance from the house. She put her arm through Sean's to steady herself. As they walked on the path of mulch, she avoided conversation by reminiscing about how she and Michelle many mornings would walk this same path. She would sit on the bench and watch Michelle throw rocks in the water. On their way back, they picked flowers to put in vases for the sun room and dining room to be enjoyed during dinner.

When they reached the water, Sean understood why this was a treasured place. The large pond was surrounded by wild flowers and then beyond, large trees. Only the chirping of the birds or insects or the frogs' croaking would break the silence. Sean followed Sophia's lead and sat on the bench.

"Sophia, I talked to your dad yesterday."

"Mmmm," her attention was off in a distance.

"Did you know he gave Leo money to leave town?"

She looked surprised, but something else—pained. "Leo took the money?"

"Did you know that your dad tried to bribe Leo to leave?"

Sophia was now looking at her hands, "No, I didn't know for sure, but when Leo didn't come that night, I thought it might have been something like that." She looked at Sean, her eyes clear, but her movements lethargic. "When I read that Leo's body had been found, I actually thought Dad had killed him."

"Did you say something to your dad?"

"Yes, I rushed over there and accused him of killing Leo."

"What did he say?"

"He denied it."

"What can you tell me about you and Leo?"

She was quiet. Sean gave her time. Then, tears began streaming down her face, "We were in love. It was July Fourth. We thought it being a night of celebration was a perfect night for us to start our new life." Sean watched as Sophia returned in her mind to July 4, 1980. "We were planning to elope that night. I was supposed to watch for him outside my bedroom window and slip out of the house when I saw him flash a light. I had a small bag sitting by my feet.

"As it grew late, I remember growing more anxious. I also knew that Dad was still out, and I was afraid when he came home, he might run into Leo. Finally, Dad pulled in and came into the house. My bedroom light was off, so I'm sure he thought I was asleep. I thought that now things would be okay, Leo wouldn't run into Dad. I'd just have to be quiet when I slipped from the house."

She paused, the pain showing in her eyes. Her voice dropped to almost a whisper, "I sat there all night, and he never showed up. He didn't call that day. Finally, that afternoon, I grew desperate. I drove up to the house where he and Byron lived. I remembered my heart rose when I saw Leo's truck sitting in the drive. I just knew he was there. I knocked on the door, and finally Byron opened the door. I told him that I wanted to see Leo. He was surprised to see me. He told me that Leo wasn't there. I thought he was lying to me. I told him that Leo's truck was there. He said he didn't know anything about it. He just knew that Leo wasn't there. I pushed past him and rushed through the house. I even looked out the back. I didn't find Leo. I started crying. He finally told me that he thought I should get on with my life. I remember driving away crying so hard I could hardly see.

"Once I got myself pulled together, I went to the only other people who might know something. I knocked on the door, and his uncle came to the door. He was a kind person. He was surprised though that I was asking him about Leo. He told me that Leo had come by the evening before and told them that he was leaving to go to Texas. That's what he thought Leo had done, because he was leaving that day."

"Did Byron tell you that your dad had given Leo money to leave?"

She shook her head no.

"Tell me what was really going on between you and Leo."

Sophia sat for a while, and then looked at Sean. "I think you know, Sean."

"Well, I'd like to hear it from you."

Sophia took a deep breath, "After spring break, Leo had come to visit me every weekend at college. It was a magical time. I was so excited to return for the summer to Bekbourg to be with him. We were so happy. I found out I was pregnant. I was so afraid to tell Leo, but when I finally did, he was happy. I knew, of course, how Dad felt about

Leo, and we both just wanted to start a new life together.

"Leo had some money coming to him for some work he had done. I had a checking account with some money. I waited for about two weeks after he didn't show and knew that I had to do something. Charles had already hinted at us getting married, even though we never seriously dated or anything. I called him and invited him over to dinner at the house. Dad was going to be at some judge's conference in Cincinnati. I seduced him. Then, for the next couple of weeks, we tried to be together alone as much as we could. He mentioned us getting married, and I leaped at the idea. I suggested that we not wait, that we elope. At first, he wanted a large wedding, but I convinced him that we could have a reception after we returned. That's what we did."

"Did he know that Michelle wasn't his?"

"I never told him. I acted like she was premature. He never said anything if he did, and he has been a good father to Michelle."

"What about your dad, did he know?"

"Again, I don't know." She paused, "You know, I have never really loved Charles. He is a good husband and a good father. I tried, Sean, to love him. I tried to be a good wife. I know that I let him down. He wanted me to be like his mother, active in all those social functions, lunches with all his friends' wives, all those things, but I never wanted to. I knew how those women made my mother feel, and their daughters were the same. Of course, I could have easily been accepted, but I chose not to. I just wanted to be a wonderful mother to Michelle—the way my mother had been for me. She was my love, my priority."

"I talked to Byron Thornton. One thing he told me Sophia was that Leo took the money from the judge so that you and he would have some extra money to start a new life. He didn't have plans of leaving without you."

Sean saw her mentally crumble as she folded over sobbing uncontrollable. He moved over and put his arms around her to comfort her. She eventually calmed, and he released her and sat back. She sat up, seeking composure. Her transformation laid bare by swollen red eyes marred by darkened smudges streaking down her cheeks. She pulled a tissue from her pocket and sought to banish the evidence of her collapse. "I'm sorry, Sean. I've held this in so long. I feel like a dam broke inside me. I am so embarrassed."

"Sophia, I have two good friends here in town who work with people on addictions."

She started to protest, but Sean shook his head. "Don't try to deny it to me or yourself, Sophia. I've seen it. Your daughter needs you even though she is away at medical school. Go see your doctor. There are programs you can get in, and once you finish those, I can introduce you to Dusty and Carla."

"Thank you for telling me about Leo not planning to leave me. I needed to hear that. Did you find my necklace when you found Leo?"

"Your necklace?"

"Yes, my mother had given me a necklace on my tenth birthday. I gave it to Leo when we decided to elope."

"No, Sophia, I've not found that." Sean thought he might know what happened to the necklace—Thornton. He also needed to ask Byron about Leo's truck.

She held onto Sean's arm as they walked back to the house. Sophia felt a burden had been lifted from her, but she still carried a lot of sorrow, pain and guilt.

"I understand that Sean Neumann was here again today."

"Please Charles, must we talk about this?"

Sophia was pushing the vegetables around on her plate.

"I find it odd that he's been here twice now. Sean's a busy person. There has to be a reason."

Sophia laid down her fork and looked at Charles. "If you must know, he was here about Leo. He's trying to talk to people who might have known Leo."

"I know you knew him, but why would he need to come here. What's this all about, Sophia?"

Sophia's hand was trembling as she picked up the glass of iced tea for a sip. "He came to ask me if I knew that Dad had given Leo money to leave town."

"What?" He laid down his fork and knife. "Is this for real? Who would be telling such an outrageous lie?"

"No, it's no lie or rumor according to Sean. Dad admitted it to him."

"My God. Surely Sean doesn't suspect your dad of killing Leo?"

"I don't know what he thinks, Charles. He didn't tell me."

Charles noticed that Sophia was trembling all over. "Let's drop the subject. Eat something, Sophia. Blaire prepared the chicken just the way you like it."

"I'm sorry, but I'm not hungry. All this has me upset."

"Sophia, I think you need to see your doctor. Those pills you're taking aren't good for you. You're taking too many." Sophia had a dullness about her. Charles knew that she often slept until noon.

"I'm fine, Charles, really."

Chapter 41

"Gentlemen, I'll show you to your table," Margo said to Judge Bergmann and Charles. "Jan will be right over. Enjoy your lunch."

"How's the banking business?"

"Fine," said Charles. "We're thinking our loan business will pick up with the Lake Meadows development, but with the lawsuits pending, you probably don't want to discuss that."

"Yes, we better not. How are Sophia and Michelle?"

"Well, Michelle is very busy. Sophia doesn't get to talk to her often, but when she does, she tells her mother that she is really enjoying her internship. I know Sophia is hoping Michelle will have time before her classes begin and can come home for a visit."

Jan brought their lunches and refreshed their drinks. After she left, Charles said, "I think it will be good for Sophia if Michelle can get the time off. Sophia has not been herself lately." When Pierce didn't comment, Charles continued, "Sean Neumann's been by the house asking her about Leo Davis. She was upset last night. She said that Sean came by yesterday asking her about you paying Leo to leave town."

"Yes, he came by and asked me about that. I told him that I gave him the money to leave, that I wasn't going to let that con man take advantage of Sophia."

"He sure seems to be learning a lot—especially given that Leo apparently was killed over twenty years ago. Do you know how he heard about you giving him the money?"

"No, I don't. I've been thinking about that. Leo had some relatives that lived here. Well, his uncle is dead, but his aunt still lives here. You've probably seen her name in the news lately, Kye Davis, one of the property owners who are part of Owen's lawsuit. He ran around with that punk, Byron Thornton, so it's possible he told him."

"Well, I don't see how Sean can solve a case that old."

"I wouldn't take that bet, Charles. He proved last year that he shouldn't be underestimated."

Cheryl looked back into the archives of the *Bekbourg Tribune* and found where the *Tribune* had reported the budget amount for the years covering Charlotte's documents. While they didn't cover the individual account items, the budget numbers were consistent. She tried to interview Harvey Bennett and Commissioner Garrison, but they declined to talk to her. Pauline Kaufmann's comment when asked about public funds being used for improvements for the Lake Shore development said, "This is all a lot of nonsense. We have followed the law, and I am confident that everything was done correctly. We are a small county with limited resources, but if the committee that is looking at this recommends that our property records be computerized, I'm sure the Commission will make it a priority to find the funds that will be necessary to implement that." When Cheryl tried to return the topic to the public funds being used in the Lake Shore development, Pauline didn't give any more comments.

The Presenter broke the story, "*Allegation of Public Funds Used for Local Development.*" The *Beckett Tribune* carried the syndicated story. Cheryl reported that there was evidence that suggested public taxpayer money had been used to pay for the private golf course, roads, and infrastructure in the Lake Shore development. As expected, the idea of another county corruption scandal caused an uproar around town. When Noel read the article, he called for a town hall meeting to discuss the latest development.

Pauline called Nickolas's personal phone line. "I'm returning your call."

"My phone is ringing off the hook. That Noel Fischner is demanding a town hall. The state's here looking at our property records. This is a catastrophe."

"I told Harvey it wasn't a good idea to so publicly push back on Owen and that reporter. If we had just let the lawyers handle it and kept a low profile, I don't think the state would be sticking their nose in."

"That's just like you—trying to blame someone. That doesn't help a bit. What is the plan to manage this?"

"Look, there isn't much property on which we changed the addresses. It's too late on Lake Shore, but the issue was never raised there anyway. So, it's just the new project. We handle a lot of property. I can say that mistakes can be made, but the property owner has some responsibility to raise the flag if they didn't get a tax invoice. But, Nickolas, I think it's time to consider a smaller development. I think we need to settle with Kye and the Steinsens without conceding any wrongdoing, and let them have the property back. We would still have one-hundred-seventy acres. We can offer to computerize our property records if it means stopping the state from this audit. We can figure out a smaller development."

"What about that reporter's claim that public funds were used in Lake Shore?"

"I don't know where she got that, but we can't panic. I'll think of something."

Chapter 42

Boone had not finished drafting all the paperwork to finalize the settlements when he read Cheryl's article. He called Kye and the Steinsens and suggested that he call Zack Norcross and tell him the settlements were off the table. He didn't think the lawsuit and complaint at the state should be withdrawn. They agreed.

The killer pulled up in front of Byron Thornton's house and killed the motor. *Thornton has been a loose end for over twenty years. It was time to eliminate that risk.* The killer slipped the gun from the glove compartment. Disappointment surfaced as the killer looked on. No vehicles were in the driveway. No lights were on in the house. No one was there. *I'll be back tomorrow night, Thornton.*

Chapter 43

Jack Rhodes had been the sheriff in Bekbourg for several years before he had retired to Florida a little over ten years ago. Sean had talked to him during his last murder investigation, and Jack's knowledge of the county and many of its citizens had broken the log jam that led to Sean solving the crimes. Now, he again felt his investigation had reached an impasse. He called Jack to see if he could visit him in Florida and pick his brain. Maybe Jack would have some information to unlocking these crimes.

As Sean stood on the front concrete pad waiting for Jack Rhodes to answer the door, he looked around at the other small concrete block homes. All seemed to be closed up until their owners returned in the fall or winter. The heat and humidity in Sebring, Florida, was stifling, and Sean could already feel moisture on his upper body.

Sean was surprised when Jack opened the door. "Come in, Sean. Let's go out back. Grab a beer or water out of the fridge if you want something."

Jack had already turned to head to the small concrete pad off the back of his house overlooking Lake Jackson.

"Wow, Jack. You seem to be getting around a lot better than the last time I saw you." Last year when Sean had seen him, he was in a wheel chair and looked frail. He had put on some weight and looked healthier.

"Yeah, Sean. I don't know what got into me after all that business last year with Thompson, but I went to a doctor. I ended up getting both hips replaced. It was rough at first, but now, I'm using this walker. He thinks I'll be able to get around without it sometime down the road."

"Well, that's great news, Jack. You thinking about doing some fishing again?"

"I sure would like to. Me and my buddies around here talked about it before they left for the summer. Maybe when they get back, I might try to get in one of their boats. We like to sit out on the lake, fish and drink beer."

Sean laughed.

Jack said, "I guess you didn't come all this way, though, to talk about fishing."

"No, but it's good to see you doing well."

Sean told him about finding Leo's body and the coins.

"What can you tell me about Leo and Byron and their dealings with Roger?"

"Well, first, that's something about finding those coins. I always wondered what happened to them. Leo and Byron were punks. They never got into serious trouble, but they were always up to no good as far as I could tell. They'd get in some fights, especially at Knuck's, and I arrested them when they were teenagers for vandalism, stuff like that. Leo was the brighter of the two by a long shot. I always suspected them of stealing things around the area, but I could never prove it. I knew they hung out at Burkhart's pawn shop. I investigated that pawn shop a few times after a theft had been reported, but I never found any evidence there. Burkhart had a smelter in the shop, so you can imagine what happened to anything stolen that was brought in there. I never knew exactly what they did for Roger, besides bringing things in to him. Leo had that place that belonged to his family. Byron lived with him. They both drove old vehicles, so it probably didn't take a lot of money for either of them.

"I guess after Roger died, Thornton's gravy train dried up, because he somehow got a job with the county doing road work. I couldn't believe that he got a job, but he did. I really never paid any attention to Leo being gone. It was just one less punk in the area. There was one thing though that surprised me. Like I said, they never seemed to have a lot of money, but about six months after Roger died, Thornton started driving a brand new Firebird. I pulled him over one evening and asked him about it, how he got it. I ran a license check on it, and it wasn't stolen. He told me that he bought it like any 'respectable, law-abiding citizen' did. I asked him how he knew how a 'respectable, law-abiding citizen' even acted. Anyway, he said he bought it. At first, I thought maybe he had stolen those coins somehow from Roger, but I never saw him with anything else flashy after that."

"Did he ever mention Leo?"

"Not that I'm aware of. Like I said, I never paid much attention to them unless they were causing some kind of problem."

"Did you know that Sophia Bergmann was seeing Leo at the time?"

"No, Sean, I don't remember hearing that."

"What do you think the judge would have thought about her dating Leo?"

"Well, knowing Pierce, I can't imagine he would have approved, but I don't know anything about that."

"What do you remember about Judge Bergmann's wife's death?"

Jack paused. "I hated what happened to Bonnie. She was a beautiful woman and nice to everyone. You know that some of the people could be real snobs there. Some thought she was from the wrong side of the track, growing up so poor. I never thought that about her. I thought she had more class than just about everyone there. There really wasn't much to tell. Her car came around the curve that evening, and she lost control. It's not in any report, but she had been drinking. She was dead before the police and ambulance got there. We didn't want to bring scandal to her or Pierce or their daughter, so she was transported on to the morgue. If what you're getting at is foul play, even though Pierce was a friend of mine, I checked out things. There was nothing other than a tragic accident."

"There's something else that I need to ask you about."

Jack laughed, "You sure stay busy, Sean."

"That's for sure. Owen Donaldson was killed recently. You may remember him. He was looking into some land that was sold through the tax lien process. He felt that maybe there were some shenanigans to make it look like taxes had not been paid, and then the property was foreclosed on. This could be going back twenty-plus years, but there's some more recent property." Sean told him about Bekbourg Enterprises buying Kye's and the Steinsen property at the tax sale as part of four-hundred acres in what looked like a new development project near where the state was considering its new conference center and lodging. He explained the exclusive deals with Pauline and Nickolas. "Any thoughts on any of this, Jack?"

Jack was surprised, "I hate to hear that about Owen. I knew he could be a pain to deal with, but I always thought he was okay. He was super smart. No Sean, I don't know of anything like that, but it wouldn't be surprising, especially since Randall and Jeff Thompson were behind that big land deal where the golf course went in and since they ran the county. So many of those local politicians were hand-picked by those two over the years."

"What can you tell me about Pauline Kaufmann?"

"Pauline. Mmm. She was tenacious, for one thing. She controlled the real estate market there in Bekbourg when I lived there. She was one of Randall's hand-picked politicians. I remember when he chose her to run for the County Treasurer. She was smart, too. I don't know if you know this, but what's interesting is that she and Owen were an item for a while."

Sean was floored, "You've got to be kidding."

Jack chuckled, "Nope. I know. It's like mixing oil and water on steroids. Owen was a black and white type guy. He knew where the line was, and he sure didn't believe in crossing it. Well, Pauline never saw a line that couldn't be moved to fit her real estate deals. They were on opposite sides of a deal, and I don't remember the details if I ever knew them, but Owen stopped Pauline from doing what she wanted to do. It was a big scandal. Not only did it cost her a big commission, but it nearly ruined her reputation. Their relationship died an ugly death after that one."

"That's interesting."

"Now, you mentioned Nickolas Garrison. He and Randall were like two peas in a pod. If there's some monkey business going on, it sure wouldn't surprise me to find Garrison involved. I don't know if this is still the case, but Nickolas used to gamble. Even went to Vegas sometimes. I don't know if that means anything to your investigation, but I thought I might mention it."

"I didn't know that, Jack. Do you know if he got in over his head?"

"No, I don't know about that. I never heard that and never saw any indication that he was."

"What about Harvey Bennett? What do you know about him?"

"Jeff Thompson knew him from college. I remember when he first moved to Bekbourg, but that wasn't too long before I retired. I can't say I know much about him other than he was a big-time developer."

"Thanks, Jack. You've been very helpful. I'm glad to see you doing so well."

"It's great to see you, Sean. I don't miss what you're doing, but Bekbourg is darn lucky to have you. Call me anytime."

After leaving Jack, Sean called his friend with the FBI, Lucky Brennan, and explained the situation. He asked Lucky if he could do a check on Nickolas Garrison.

On his drive back from the Columbus airport, Sean called Alex and told him to bring Byron Thornton in for questioning and described other information he needed.

Byron was not patiently waiting in the interrogation room.

"What do you think you're doin' havin' your jackass deputies draggin' me down here?" Both Alex and Syd were in the interrogation room sitting at one end of the table watching Thornton—who was sitting at the other end. "This is harassment."

Sean sat down right across the table and nodded to the deputies to leave. Byron suddenly got nervous. "Why're they leavin'?"

"You and I are going to have a talk, Thornton. Whether I arrest you within the next few minutes for the murder of Leo Davis is going to depend on your answers. I'm through with your playing games."

Byron seemed to relax and snorted.

"What did you do with Leo's truck?"

That got his attention, "What truck?"

Sean banged his hand down on the table, sending a boom around the room and causing Byron to shudder. "That's strike one, Thornton."

"Okay, okay. Can I smoke?"

"No. Answer the question now!"

"Okay, man. Leo told me that he was goin' to drive him and Sophia to the airport in Cincinnati. They were goin' to fly somewhere from there. That truck was a piece of junk. It ran okay, but it was shit. He told me that he would call me and tell me where he left it—that I could have it if I picked it up. I didn't know if I wanted to go to that trouble, but that's what he said."

"But he didn't do that, did he? It was there. You didn't think to tell me about the truck. How was Leo supposed to have left without his truck? You told me that he was leaving, but the truck was there, Thornton." Sean demanded in a clipped voice.

"Well, I thought maybe they used Sophia's car."

Sean looked incredulous, "She came by the next day. They didn't leave in her car, Byron."

Byron was sweating and was fidgety. "Man, I don't know. I didn't think about it. Leo wasn't there. I didn't know. He had that money the judge had given him. How was I supposed to know? For all I knew, he left town, left Sophia. I didn't know what he did. I even believed Leo might have stolen Burkhart's coins and jumped a freight train to get out of town. That was the night that Roger was killed. I never much thought Leo killed him, because Leo couldn't shoot like shit, but I didn't know what he did. I just knew he wasn't around."

"What happened to the truck?"

Byron looked uncomfortable. "Don't lie to me, Thornton!" shouted Sean.

"Hey, man, I need a smoke."

"Answer the question, Thornton!"

"Okay." Byron was perspiring and finished drinking all the water. "Okay. After Leo didn't come back, I sold it. It wasn't worth much. I figured he had abandoned it."

"When did you move out of Leo's place?"

"I'd been seein' Peggy. I knew Leo didn't own the place. I didn't want his uncle to come up there and threaten me or somethin', so after a couple of weeks or so, I moved in with her."

"What about Leo's truck?"

"I told you, I sold it."

"When?"

"About a half a year or so."

"About six months later? Where was it during all that time?"

"Man, can I have a cigarette?"

"Where was the truck, Byron?" Sean demanded.

Byron was wiping his brow, "I took it and parked it at Peg's. He had told me I could have it. I didn't sell it until I thought for sure he wasn't comin' back. At least give me some more water, man."

Byron watched warily as Sean walked over to the door. He stuck his head out and said something that Byron couldn't make out. Sean closed the door, and in a minute, Syd brought in a water bottle and a file folder. She left, and Sean slid the water bottle toward Byron, who was eyeing the file folder.

"You came into some money around the time that Leo was killed, didn't you Byron?"

"What are you talkin' about?" Byron was rattled.

Sean slammed his hand down so hard on the table that the unopened water bottle tipped over. "That's strike two, Thornton. Let me tell you what happened." Sean was now shouting. "You saw that money lying on the table that the judge had given Leo. Leo had already told people he was leaving, so you saw it as your chance to kill him and take the money. Who would know? That's what you were thinking, wasn't it? So, you'd just hide the body in the trunk of that car for a while. Did you forget to bury it, Thornton, or did you just take the lazy way out and leave it in the trunk?"

"No," he yelled. "I didn't kill Leo!"

"You had a surprise when you found the necklace that Sophia had given Leo. How much did you pawn that for? You knew all the pawn shops around. They didn't ask any questions—did they, Thornton?" Sean was leaning up on the table toward Byron.

"What necklace?" Byron screeched.

Sean's voice could be heard down the hall. "With the money the judge gave Leo and the money from the necklace, you bought that fancy new Firebird, didn't you? Didn't you?" Sean was stabbing to the file folder on the table, which contained a copy of the record from the state's motor vehicle office of Byron owning the Firebird.

Byron now looked like a cornered animal. He was looking between Sean and the file folder. Finally, for the first time ever, Sean felt he had Byron's undivided attention.

"No, you've got it all wrong. There was nothing like that!"

Byron opened the water bottle and took a drink. "After Leo had been gone a week or so, I went into his bedroom and looked around. Leo traveled light. He never had much. Like I told you, he had a duffle the last time I saw him, so there weren't hardly any clothes left. I pulled open a drawer in the chest sittin' next to the bed. There was an envelope. I recognized it, because it looked just like the one Roger had given me for the work we did on gettin' things from the pawn shops for him, those coins and all. He paid us each a fee. Anyhow, I picked it up, and sure enough, it had money in it. I counted it, and it was the same amount that Roger had given me. I never saw the money the judge had given Leo. I only saw the envelope, and I don't know nothin' about a necklace. Leo never came back for his money. After he was gone six months, I figured that he wasn't coming back. I took that money and used it to buy the car. I swear."

Sean yelled, "I don't believe you. You were there, Thornton. You couldn't resist that much money. You and Leo got into a scuffle and you shot him. You even got rid of the gun, didn't you? Maybe you even saw it as a chance to be Roger's sole runner, only you didn't know that Roger got killed the same night, did you? This was the chance you had been waiting for: kill Leo, be Roger's number one side-kick, and have all that money to yourself! You took his duffle, cleared out all his things to make it look like he left. You even took his truck away. Did you ever feel guilty driving around in that shiny new Firebird knowing you had killed Leo for it?" Sean was yelling at the top of his voice.

Byron could see the noose closing around his neck. He panicked. "That's a lie! All of this is a lie! The judge could have done it. It might even be that woman, Sophia, who did it. Maybe she found out her old man paid him to leave. Maybe she killed him for another reason. I told that banker's son who married her that they were leavin'. It could have been anyone! Roger was blackmailing someone. Leo may have been workin' with him on that!"

Sean got eerily quiet—his eyes penetrated Byron's, "What blackmail? What do you mean you told the banker's son? What the hell are you talking about? When did you see him?"

"That night after I left Leo's place, the night Leo was leaving. I drove to Knucklepin's to tie one on. The banker's son came in and sat down next to me. I know Leo sure didn't like him. He asked me if Leo was with me, but he didn't say it just like that.

He called Leo a SOB. It made me mad. I was already out of sorts with Leo leavin' and all. I told him he was half the man Leo was. Proof of it was that Leo got the girl. He said, 'That SOB isn't good enough to wipe her shoes.' I was so ticked. I swore to Leo that I wouldn't tell no one, but I wanted to rub it in his face. I said, 'He's probably goin' to be screwin' her tonight. They're leavin' tonight and not comin' back."

Flabbergasted, Sean roared, "Why didn't you tell me about this before?"

Byron shrank back, almost causing the chair to tip, "I didn't see no need. What difference did it make? That banker's son got the girl after all."

Sean replied angrily, "It's not your place to decide what makes sense! You need to tell me everything you know. You don't lie to the police when they ask you questions. I could get you on an obstruction of justice charge, if nothing else. What did Martin do then after you told him this?"

"He didn't do nothin'. He just left."

"What's this about Burkhart blackmailing someone?"

"I don't know nothin' bout that, I swear. Roger was always braggin'. We never knew if he was lyin' or not. We were all drinkin' one night. He was braggin' about the amount of money he was goin' to make on sellin' the coins. He said somethin' about it didn't hurt either that he had the squeeze on someone. I took that to mean he was blackmailin' someone.' He sometimes worked with Leo on things. I don't know if Leo knew what he was talkin' about or not. I meant to ask Leo 'bout it, and then Leo told me he and Sophia were leavin' town, and I just never did." He took another swig of water. "I've told you everythin' I know. That's all."

"Byron, I'm done with you. If I find out your holding out on me again, that will be strike three." Sean was furious.

Sean rose and stuck his head out the door. Alex and Syd walked in, and Sean told them to charge Byron and take him to a cell. "What for? You don't have anythin' on me."

Sean said, "Yes, we do. You're driving on expired tags. We've impounded your car. That's just for starters."

He was yelling, but Sean didn't care. Sean was striding toward the front door.

Chapter 44

On his was to see Charles Martin, Lucky called. “Hey, Sean. How are things going?”

Sean laughed, “Oh, about the same as the last time I talked to you, Lucky. Gravity’s not impacting any of these balls I have up in the air.”

“Well, maybe what I have for you might help. Here is what I found out about Commissioner Nickolas Garrison. He has refinanced his house there several times. He is maxed out on four of his credit cards.”

“Financial problems,” said Sean.

“Oh, it gets more interesting. There was a casino that opened in Vegas about five years ago. He’s a regular there. Goes three or four times a year. He’s a good customer—he’d lose some, but nothing he couldn’t pay off. Gets the red carpet treatment. However, he’s not been back for about seven months, so that made me suspicious. Come to find out, last time he was there, he hit a losing streak. He kept trying to dig out, but he got to where he was betting on credit, and the management closed him down. Turns out, he had two-hundred-thousand dollars in losses on that one trip.”

Sean whistled.

"Yeah, I know," replied Lucky. "I don't know how much interest he's paying, but knowing the way it works, it's probably steep."

Chapter 45

The bank had closed for the day, so Sean went to Charles and Sophia's home. He wanted to talk to Charles about Byron's revelation that Charles knew that Leo and Sophia were planning to leave town that night. Sean pulled up in front of the house. He didn't see a car, but he figured the cars were parked in the garage. The housekeeper must have left for the evening.

Sean walked up the steps and was getting ready to ring the doorbell when he heard a shot ring out from inside the house. To his relief, the door was unlocked. He rushed in, following loud voices coming from down the hall. He rushed to the open door to Charles's office. Charles was standing behind his desk holding his arm with blood showing under his hand. Sophia was shakily pointing a pistol toward Charles with tears running down her face. Her hair was unkempt, and she wore no makeup. Her robe now hung large on her shrinking frame. When Charles saw Sean, he yelled, "Sean, she's on something. She's lost her mind. She's tried to kill me."

Calmly, Sean said, "Sophia, put the gun down. We need to talk, but we can't talk with you holding the gun."

During this, Sean was keeping an eye on both Charles and Sophia, because he didn't know what Charles might do.

"He killed him. He killed Leo." Her voice was quivering but loud.

Sean was concerned that she would shoot again.

"Sophia. I need you to give me the gun. Don't make this worse. Think about Michelle. We can sort this out, but I need for you to give me the gun."

Sean wasn't sure she heard him, but she finally said, "He killed Leo, Sean. He's not going to get away with it." Still looking at Charles, "Tell him," she screamed. "Tell him how you got my necklace that I gave Leo."

Charles barked, "She's crazy, Sean. Do something, damn it! Get the gun!"

Sophia quit crying and calmly, in a lower-toned voice, said, "Sean, this is the gun I found with this necklace I gave Leo." She was wearing the heart-shaped pendent. "He had them both hidden behind that drawer in his desk."

"How did you find them, Sophia?"

"He came in last night. He didn't know I was in the kitchen. I saw him go in, and I slipped over and saw him pull the drawer out of the desk and pull out a box. I saw him put something in it. I never knew there was anything there. I waited until after Blaire left this evening. He wasn't here, so I went and found the gun and my necklace and a note I had written Leo."

Sean wanted to diffuse the situation and get the gun, "Sophia, I can have the gun tested. We can match the bullets. That'll be proof. We can send him to prison for a long time. Don't destroy your life over this. Don't do this to Michelle."

"Sorry Sean, that's not good enough. He'll hire the best attorney. I'm not going to let him escape what he did to Leo." Her voice became more determined, "You're not going to get away with this, Charles. If you don't tell Sean that you killed Leo now, it won't matter to you, because you will be *DEAD*!"

"Okay Sophia. I didn't mean to kill him. I heard that he and you were planning to elope that night. I didn't want that SOB to ruin your life. He would have made your life miserable. I went there to talk to him, to convince him to leave without you. I told him I'd pay him, that I'd get him the money. He laughed. Said he wasn't interested, that he had enough money. He told me to leave. I had the gun with me that I always carried back then. I can't explain it, Sophia. I just shot him. I rushed to him. I could feel blood. I grabbed my flashlight. I knew it was a grave wound. I saw your necklace around his neck. I took it."

Sean asked, "What did you do next?"

"I checked his pockets to make sure there wasn't anything else from Sophia. I found the note from Sophia in his wallet. I knew I had to hide the body. I knew the old barn was out back, so I went to get a shovel to bury him and saw the old car. I figured it was easier to put him in the trunk than bury him." Sean was wondering if he had help.

"How'd you manage that by yourself?"

"It wasn't easy. I put his body in the wheel barrow. I finally managed to drag his body from the wheel borrow to the trunk."

"What about the money? Did you find the money that the judge gave Leo?"

"Yeah. It was in the coat pocket, but I didn't know Pierce had given it to Leo. I took the money and the necklace."

"What about his wallet?"

"I threw it away."

Sophia was awkwardly pointing the gun at Charles, and tears were streaming down her face. "How could you? How could you kill him?"

Sean gently moved toward her, gently coaxing, "Sophia, give me the gun. It's over."

Her shoulders were shaking from her sobbing. She lowered the gun and sank to the floor. Keeping his eyes on both Charles and Sophia, Sean took the gun from Sophia. He called for backup and the EMT. As they sat there waiting, Sean reflected on how murders affect people and thought this one was like a Greek tragedy where the pathos of murder had touched many people.

Chapter 46

"Hi, Honey." Cheryl put her arms around Sean, and Buddy was weaving all around Sean, wagging that strong tail.

"This is sure a nice way to be greeted," he said kissing Cheryl and then patting Buddy's head and neck.

"Let's go to the kitchen. I've put your dinner in the refrigerator. I'll heat it up. You must be hungry. It's almost 9:30."

"Yeah, I'm pretty hungry now that you mention it. I was hoping to get home in time to talk to Kye, but I don't feel right knocking on her door this late."

"You can talk to her tomorrow, but Martha called. She would like for you to call her. I told her it would be late, but she said that was okay."

"Mmmm. Well, I'd better call."

Martha answered on the first ring. "Hi, Sean. I've been thinking about something that came to me. I don't know if it's important, but I thought I should tell you."

After Sean got off the phone, he seemed distracted. "Is everything okay, Sweetie?"

"Yeah. She remembered something that she thought I should know. Thought it might be relevant in Owen's murder."

"You think it is?"

"Might be. I need to think about it."

"Well, I'll get your dinner ready. Actually, I've got a surprise. Milton brought us a bottle of his favorite Irish whiskey to celebrate my becoming the new owner of the *Tribune* and him moving to Bekbourg. He's been asking a lot about Martha. I think he might be sweet on her."

Sean laughed, "So are you going to share some of that delicious whiskey?" He started to get two glasses.

She laughed and walked over to a cabinet and pulled out a bottle. "Ta da. Bushmills!"

The smile on Sean's face froze. Cheryl didn't know what had happened. "Sweetie, is something the matter?"

Sean stood there, thinking. She saw the light bulb go on. Sean looked at her, "That's it. I've got to go to the station, Babe. There are some things I've got to review. Don't open that. We'll celebrate another time."

He gave her a big kiss and patted Buddy's head and left.

The next morning, Sean called Martha and asked to run by the office. When he got there, he found Martha with a large stack of files on her desk. "Hi, Martha. I'd like to see Owen's office again."

"Sure Sean. She led him back down the hall and opened the door to Owen's office. "I've kept the door closed. I had to get his active files, but I haven't wanted to go back in. At some point, I'm going to have to. I thought I'd wait until Drew gets back. He can help me go through Owen's things."

Sean looked around the office. On top of the filing cabinet was a bottle of Canadian Club, the whiskey he always had in his office. A bottle of Bushmills was sitting on his desk. The glass that he had been drinking from had been taken by Forensics. "I never saw anything but Canadian Club in Owen's office."

Martha looked and saw the Bushmills. "Oh my," she stuttered, "I didn't think about the reference to Bushmills when I told you last night that the person mentioned to me at the wake that 'at least he died happy drinking Bushmills.' Canadian Club is what he kept here. I wonder when he got that. Does this mean that this person knew he had it in the office?"

"Had this person been to see him here recently?"

"Sean, I don't remember that person ever coming to his office."

Sean called the station and spoke to someone. After he hung up, "Martha, I'm going to take you home. One of my deputies is going to sit in front of your house. Let's lock up here."

"Sean, do you really think I could be in danger?"

"If this person remembers saying that to you, you definitely could be. I'm not going to take any chances."

Sean wanted to be sure about the Bushmills. He called Milton.

"Hey, Milton. This is Sean Neumann."

"Hi, Sean. How's it going?"

"Pretty good. Well, actually real good with that bottle of Bushmills you sent me and Cheryl. Thank you for that."

"Well, a good bottle of Irish whiskey can never hurt."

Sean laughed. "Did you send Owen a bottle of Bushmills too?"

"Yes."

"Can you tell me when you sent that to him?"

"I don't even need to look at a calendar for that one. Owen called me to catch up. I guess with Cheryl working on that story, and her knowing me and all, he got to thinking old times. Well, we had a good talk. I was even thinking about coming to Bekbourg to see him. Sorry that I didn't make that trip. Anyhow, I sent him that bottle. He called me that evening after he'd helped himself to a glass or two. Told me he would think about me every time he took a drink." Milton's attempted chuckle was tempered. "That was two days before he was killed. I sure hope he got to drink some more before he died."

Sean said, "He did, Milton. Well, thanks for your time."

"Say, Sean. That Frau's serves my kind of food." He and Sean both laughed.

Sean said, "Yeah, it's been here my whole life, and I still eat there."

Sean's next call was to get a warrant.

Chapter 47

She was not happy to see them when she opened the door. Sean showed Pauline the warrant. "What is this about, Sean? You surprise me. I never thought you were so easily duped. That girlfriend of yours is printing stuff that I'm going to ask my attorney to check on as libel."

"Pauline, where is your gun?"

Pauline looked sharply at Sean, "Gun?"

"Yes."

"Why would you need to know that?"

"Just answer the question."

"I'm not answering any of your questions, Sean. I'm calling my lawyer."

Once Sean learned about her reference to the Bushmills whiskey, he needed to find the weapon.

"Pauline, I have a warrant to search your home. We also have search warrants for your real estate office and county offices, which are being searched right now. These are officers Johnson and Ogle."

A suitcase was sitting on the bedroom floor, packed with clothes.

Syd found a 9mm gun in the glove compartment of Pauline's car. The following morning, Sean drove the gun to Columbus to be tested by Ronnie's team. Only the killer would know that Owen was drinking Bushmills.

Chapter 48

There were a couple of people that Sean needed to talk to. Sean went to see Judge Bergmann. Even with his son-in-law being charged with murder, and Sophia being admitted to a rehabilitation facility, Pierce Bergmann was his usual stoic self. "Sheriff."

"Judge, I know this is a difficult time for your family. I met Michelle when she was in town to help Sophia pack to go to the treatment facility. She is an accomplished young woman with a bright future ahead of her. I've known Sophia a long time, and she, too, is a special person. This can't be an easy time for them. They need you. I'm sure I don't have to tell you that, but sometimes it's difficult to think of the pain that others are feeling when a person is also experiencing his or her own pain."

The judge's expression didn't change, "You're right, Sheriff. You don't need to remind me of my obligations."

"There's one more thing I want to mention, Judge. During my investigation into Leo Davis' murder, I made a trip to Akron. I talked to Faith Powell." A flash of surprise crossed the judge's otherwise stoic façade. "There's a young man who recently graduated from law school who you might want to meet. My suggestion, Judge, is that you quit trying to control people. Sophia and these two young people could use your help."

Judge Bergmann remained silent as Sean left his chambers.

Cooper was working in his mother's yard when Sean pulled up. He watched as Sean walked over to him.

"Hi, Cooper. I need to talk to you. I don't like the way you have been carrying on around town. You've been given a second chance to get your life straightened out." Cooper started to say something, but Sean held up his hand. "Don't make it worse for yourself or your mother. She's had enough stress. What's done is done."

"That's easy for you to say. You ain't the one who rotted in prison for no reason."

"You were guilty, Cooper. Maybe not of drug possession, but of embezzling from the Thompsons. You're lucky they didn't kill you." Cooper looked shocked that Sean knew about his stealing from the Thompsons.

"How'd you hear that?"

"I know, Cooper. You need to get over it and move on with your life."

"It'd be a lot easier if you could get my record cleared. You know I was framed for those drugs."

"I'm going to see what I can do, but it's going to be difficult. Quit fooling yourself about being free of guilt and get the chip off your shoulder, Cooper. If you don't, you'll lead yourself down a wrong path."

Chapter 49

Hans had gone to his workshop this morning, as he always did, but for the first time in memory, the creativity wasn't there. He sat looking at the clocks in various stages of completion but could not muster the desire or energy to pick up a tool. The last several days had drained him with the realization that his past had finally caught up with him. After lunch, he didn't return to his workshop but sat in a chair in the backyard as the weariness continued its assault. Hilda kept glancing at him during dinner, concern in her eyes, but he assured her that tomorrow would bring a better day.

As was his after-dinner routine during the summer months, he was sitting in the rocking chair on his front porch enjoying the peace brought on in the evening. Hilda was putting away the dinner dishes, and the sounds of an occasional pan or dish clang against something was soothing along with the chirping of the crickets. As he often did during this time while he waited for Hilda to join him, he drifted off, his rocker coming to a gentle stop. His slumber this evening took an unsettling turn—to a place in the far reaches of his consciousness not breached in over fifty years.

He was drafted into the SS when he was only sixteen. He was sent to the Russian front lines where he spent three hellish years. He didn't know there were degrees of hell until he was sent in 1945 to a far worse hell than he ever imagined—a concentration camp in northern Germany. He had heard rumors of the SS concentration camps, but never could he have imagined such death and degradation to human beings. The stench of filth, rot and decay never left his nostrils, and the abject despair telegraphed from the vacant and lifeless eyes of the wasted, ragged-clothed souls made him reflect that perhaps depravity had no bounds. Although he was assigned strictly to guard duty, he would never escape the weight of knowing the uniform he wore.

Hans, a young SS officer, remembered the day very clearly. He climbed to the watch tower at the concentration camp on the pretense of scoping the surroundings, but in fact to gain momentary solace. Rumors were circulating that despite the propaganda from Hitler's command, the Allies were winning, and it was just a matter of time until their advancement led them to the camp. Looking out over the site below, he knew what had been done to those brought to this hellhole was indefensible. Even if he escaped imprisonment or death when the Allies eventually won, he would be forever trapped in his own private hell wearing like a second skin the barbarism and inhumanity he had witnessed here since being transferred two months prior.

"Herr Obersturmfuhrer," being yelled up to him brought him out of his stupor. "The Commandant wants to see you."

As Hans descended, he dreaded what heinous deed he was going to be tasked to perform.

Once inside the Commandant's office, he was ordered to take two guards to an isolated location and bury their remains. Upon arrival, they found nine Wehrmacht soldiers that a returning SS patrol had come upon and executed them on sight for desertion. As the other two set about the grim task of digging the mass grave, Hans searched the victims for anything of value. The Russians were advancing—the distant artillery fire bore truth to that—and it was just a matter of time until Germany's defeat. He knew, of course, that members of the SS would be harshly dealt with by the Russians as well as the Allies.

He credited the dire environs to the actions he next took. He rolled the man over and stared into a face bearing a close resemblance to his own. It might just work—a way out. Out of sight of the other two men, he stripped the dead man of his uniform and identification and took off running. He never knew whether the SS tried to track him too for desertion. Once he felt he was at a safe distance, he changed into the dead man's uniform and, as luck would have it, found the coins sewed in the coat's lining. Wilhelm Krutzjans became Hans Mueller and eventually made his way to the United States.

Hilda finished in the kitchen and joined Hans on the porch. His rocker was still and his head dropped forward on his chest. She spoke his name. When he didn't stir, she gently put her hand on his. Tears filled her eyes.

Chapter 50

Charles was charged with Leo's murder. No charges were filed against Sophia. Sophia told Michelle everything. She came to Bekbourg to help her mother. A couple of days later, Sophia checked herself in to a private drug treatment program.

When the forensics came back on Pauline's gun, the murder case against her was sealed. When she realized she had no way out, the dam of loathing that she had carried against Owen broke. Her bitterness toward him for nearly ruining her all those years ago ran deep, and the thought that he might do the same again, was too much for her. When Sean showed up that day with the warrant, she was in the process of fleeing to South America.

The state auditors were able to confirm that public funds were used to construct the golf course, amenities and road and related improvements. The taxpayer monies totaling approximately two million dollars were diverted from the inflated budget line items and paid for these projects. The corruption didn't stop there. The state further uncovered that the two million dollars was shown on Bekbourg Enterprises balance sheet as an expense, when it had not actually incurred those costs, and therefore under-reported the company's actual profits. This misrepresentation gave them cover to under-report their income on the state and federal tax filings.

Harvey Bennett, along with his powerful legal team, were claiming that it was the Thompsons who set up everything and did all the reporting, that he didn't know about the public funds being used or the profits being underreported. Nickolas Garrison claimed ignorance, also putting the scheme on the backs of the Thompsons. He said the Thompsons knew he had a gambling problem and kept him out of the loop.

It was proven that Pauline had changed the tax bill mailing addresses to the property itself so that Kye and Steinsen wouldn't receive the tax invoices or notices of forfeiture. The property was then purchased by Bekbourg Enterprises at the Sheriff Sales to be included in the Lake Meadows development. Boone worked with the county, and ultimately, Kye and the Steinsens got their properties back after paying back taxes.

Bekbourg Enterprises's Lake Meadows development was stopped. Nickolas resigned from the Commission, and an interim Commissioner was appointed.

The newspaper profited from people's interests in Cheryl's syndicated columns in the *Bekbourg Tribune* about the tax forfeiture wrongdoings by the county officials and what was happening in the various lawsuits and criminal prosecutions.

The Reform Party used the turn of events to campaign that they stood for growth and development, but transparency was necessary as well as adherence to the law. Their original supporters were flocking back, and new people were showing support.

Danny and Sally donated the coins to Mary's foundation, except for the ones once believed owned by Salomon Matzner. Those coins were turned over to the State Department to determine the appropriate next steps.

Drew passed the CPA and was emotional when he learned that Owen had left a will giving him his CPA business and office and his house. Owen never had any children, and even though Drew only worked for a short time with Owen, he took a liking to him. He was impressed with Drew's work ethic and the way he cared about people and the foundation. The law practice part of the business was transferred to Boone's firm. Martha agreed to stay on as Drew's assistant.

Everyone got a laugh out of what they learned about Owen. Drew had an old computer in his office that sat on a table. Owen had approached him one day and asked him to show him how to work "that contraption" but Drew wasn't supposed to tell anyone. Martha and Drew called Sean over and Drew explained, "I guess I shouldn't be surprised at what I found, because he was a very fast learner, but I never thought he touched it unless I was around. Anyway, I needed to find some notes from one of my accounting classes for my CPA exam. When I opened it up, I found a file that I had never seen." It contained Owen's notes from his meeting with Charlotte Mooney. Even though she had not yet given him the documents, he had started to draft a bombshell legal action regarding the improper use of public funds in the Lake Shore development.

Sean walked into the *Bekbourg Tribune*. Patti Richards, the receptionist, looked up and smiled. "She's in her office. Do you want me to let Ms. Seton know you are here?"

He smiled, "That's okay. Is she in a meeting?"

"No, and not on her phone," she said after looking at the phone lines.

"Then, I don't think she will mind," he said.

Patti grinned, "I don't think she will either."

Sean walked back to the big office. She was intently reading something. He knocked on the door. Without looking up, she said, "Yes?"

Sean smiled, "I understand you are the new owner?"

She looked up and laughed. "Yes. What can I do for you, Sheriff?"

ABOUT THE AUTHOR

Sherrie Rutherford lives on Florida's Gulf Coast and has ties to Ohio, East Tennessee and Houston. She and Larry love traveling, hiking (especially in the Great Smoky Mountains), and playing Bridge. She is a retired attorney. Her passion for Appalachia and railroad history inspired the Bekbourg County Series.

Sherrie's website
http://www.sherrierutherford.com